MORTAL
CONSPIRACY

NOEL C. SCIDMORE, M.D.

Mortal Conspiracy

For information about this title or to order other books and/or electronic media, contact the publisher:
Noel C. Scidmore, M.D.
authornoelscidmore@gmail.com

Library of Congress Certificate of Registration: TXu 1-003-675

ISBN: 978-1-7326118-0-1

Printed in the United States of America
Cover and Interior design: 1106 Design

Publisher's Cataloging-In-Publication Data
(Prepared by The Donohue Group, Inc.)

Names: Scidmore, Noel C., author.

Title: Mortal conspiracy / Noel C. Scidmore, M.D.

Description: [Rogers, Arkansas] : Noel C. Scidmore, M.D., [2019]

Identifiers: ISBN 9781732611801 | ISBN 9781732611818 (ebook)

Subjects: LCSH: Physicians--Tennessee--Nashville--Fiction. | Chief executive officers--United States--Fiction. | Insurance fraud--United States--Fiction. | United States. Federal Bureau of Investigation--Fiction. | Conspiracies--Fiction.

Classification: LCC PS3619.C54 M67 2019 (print) | LCC PS3619.C54 (ebook) | DDC 813/.6--dc23

----

*I would like to dedicate this book to all my patients
whose bravery in the face of tremendous suffering
taught me a great deal about life and love.*

Chapter 1

That autumn day in Nashville, Tennessee, had been breezy and sunny. Now at midnight, a full moon stood tall in the sky, casting its golden beams earthward and creating reflections of the skyline in the swirling waters of the Cumberland River as it patiently carved its way through the downtown area. Even at this late hour, the din of heavy traffic echoed along the shores of the Cumberland.

The relative tranquility was shattered by the sound of gunfire. Bursting from the shadows two hundred feet from the shores of the river, a solitary figure ran from a four-door burgundy Cadillac sedan. Outstretched arms brandishing handguns protruded through the car's open windows. The young man barely escaped death as he jumped down the stairway leading to the river. With a fierce effort, he landed aboard a river taxi just leaving its dock. Two men emerged from the Cadillac and chased the young man. Their bullets had failed to hit their mark.

Five months earlier, a mid-May morning starts out much as it always had for Butch Kennedy. The air is unusually cool and damp when he arises, chilling him as he pushes aside the warm bedcovers. While he showers, his wife, Elinor, prepares breakfast; later, she sits beside him during his meal. Before leaving for work, Butch reaches for a lightweight jacket and a thermos of freshly brewed coffee. At the back door, he kisses Elinor, still dressed in her bathrobe and floppy slippers, and tells her he loves her. On the way to his well-worn pickup truck sitting in the driveway, he notices that the darkness is just beginning to fade as the sun's first light appears on the horizon. Butch's warm breath fogs the air as his gloved hand reaches for the steering wheel of his truck.

On the way to work, Butch travels along a series of winding country roads that, up until recently, have gone mostly unpaved. Passing one sprawling farm after another, Butch waves to some of his early rising neighbors, many of whom are already out on their tractors or tending to their cattle. The morning air coming in through the truck's ventilation system is ripe with the fresh scent of pollen, mixed with the pungent aroma of cow manure. Small flocks of birds dot the fields on either side of the roadway.

As Butch approaches his workplace, the Nissan plant in Smyrna, Tennessee, he thinks ahead to the schedule and hopes it will be an uneventful day. Slightly behind on their monthly production quota, the laborers have been grumbling to him about having to work longer hours for the past several weeks.

After finding a parking spot in the employee lot, Butch wastes little time getting inside. He reaches his locker and quickly changes into the familiar attire of blue coveralls and an orange baseball cap. Before leaving the locker room, he pulls a clipboard from the wall with the day's work assignments and, over his first cup of coffee, sits down to briefly review the list. Satisfied that everything seems to be in order, he stands and hurries to organize his team.

Butch then walks toward the large manufacturing portion of the facility. The cavernous interior is initially dark, with some early daylight streaming in through the windows on the south side of the building. Upon entering, he reaches up to throw the main breaker on the inside wall; the room becomes brightly illuminated by long rows of humming fluorescent lights. The air within the facility, heavy-laden with the scent of machine oil, paint fumes, and metal dust, instantly permeates Butch's sinuses.

Several of the men and women who assemble the passenger cars and light trucks are already gathering their tools and getting situated. Butch briefly inspects each station before allowing any work to commence. For the past fifteen years, Butch has served as the line foreman for the Japanese company's large facility in Smyrna. To those he supervises, he is known as tough but fair. They greatly respect him. Because of his dedication to the job, he has won more productivity awards than any other Nissan employee.

After another thirty minutes or so, all the workers have arrived and taken their positions on the floor. Once Butch determines that everything is in place, he visually scans the floor one final time. With a nod, he reaches upward to pull a long cord hanging from the ceiling. A horn blares, and the steel automobile shells begin their slow, linear march forward. Teams of two or three men and women perform a single task at each stopping point. They work ceaselessly; the only hint of their fatigue is the perspiration that falls uninterrupted from their foreheads. From all across the building, mechanical wrenches sound out a type of crude melody as bolts are snuggly fit into place. Loud hammering and high-pitched metal sanders add to the clamor. As Butch strides back and forth to check on his laborers, showers of sparks are sent high into the air beside him, with huge robotic arms swinging into place to weld the steel frames.

Suddenly, Butch catches a glimpse of something that greatly concerns him. As he sprints across the concrete floor, his cap blows off, but that doesn't slow his progress. Just in time, he reaches one of the newer employees, who was in the process of installing a steering column. The young man had gotten his pant leg caught in one of the machines and was about to fall backward before Butch caught him. Acting quickly, Butch releases the man's foot, which a moment later would have been crushed. Remarkably, the assembly line has to be halted for only a moment. With Butch's assistance, other workers guide the long metal tube into place. Shaken but grateful, the man peers over at his boss. Butch pats him warmly on the back and gives him a couple of suggestions. He then retrieves his cap and continues his surveillance.

As the morning wears on, Butch begins to feel slightly nauseated, and soon an ache develops in the left side of his chest. For the past two weeks, this pain had been nagging at him. It seemed to strike him at nearly the same time each day, which confused him. Believing he had an ulcer, Butch had been gobbling up antacids. He had even made an appointment with the company doctor for later in the week. Today, however, the pain is much more severe than it has been before, and it is accompanied by some lightheadedness. He waves at the plant supervisor, who is standing in one corner of the building. The man immediately walks over to Butch.

"Harvey, I'm not feelin' so good. Could you take over my shift for a few minutes so I can see the nurse?"

"Sure, Butch. You go and get seen. You don't look so good. What's the matter?"

"I think I've got an ulcer, and it's just killin' me today. I'm feelin' a little dizzy, too."

"You hurry on, Butch; I can take over for the rest of the day if I need to."

"Thanks, Harvey; you're one great guy."

Butch turns and walks toward Employee Health. After only a few steps, the ache in his chest dramatically escalates to an excruciating pain that squeezes the breath out of him. Without uttering a sound, he falls to the floor, gasping for air. He grimaces as he feels his face strike the cold concrete floor. Lying on his side, he rocks back and forth, hoping to find relief from the crushing tightness in his chest. He mumbles loudly to himself as he struggles to comprehend what is happening to him, "Oh God, I can't breathe. Let me get some air before I suffocate. Please, please, Lord, stop the pain! Why does my head hurt so bad? Am I dying? Dear God, am I dying?"

While Butch writhes around on the floor, he can barely hear the alarms ringing or the cries of his coworkers as they rush to his side. Harvey is the first to reach him. Butch can feel Harvey's hands on his side as he rolls him over onto his back. Then, feeling another set of hands support his head, Butch strains to look up to see who it is. The fuzzy image of braided red hair comes into focus. He slowly recognizes the face of one of his longtime friends and coworkers, Linda, who is sitting beside him. Next, he feels his coveralls being pulled down to his waist and his T-shirt being raised to his neck. He hears Harvey yell at the workers, "Come on, everyone, stand back and give Butch some room to breathe!"

Butch's brain is swimming at this point, and everything seems to be happening in slow motion. Butch's thoughts drift to his family.

Where's Elinor? I want to see my wife! Where is she? Someone please call her! What about David and Suzie? I want to see my children!

By now, Butch can barely hear anything. He futilely struggles to listen to the conversation of several men who stand over him. Without warning, their discussion ends and his pain worsens as one of the men begins to vigorously compress his chest to get his heart back in rhythm. The compressions are initially uncomfortable, but then Butch's chest pain begins to wane and his breathing becomes easier. It seems dark inside the plant. He wonders why he can only make out the shadowy outlines of the people who stand nearby.

At about that time, the circle formed by the crowd of factory workers around him opens. So profound is Butch's weakness that he doesn't hear the wailing siren or see the flashing red lights when the ambulance arrives. He does, however, notice two large male paramedics when they kneel beside him.

Unbeknownst to Butch, the men work at a furious pace. There is, at first a pinch in one of his arms as they insert an intravenous line, and then comes the feeling of something cool running into his vein. Next, beneath his nostrils they place plastic tubing containing oxygen, relieving his struggle for air. He barely notices when the paramedics lean over him to strap electrodes across his chest that they will use to check his heart's rhythm. Then, after prying his eyelids open, they shine a bright light into his eyes.

Butch's next sensation is of being hoisted up onto a gurney and then being wheeled briskly across the plant floor. For the first time, he opens his eyes to look around. In close proximity are the anguished faces of his friends and coworkers. They are quickly left behind as he is rushed to the waiting ambulance. As soon as the back doors are securely fastened, the driver quickly accelerates. Butch now looks up at the men who are working furiously to save his life. John, the younger of the two paramedics, continues to check Butch over carefully, while his older and bearded partner, Charlie, calls into the Deaconess Hospital in Nashville by two-way radio.

"Let me speak to Dr. Sterling."

A moment passes. "Yes, Charlie. I'm here. Whatcha got?"

"Late-forties black male. Collapsed while at work. Severe chest pain. Looks like an MI. Initial pressure 220/118. Pulse 110. Mental status: intact but lethargic. Rhythm regular. ST-segment elevation in anterior leads. We've given two milligrams of morphine IV and three inches of nitropaste with good reaction in both systolic and diastolic BPs. We're running five liters O_2 through binasal cannula. I'm sending the rhythm strip to you right now by fax."

"You got any TPA on board?"

"Sure do."

Dr. Sterling pauses as he reviews the EKG tracing that is now coming off the fax machine. After his analysis, he returns to speaking to the paramedics.

"Charlie, you're right, looks like an anterior MI. Give a fifteen-milligram dose of TPA over two minutes' IV, and then start a drip at two milligrams per minute. We'll aim for a total dose of one hundred milligrams."

"Got it. Our ETA is about ten minutes. I'll see you then, unless something comes up."

John then instills an initial dose of the lifesaving tissue plasminogen activator through the line in Butch's vein, hoping to break up the clot that has formed in the arteries of his heart. As the loud siren wails and the countryside races by in a blur, Butch stares out the back window of the ambulance, wondering what will happen to him. The morphine and nitroglycerin go to work in his body, and his pain begins to subside. He turns his head to watch the clear bag of fluid that drips slowly into the vein of his left arm. In his sleepy state, the trip passes quickly. Closing his eyes, Butch prays silently to himself: *Dear God, let me live. You've gotta let me have more time with my family. I've gotta see my children grow up. Please, Lord, don't let me die.*

Moments later, the automatic doors of Nashville's Deaconess Hospital's emergency room fly open as two young paramedics propel Butch swiftly inside. The loud commotion of the ER startles Butch. Off to his left, a young girl screams, while from all over the room, doctors and nurses yell to one another. Meanwhile, multiple patients stream in the doors beside him. Along one hallway, a long line of people sit with their families, waiting to be seen by a doctor. On a stretcher just in front of Butch a young man is groaning loudly. He wears a rigid neck collar, his body strapped to a long wooden board. Over his face and chest are several large bruises and lacerations, and on his torn trousers are multiple dark bloodstains. Beside the man are two firemen, who describe how they had to cut the young man out of his crushed automobile.

Stopping only momentarily, the paramedics wheel Butch directly into patient room number one. Paramedic Charlie hollers loudly, "Kennedy in one!"

Dr. James Sterling, tall and thin, with black hair, runs into the room with two nurses alongside him as they transfer Butch to a hospital bed. Sterling wastes no time in shouting out orders. "O_2, six liters a minute— oxygen SAT monitor—twelve-lead EKG—cardiac isoenzymes—Troponin

I—electrolytes—magnesium—fibrin splits—fibrinogen—and PT, PTT, and CBC—*stat!* Get Dr. Peters down here!"

The team works rapidly. While the EKG technician places more leads across the chest, Butch is taken off the portable monitors and transferred to stationary wall-mounted devices. Dr. Sterling compares the EKG tracing to the rhythm strip obtained at the Nissan plant. He, too, notes the presence of an anterior heart attack, but he is delighted to see there has been dramatic improvement with the clot-busting therapy. As the two paramedics get ready to depart, Dr. Sterling lifts his head briefly. "Nice work, Charlie, John. You did a great job with Mr. Kennedy."

The men wish their patient the best of luck as their dispatcher sends them on their next task. Knowing the paramedics have saved his life, Butch struggles to get out the phrase *thank you* before they are gone. By now, Butch's mind is clearer and he is beginning to hope that he might live.

After quickly assessing Butch's status, Dr. Sterling performs a cursory physical exam that includes a neurologic check, listening to his lungs and heart with his stethoscope, and an abdominal exam. He notes Butch's slightly overweight physique and then begins Butch's patient interview.

"Mr. Kennedy, I'm Dr. Sterling. I will be taking care of you here in the emergency department. Can you tell me how long you've been having chest pain?"

Butch stares up at Dr. Sterling before he answers, noting the look of concern in the doctor's eyes. "A couple of weeks."

"What about this episode?"

"It came on about twenty minutes before I got dizzy and fell down."

"Did it radiate into your jaw or shoulder, or cause numbness in your left arm?"

"This time it hurt my left shoulder."

"Do you have any history of high blood pressure, prior heart attacks, or strokes?"

"No, sir."

"Do you have a history of high cholesterol or triglycerides?"

"Not that I know about."

"Anyone in the family with heart disease?"

"My father died of a heart attack when he was sixty-two."

At that moment, the cardiologist, Dr. Leonard Peters, walks in. He and Dr. Sterling initially move to a corner of the room to discuss the case.

"Thanks for coming down, Leonard."

"What's the story, Jim?"

"Forty-eight-year-old black male with a history of chest pain for two weeks. Anterior MI forty minutes ago while at work. Pain into left shoulder. Paramedics on scene in eight minutes. One hundred milligrams TPA given, with subsequent improvement in EKG and pain. Lab work pending. O₂ SAT on six liters 95 percent. Normal neuro and cardiac exam."

"Where's the rhythm strip and EKG?"

Dr. Sterling hands the chart to his associate. After reviewing the data, Dr. Peters examines Butch thoroughly, holding his stethoscope against Butch's chest for a long time. After that, he compliments Dr. Sterling on his management of the case and asks for Butch to be transferred emergently to the cardiac lab, where he'll undergo a cardiac catheterization to document the extent of atherosclerotic blockages of the arteries of his heart. At the same time, an angioplasty might be performed, where the blockages will be reduced by an inflatable balloon to improve blood flow.

Transported briskly by two attendants, Butch arrives in the cardiac suite a few minutes later. Following a thorough explanation of the procedure, he is transferred to the cold, hard surgical table. The initial preparation is skin sterilization of the right groin, followed by injection of a local anesthetic. After a small skin incision is made, Dr. Peters inserts the long metal and plastic tube-shaped heart catheter into the main artery of the leg and guides it into position with the help of a fluoroscopic X-ray machine. Once the catheter position has been verified by Dr. Peters, contrast dye is released, appearing dark gray on the black-and-white fluoroscopy screen. Plain X-rays are then taken as the dye runs the gauntlet of vessels. The study shows that Butch has significant narrowing of the main artery to the heart, the left anterior descending artery. There is also significant obstructive plaque formation in one of the other major arteries. Proceeding swiftly, Dr. Peters is able to successfully perform angioplasty on both arteries. Without sustaining a single complication, Butch is soon on his way to one of the coronary care units for close monitoring.

Having been called by one of the Nissan plant managers shortly after Butch's heart attack occurred, Elinor Kennedy arrived at the Deaconess Hospital only a few minutes behind Butch. There, she sat anxiously in the cardiac intensive care unit waiting for Butch's procedure to be over. When the nurses informed her that Butch was in his room following the angioplasty, she ran in and threw her arms around her husband, shouting out; "Butch, you look so good! I've been so worried. Are you okay?" Stoically, Butch nods to the affirmative, as he is still groggy from the anesthesia; "Elinor, I love you! I think things are goin' to be all right." Elinor then takes a seat beside Butch's bed and grasps one of his hands between her two.

Because of the extent of Butch's disease, Dr. Peters feels that consideration should be given to cardiac bypass grafting. Luckily for Butch, one of the most eminent cardiothoracic surgeons in the nation practices medicine at Deaconess Hospital in Nashville. Dr. Edward Westmoreland happens to be on duty today. Dr. Peters calls him personally to review the case with him. Dr. Westmoreland arrives late that evening after finishing his scheduled surgeries for the day. Prior to evaluating his new patient, he spends a great deal of time reviewing Butch's angiography films and chart. Somewhat abrupt, but extremely professional, the silver-haired Edward Westmoreland introduces himself to Butch and his wife upon entering their room. First, he asks a series of questions and then performs a thorough examination. His initial assessment is that Butch may be a candidate for surgery, but he recommends that a few additional tests be run first. Next, he pulls out a detailed anatomical diagram of the heart from his pocket and shows Butch and Elinor the sites of Butch's significant arterial disease. He explains that the heart attack was severe, adding that fortunately the clot-busting therapy given to him in the ambulance has made a significant impact, thereby minimizing the damage to the heart.

Dr. Westmoreland then explains that the first test, an ultrasound of the heart, will provide a rough measurement of the functional strength and anatomy of the heart. If all goes well at that step, then bypass surgery could be considered. Just before Dr. Westmoreland departs, he asks one final question: "Most insurance companies now require authorization before I'm allowed to order any tests. If you can tell me who your carrier is, I'll get my nurse working on the approval process right away."

Elinor answers, "We're insured with AmericaHealth. All the workers at the Nissan plant have been transferred to that insurance company."

With a nod of his head, Dr. Westmoreland dashes off to see his next consult. The clock on the wall of Butch's room now reads 10:00 p.m.

Chapter 2

Aware of the urgency, Dr. Edward Westmoreland presses on. The elderly man on whom he is currently operating is in dire need of cardiac bypass surgery, and each passing minute means more risk of complications from the anesthesia. This is Dr. Westmoreland's third procedure of the day. Under the intense effort, his face reddens and beads with sweat. The muscles of his back and neck cry out in pain from being kept in one position for too long. Beside him stand two surgical scrub nurses, who swiftly transfer instruments to and from his hand at his request. Across the table from Edward is the tall assisting cardiothoracic surgeon, who also works at a furious pace. Positioned beside the patient's head, the anesthesiologist passes along critical data on blood pressure, pulse, and lab work on a moment-by-moment basis.

Beneath the sterile green draping, the patient lies rigidly still, aside from his chest, which moves rhythmically up and down with the anesthesia respirator. Splayed apart at the breastbone, his chest lies wide open, his ribs jutting eerily upward. In Edward Westmoreland's hands lies the man's nonbeating heart. The job of perfusing the body with oxygenated blood has been assumed by the metal bypass pump, a tall canister punctured by multiple rows of normally clear hoses that are now a crimson color from the flowing blood. Beside the operating table, the glistening surgical instruments, awash in red, lie neatly organized at the fingertips of the assisting nurses.

Despite the presence of all the personnel required to carry out a case of this magnitude, the room remains remarkably calm and orderly. Edward

Westmoreland is well-known not only for his surgical skills but also for his calm, cool demeanor. And he is respected for both his professional manner and his compassion for his patients. As opposed to the way many other surgeons behave, Dr. Westmoreland never considers using foul language or throwing instruments in the operating room.

This case, in keeping with the two previous surgical procedures of this hectic day, proceeds smoothly. To maximize the long-term success rate of the operation, Edward Westmoreland plans to forgo the traditional venous graft for the principal artery of the heart and use instead an arterial one. Dr. Westmoreland wears specially manufactured magnifying eyeglasses as he begins to sew the artery into place with the tiniest of silk sutures. As the third stitch passes across the heart, Edward's beeper goes off in rapid succession. Over the intercom system, the hospital operator calls loudly into the operating room: "Dr. Westmoreland! You're needed in the emergency room right away. Trauma case."

Glancing across the table, Edward can see in his colleague's eyes his unspoken willingness to take over the case. Immediately breaking scrub, Edward thanks everyone in the room and runs in the direction of the nearest stairwell. He hurries down two flights of stairs to come out near the entrance to the emergency department. Awaiting his arrival, one of the nurses leads him directly to room number five, where from outside the room, Edward can hear a commotion within.

As he pushes the door open, Edward sees a large group of doctors and nurses completely encircling the victim of a motor vehicle accident. The pace in the room is frantic. Quickly reaching the bedside, Edward witnesses a sight that is horrifying at first. Completely bathed in his own blood from a massive chest injury is a young man, possibly in his twenties. The left chest wall has a gaping hole in it, with jagged fragments of ribs encircling the wound. Assessing the situation, Edward's first goal is to get the bleeding under control. He reaches into the chest cavity to clamp off several of the sheared arteries and blood spews forth, splattering his face mask and soaking his neck and chest. Struggling to see, he manages to successfully stop the blood loss. Afterward, he places two large-bored chest tubes in each lung while yelling out to the staff to get one of the operating rooms ready to go.

Four hours later, with sweat and blood caked all over him, Edward is finally able to get the chest wound closed. Because of the man's young age, Edward feels that there is a good possibility he will survive the trauma. However, it is likely that the patient will need to be in the closely monitored intensive care unit for several weeks during his recovery.

Having had to cancel his other, previously scheduled surgeries for that day, Edward immediately goes to the physicians' locker room to shower. The warm water flowing across his back and neck helps release some of the strain. For the first time that day, his mind has an opportunity to relax.

Exhausted, but partially refreshed after his shower, Edward returns to the intensive care unit to look over his patients, beginning first with the emergency case. Less blood is coming out of the tubes draining the chest—a good sign—and, remarkably, the vital signs are stable. Given the extent of the injury, Edward expects the young man to be unconscious at least another twenty-four hours. His three other patients are recovering nicely. Edward spends nearly thirty minutes analyzing their postoperative blood work and heart rhythm tracings.

With the more pressing matters attended to, Edward can now go and see his less critically ill patients on the hospital wards and catch up on routine duties. Twenty-four hours since his first meeting with Butch Kennedy, Edward pulls Butch's chart down from the rack at the nurses' station and walks toward his room. On entering, he reintroduces himself to Butch and his wife, Elinor, and then takes a seat beside the couple. Dr. Westmoreland explains that this evening, he would like to perform one of the most critical tests in Butch's workup, an echocardiogram. In order to accurately define the heart's internal anatomy, ultrasound waves are bounced off the muscular organ, and the images are then recorded. The degree of accuracy is astonishing and will give Edward needed information about the shape and size of the heart's four chambers, the strength with which the heart contracts, and an idea of the appearance of the heart valves. With the handheld ultrasound probe in his right hand, Edward inches it across the left side of Butch's chest while staring intently at the black-and-white monitor screen.

Echocardiograms are normally performed by a specially trained technician, but Dr. Westmoreland is known by the Deaconess Hospital's medical staff for his insistence on performing this test himself. The quality of this study is crucial in identifying patients who are surgical candidates and, in some cases, how extensive the surgery will be. Substantial damage to one of the heart valves means the surgery might involve replacement of that diseased valve. Subtle perforations of one of the walls of the heart chambers following a heart attack would entail a delay in the surgery and also involve an entirely different surgical approach. Such a situation would lead to substantially higher risks than a more straightforward bypass surgery alone. Edward Westmoreland's outstanding reputation has been built on his careful attention to each and every detail of a patient's case.

The echocardiogram goes smoothly. After ejecting the study results from the ultrasound machine, Edward stands up and drops the disc into the lower left pocket of his crisply pressed white lab coat. He tells Butch and Elinor that he will return to discuss the results once he has had a chance to thoroughly analyze the disc. Walking quickly to his office, he carefully reviews the study, often pausing to clarify certain details. Then, he places a call to the hospital operator and instructs her to page Dr. Peters. While awaiting the return call, he dictates his interpretation of the study. Within several minutes, his office phone rings.

"Good evening, Leonard. I just managed to get the echo done on Mr. Kennedy. I'm afraid I have a bit of bad news. In addition to the MI, his heart appears severely dilated, especially the left ventricle, with an ejection fraction of only 38 percent. I really don't think he could withstand bypass surgery at this time. My recommendation would be to consider an atherectomy at each site and stent placement. … I'm terribly sorry, Leonard. I wish there was more I could do for this fellow."

"Edward, thank you for your quick and thorough evaluation, as always. I'll come by and break the bad news to Butch and his family tomorrow. He's such a nice guy. I know this will devastate him."

The following morning, Dr. Peters enters Butch's room a few minutes before eight o'clock. Already awake, Butch is sitting up in bed with cardiac monitors strapped across his chest. Standing beside her husband, Elinor has her arm draped across his shoulder. In their eyes, Dr. Peters can see their anxiety in wanting to understand how serious Butch's condition is. He calmly reviews the results of the echocardiogram.

"The test that Dr. Westmoreland performed last evening shows an enlargement of the main pumping chamber of the heart, the left ventricle. This chamber has been weakened enough that Dr. Westmoreland feels that, right now, bypass surgery is too risky. We both feel that the best option at this point is to perform a procedure called an atherectomy. This is very much like the cardiac catheterization you just had, Mr. Kennedy, except in this case we'll use a very specific type of catheter that has an instrument that can actually cut away the blocked portion of the artery. Following that, a device to keep the artery open, a stent, can be placed. We think the atherectomy and stent placement is much superior to an angioplasty alone in keeping the arteries open."

Butch then asks, "The weakness in my heart, how serious is it?"

"It is of moderate severity, but with the right medicines and cardiac rehabilitation, we can probably get you back to most of your routine activities. However, I hate to break this to you, Butch, but you can't go back to your job. It's too physically demanding."

Obviously upset, Butch's speech is loud and agitated. "But, Doc, my job is my life! How can I go on living if I can't work? My best friends are at the factory. I've *got* to go back to my job. They can't make it there without me!"

Calmly, Dr. Peters tries to encourage his patient. "As outstanding an employee as I'm sure you are, Butch, I'm certain Nissan will find the perfect job for you, one with a little less stress."

In an effort to hold back the flood of thoughts clamoring to be heard, Butch stops speaking and closes his eyes. He reflects back to when he and Elinor were just married, right out of high school. Their innocent happiness was interrupted less than a year later by the Gulf War. Butch earned his nickname from the haircut he'd acquired from his days as a sergeant in the Marines. He spent sixteen months in Iraq and Kuwait and received numerous citations and medals for bravery under fire. The men under Butch's command felt secure with him. They knew he would give his own life for theirs if necessary.

Butch's mind then races back to the day when he arrived home from the war. Euphoria overcame him when he saw Elinor; it felt as if they'd been apart for a lifetime. When she handed him their four-month-old son, David, it was the first time Butch held the infant in his arms. He remembers thinking how beautiful his little boy was. His daughter, Suzie, was born two years later. At her delivery, he reveled in the newness of fatherhood, not having witnessed the birth of his son.

Next, Butch's recollections jump to the day he started work at the Nissan plant. He remembers how anxious he was to do a great job. The night before, his sleep was fitful. He'd ironed and reironed his clothing to make a good first impression. Now, as a fifteen-year veteran of the plant, he serves as a role model for the younger men.

Being a hardworking, disciplined individual, Butch has always centered his priorities around his job and his family. Soon, he and Elinor will be celebrating their twenty-eighth year of marriage, a marriage that has only strengthened over time. While his children were growing up, he spent rainy Saturdays under an umbrella watching David's football games or proudly dressed in a suit at Suzie's ballet recitals.

Dr. Peters's voice, signaling his departure, interrupts Butch's pleasant memories, bringing him back to reality. "Butch, don't worry. Everything's going to be okay. I'll check on you later this afternoon."

Chapter 3

While Butch Kennedy lies in his hospital bed at the Deaconess Hospital recovering from the initial phases of his heart attack, the early Friday morning pace at Vanderbilt Hospital's pathology department remains unabated. Seated at rows of microscopes in the main reading room are multiple physicians, busily analyzing the seemingly endless supply of glass-mounted tissue samples constantly being delivered to them. In addition to the usual requests for inpatient bone marrow biopsies and the occasional autopsy or two, the number of ongoing operative procedures seems inordinately high. Surgeons anxious to know whether they have clear margins in cancer surgeries before completing their cases call in from the operating rooms on a regular basis. As soon as one pathologic specimen can be evaluated, another follows quickly thereafter. Routine work is pushed aside to adequately address the more pressing responsibilities.

Standing squarely in the center of the room is a tall, young physician who, by all appearances, is responsible for organizing much of the work that comes into the pathology department. Confident in demeanor, the trim but muscular dark-haired man remains surprisingly collected under the pressure. Evidence of his difficult work schedule is readily apparent in his appearance; fatigue hangs lightly on his handsome angular face, and his cobalt-blue eyes are slightly recessed and red. While advising other physicians on their cases and offering assistance to several of the lab technologists, Dr. Brad Pierson, a physician-in-training, then tries to complete his own work. Hunched over one of the microscopes, Dr. Pierson thoroughly evaluates a series of pathologic tissue samples, intermittently speaking into a handheld dictating device in a nondescript Northeastern accent.

Not easily discernable in Dr. Pierson's behavior is the fact that he is under a great deal of pressure. In a mere forty minutes, he is to meet with the chairman of the pathology department, Dr. Robert Collins, to review all the cases currently being studied. During that conference, he is expected to present each patient's medical history in detail and explain what he believes the exact disease process to be. Today's cases involve the diagnosis of leukemia and lymphoma. Brad Pierson is well aware that Dr. Collins is regarded as one of the world's leading experts in the area of those types of blood cancers.

Doing his best not to be distracted by all the noise around him, Brad takes copious notes as he reviews each case, pausing frequently to refer to a series of pathology textbooks beside him to help discern the subtle distinctions between various diseases. All the while, he keeps an eye on his watch because of the time constraints. Five minutes prior to Dr. Collins's scheduled appearance, Brad hears a taunting voice behind him. "Better hurry up, Bradley. The chairman's on his way. Don't screw up or you might get fired."

Brad reels around when he hears the familiar voice. Standing directly behind him is Dr. Sanford Starke, better known to his friends as Sandy, who is also a resident physician in the pathology department. Sandy's chestnut-colored eyes are aglow in mischief. And to be as aggravating as possible, he wags one index finger in Brad's direction. Irritated, Brad reaches backward and tries unsuccessfully to grab hold of his colleague's lab coat.

"Dang it, Sandy, how do you always manage to show up when I'm under some kind of pressure?"

No one would guess from their interaction that the two young men are best friends. They first met nearly seven years ago when they both began medical school together at Vanderbilt.

"Come on now, Bradley, you're up to the challenge, aren't you? After all, Dr. Collins is probably *only one of the best hematopathologists in the world!* Don't let him make you look stupid now."

That last comment achieves its desired effect. Brad jumps up from his chair to chase after Sandy. Brad barely lands one soft blow on his friend's back before Sandy is down the corridor and out of sight. Deciding his pursuit is futile, Brad quickly turns around and begins walking back to his workstation to finish up his work. As he reenters the pathology department, his heart nearly stops when he sees Dr. Collins waiting for him. Doing his best to remain calm, Brad flushes while apologizing for his absence. "Dr. Collins, please forgive me. I just had to step out for a moment. I'm almost ready for you."

With the gracious manner for which he is well-known, the tall, gray-haired Robert Collins reassures the younger physician. "Brad, don't worry. I'm a little bit early. Let's get started. I'll help you with anything you haven't quite finished."

Brad then sits down across from his chairman at the two-headed teaching microscope. The slides have been organized to begin with the simpler and more routine diagnoses. Brad wants to build some confidence before matching wits with Dr. Collins on the more complex cases.

Over the next three hours, the tall mound of glass-mounted tissue samples passes from one side of the microscope to the other. All the while, Brad constantly jots down notes, delineating his chairman's comments beside his earlier impressions. This information will be needed later on this afternoon when the final diagnostic reports are dictated. As he reaches for the final slide, Brad feels intellectually and physically drained.

Once that last case comes to rest, Dr. Collins stands, looking remarkably refreshed. His only parting comment: "Nice work, Dr. Pierson. See you tomorrow morning."

After his attending physician has left, Brad straightens his desk beside the microscope and returns the slides to their original order. He then embarks on his next task, which is to dictate the complex reports that will go into the hospital chart and permanent pathology file. Ninety minutes later, he takes a short breath and glances at the clock. Startled by the time, he reaches up to snap off the engineering-style lamp over his desk. He gathers his soft-sided nylon briefcase and rushes out of the pathology department in the direction of the parking lot. A few minutes later, he arrives home. He tosses his briefcase on the sofa while his keys are left dangling in the front door. Moments later, he emerges from his bedroom partially dressed, tying his necktie as he walks.

He hurries across town on West End Avenue hoping he will not be late for a dinner engagement. Several miles later, he makes the familiar right-hand turn onto Lauderdale Road to enter a well-manicured neighborhood composed of modest-size houses. He parks halfway up the block in front of a tiny European-style gray stucco home and checks his watch, noting with relief that he's on time.

After walking up the half flight of concrete front steps, Brad gently knocks on the tall oak-paneled front door. Soon comes the sound of footsteps inside on the wooden floor. Through a tiny window in the top of the door, Brad sees olive-colored eyes peer out. He hears his name called aloud, and the hinges sigh as the front door pops open. Standing before him with her arms wide open is the woman he has been dating for quite some time, Julie Christensen. Tall and slender, she is wearing a knee-length royal blue silk dress that nicely complements her figure. Her wavy blond hair is worn down tonight, nearly touching her shoulders. Bubbly and outgoing, she reaches for Brad's hand and pulls him inside while kissing him. "Hey, handsome, come on in. I'm almost ready."

"*Almost* ready? You look gorgeous."

The compliment brings a smile to Julie's face. "I need to have dinner with you more often. You're really good for my ego."

Following his date into the living room, Brad relaxes on the couch while Julie stands in front of a large gold-framed mirror in the corner of the room. After brushing her hair a final time and making some last-minute adjustments to her makeup, Julie announces she's ready to go. Brad stands, reaches one arm around her waist, and escorts her to his car. Now in less of a hurry, he drives leisurely as they continue out of town on West End Avenue. Julie's curiosity soon gets the better of her.

"Now, where exactly did you say we were going again?"

"You know tonight's a surprise, so you'll have to hang in there just a few more minutes."

Wrinkling her nose in displeasure, Julie responds playfully. "That's not any fun."

Several miles later, they reach Belle Meade, one of the oldest and most affluent of Nashville's many suburbs. On the outskirts of this intimate township,

Brad turns onto a short side street to arrive in front of a tiny intimate restaurant known as the Belle Meade Brasserie. The restaurant's name is artfully presented in bright pink neon script across the front of the building. Julie sighs aloud with pleasure when she sees where they'll be dining.

"I've heard this place is incredible, Brad. How did you find out about it?"

"Let's just say I did a little research."

Inside the restaurant, the atmosphere is one of hushed elegance. The tuxedo-clad maître d' welcomes them and then directs them to a table in the cozy main dining room. Surveying the room, Julie takes note of the decorative furnishings. The floor, composed of black-and-white marble tiles, is polished to an impressive shine. Complementing the décor are black-lacquered dining tables covered by pink linen tablecloths. Dim lighting, in part due to the burning candles, adds to the charm. As she settles into her chair, Julie feels completely at home.

"Thanks for bringing us here, Brad. It's simply charming."

"You're welcome. I'm happy you're enjoying yourself."

In the midst of looking over some of the antique chandeliers and furniture, the couple is interrupted by their waiter, who reviews the menu with them. After he leaves the table, the pair's conversation drifts to their work. Also a physician-in-training, Julie is nearing her second year of specialty training in the radiology department at Vanderbilt. In her soft Southern accent, she says, "I'm curious: how did the first week of your new rotation go?"

Brad smiles at the question. "Dr. Collins is so brilliant that I was a little intimidated at first, but he's remarkably generous in his teaching, so all in all, things have gone pretty well so far."

"That's great. I know you'd looked forward to this for a long time, so I'm glad things got off to a good start." With an animated expression, Julie continues. "I think I've decided what specialty I'm going to choose in radiology. For the past two months while doing pediatrics, I've been reminded of how much I love working with children. I think it's right for me."

Smiling, Brad glances directly into Julie's eyes. "I had a feeling that's what you'd choose; you're a natural with children."

At that moment, they are distracted by their waiter, who appears with colorful mixed green salads. After taking a few bites, they resume their conversation, which drifts to more carefree topics. The combination of Julie's company, the plush surroundings, and the remarkable food melts Brad's tensions away, affording him a feeling of deep relaxation. Toward the end of their meal, he remembers something he meant to ask Julie. "How did dinner go with your mom on Wednesday night?"

"We had a great time together. She's all excited about going to Atlanta next weekend to see my sister, Lauren, and her family. Lauren's daughter, Elaina, is almost two; she's just darling."

"Is her business still going well?"

"Mom's been extremely busy lately, but she loves it. I got to see photographs of some of her recent interior design work; they were incredible."

Julie then detects a wistful look in Brad's eyes, which is mirrored in his voice. "It's great that your family's so close that you get to see them often. I miss that. The last time I was home was almost six months ago."

"I don't know if I could ever be away from my family again. When I went off to Virginia for medical school, I was miserable being so far from home. I know that being apart from your family must be hard for you."

"It really is."

After a momentary lapse, Julie reaches for Brad's hand. Brad detects an element of excitement in her expression.

"I'm gathering that by bringing me to this wonderful restaurant and with all your secrecy, tonight represents some kind of special occasion."

Lifting both eyebrows, Brad smiles faintly before he responds. "Taking you out to dinner is *always* a special occasion."

Julie then stares intently at Brad, searching for the answer to her question. Disappointed when she is unable to detect any emotion, she says, "I thought you might have been celebrating the fact that we've been together for almost a year."

Brad's lack of response produces a hurt look in Julie's eyes, which she quickly tries to cover by tilting her head down. At that point, while she is distracted, Brad raises his hand to call attention to their server. A moment later, a frosted cake with a single lighted candle appears at their table. When Julie catches a glimpse of the cake, she smiles and tears up. Getting up out of her chair, she walks over to Brad. After gently swatting him on the shoulder, she kisses him softly. "Thank you. That was wonderful."

When Brad's car is again in front of Julie's house, he is struck by the sense that the evening has flown by, both of them feeling as if they were together for the first time after a long separation. Brad walks Julie to her door, reflecting on how they'd first met. One afternoon over a year ago, he was walking through the radiology department on the way back to work after lunch. As he rounded a corner, he saw one of the female attending physicians standing in front of Julie, loudly chastising her in the middle of the room. It was obvious that Julie had done nothing wrong; the staff radiologist was taking out her frustrations on her. After the woman finished yelling, she stormed off, leaving Julie standing there, visibly shaken. Brad went over to Julie and convinced her to step outside the hospital for a few minutes. There, he offered her his support and tried to convince her the incident was the attending physician's fault, not hers. Having been a medical student at Vanderbilt, Brad explained to Julie that he had witnessed the woman blow up on multiple occasions in the past. His words seemed to provide some relief, but Julie was too embarrassed by the whole matter to say much.

Several weeks passed before Brad saw Julie again. He ran into her in the cafeteria, and she seemed to have sincerely appreciated his concern. She mentioned that their talk had given her the necessary perspective on the situation, allowing her to return to work that afternoon. They ended up having lunch together that day, and although initially it was somewhat awkward, they enjoyed their time together, discovering that they had a lot in common. Brad invited Julie to have dinner with him not long afterward, and she readily accepted.

On reaching Julie's front steps, Brad knows he'll need to leave soon. Work in the operating rooms is scheduled to begin at 6:30 in the morning, and he's expected to be there to assist the surgeons. Standing under the dim light of the front porch, Brad pulls Julie close to him. As he places his lips on hers, he can smell the light scent of perfume on her neck. He feels the silkiness of her hair on his fingertips. Reluctantly, Brad ends their kiss a moment later. While holding on to Julie, he stares into her eyes, wondering where their relationship will lead them. Sensing that Brad's contemplations are something of a serious nature, Julie searches his eyes.

"What's got you so distracted, Brad?"

Somewhat evasive, Brad's response is still truthful. "I wish our schedules were a bit less hectic so we could spend more time together."

Still looking up at him, Julie smiles and rests her head on Brad's chest while she holds him around the waist. As Brad regretfully walks to his car in the darkness that is only partially punctuated by the dim light of a single streetlamp, he feels a lightness in his chest. After opening the driver's-side door, he glances back a final time at Julie, who is still standing on her front porch, staring in his direction.

Chapter 4

Feeling as if his head had just landed on the pillow, Brad groans loudly when the unpleasant buzzing of his alarm clock awakens him at 5:30 on Saturday morning. After hitting the snooze button, he rolls over onto his back to rest a moment longer while it is still quiet. His body feels heavy and tired; his brain, achy. Little effort is required for him to drift back into a pleasant sleep. All too soon, the irritating alarm startles him awake a second time, and he grudgingly makes his way toward the shower, leaving behind the enticingly warm bed. Efficiency will be necessary this morning; he's scheduled to begin collecting tissue samples in the operating room in less than an hour.

The only consolation Brad can find under the unpleasant circumstances is that his friend Sandy Starke is also scheduled to work this morning. On the way to the hospital, he drives by Sandy's apartment, which is not far from his own. Sandy's foul mood is evident as he climbs into Brad's car.

"Dag nab it, Bradley, it's barely sunrise and the two of us have to go to work while the rest of Nashville is still sleeping. Did we make a bad career choice or what?"

Initially quiet, Brad decides to tease his friend. "It is pretty miserable, and I really feel like whining myself, but you've done such an admirable job of it that I don't know if I could do any better."

Not to be undone, Sandy rubs his tired eyes and frowns. "Don't you ever get tired of working all the time? I mean, I worked myself to death in college while everybody else was out having fun all the time, and then in medical school, I barely even had time to sleep. Now that I'm a resident, I'm at the hospital all the time—and I get paid less than the guy down at McDonald's."

"You know something, Sandy, you're absolutely right. Open the glove box; there's a folded-up road atlas in there. I'm turning south; we're heading for Florida for an extended vacation on the beach."

As Brad swerves and changes direction toward the interstate highway system, Sandy's mouth hangs open in disbelief. "Come on, Brad, what are you doing? We're going to be late."

Turning his head to conceal his smirk from Sandy, Brad comments, "Listen, Sandy, it's time we ventured out of our boring lives and did something a little spontaneous."

Confused by behavior that's so out of character for Brad, Sandy stares at him with an expression of complete disbelief. When Brad eventually slows down and turns back toward the hospital, he notes, with great satisfaction, that Sandy begins to relax.

After reaching the pathology department, the two barely have time to drop off their belongings before they're immersed in the fast pace. The workload is surprisingly heavy this morning. In the hectic schedule, Sandy quickly has to push his disgruntled feelings aside as he struggles to keep up.

To improve their efficiency, the two divide the major responsibilities between them. Brad initially runs between the operating rooms to collect tissue specimens while Sandy stays behind in the pathology department to process them or give expedient frozen-section diagnoses. Dr. Steve Albertson, the attending physician on call, assists Sandy in the main pathology lab. After a ten-minute lunch break to catch their breath and get something to eat, the two switch tasks. Unfortunately, first thing in the afternoon, Sandy crosses paths with one of the senior general surgery attendings who is known to be intimidating. The case involves an older man who presented to the emergency room with uncontrolled rectal bleeding. Normally, an extensive workup would determine the cause of the blood loss, but this fellow was too unstable. Immediate surgery was required to keep him from bleeding to death. When they opened the man's abdomen, they found a large, shaggy-appearing cancer in the sigmoid colon. Sandy had been called in to collect the specimen after the mass had been removed. The surgeon, Dr. Hartmann, treats all subordinates, including resident physicians, like half-witted imbeciles, and Sandy is no exception. As soon as Sandy enters the operating room, he is assaulted by the gruff, moderately overweight Dr. Hartmann.

"*You*, what's *your* name?"

"Dr. Sanford Starke."

"Well, Dr. Starke, don't screw up my case. Make sure the proximal and distal margins of the colon specimen are carefully labeled and examined microscopically. Also, specimen number two is the lymph node dissection, and number three is the wedge biopsy of the liver. Do you think you can remember all that, Dr. Starke?"

Angered, but not willing to risk displaying his emotions, Sandy responds curtly while he daydreams about choking Dr. Hartmann. "I believe I can handle that amount of information without *any* difficulty."

"Since you're so intellectually gifted, then repeat it back to me before you leave *my* room, *son*."

Treated like a misbehaved first grader, Sandy grudgingly reiterates what was said. Struggling within himself, he fights back the overwhelming urge to tell Dr. Hartmann what an intolerable buffoon he is. Before taking the specimens back to the pathology department, Sandy carefully labels and organizes them. Just before the resident leaves the room, the surgeon repeats his inappropriate warning: "Remember, Starke, don't mess up or you'll have me to deal with."

Under his breath, Sandy mumbles, "And God said there was only going to be one true Antichrist. I guess he hasn't met Hartmann yet."

After that one unpleasant experience, the remainder of the afternoon is busy but goes relatively smoothly. By 2:00 p.m., the one-after-another pace of the surgeries begins to slow down. Brad and Sandy breathe a sigh of relief as they finish up their work for the day. Exhausted, but not wishing to have his whole day ruined, Sandy tries to talk Brad into some outdoor recreation when they leave the hospital.

"Come on, Bradley, it'll be fun. It's a beautiful day. Let's go play Frisbee for a while. You deserve it; you've been working hard."

Silent at first, Brad's face assumes a contemplative look as he weighs Sandy's words. After a brief lapse, a boyish grin crosses his face and a glimmer appears in his blue eyes.

"All right, you convinced me. Where do you want to go?"

"How about Percy Warner Park?"

"Sounds good. Let's go, but remember, I can't stay long."

Sandy, now ecstatic to have a diversion from the mundane routine, agrees to make the outing a brief one. After quickly visiting their respective apartments to change clothing, the two young men are soon on their way to the western outskirts of Nashville. Not long afterward, a sign on the shoulder of the road indicates they've entered the prestigious Belle Meade suburb, and a short distance later Brad turns left onto Belle Meade Boulevard. Several miles pass while Brad and Sandy wind along gently curving roadways on the way to the park. In this unique part of Nashville, opulence is everywhere, evidenced by the hand-forged iron street signs and tall gas-lamp-style light poles. Only patches of daylight are sprinkled on the pavement before them, heavily filtered by the dense foliage of grand arching Southern magnolias and the bountiful blooms of tall camellias. Eventually, the heavily woven tree cover retreats from above, and in the clearing ahead is an ornately carved thirty-foot granite archway, which marks the entryway to Percy Warner Park.

Wasting little time, Brad chooses a parking spot and flings his car door open, embracing both his freedom and the outdoors in one deep breath. Before any activity ensues, Brad stands a moment beside his car with his eyes closed and his chin up, basking in the soothing midafternoon sunshine. His dawdling is short-lived, though, because his colleague and friend, impatient as usual, yells for him from the manicured lawns nearby to begin their game of Frisbee.

Sandy is the more competitive of the two, even when it comes to play. To keep the Frisbee from landing before being caught, he manages to get grass stains on his knees, and there are even a few clumps of dirt in his hair. Brad, because of his longer arms, is more comfortably able to reach the floating disc without resorting to a slide on the grass. After an hour or so, the two men have completely forgotten the unpleasantness of the earlier part of their day. Their aerobic activity has left them physically refreshed but a bit tired. With the final toss, Brad races Sandy to a spring-fed water fountain nearby, where the two fight for the first gulp.

After their thirst is quenched, they rest under the broad shade of a nearby oak tree before returning home. It feels pleasant just to relax and allow the light afternoon breeze to run across their bare arms and legs. Sitting beside one another, their physical differences become readily apparent. Taller and more athletic-looking, Brad has a slightly darker complexion than his blond-haired friend and keeps his black hair more conservatively styled.

When it is finally time to leave, Brad is now the one who resists, as Sandy stands up and takes a couple of steps in the direction of the car.

"I'm not ready yet, Sandy. Can't we just sit a few more minutes?"

"I really need to get back, Bradley. Sorry."

Understanding his friend's needs, Brad groans slightly as he gets to his feet. "Okay, off we go."

On their drive back through Belle Meade, the two take their time marveling at the architecture and landscaping of the estates. Just when they think a home is the largest and most lavish they have ever seen, along comes another that is even grander. At one point, Brad becomes so preoccupied with sightseeing that he nearly drives off the road into a clump of tall bushes. He swerves back into his lane with a jerking motion, causing Sandy to slam into the side of his car door. Startled, Sandy yells at his friend, pretending to be angry.

"That's right, Bradley, get us both killed while you're over there dreaming about being rich."

"Sorry, Dr. Starke, but I wasn't dreaming about owning one of those fancy estates. I was just wondering if they'd let me live there if I agreed to be the butler."

Now laughing, Sandy can barely get his words out. "I can just see it now, you in a tuxedo walking the poodles and fetching the morning paper with some rich woman calling after you: 'Come here, Bradley, do this, Bradley, do that, Bradley.' I think you'd be perfect for it."

Exhausted, Brad is a bit giddy. He chuckles at the remark. "I don't know if you knew this, but I used to have a place out here. Eventually, I had to downsize to my six-hundred-square-foot apartment to avoid being ruled by my possessions."

Sandy, now grinning, responds, "Let's face it, Brad, you and I were born with wooden spoons in our mouths."

Approaching the end of Belle Meade Boulevard, Brad and Sandy reach Harding Road and leave behind the peaceful, almost tranquil neighborhoods.

The bustling traffic of multiple lanes of fast-paced passenger cars and commercial trucks proves to be an abrupt transition. As the two friends continue their journey back to their apartments, Brad changes the topic of conversation.

"What are you and Joanie up to this evening?"

"My mom and dad are coming into town this afternoon from Chattanooga, and we're all going out to dinner. Until then, I'm afraid I'm going to have to crack the books."

"Are your parents excited about you and Joanie getting married?"

"Absolutely. They love her."

"Have you decided on a date yet?"

"Well, with our darned work schedules, it's probably going to be about six months."

A few minutes later, they arrive in front of Sandy's apartment. Brad says jokingly, "See you on Monday. And give Joanie my love. Oh, by the way, I'm available for Frisbee lessons anytime."

Sandy lightly flings the Frisbee at Brad, barely missing his head. "Nice try, my friend, but I'm the *king* of Frisbee."

At about the time Brad and Sandy leave Belle Meade, a major social and athletic event gets underway in another part of the several-thousand-acre Percy Warner Park. Today marks the fifty-ninth annual running of the National Iroquois Steeplechase. This amateur horse race is a charitable event, with all proceeds going to benefit the Vanderbilt Children's Hospital. Held each year on the second Saturday in May, this national attraction is generally well attended, and this year is no exception. The city's elite faithfully appear, daring not to miss a chance to rub elbows with their affluent brethren.

The steeplechase arena lies on the southwestern edge of Percy Warner Park. A granite amphitheater, built into the side of a nearby sloping hill, provides extensive seating for the visitors. The course itself is laid out in a circular pattern on a level grassy field marked by tall hedges, water-filled trenches, and black-and-white painted wooden barriers. Off to one side of the field, dozens of empty horse trailers sit behind idle pickup trucks. Visible throughout the fenced-in arena are short-statured jockeys wearing colorful numbered jerseys and caps, walking beside their long-legged thoroughbreds.

With only moments remaining before the event begins, the atmosphere becomes rife with excitement. The stadium is brimming with spectators, whose animated conversation fills the air. Small packs of young children dash among the attendees, while anxious parents call out their names. Vendors hawk hot dogs and soft drinks from behind large rolling carts.

Along the edge of the steeplechase course at the first turn is an area designated for the exceptionally well-to-do. Large clusters of portable white canvas tents have been erected to provide shelter from the searing late afternoon sun. While seated in comfortable wooden armchairs, this group is served a catered dinner of local delicacies by formally dressed waiters donning white gloves. Accompanying the first course is the sound of corks popping, soon followed by effervescent bubbling as champagne is poured into crystal flutes. These guests are ostentatiously dressed, even for this casual affair. The men are wearing blazers and expensive piqué polos, while their wives wear traditional linen—freshly starched—or silk dresses. Their children are manicured in both appearance and manner. Nearby, in the parking area, chauffeurs proudly stand guard beside rows and rows of gleaming European luxury automobiles.

Unexpectedly, the deafening roar of the crowd comes to a quiet hush. Over a primitive static-riddled intercom system, a man with a distinctly Southern accent welcomes the visitors and announces the start of the race.

"Folks, thank y'all for showin' up today! We're 'bout to get this thing under way. Lemme tell y'all how great it is to see so many happy faces here this afternoon."

A brief pause on the part of the announcer prompts the spectators to stand and clap loudly. Their attention is then drawn to the center of the field where an older man wearing a dark gray suit ambles toward the starting line. Following a brief inspection of the horses, he gives quiet instructions to the jockeys and the trainers. The loud stadium quiets again as the man raises a starting pistol into the air. Tension is evident in the faces of the jockeys as they wait for the start of the race. They stand rigidly forward in their saddles, with their chins nearly touching the heads of their steeds below. One of their hands firmly grasps the reins while the other carries a short, black riding crop. Within the multiple gates, the horses, with flared nostrils, anxiously kick the ground beneath them. The loud blast from the starting gun sends the giant beasts lunging forward.

Thundering hoofbeats shake the earth as the horses reach the first jump. Lapses of silence occur as their sinewy leg muscles tense to make the graceful leaps. Frighteningly, one jockey loses his grip and falls to the ground as he reaches the first barrier. Once the cloud of dust clears, everyone sighs in relief as they see him arise unharmed. Undaunted by his certain last-place finish, he runs to his horse and jumps back on.

As the riders reach the final stretch, the spectators again come to their feet and cheer fervently. The large red digital numbers on the huge clock on the infield stop when the winner crosses the finish line. Only a few minutes lapse before the second group of horses and jockeys are ushered onto the field.

Seated contentedly beneath one of the tents is Dr. Edward Westmoreland, accompanied by his wife, Patricia, and their three teenaged daughters. Despite being on call this weekend, he has been able thus far to enjoy most of the afternoon. While savoring their late luncheon meal, Edward and Patricia are engrossed in conversation with several other couples. As the day wears on, the men slowly congregate off to one side and tell stories of recent international hunting ventures or share their latest conquests on Wall Street. The women are left behind to oversee the children and catch up with their female friends. The Westmorelands are typically a very popular couple. Born into an influential and wealthy family, Edward has preserved the tradition by becoming the third generation of Vanderbilt-trained cardiothoracic surgeons. His remarkable success as a physician, as well as his family name, makes him a powerful force in Nashville's political and social circles.

Relaxed, and with his feet propped up, Edward enjoys the sporting event as well as conversation with friends and colleagues. With the rising heat and humidity, his pearly white complexion is highlighted by scarlet-colored cheeks. Despite hair that has prematurely turned gray, his slate-blue eyes are vibrant and sparkle with life, giving evidence of his true age. At one point, he glances over to his wife, contemplating how lucky he is to have ever met her. Her natural grace and elegance still amaze him. He finds himself staring at her youthful, slender figure and shining, shoulder-length, deep-brown hair that complements her sensitive, deep-brown eyes. To Edward, she is the most beautiful woman in the world.

As the final race comes to a conclusion and many people get up to collect their belongings, a visitor approaches Edward and Patricia. Out of character for the setting, the tall, almost gaunt man wears a dark-colored three-piece suit and black wingtip shoes. Edward's back is initially to the fellow. Patricia notices him and gently taps her husband on the shoulder. As Edward turns around and asks, "What is it, dear?" Patricia sees her husband stiffen slightly. With a slight tension in his voice, Edward stands and extends his right hand out to the man.

"Robert, I'm delighted you were able to make it out here this afternoon. Let me introduce you to my wife, Patricia."

The visitor, who has dark curly hair, nods politely and formally in Patricia's direction while Edward continues.

"Honey, this is Dr. Robert Altman. He's the head man down at one of the big insurance companies in town, AmericaHealth. He's been doing a good job of keeping them on track."

Patricia's gentle manner puts Robert Altman immediately at ease. After standing up and stepping beside him, she rests one hand on his arm and chats with him as if he were an old friend.

"Robert, may I offer you a glass of iced tea?"

"That's very kind of you, Patricia."

"I'm certainly pleased that we've had an opportunity to get acquainted, Robert. Tell me, how long have you been in Nashville?"

By this time, Robert has begun to relax. He loosens his tie.

"I was transferred down here from Boston a year ago when we moved our corporate headquarters to Nashville. I was put in charge of the move as well as day-to-day operations."

"That sounds like a great deal of responsibility. Do you enjoy your work?"

"Despite the long hours, my job has been, up to this point, reasonably satisfying."

Robert Altman then removes his suit jacket and drapes it over one arm. Patricia continues her polite questions. "Has the transition to Nashville gone well so far?"

"Having spent most of our lives in the Northeast, my wife, Anne, and I expected not to like Tennessee very much, but we've actually been pleasantly surprised."

"Wonderful. Is your wife with you this afternoon?"

"I'm afraid not. Anne is up visiting family in the Providence, Rhode Island, area this week. I know she'll be terribly disappointed that she missed an opportunity to meet you and Edward."

A concerned look then appears on Patricia's face. "Robert, I'll speak with Edward and see if we might possibly get you out to the house for dinner when your wife gets back. You two need a real welcome to town. I'll arrange everything and have Edward phone you, if that would be acceptable."

"Anne and I would just love it, thank you."

Robert then glances at his watch and grimaces. "Oh my gosh. I'm late for a meeting. I hope you'll forgive my rude departure, Patricia. I've enjoyed getting to meet you."

With that, Robert pats Edward on the shoulder and, saying goodbye, hurries in the direction of the parking area. Once Robert is out of hearing distance, Patricia turns to her husband. "Now, Edward, why were you so tense around Robert?"

In a casual manner, Edward attempts to dismiss his wife's concerns. "I've had some difficult business negotiations with Robert's company in the past and he's a reminder of that; that's all."

Without saying another word, Patricia glances at her husband out of the corner of her eye. At that moment, she is distracted by Edward's beeper going off. After staring briefly at his pager, Edward retrieves a compact cellular phone and places a call. During the exchange of several sentences, his brow furrows. As he closes his phone, he looks over at Patricia, who speaks before he manages to get a word out.

"Please drive slowly on the way to the hospital, Edward. There's a lot of traffic this afternoon. Don't worry about me or the girls; we can pack everything up. If you have time, call me later and let me know how things are going."

After kissing Patricia on the cheek and saying goodbye to his daughters, Edward moves along quickly. One of his patients who'd had a heart valve replacement earlier in the week is unstable in the intensive care unit and may have to be reoperated on this evening. Edward is just thankful he made it as long as he had without being called in.

As he accelerates along the curving roads of Belle Meade with the late-afternoon sunshine streaming in through the windshield of his long Mercedes sedan, he thinks about how remarkably patient his wife is. He ponders all of the hardships he's put her through during their twenty-one years of marriage—the missed dinners, the canceled vacations, the absent weekends. He reflects on how lucky he is to have such a devoted wife. Someday, he hopes he'll have an opportunity to make it all up to her.

Chapter 5

The enchanting weekend of steeplechase activities and Frisbee playing is ended too soon by Monday's abrupt arrival. While she strolls through her home, a young woman savors her last sip of coffee. The house is quiet and still as her husband left for work earlier this morning. Standing at the bottom of a staircase lying adjacent to the foyer, she presses her mug against her lips with both hands while obviously lost deep in thought. Then her expression changes, and she hurries up the stairs to a small bedroom on the second story. There, standing with her arms crossed, she visually weighs each detail of the room. Faint morning daylight streams in from the windows, beside which are hung cream-colored curtains printed with images of teddy bears, bicycles, and toys. The color of the walls, sky blue, is now becoming discernable in the partially darkened room.

In the center of the nursery is a tall crib. Walking to it, the woman runs her fingers along the smooth slats of wood that shine from a fresh coat of white paint. Within the crib is a large, colorfully dressed doll, which she picks up and rocks in her arms while humming a lullaby. Then pain spreads across her face. She draws her eyelids tightly closed over her deep brown eyes. Several quiet tears stream down her cheeks. As she tilts her chin down, her long, wavy red hair falls forward, covering her face. During their eleven years of marriage, Tracy Kilpatrick and her husband have desperately wanted children. At the age of thirty-three, Tracy has yet to fulfill her dream of motherhood. From deep within her skirt pocket, she retrieves a paper tissue to blot her tears dry, which are now darkened by mascara. With a look of resolve, she rubs her eyes forcefully, pushes her hair back, and then returns downstairs to the kitchen.

After placing her ceramic coffee mug in the sink, Tracy pauses momentarily in front of a window overlooking a flower garden in the backyard while she struggles to pull herself together. Several minutes later, she closes and locks the front door of their home on Eighteenth Avenue South and walks briskly across the street toward the Peabody campus of Vanderbilt University. It is only a short distance to her workplace in the undergraduate History department. She knows she'll need to hurry; soon the chairman will be looking for her, his executive secretary, to organize his day.

Three days have now passed since Butch Kennedy's heart attack, and his recovery continues to be nothing short of remarkable. Yesterday, Dr. Peters performed an extensive examination on Butch and was amazed at his progress. Because Butch was not felt to be a suitable candidate for bypass surgery, Dr. Peters has scheduled him for a second cardiac catheterization, which will take place this afternoon. An attempt will also be made during the procedure to strip away the arterial blockages in Butch's heart and to place metal mesh stents across those blocked areas to decrease his risk of having a second heart attack.

Ninety minutes ago, Butch was wheeled down by wheelchair to the cardiac suites at the Deaconess Hospital, and since that time, he and his wife, Elinor, have been waiting in the preoperative holding area. Dressed only in a skimpy hospital gown and white cotton athletic socks, Butch is beginning to shiver. He is a little nervous about the upcoming procedure, though he won't admit it. Uncharacteristically, he squeezes Elinor's hand tight, barely saying a word. Attempting to distract her husband, Elinor chats about everyday events.

"Honey, you know David's got a graduate school presentation on Friday. ... He's looking forward to his dad being there."

Unfettered, Butch remains hunched over in his chair and continues to stare at the floor. He doesn't respond until Elinor prompts him. "Butch?"

"Sounds good, Elinor."

"What sounds good?"

"Whatever you just said."

"That's the question: what did I say?"

"Something about having lunch with one of your friends next week."

Not anxious to add to her husband's burden, Elinor tries to soothe him. "Yes, Butch. Would you like to have lunch with me and my friends next week?"

"Love to."

"What about going to David's graduate school presentation this Friday?"

Butch now looks over at his wife with a surprised look on his face. "You mean he's gonna give a speech at school this week?"

"He sure is."

"Well, I plan to be there to cheer my son on. How come you didn't mention this to me sooner?"

"You're right. I'm sorry, honey."

At about that time, a young female nurse dressed in a white uniform walks over to Butch and Elinor with a clipboard in her hand. She touches Butch gently on the shoulder and in a kind manner gives him instructions.

"Mr. Kennedy? Good afternoon. I'm Pat, your nurse. They're almost ready for you; would you please follow me? … Mrs. Kennedy, you can stay right here; the doctors will come out to you once the procedure is over."

As Butch stands, he feels a little wobbly on his feet. Observing this, Pat eases him back into his wheelchair. She then wheels him back to the cardiac suites, where Dr. Peters awaits him. Once Butch is in the room, Dr. Peters walks directly over to him.

"Don't worry, Butch, this should all go very smoothly. It will be just like the first catheterization you had done a couple of days ago, only this one will be easier for you since you know what to expect. Come on over here and take a seat for me."

After Butch sits down on the edge of the table, Pat helps him lie back while another nurse assists Dr. Peters in putting on a sterile gown and gloves. Through the back of his thin cloth garment, Butch can feel the biting coldness of the hard table beneath him. Things move very swiftly from that point on. Not long afterward, Butch feels the cold antiseptic solution being applied to his right groin area, followed by a slight sting as the local anesthetic agent is injected. Then, Dr. Peters moves in beside Butch. Within several minutes, the patient hears the doctor's reassuring voice tell him that the catheter is already in good position. With fear still gnawing at him, Butch looks around the darkened room at the complex equipment and the monitors that resemble small television screens. A wave of last-minute anxiety passing over him, and he slides his right hand behind his thigh and clenches tightly, in an effort to stay calm. Dr. Peters's voice again calls out to him. "Butch, we are set to release the contrast dye. You may feel a little bit warm from the dye itself. Don't let that worry you."

Then Butch hears what sounds like a bell go off, signaling that an X-ray is being taken. Several minutes pass. Dr. Peters halts the procedure momentarily.

"Butch, we've outlined where your blockages are. I'm now preparing to strip away the obstructed area with a special device containing tiny rotating blades. Everything looks good so far."

Lying in the dark, with people standing all around him, Butch begins to focus on the thought of the spinning blades entering his heart. In a controlled panic, he breaks out in a sweat and holds his breath. The pulse rate monitor immediately picks up his rapid heart rate. Dr. Peters pulls off his goggles and looks down at his obviously frightened patient. "What's wrong, Butch? Are you having chest pain?"

Speaking quickly and slurring many of his words, Butch blurts out, "Those blades ... do they ever put a hole in your heart? Can they kill you?"

In a calm, supportive tone, Dr. Peters tries to soothe his patient. "Butch, let me reassure you: we'd never do anything to hurt you in any way. Over the past year, I've performed close to three hundred atherectomies, and I haven't put a hole in a single artery."

After listening to Dr. Peters, Butch's fear begins to lessen and he relaxes. Restoring his protective eyewear, Dr. Peters proceeds while keeping one eye on his patient. A dull ache appears in Butch's jaw muscles as he releases the tension in his clenched teeth. Dr. Peters, now watching the monitor, feels confident to resume the procedure. The first calcified obstruction is stripped away from Butch's left anterior descending artery without difficulty. Dr. Peters calls it a success. The special catheter is then repositioned in a second artery, and dye is again released to precisely locate the blockage. Just as before, the device, with its diamond-sharpened stainless steel blades, spins at a high speed inside the artery to shear away the plaque. Afterward, at the site of each obstruction, a long thin mesh-wire stent is inserted to keep the arteries open. Again, Dr. Peters is happy with the outcome.

Before long, Butch is in the recovery room, groggy from the light anesthesia. The minute Elinor hears the recovery room nurse call her name, she looks up. Seeing her husband, she runs over to him. She grabs onto the metal arm rails of his gurney with both hands and nervously looks him over. "Butch, honey. … How did it go? Are you all right?"

Still sleepy, Butch looks up at his wife at the same time that Dr. Peters arrives. Before Butch has an opportunity to speak, Dr. Peters begins reviewing the results of the procedure with the couple.

"Mrs. Kennedy, things went really well. Your husband came through without any problem at all. After we were finished, we took a second look at the arteries, and we found that they were wide open."

A big grin passes across Butch's face. Elinor, delighted with the news, hugs Dr. Peters. Butch then struggles to sit up, telling Elinor that he's ready to go home.

"Honey, would you get my clothes for me? I can leave now, can't I, Doc?"

With one arm outstretched, Dr. Peters gently nudges Butch back into the lying position and checks the catheter insertion site for any sign of bleeding. "You're not going anywhere just yet, Butch. You'll need to stay for a while to be certain that no problems arise. Just relax and lie flat on your back for at least four hours."

"But Doc, I feel great. Let some person who's really sick have my bed. I'll be just fine at home."

Without being prompted, and much to the relief of Dr. Peters, Elinor jumps into the conversation and encourages Butch to stay. Grumbling, Butch relents, insisting on leaving once the four hours have passed.

Ten days later, Butch uneventfully begins a structured cardiac rehabilitation program, which will go forward on a daily basis for the next three months. While filling out routine paperwork at the Deaconess Hospital's outpatient department, Butch is startled by the sound of a young woman's voice loudly calling out his name. As he looks up, he sees a petite, fit-appearing woman in her mid-twenties with short brown hair and hazel eyes standing directly in front of him. With her feet firmly planted and her arms crossed, she addresses her new patient in a confident and authoritative tone. "Mr. Kennedy? I'm Toni. I'll be working with you for the next twelve weeks. What do you think about that?"

Butch instantly likes her energetic take-charge personality and feels comfortable joking with her.

"Whatever you say, Toni. What do we do first—a round of push-ups and sit-ups?"

Enjoying the interaction, Toni responds playfully. "No. First you learn respect for your drill instructor, and after that, we begin the really tough stuff."

Before getting started, Toni gives Butch a guided tour of the gymnasium-style fitness area, showing him the rows of exercise bikes, treadmills, and stair climbers, and finally the swimming pool. Then she describes the program to him, explaining the slow and careful increases in aerobic exercise she will take him through over the next three months. Next, she directs Butch to an exercise bike. Before having him begin, she straps a wide, nylon blood pressure and pulse rate monitor cuff to his right arm. She then explains that there is a target heart rate that Butch should not exceed while exercising and instructs him to stop exercising temporarily if he gets above that target number. Under Toni's supervision, Butch is soon pedaling away. The two continue their jovial bantering.

"Kennedy, you're slackin', you're slackin'. Now let's see some effort."

"But Sarge, I'm one of the newer recruits. Please show me some mercy."

While walking in a circle around Butch as he exercises, Toni laughs at some of his remarks.

"You're one of the sorriest patients we've had in years. Now finish riding that bike so we can get into something a little more challenging."

Twenty minutes later, a tired, perspiring Butch climbs off the bike. She checks his final pulse rate and blood pressure. Then Toni puts him through some light weightlifting exercises before dismissing him for the day.

"Good first day, Mr. Kennedy. See you tomorrow at the same time."

One month after his heart attack, Butch returns to work, which proves to be a rather difficult day for him. The night before, he awoke on several occasions, remembering his last day on the job, the day of his heart attack. For the first time in his life, while getting ready for work, he reaches into his closet for a suit instead of casual clothing. Nearby, his blue coveralls hang washed and pressed. Butch stares at his name tag on the front of them for a long time. He likely would have stood there for hours had Elinor not called his name. No longer able to keep up with the physical demands of the vehicle assembly, he has been given an administrative position in the automotive design division of the Nissan plant. There, it will be his responsibility to act as an interface between the designers and the assembly workers. The engineers, familiar with his extensive experience, are relishing the opportunity to work with Butch. He will be able to give them the hands-on perspective that they have desperately desired.

On Butch's first day back, he nervously parks his truck in his old parking spot and then walks slowly into the building. No one seems to notice him at first as he quietly inspects the heavy equipment on the assembly floor. Then he walks toward the locker room. As soon as he enters, several of his coworkers encircle him, patting him on the back and offering their congratulations on his return. Butch can feel the tension that had gripped him for the past several days melt away. He feels overwhelmed by the show of affection and can barely put together the words to thank everyone.

By the next day, however, things are substantially different for Butch. From high above the manufacturing floor, he stares out of his office window, looking at his former coworkers below. He longs to be back with them, to be beside them, to do the thing he loves best. Anguished, he struggles not to rush back down there and take over, willing to risk his health in the process. The first week is a lonely one for him. He cannot get used to wearing a tie and sitting in an office all day, away from the excitement of troubleshooting the problems of the assembly line. Anxiety is only one part of Butch's unhappiness; terrific boredom and loneliness also plague him.

When Butch returns home each night after work that week, Elinor has cause for concern. In years past, Butch would typically run into the house full of life and rush to kiss her on his way upstairs to check on David and Suzie. The man who struggles through the front door now is a changed man, a different man from the Butch Kennedy she has been married to for the past twenty-eight years. Now, he barely mumbles hello as he comes in from his exercise class. His preoccupation is so profound that Elinor can barely get a word out of him while he sits in the darkened living room for hours on end, staring blankly at the television.

Knowing that it might only add to the problem, she doesn't dare say a word to her husband. The children are also well aware of the change. Dinnertime brings only intermittent strained conversation, with long lapses of silence.

After several painful weeks have passed, Butch's personality slowly reappears. He unintentionally discovers a role for himself at work that gives him a newfound sense of purpose. In the mornings, he listens carefully to the design engineers and reviews the blueprints for potential new vehicles. Then, from his perspective as an assembly line worker, he proposes changes to cars or trucks that would make them easier to assemble. He spends afternoons discussing the plans with the workers on the floor, getting their feedback. Finally, using the three-dimensional computer modeling available in the engineering department, he incorporates suggestions directly into the vehicle structure prior to constructing expensive scaled models. This interface between engineer and worker has proved so successful that the time required, as well as the cost to produce prototype vehicles, has dropped significantly thanks to the simplification of the assembly procedure. Additionally, the quality has become much more predictable.

With the ability to work on a daily basis with his former colleagues, and his newfound sense of direction at the plant, Butch returns to his old self. Lighthearted and proud, he nearly yanks the door off its hinges when he walks in the house at night. Elinor's concern gradually fades away.

On the first Wednesday in June, the annual Davidson County Medical Society meeting takes place, typically attracting a large physician turnout from all over central Tennessee. Time-honored tradition places the gathering at the Opryland Hotel Complex, located on the northeastern periphery of Nashville along the shores of the Cumberland River. Edward Westmoreland has looked forward to the event for many months, and even to consider attending, he had to substantially trim his schedule for that day. Despite his advance planning, he is far behind that afternoon because of the usual unexpected emergencies. Once he is comfortable that his patients are stable, he hurries to his home in Belle Meade to change into the appropriate attire. With a smile on her face, Patricia, his wife, stands at the front door awaiting her husband. Her trim, youthful figure is highlighted by a floor-length black-sequined dress. With a long strand of white pearls dangling from her neck, she holds Edward's black tuxedo in one hand and a pair of his formal black patent leather dress shoes in the other. She's been married to a surgeon long enough to know that it is unusual for them to arrive anywhere on time.

With aggressive driving, Edward manages to maneuver his way across town with surprising speed. A few minutes past 7:00 p.m., Edward's long, midnight-blue Mercedes-Benz sedan eases up to the main entrance of the large Opryland Hotel. It is still quite warm outside with the sun standing high in the sky. A light breeze unfurls the row of flags that line the circular entrance. Even before Edward manages to bring his car to rest, one valet stands ready to take his keys while a second is poised to open the passenger door for Patricia. They are arriving late, so the couple wastes little time in traveling toward the ballrooms at the far end of the hotel.

Despite their rush, the Westmorelands can't help but notice the unique architecture and décor of the hotel. Patricia glances briefly at the thirty-foot-long crystal-laden chandelier hanging from the ceiling of the antebellum-style three-story foyer. Along the hallways, she takes note of the six-tiered crown molding stretching along the junction of the ceiling and wall, and of the plush Oriental carpeting that lines the long hallways. On their way to the first-story conference rooms, she and Edward pass by the entrance to the three large indoor arboretums for which this hotel has become so famous, barely having a chance to glance inside. They have quite often made a special trip out here for lunch or dinner, primarily to enjoy the gardens accented with man-made streams, rivers, and waterfalls.

When they finally reach the ballroom, they are dismayed to find dinner already being served. Fortunately, one of Edward's associates, who is seated at their table, took the liberty of ordering for the couple, for which the Westmorelands express their appreciation. Before Edward can get a single morsel in his mouth, the lights dim and the keynote speaker walks to the podium at the front of the room. Tall and distinguished, Dr. Holcomb Carruthers, in his formal attire, has the appearance of a true gentleman. His manner of speech, precisely enunciated with the faintest of Southern accents, hints at his extensive education. With his first words, the room becomes silent.

Following a brief historical preamble, he announces all the new members who have joined the medical society over the past year. He then reviews previous accomplishments and future goals of the organization. Dr. Carruthers becomes momentarily silent as he stares blankly at the written speech in his hands. After a short deliberation, he straightens his back and puts the typed pages aside. Previously relaxed, his face becomes taut and his eyes take on a resolute look. Even before his voice is again heard, his lips purse in anticipation, his right hand tightly clenched into a fist. Initially there is a struggle to get the words out, but his determination builds to an impassioned momentum.

"First of all, I would like to thank everyone for their attention this evening.... I had prepared a speech that celebrates the miraculous achievements of medicine that have come about in my lifetime and the new discoveries looming on the horizon. The things I have witnessed have truly been remarkable. I must, however, in good conscience, relinquish that subject in favor of something that weighs heavily upon my mind."

Looking down, Dr. Carruthers pauses to take a sip of water while gathering his thoughts.

"We, as physicians, have faced many obstacles over the years. I believe that most of us have chosen this honorable profession to be of service to our fellow man. Over the past several decades, we have faced the unpleasantness of a growing number of frivolous lawsuits, ever-increasing malpractice insurance premiums, and unprecedented government regulations. We have all patiently withstood these attacks not only on ourselves but also on our profession. But recently, new atrocities, unlike any we've seen before, are being committed in the name of so-called health-care reform in this country. At no time in my memory have the healers of our society been under such attack.

"The insurance industry thwarts every attempt we make to provide quality health care for our patients. We have been forced to ask the permission of these companies just to see our own patients. Each and every test we order is carefully scrutinized by people with little or no formal medical training, often resulting in our patients not receiving valuable diagnoses or treatments. Referrals to specialists have been drastically reduced to 'save money.' I daresay that if patients die because of inadequate treatment, the only winner is the insurance industry's bottom line, *because money will indeed be saved!* Patients are being denied care they deserve, all in the name of 'saving medicine.' Politicians have introduced legislation limiting lawsuits against health insurance companies, further enhancing the latter's willingness to commit unthinkable acts against our patients so that they may increase their profit ratio."

Now with a staid anger, Dr. Carruthers gently taps his fist against the podium as he continues.

"And what about us? What about the health-care provider? We are not even given the opportunity to help our patients, and if we order the appropriate tests and consult specialists when necessary, the insurance companies drop us from their provider list, telling us we are 'too expensive.' They then proceed to take our patients away from us and give them to a physician who just doesn't care, often a poorly trained physician, someone who will 'follow the rules' and won't question their authority.... Each and every day, I reach within myself to pull out the absolute best I am capable of to take care of the people who put their lives in my hands. I worry about costs for every patient I see and am careful with the precious health-care dollars I choose to spend. For whatever reason, that does not seem to be enough. This, all in the name of 'saving medicine.' When it's all over and done with, the kind of medicine that's left *won't be worth saving!* Health care in this country is the best in the world, *and I believe it is worth fighting for!*"

With that final word, Holcomb Carruthers's voice falters, and he glances down momentarily. When he again lifts his eyes, he is startled to find that every man and woman in the audience is proudly standing and applauding. Overwhelmed by the show of support, Dr. Carruthers's stern expression melts into a smile. He leaves the stage to take his seat at one of the private dining tables. The crowd continues to cheer loudly and clap long after he is seated. A second physician, Dr. Curtis Edmundson, the current president of the Davidson County Medical Society, approaches the microphone. It is necessary for him to stand for several minutes until the room quiets down. At that point, with a big smile, he begins.

"I would like to thank everyone for being present this evening. ... And Holcomb, thank you for such an inspirational speech. Everything I say from this point forward will be somewhat of a letdown, but we do have some other business to conduct.... One of the highlights of this evening's meeting, as anyone who has been a member of this organization for very long knows, is to give an award for the Davidson County Physician of the Year. Each June at this get-together, we give special recognition to an individual physician who has brought forth a substantial advancement in the field of medicine. The list of former recipients is an impressive collection of history-making pioneers, and this year's winner is no exception. Besides his unprecedented character and superb talent, the man we honor tonight has made a special contribution. This surgeon was one of the first to develop successful human heart transplantation. Initially beginning his career in the university setting, he has, over the past five years, moved into private practice, where he has continued to perform cardiac transplantation with an unparalleled success rate. Currently practicing at Deaconess Hospital, he is a leading expert in this field and is consulted by physicians all over the world. Please welcome my friend and colleague, Dr. Edward Westmoreland."

It is obvious that the award has come as a shock to Edward. He is so taken aback by the whole matter that he doesn't get out of his chair until his wife, Patricia, nudges him. Once on the stage, his typical confident demeanor quickly returns, and he heartily shakes Dr. Edmundson's hand as he receives the large gold-and-crystal plaque. Camera flashes from all over the room temporarily blind Edward as he stands beside his presenter. Exhibiting sincere humility, he pauses, searching for the appropriate words with which to express his gratitude.

"I'd, I'd like to say what a great honor this is for me. ... Thank you very much for thinking of me at such a time. With so many well-trained, dedicated physicians who are here this evening, I consider myself very lucky to have been chosen for this special award. I can personally think of at least a dozen men and women who are more deserving of this distinction than I ... I would like to humbly accept this plaque on behalf of my patients, to whom I am deeply indebted. Through their courageous struggles, I have witnessed great strength and dignity. They exhibit a remarkable tenacity to overcome the tragedies they face, and I have learned a great deal from them. I consider it an honor to be of help to those fine people." Motioning toward the audience, he finishes by saying, "Thank you all, and God bless you!"

Edward's acceptance speech is met with a standing ovation, which goes on long after he is seated. The breakthroughs that are accredited to him—heart transplantation and minimally invasive heart bypass surgery have truly saved the lives of countless patients throughout the world.

Chapter 6

Fridays in the pathology department at Vanderbilt Hospital are generally quite hectic, and this Friday proves to be no exception. It is not until well after 7:00 p.m. that Brad Pierson is able to slow down long enough to catch his breath. Fatigued by day's end, he drags himself back to his office to finish any remaining paperwork. Brad sighs aloud when he discovers a tall stack of haphazardly arranged reports, charts, and lab work piled high on his desk, most of which will need to be organized, dictated, and signed before tomorrow at noon. Certain that it will take him at least three or four hours to properly complete this amount of paperwork, Brad finds himself feeling a bit overwhelmed. Uncertain where to begin, he first surveys the lofty mound of papers, trying to get himself mentally prepared. Pushing aside his growing weariness, he resolutely decides to tackle what is before him and reaches for the telephone-style dictating machine. While mentally composing his first words, he feels something soft touch the side of his face. Completely startled, he twists his neck around to see Julie's green eyes and smiling face.

"Hey, stranger, I thought I'd come check on you before I went home. I know you've had an awful week, so I wanted to make you an offer you couldn't possibly refuse. … If you take me out to dinner, I'll let you pay."

Feigning indecision, Brad reaches up to rub his chin. "Let me see what my options are. … I can either stay here in this stinky, formaldehyde-filled pathology lab on Friday night and dictate reports for a couple of hours, or I can go out to dinner with a good-looking woman who understands my ridiculous lifestyle. ... That's a tough one. I'm really not sure what to do."

Quick to respond, Julie places her hands on her hips. "Well, I'm only going to ask once, and then I'm on my way."

Standing up, Brad grabs Julie around the waist and kisses her. "Not without me, you're not. Let's get out of here."

Hand in hand, they walk to the elevators, while Brad asks Julie if she has a dining preference.

"What about San Antonio Taco Company? It's a beautiful night. We could walk there from here. It would be fun to be outside for a while."

Smiling, Brad glances over at Julie. "Great idea! Let's go."

Popular with the student crowd, the casual restaurant is only two blocks from Vanderbilt Hospital, along Twenty-First Avenue South. On the large wooden outdoor deck on weekend nights, a live band plays, and tonight, somehow, Brad finds the loud guitar music rather relaxing. While standing in line at the entrance of the restaurant, Brad and Julie see a group of friends seated at an outdoor table. Among them are his friend Sandy Starke and Sandy's petite fiancée, Joanie, who wave to encourage the couple to join them. Sandy stands up as soon as they arrive.

"Hey, Bradley, glad to see you finally got away from work. Boy, it sure looked like you were having one miserable day. Why don't you sit with us? ... Julie, you look great, as always. How are things in the world of radiology?"

Glad to see Sandy, Julie hugs him briefly. "Radiology's fine, Sandy, thanks. I could really use a vacation right about now, but otherwise, I'm doing great. ... What about you and Joanie? How are the wedding plans coming along?"

Sandy frowns at the question. "You better not say anything about it to Joanie right now; her mom's got her all wound up over a couple of trivial details. Aside from that, things are going pretty well."

Seated at the table with Sandy and Joanie are two other couples whom Brad knows well. Directly across from him is Brian Osmund, a dark-haired athletic-looking fellow who was a classmate of Brad's in medical school. Currently a general surgery resident at Vanderbilt, Brian eventually aspires to become a plastic surgeon. Beside him is his latest blonde girlfriend, Candace. As usual, Brian has chosen a woman whose striking appearance clearly overshadows her intellectual prowess. To Brad's right is the fair-haired Dr. Brett Barnett, also a former classmate, who sits beside his wife, Susan. More reserved than Brian, Brett is currently in his third year of internal medicine training at Vanderbilt Hospital. During the introductions, Julie discovers that Candace is employed as a secretary in the undergraduate education department and works with one of Julie's high school friends from Franklin, Tennessee.

Halfway through their meal, the conversation gradually drifts toward unusual experiences that each has had in the medical profession. Eager to tell the first story, Brian first warns Candace about the graphic nature of what he is about to convey. Then he proceeds, saying, "Two months ago, when I was over at the VA hospital, we were operating on this guy for what looked like a large left-side colon cancer. The workup, including a CT scan, had demonstrated a large mass consistent with a cancer. Anyway, before we could do a colonoscopy to get a tissue diagnosis, the guy started bleeding profusely. We had to take him to emergency surgery. ... He failed to mention to us that he had recently been traveling in Nepal. When we opened him up, there was this giant tapeworm in his colon. ... *Ooh,* it was grotesque!"

Breaking out into laughter, Sandy manages to stop laughing long enough to get a few words out. "I heard about that case at our monthly pathology conference. I heard you guys cut the worm out. ... Don't you usually treat those things with pills? Ha-ha-ha."

Breaking once more into full-blown laughter, Sandy's comment causes Brian obvious embarrassment.

"Well, what were we supposed to do, leave it in there while the guy was bleeding?" Now irritated, Brian directs a sharp criticism at Sandy. "What about when you and I were doing internal medicine together at Vanderbilt in our third year of medical school?"

While he gasps for air in between his snickering, Sandy asks, "What are you talking about?"

"Remember when our attending cardiologist asked you to describe the heart murmur in that young woman?"

Realizing what is coming, Sandy suddenly becomes quiet.

"Well, there we were, a dozen or so medical students surrounding this twenty-eight-year-old fashion model who had been admitted because of repeated episodes of dizziness. Her cardiology attending, Dr. Fitzpatrick, asked Sandy to do a thorough cardiac exam in front of all of us and describe her prominent aortic valve murmur. Sandy was so nervous when he got near her that he couldn't even talk. After he put his stethoscope up to her chest, he listened for a long time and then described the murmur for us in perfect detail."

Confused, Brad interrupts. "What's so funny about that?"

"After we left the woman's room, Dr. Fitzpatrick commented that Sandy had exceptional hearing capabilities. He pointed out that Sandy had been so distracted that he had forgotten to actually put the earpieces of the stethoscope in his ears. They were hanging around his neck the whole time!"

Much to Sandy's displeasure, the whole group begins laughing loudly. To distract attention away from himself as quickly as possible, he offers up a story about Brad. With his ears perked, Brad locks gazes with Sandy, who continues, unfettered.

"One particular night when Brad and I were third-year medical students comes to mind. We were on the internal medicine service at Vanderbilt Hospital at the time and were running urine specimens on the centrifuge. ... Somehow, Brad forgot to secure one of the tubes before he started spinning the machine. Within seconds, there was urine splattered all over him. We were on call that night, and we were so busy that he never got to take a shower. He had to walk around with dried urine on him until the next day! When we went to medicine grand rounds the following Saturday morning, no one would sit anywhere near Bradley because of his penetrating aroma."

Once again, there is prolonged laughter, while Brad, self-effacing person that he is, joins in. He even comments that he could barely stand his own stench.

After several more stories have been shared, the June sun finally wanes, and the couples decide to call it an evening. After saying goodnight to their other friends, Brad and Julie, accompanied by Sandy and Joanie, walk together back up Twenty-First Avenue South toward the hospital parking lot. By now, it is quite dusky, and in the warm, humid air, the streetlights cast a diffuse hue on the sidewalks below. Tonight, traffic is more moderate than usual. Except for the occasional passing car, it is relatively quiet. At their respective automobiles, the couples part. When Julie reaches her car, she invites Brad to follow her home, hoping they might have some time alone.

Once they've gotten comfortably relaxed on Julie's living room couch, they sit together and chat quietly for several hours. At one point, Brad gets up to stretch and walks across the wooden floor of the living room in his stocking feet. On the opposite side of the room, he pauses before a pair of tall built-in bookcases, where he studies several rows of neatly arranged antique sterling silver picture frames. One photograph in particular catches his attention. When reaching behind several others to lift it, he is surprised at how heavy the frame is. Lined by seashell motifs, the decorative frame contains a family portrait taken when Julie was only five or six years old. The silver is partially marred by dull gray tarnish, and the glass is a bit dusty.

Before long, Julie leaves the comfortable sofa to nestle in beside Brad, who reaches one arm around her while he continues his perusal. Intrigued by Julie's childhood appearance, he brings the photograph up close to his face for a better look. Her attire of blue denim overalls and a white cotton T-shirt amuses him.

"Julie, is that you, or is that some farmhand?"

She laughs, acknowledging that she had been a tomboy at that age. "The only thing I cared about back then was riding horses and climbing trees. My sister, Lauren, did a much better job of being a little girl. She had a wonderful doll collection and actually enjoyed helping my mother cook and sew."

After staring at the photograph a bit longer, Julie becomes silent, prompting an inquiry on Brad's part. "What's the matter, Julie? Did I say something wrong?"

Several seconds lapse before Brad hears her quiet voice.

"No, of course not. I still have a difficult time seeing a picture of my father without getting upset. He was a wonderful father and a great doctor, Brad. All the people around Franklin really loved him; he treated them like family."

A painful look now crosses Julie's face. She tilts her chin down. "I remember the night he was killed. ... I was a senior medical student in Virginia at the time. My mom called. It was horrible; I'd never heard her so upset. I could barely understand anything she was saying, she was crying so loudly. ... She told me that my father had gone out on a routine call late one night and that on his way home, a drunk driver crashed into his car. It felt as if my heart had been torn to pieces that night. ... I'm not certain I'll ever get over it completely."

Putting the photograph down, Brad leads Julie back in the direction of the couch, where he holds her. "Julie, I'm really sorry about your dad. I've wanted to ask about him for a long time, but I was afraid to bring it up."

Uncertain if what he's about to say will be of help, Brad asks Julie to tell him about her father, hoping the pleasant memories might provide a distraction.

"Brad, he was an incredible man, kind and gentle, yet passionate about everything he did. When I was around seven or eight, I remember hurrying to grab his worn leather doctor's bag when he got a call. I would then run and stand by the front door, hoping that he'd let me go with him. One day, one remarkable day, he looked over at my mother and she nodded her approval. And off we went. I'll never forget it."

Pausing, Julie walks to the bookshelves and pulls down a large leather-bound photo album. On her return to the couch, she flips back and forth through the pages for several minutes. With the album opened on her lap, she intently scrutinizes several photographs on the same page. Her facial expression then softens, and a smile appears as she hands the album to Brad. From the yellowish light of a dim table lamp, Brad gets a glimpse of the varied gardens that Julie's father had planted around their wooden farm-style home in Franklin. Dotted in among colorful azaleas are camellias the size of trees, so overrun with blossoms that their shining dark-green leaves are barely visible. In another photograph is Julie's father standing beside a rosebush with a shovel in his hand. One arm is wrapped around Julie's older sister, Lauren, who stands beside him. As Julie points to the pictures, it is apparent to Brad that she is enjoying herself.

"My father really loved the outdoors; he spent every spare moment either gardening or with the horses. For him, it was a great distraction, the way he got relief from his stressful job. I remember how contented he looked when he was out in the yard, whistling away while he was planting or pruning."

"He must have been quite a man."

"Oh, he was, Brad. I'm sorry you never got to meet him. I know you two would have gotten along very well; he was such a talented and interesting man."

A startled look then appears on Julie's face as she notes the time. "Brad, it's almost midnight. I'm sorry, I didn't mean to keep you up so late ... I know you've got to be at work early tomorrow, and I'm sure you need to go so you can get some sleep."

"Yeah, I guess I'd better. I'm supposed to be in the department by seven o'clock."

At the door, Julie kisses Brad and makes him promise to be careful driving home. Nodding, Brad steps out. From the living room window, with the curtain pulled back, Julie lovingly follows his progress to the car and eventually out of view. She will also need to be at the hospital early in the morning, so she hurries to get ready for bed. After the alarm is set, she slides on a lightweight cotton nightgown and walks to the bathroom. While the warm water soothes her tired face, she reminisces again about her father and thinks of how much she'd cherished the opportunity to share a part of him with Brad.

Chapter 7

Dawn's arrival brings with it an eastern sun that peaks out from just above the horizon. A charcoal sky is pierced by streaming colors of yellow and orange that highlight the outline of the buildings that comprise Nashville's downtown area. Along Front Street, which runs behind the banks of the Cumberland River, a thirty-five-story gleaming white skyscraper with smoky gray mirrored glass streaks upward from the pavement below. Chiseled in polished granite over the entry doors on the first story is the company's name, AmericaHealth.

Located in the penthouse of this impressive building is the office of the chief executive officer of the AmericaHealth Corporation, Dr. Robert Altman. A physician-turned-administrator, Robert Altman has become the head of the largest private health insurance company in the United States. In addition to being responsible for making all the major decisions for the company, he must also supervise day-to-day operations. He begins each workday much earlier than most people. Having arrived this morning at 5:30, he has already sifted through many of the documents piled high in his office. Seated behind an expansive mahogany desk, he takes notes and signs paperwork with his favorite pen, an eighteen-karat-gold Mont Blanc roller ball. With only a handful of employees in this large building at this hour, his office is remarkably quiet, giving him an opportunity to think without interruption.

Surrounding Robert is a lavish and luxuriously appointed office with an ostentatious array of expensive antique furnishings, Oriental rugs, and modern original works of art. The size of the office is also impressive at nearly three thousand square feet. One wall is composed entirely of a long row of tinted glass windows, beside which lies an elongated wooden boardroom-style table. Encircling the table are fourteen unoccupied reclining black leather executive chairs. Nearby, in one corner, is an area containing a full bar with an array of prized liquors in cut-crystal bottles displayed on rows of lighted glass shelves. On the opposite wall is a door leading to a well-equipped personal gymnasium and a private bathroom, which contains its own shower and sauna. Hanging directly behind Robert Altman's desk is an oversized cubist painting of an elderly woman in odd geometric shapes and sharply contrasting colors. The intentionally sloppy bright yellow signature in the right-hand corner reads, "Picasso."

This morning, Robert hurries to complete a proposal for a potentially important client. It had previously taken him several hours to do some final number crunching and put the finishing touches on a series of preliminary contracts. After penciling in tentative figures and drafting a couple of additional paragraphs, Robert summons his secretary. Barely looking up when she arrives, he hands a stack of papers across his desk to her.

"Ms. Jamison, could I give you these to finish up for me? I'll need them relatively quickly."

Pleasant and efficient as always, the trim, middle-aged Victoria Jamison responds, "Yes, sir, right away. Would you like to see the preliminary draft before I make final copies?"

With a wry grin, Robert Altman glances up for an instant. "As your work is always superlative, I do not believe that will be necessary, Ms. Jamison."

Back in her outer office, when she is certain that her employer cannot see her, Ms. Jamison allows herself a smile over the flattering comment. Less than twenty minutes later, the final documents, in crisp laser print, are in Robert Altman's hands. Just as Robert finishes reading over his copy of the contract, Ms. Jamison calls back into his office to announce the arrival of Jacob Pritchard of Pritchard Construction.

Shortly thereafter, the massive wooden doors leading to Robert's office swing open. Ms. Jamison leads in Mr. Pritchard, accompanied by his attorney, Hampton Burns, and his accountant, John Markowitz. Robert's preconceived mental image of Jacob Pritchard from their many phone calls had been completely inaccurate. Because of Jacob's rural Southern accent, and because Robert had assumed an older man would own such a prominent company, he had envisioned a cane-carrying Southern gentleman with a gray receded hairline, dressed in a conservative suit. In his place stands a tall, solid-appearing, tanned man in his early fifties, wearing an expensive short-sleeved golf shirt and pleated twill slacks. His two associates, by contrast, are both dressed more formally. On their entry, Robert immediately gets up and walks to his guests. In his toned-down Northeastern accent, he cordially welcomes them.

"Mr. Pritchard, thank you for sharing some of your valuable time with me this morning. Come in and make yourself at home."

Equally gracious, Jacob Pritchard responds in his distinctive Tennessee vernacular. "Robert, we appreciate your takin' time out to meet with us. I've been lookin' forward to us gettin' together for quite some time."

With the formalities completed, Jacob Pritchard introduces his two associates and then eases down into one of the three upholstered armchairs facing Robert's desk. The other two men take a seat on either side of him. After a few minutes, Jacob Pritchard whistles and then exclaims loudly, "Wow, Robert, this is one amazin' office you've got here. ... I don't know if I could work in here with all o' this fine artwork all over the place."

Not exactly certain how to respond, Robert politely adds, "Thank you, Mr. Pritchard."

In contrast to the more formal posture of his accountant and attorney, Jacob Pritchard slinks down low into his chair and extends his crossed legs. After Ms. Jamison comes in with copies of the contracts, Robert prepares to distribute them, but while doing so, he is interrupted by Jacob Pritchard.

"Now, Robert, please give Mr. Burns here my copy. He's the legal expert on this sort of thing. ... Me, I can build a fifty-story office building or a gigantic shoppin' mall and tell ya exactly how the girders ought to be, and where the plumbin' and electrical need to go, but the technical language of these type of documents is beyond me."

While Hampton Burns and John Markowitz quickly scan the multipage proposal, Robert shrewdly attempts to size up his guests. Hampton Burns, a graying man in his early sixties, is thin and fit-appearing and wears a very expensive, dark-colored, English-made double-breasted suit. Robert surmises he is a tennis player, and very likely a highly competitive one at that. On the other hand, John Markowitz is younger and less manicured. His dirty-blond hair is not precisely cut, and his sports jacket and slacks are not an exact match. Slightly overweight, and with little visible muscle tone, Markowitz, Robert assumes, likely spends a great deal of time at work and pays little attention to anything else in his life, meaning that his assessment will probably be quite thorough. With Jacob Pritchard looking all around the room and paying little attention to the discussion, Robert feels he can easily sway Markowitz's opinion.

As the men finish their reading and set the paperwork aside, several questions arise. Pulling off his thick eyeglasses, the accountant, John Markowitz, begins. "I see that you have correctly identified Mr. Pritchard's employees at five thousand two hundred and seventy-one from the data we faxed over to you last week. Your preliminary quote for one year's health coverage comes in at eighty four million three hundred thirty six thousand dollars a year."

Pulling a calculator out of his briefcase, he punches in a few numbers and jots down several figures on the margin of the contract. "That's sixteen thousand dollars per employee per year. … That seems a little high, doesn't it?"

Barely showing any emotion, Robert slides open his center desk drawer and withdraws a single typewritten page, which he lays on the center of his desk to refer to.

"Forgive me for doing my homework, Mr. Markowitz, but according to my research, you are paying close to one hundred ten million dollars a year for your current health care plan. I believe I just offered you a 20 percent discount, which is a pretty substantial chunk of money. … So, in deference to your question, I do not believe my quote is too high."

The last comment gets Jacob Pritchard's full attention. He pulls himself straight up in his chair.

"Dr. Altman, I'm impressed! How did you manage to get that information?"

Before Robert has a chance to respond to Jacob's question, John Markowitz continues to fire questions at him.

"What about prescription medications for our employees?"

"Included, but I forgot to detail it. I'll fax you an addendum."

"Are there any drugs excluded from your plan?"

"There are, and I'll be certain to include that list with the other information."

Tenaciously scrutinizing each detail, the accountant continues. "What are the individual and family financial caps?"

"Two million per person per lifetime; three hundred thousand dollars in a single year."

"Hmm ... reasonable enough."

At that moment, Hampton Burns leans forward slightly in his chair and glances over at John Markowitz, who nods. He then begins to make inquiries of his own.

"If I might ask, which hospitals does your company utilize in the provision of its health care?"

"We try to use only the finest facilities available in Nashville. We have contracts for various services with Vanderbilt, Saint Thomas, Baptist, and the Deaconess Hospital, as well as with some of the smaller regional hospitals on the outskirts of town to make care more convenient for our clients who live in those areas."

That last bit of information brings Jacob Pritchard to life again. "You mean that my employees will get to go to Vanderbilt, Baptist, and Saint Thomas with your plan?"

"Absolutely, Mr. Pritchard."

Not to be distracted, Hampton Burns continues his queries. "Are all services covered at each participating hospital?"

"Not exactly."

"Could you please clarify what is meant by 'not exactly'?"

"Well, each of our hospitals is extremely strong in certain specialties of medicine, and we have chosen to contract for those particular services at each facility."

"Obviously, before even considering your plan, we would need those hospitals and doctors clearly specified. ... I'm shocked we had to ask for that information, Dr. Altman. Normally, it is more precisely specified in this type of contract."

Reaching up toward his face, Hampton Burns then pulls his reading glasses farther down on his nose and looks directly at Robert. His next question is quite pointed. "Besides the quality of services rendered, does economics play a role in which hospitals and doctors you choose to contract with?"

Caught temporarily off guard, Robert grins slightly. "Of course part of the decision is monetary. If one hospital charges exorbitant fees for radiology, for instance, we get all of our X-rays, CT scans, and MRI scans done at a hospital that offers us more competitive rates, but before selecting that facility, we ensure that the quality is good first. ... And you realize that our securing lower costs for various procedures allows me to pass the savings directly on to you."

Having listened very carefully to the discussion, Jacob Pritchard has several questions of his own.

"Speaking of savings, how is it that you can undercut your competition by 20 percent and *supposedly* offer the same quality of care? How exactly are you able to pull that off?"

"You gentlemen are familiar with the construction of large buildings, so please allow me to provide you with an analogy if I may. ... Let's say you were to order ten thousand bolts from a particular distributor. You might normally ask for and receive a large discount off what you would normally pay for the unit cost of a single bolt. This adheres to the principles of supply-and-demand economics. ... The same is true of health care. If I can go to a hospital or group of doctors and tell them that I can guarantee them a certain number of patients, reflecting a certain number of health-care dollars per year, they are willing to cut me a deal to get my business. It's as simple as that."

Remarkably practical, Jacob Pritchard puts Robert on the spot. "So what you're telling me is that *you* can outcompete the big boys, like Blue Cross and Blue Shield, because you have *more clout*? Come on now, Dr. Altman."

Unclear on how to substantiate his position further, Robert blithely reaches into his desk and pulls out several more papers.

"Mr. Pritchard, forgive me, but since you asked, let's get down to the bottom line. I've done my research with regard to your company—that's my job. We offer a very high-quality product at a very competitive rate. The documents I have in front of me detail how much you paid for health insurance for your employees over the past five years. As we've already discussed, I'm offering you comparable health-care coverage while undercutting your costs by roughly 20 percent. Those are the facts, and that's with the assumption that your current premium doesn't go up in price this year. ... Not only that, but also I have copies of quotes you asked for from three other major insurance companies, documenting substantially higher figures than I just gave you."

John Markowitz's jaw falls open in surprise, but Hampton Burns covers his shock more cleverly by rustling papers in front of him. At first, Jacob Pritchard is quiet and pensive, staring directly into Robert's eyes. Then, he leans forward and guffaws loudly, instantly breaking the tension.

"Why, Dr. Altman, you certainly have done your research. ... John, Hampton, I think he's outfoxed us, eh? ... I like a man who knows his stuff. I'm very impressed, Robert. I think I *will* take a copy of that contract you offered me. I'll need to study up on this. It's possible that we may be doin' business after all."

Still chuckling, Jacob gets up and excuses himself, motioning to his associates that it's time to leave. On his way out, he makes a final comment about Robert's office, which he likens to a modern art gallery.

Ms. Jamison leads the three business guests back to the main elevators and thanks them for their visit. On their way down in the brightly lit elevator car to the marble-tiled lobby, Hampton Burns and John Markowitz celebrate the success of their meeting, hammering out the final details in loud, jocular conversation. All the while, Jacob Pritchard makes no comment. Once the elevator doors open, Jacob's chauffeur, who is awaiting them in the lobby, dashes to open both the front doors and the limousine doors ahead of the three men.

After giving the driver brief instructions, Jacob Pritchard eases back in his cushioned leather seat and listens to the conversation of his two associates. Halfway to their destination, Hampton Burns finally notices Jacob's quietness. For the first time since they left Robert Altman's office, he and John Markowitz pause their discussion. First looking at Jacob, Hampton Burns comments, "Jacob, it looks like you've done it again. You always manage to come up with great deals."

With a look of contemplation, Jacob turns his head to meet Hampton's gaze. Several seconds lapse before he concludes his thoughts. "I'm not convinced."

Jacob's associates look over at one another, each wondering if the other understood the remark. John Markowitz then bravely asks, "I'm sorry, Jacob, but what do you mean?"

"I'm not convinced that this Altman fellow is tellin' the truth. I've built a business on not only knowin' how to build buildings but also on knowin' how to read people. There's somethin' about this guy I don't quite like. Not only that, but what he's tellin' us doesn't sound right to me. How can he get the best doctors at each hospital to take the kinda pay cut he's talkin' about? ... I don't think so. He's cuttin' corners somewhere, and I don't want it happenin' to one of *my* workers, that's for darned sure! My guys risk their lives puttin' up *my* buildings, and it's *my* job to look out for them!"

Surprised, Jacob's accountant and attorney sit quietly, waiting for the next statement. Jacob then begins to spit out specific instructions for each man.

"Hampton, this guy's up to somethin' funny. I want you to research all the lawsuits against his company for the past coupla years, and I want you to contact other businesses that have their health insurance with AmericaHealth. See what their experience has been. And let's find out about Dr. Altman's personal history—how he got where he is. ... And also, find out how it is he got a hold'a our other insurance quotes and how he found out about how much we paid in premiums for the past five years. It really pisses me off that he got a hold'a that! Whoever gave him that information will answer *to me!*"

"Yes, sir, I'll get to work on it immediately."

"John, your job's a little easier. I want you to find out for me the company's financial strength and how quickly it pays its claims to doctors and hospitals. I want you to call the local hospitals and see how easy this company is to deal with. All right?"

"Certainly, Mr. Pritchard."

By that time, the limousine has reached Jacob's office. He excuses himself. With Jacob having exited the vehicle, the driver knows to take the other two men back to their respective offices. As they drive off, the two colleagues' shock is still evident. Jacob Pritchard's quick intellect continually amazes them.

The very minute his guests have departed, Robert wastes little time in summoning his secretary. He instructs her to locate Brian Sanders, who's the highest-ranking executive of the AmericaHealth Corporation's operations in Nashville after Robert. While Ms. Jamison is trying to locate Mr. Sanders, Robert reaches into his desk drawer for a calculator. White paper spews forth furiously as rows and rows of numbers are printed. When his eyes catch the bottom figure, they become positively vibrant. At that moment, a light knocking at the door distracts him. Without standing, he barks, "*Come in.*"

Gingerly, Brian Sanders opens one of Robert's outer office doors. He walks to his boss's desk and stands there for several seconds until Robert looks up and acknowledges him. Robert's voice exudes optimism.

"Brian, why don't you sit down over here. ... You know, I think we may have gotten into the Pritchard deal. What a coup! I gave them the higher figures, knowing they would try to negotiate. Even if they get me down another 5 percent, we could potentially make 10 million dollars a year on this deal alone! ... Now, here's what I want you to do: find out what Jacob Pritchard's favorite wine or liquor is and send him four cases today with a note from me on our corporate stationery attached. Got it? ... Now get going and also pick up a copy of the final contract from my secretary on your way out. We can fill in the negotiated numbers later."

Signaling his understanding without a saying a word, Brian hurries along. Aware of how intolerably impatient Robert Altman can be, he knows he'll need to work quickly.

Later that morning, billowing white cumulus clouds drift slowly across the expanse of the pale blue sky overhanging central Tennessee. Throughout the Vanderbilt campus, hordes of summer students traverse the well-worn paths and paved walkways on their way to class. At this time of year, the pace of the college campus is typically quite leisurely. Besides the frequent sunbathers scattered throughout the grassy lawns and courtyards, there are multiple Frisbees flying overhead, accompanied by music blaring from nearby dormitory rooms and portable radios. Groups of casually dressed young men and women are clustered throughout the tree-lined campus, engaged in casual conversation.

English 301, a course on early Russian literature, begins promptly at 10:00 a.m. in Calhoun Hall. Coveted because of its articulate and inventive professor, this course is one of the few that is forced to turn away applicants every year because of its popularity. After climbing up five flights of the

Gothic-style building's stairs and reaching the top floor, the students quickly take their seats in the auditorium-like classroom. With his back to his class as they enter, William Lockwood completes the outline of the morning's lecture on the chalkboard.

Barely giving his audience time to settle in, Professor Lockwood delves swiftly into today's subject matter. After introducing Tolstoy's masterful work *Anna Karenina* as the topic of discussion, he begins a theatrical overview of the book, set in time of great oppression in Russia's history. Expressing great interests in his subject, his brown eyes appear large through his thick horn-rimmed eyeglasses, capturing the students' full attention. While he dashes enthusiastically back and forth from the front of the classroom to the four blackboards behind him to jot notes, locks of his moderate-length curly brown hair group intermittently across his forehead. Not long into his lecture, his efforts require him to loosen his canary-yellow bow tie and shed his blue blazer, exposing the partially untucked shirt that overlies a mildly bulging waist.

After reviewing the first chapters of the book, the professor pauses and dims the lights. He then begins a PowerPoint presentation on a screen that comes down in front of the blackboards. Photographs of Tolstoy, his family, and rural scenes of Russia in the early 1900s are cast onto the large screen. Using historical landmarks to shed light on the author's life, Professor Lockwood begins to weave his gripping tale. Spellbound by the presentation, the students' eyes grow wide in anticipation of the next anecdote. They lean forward in their seats, as if by doing so they might hear what is being said more clearly. William Lockwood depicts how the novel parallels the author's life and how many of the tragic events are semiautobiographical. All too soon, to the listeners' disappointment, the lecture is over and the week's homework assignments are listed on the board. While using a handkerchief to wipe the perspiration from his forehead, Professor Lockwood dismisses his class.

"Thank you, ladies and gentlemen, for your attention. Please note the chapters we'll be covering in Wednesday's lecture. Read ahead so that you will understand the material better. Good day!"

At about the time that William Lockwood finishes his last class that afternoon, Tracy Kilpatrick leaves work a bit early for a scheduled doctor's appointment.

She is to meet her husband, Tom, at their obstetrician's office. Having arrived several minutes ahead of his wife, Tom Kilpatrick is already in the waiting room filling out routine paperwork when Tracy appears. It is obvious that this is not a happy meeting. Tom gives his wife a supportive hug while they wait. Not long afterward, a nurse calls out their names, and they are escorted back to Dr. John Greer's office, where they wait for an additional twenty minutes. Somewhat quiet, Tracy will speak only if prompted by her husband, who struggles to know how best to be supportive. A long uncomfortable silence ensues, during which time Tom distracts himself by reading the titles of all the books lining one wall of their physician's office. Then, the well-tanned, nearly bald John Greer, wearing a blue surgical scrub suit, walks in and sits down at his desk. While speaking, he leans forward and places both elbows on the desktop. Empathy is evident in his expression.

"Tom, Tracy, I'm sorry for being late." He pauses. "I hope you'll forgive me; I've had a couple of emergencies that have put me behind."

Looking across at the couple, he clearly discerns the mood of the meeting. Tracy's anxiety is quite evident, paralleled by her husband's look of concern. While biting his upper lip, Tom grips his wife's hands tightly. Without a single word spoken, the message is quite clear. Despite months of fertility drugs and four separate attempts at in vitro fertilization, Tracy is still not pregnant. Dr. Greer then describes the next steps in the workup.

"Right now, I think we ought to check Tracy's blood levels of estrogen and progesterone. ... We should also consider an endometrial biopsy and curette to determine the receptibility of the uterus to a fertilized egg. Also, Tracy, I want you to keep temperature charts like the ones you've done in the past."

Before asking the several questions on his mind, Tom looks over at his wife to see how she is handling the discussion; unfortunately, she remains stoic and withdrawn. Then he begins.

"How soon should we do all this?"

"The blood work can be done today, and the biopsy could be scheduled for as early as next week, whenever it is convenient for you and Tracy."

"Does the biopsy hurt?"

"Oh no, Tracy shouldn't feel a thing."

To gauge her thoughts, Tom nervously glances over at his wife, who is now leaning forward in her chair.

"Tracy? . . . What do you think, honey?"

Seemingly emotionless, she responds quietly, "If that's what Dr. Greer recommends, I guess that's what we ought to do."

On the following Tuesday, Tom and Tracy are once again in Dr. Greer's office. This time, however, they're in an exam room. Tracy has already changed into a patient gown. The scanty clothing and the cool temperature cause Tracy to shiver while she waits for Dr. Greer to arrive. With Tracy's head against his shoulder, Tom holds her gently and strokes her long red hair. After a light knock, John Greer and his nurse enter the room. Before proceeding, Dr. Greer pats Tracy on the shoulder and reassures her that this is merely a minor procedure. Once things get under way, Tom excuses himself, and the nurse assists Tracy. All goes smoothly.

Afterward, the Kilpatricks sit down again with their physician in his office. As they get comfortable, they notice that John Greer is not as relaxed as usual. He is more solemn and holds himself rigidly in his chair, with his hands folded on the desk before him. His usually booming voice is toned down to a much more serious level. Speaking slowly, he begins. "Tom, Tracy, there was something on the exam today that concerned me. There was … a reddish area on the cervix."

Anxiously, Tom interrupts, asking, "*A reddish area*? What does that mean?"

"To be honest with you, it could be any number of things. It wasn't there two months ago on Tracy's last exam. I took the liberty of taking a biopsy to determine the exact cause. The results should be out on Thursday."

Now flushed and a little nervous, Tom begins to speak more quickly. "What do you think it could be?"

Before answering, John Greer drops his gaze. "It could be infection or an irritation, or a response to some of the procedures we've done."

Sensing that their physician is withholding something, Tom presses Dr. Greer. "Could it be anything else?"

This time when he answers, John Greer looks directly at Tom. "It could … it possibly could, but not very likely, represent an early cancer."

"*What?!*" Tracy exclaims.

To calm the couple, Dr. Greer moves from behind his desk and sits down beside them, reaching for both of their hands. His tone is fatherly and reassuring.

"Tom, Tracy, cancer is the least likely possibility." He pauses. "In a few weeks, everything will be fine and we'll be back to trying another in vitro procedure. Please don't worry unnecessarily."

Two days later, at their next meeting, John Greer is serious and much more reserved. Sensing their physician's mood, the Kilpatricks sit mutely before him, trying to brace themselves for what they're about to hear. Dr. Greer struggles initially to get his words out.

"I don't really know where to begin. ... I'm afraid I have bad news today. ... I can't even believe the results myself. The cervical biopsy confirmed my worst suspicion. It appears that Tracy has an early cancer of the cervix, with invasion much deeper than I would have guessed by the physical examination. ... It concerned me so much that I had the pathologist pull the slides for me to look at myself. It can't be treated by a simple cone biopsy. ... I'm afraid the only option that would adequately treat the cancer would be to perform a hysterectomy."

Those last words instantly strike terror in Tracy's heart. Gasping aloud, she stands and runs from Dr. Greer's office, her eyes wild with fear. After a brief apology, Tom jumps up to chase after his wife. Standing in front of the glass double doors at the main entrance of the building, he visually searches for her. Several minutes later, he discovers Tracy tucked up in a tight ball underneath a tree on the front lawn of the office building next door. His heart sinks when he gets close enough to hear her quiet sobbing. Sliding in beside her, he cradles her in his arms and gently rocks her back and forth. As she buries her face deeply into his chest, he can feel her warm tears against his skin.

With his own emotions running wild, Tom realizes that he must remain calm for Tracy's sake. Desperately searching for happier thoughts, Tom allows his mind to drift to his first recollections of the day when he and Tracy first met, how gorgeous she looked on that autumn morning outside their high school. She wore a pale pink sweater and a long white skirt. He recalls how her long red hair shone in the morning light and how angelic her face looked. When one of his friends introduced them, Tom was so awkward that he could barely get a word out. Afraid that she considered him to be socially inept, he never expected to get another chance to speak with her. Several weeks later, a second opportunity arose and he forced himself to overcome his shyness and strike up a conversation. They began dating soon after, and their relationship blossomed.

Following graduation from the high school on the outskirts of Knoxville, Tennessee, the two attended David Lipscomb University together in Nashville. Being a practical individual, Tom chose to study accounting. At the completion of his education, he managed to land a job with a prestigious firm, Hayes and Cromwell, located in downtown Nashville. Because of his strong dedication to work and his honest, soft-spoken demeanor, Tom was made a partner early with his company. Tracy's interest lay in U.S. history, and her goal was to become a high school history teacher. Secretarial work has only been a temporary occupation until she can find an appropriate teaching position. It was only a month after college graduation that the two began to plan their wedding.

Now, as Tom sits in the grass with the late afternoon sunshine streaming into his eyes and his limp wife beside him, he allows himself to face his own fears head-on. Since they were first married, he and Tracy have dreamed of a family of their own. Both have shared their own special dreams of parenthood. Tracy longs for the day she can hold her baby in her arms and rock it to sleep, and for spelling bees, Christmases, the happy sounds of youngsters at the playground . . . . After a long day's work, Tom looks forward to having his son or daughter sit in his lap. He relishes the thought of bedtime stories, family vacations, and outdoor sporting activities. With the cold reality of their earlier meeting sinking in, Tom can see his daydream vanishing before him. He can bear it for himself but not for his sensitive, gentle wife.

As the graying sky brings the cooler dusk, Tracy has not yet moved or spoken. Realizing their need to go, Tom lifts his wife and supports her as they walk in the direction of their car. Before heading home, he leaves Tracy in the car and returns to Dr. Greer's office to apologize to him over their abrupt departure. He then grapples for a way to cope with the unbearable situation.

Chapter 8

O n the Saturday following Brad and Julie's dinner together at San Antonio Taco Company, Brad manages to complete his work ahead of schedule. Leaving the Vanderbilt pathology department shortly after 3:00 p.m., Brad takes advantage of his unexpected freedom and hurriedly makes a straight path for home. Despite heavy fatigue, he decides to go for a six-mile run, hoping it will perk him up. Even though he has only enough stamina to run very slowly, he finds that the aerobic activity rejuvenates him. After a shower, Brad strolls toward the living room, wearing only a loose pair of shorts. Sinking down into a chair, he reaches for the phone to call Julie. Aware that she's likely to be at the hospital, he is surprised when he hears her answer.

"I'm glad it's you, Brad; I hoped I'd get to talk to you today. Don't tell me, I'm guessing you're still at work and needed a distraction, so you decided to call me."

"Believe it or not, I'm actually home, and I've even gotten in some exercise. Isn't that a miracle?"

"I'll say. I just got home from work myself a minute ago. What did you do, bribe someone into giving you the afternoon off?" "I did, and it was mighty costly, but since I'm free from the shackles of work, what do you think about having dinner with me?"

"I don't know about this, Brad—two nights in a row for dinner? You'll start taking me for granted if I don't watch out."

"Now *that* would be awfully hard to imagine."

Julie laughs. "In that case, you've got yourself a deal. What if I came by your place in about twenty minutes?"

"Perfect. I'll be waiting for you."

Not long afterward, Brad hears a gentle tap on the front door. He is by this time more presentable with the addition to his attire of a polo shirt and sneakers. After a big hug, the two are on their way to a restaurant near the Vanderbilt campus on West End Avenue, J. Alexander's Redlands Grill. Famous for its good-quality food and generous portions, the restaurant has become a favorite of the Nashville locals.

Waiting in line at the restaurant's main entrance, Brad glances over at the large Centennial Park located just across West End Avenue. Situated in the center of the park is the only known full-scale replica of the Parthenon, erected nearly a century ago for the World's Fair. The reproduced sculptures and motifs gracing the front of the structure are exact duplicates, as are the long rows of ornate Corinthian columns that completely encircle the building. As Brad scans the remarkably intricate architectural details, something distracts him. Immediately adjacent to the park is a building strikingly different from the Parthenon. Rising from the center of the structure, in bright yellow plastic and aluminum, is a giant letter *M*, designating the location of a McDonald's restaurant with multicolored plastic playground pieces in front. Brad finds it difficult to imagine anything more vulgar. The contrast of the two structures, one a timeless Greek masterpiece and the other a modern iteration, is jarring. Noticing Brad's preoccupation, Julie inquires about it. After a brief explanation, he poses a question: "Can you imagine what would happen if this area were buried by an avalanche or an earthquake for a century or two, and then it was unearthed by a team of archeologists? I wonder which civilization they would consider to be more advanced on the basis of the architectural styles?"

Curious, Julie looks briefly at the park and laughs. His name is called shortly thereafter. On entering the restaurant, the couple is treated to the pleasant aroma of herbs and spices, seasoned tomato sauces, and freshly baked breads. They are quickly seated by a friendly college-aged woman, who takes their drink orders. Their waiter is not far behind, and their food is soon on its way. After they are settled, but before their meal arrives, Julie temporarily becomes more serious.

"Brad, thanks for letting me talk about my father last night. I often avoid thinking about him because it hurts so much."

Reassuringly, Brad reaches across the table for one of Julie's hands. "I'm really happy you did; I enjoyed hearing about him, and it made me realize how lucky I am to still have both of my parents."

Their waiter arrives with their main courses, temporarily interrupting their conversation. After a few bites, Julie changes the subject. "Brad, tell me more about your family. You've talked some about your parents and your brother and sister, but I've never heard you say much about your childhood. What was it like?"

While savoring the taste of filet mignon and garlic bread, Brad notices that his mind begins to wander. He pictures how his hometown, Cooperstown, New York, appeared to him when he was five or six years old. He remembers how their white Greek-style wooden house, located at One Main Street, looked to him as a child. With its long arching porches and wooden columns in front, the house seemed to stretch the boundaries of his world. On carefree summer mornings, he and his older brother, Matt, would leap from the front porch and run in search of play. They might head for the park by the shore of Lake Otsego and climb the life-size statue of James Fennimore Cooper, or they might scour the streets of Cooperstown, looking for other youngsters to join in a game of kickball or hide-and-go-seek. Past the fastidiously maintained Victorian homes on Main Street, the boys would race one another. They barely took notice of the long American flags that waved from the front of the homes all summer, their occupants proud to call themselves American citizens.

Nearly every week, Brad and Matt and their young friends would end up at either the Baseball Hall of Fame or Doubleday Field, the first baseball diamond ever created. According to local legend, Abner Doubleday, in the mid-1800s, plowed under a portion of his farmland to form the foundation for the field. It was rumored that some of Abner's neighbors questioned his sanity at the time. The boys would show up at the entrance to the field early in the morning, and Mr. Perkins, the gatekeeper, would let them in without charge. Brad and his friends never grew weary of running the bases at the stadium, each dreaming of becoming a major league hero someday.

Play was certainly a tiring venture. When it came time for a soft drink, Brad and Matt would make a trip to the antique-style Withey's Pharmacy in the downtown area. Invariably, they would run out of money and would require an advance on their allowance. The two would take turns visiting their father at work for additional funds.

Brad can picture himself standing in front of the Romanesque red sandstone Wilber National Bank, trying to get up the nerve to interrupt his father at work. At Matt's urging, he would forge ahead, still a bit nervous. On entering the dimly lit bank, he would see the rows of tellers' windows off to the right and the giant polished silver bank vault from the 1800s that occupied the center of the room. Gingerly, he would make his way toward the far right-hand corner of the building, where his father's office was located. There, he would announce his presence to his dad's secretary, Mrs. Doris Mitchell. Wearing her stylish cat-eye glasses, Mrs. Mitchell would always, in her polite manner, ask how "Master Brad" was doing. While awaiting a break in his father's busy work schedule, Brad would sit in a tall slat-backed wooden chair next to Mrs. Mitchell's desk with his short legs dangling in the air.

Eventually his father's seemingly massive wooden door would swing open, and Brad would be escorted in. His eye level was nearly at the same height as the ornate brass doorknob of his father's office. He can recall just what his father looked like in his staid three-piece pinstripe suit and his conservatively trimmed dark-brown hair. In the afternoon, the light would stream in from a window beside his father's desk, and Brad could see an endless array of dust particles floating in the air. Mr. Pierson would direct Brad to a chair beside him, while his son discussed his financial shortfall. Patient and loving, David Pierson would ask about the necessity of this monetary advance. After being satisfied that the cause was legitimate, he would reach into one of his long trouser pockets to retrieve two shining quarters, surrendering them only after Brad agreed to be more judicious with his spending, and "in the future exhibit better fiscal responsibility." With the burdensome task of troubling his father over, Brad would slide down from his chair, express his profound thanks, and dash outside to celebrate his newfound wealth with his older sibling.

During warmer months, at the crack of dawn on Saturday, Brad would hear his father whistle classical music while he rustled up their fishing gear in a downstairs hall closet. From the kitchen, Brad's mother, Jean Pierson, would be whipping up pancakes and bacon, and the house would be permeated by the aroma of freshly brewed coffee. After climbing into David Pierson's forest-green wood-paneled Plymouth station wagon, the family would drive toward their favorite fishing spot on the far side of Lake Otsego. Brad remembers all too well his brother Matt's skill as a fisherman. With great curiosity, he would carefully study the exact technique his brother used to bait his hook and how he casted his line. Kristin, Brad's younger sister by three years, also became adept as a fisherwoman once she received help with baiting her hook.

At that instant, Brad's daydream comes to a crashing halt. Julie's voice jolts him back into reality.

"Brad, where have you been? I lost you there for a couple of minutes."

"I'm sorry, Julie. I was off daydreaming."

After sharing with Julie many of his recollections, Brad continues. "One of the things that I was especially fond of as a child was listening to my mother and my sister, Kristin, read poems and short stories they had composed for one another. My mother had been a high school English teacher before we came along, but she took time off until we were all in school ourselves... Anyway, she spent a lot of time teaching Kristin to write, and Kristin actually became quite talented."

"What's Kristin doing now?"

"She's still writing for that same magazine in Burlington, Vermont, but she isn't sure if she'll stay with the company or not. I think she wants something a little more exciting."

"Have you talked to her recently?"

"I got a call from her last weekend. She's thinking about buying a new car and wanted some advice."

"Tell me more about Matt."

"Matt. Wow, I'm not really sure where to start. Matt was a great older brother. As I've told you before, he and I were best friends when we were children. Given that he was only two years older than me, we essentially grew up together. We did everything together. We played baseball, went fishing, and we even got in trouble together."

"In trouble?"

"I hate to admit it, but yes. ... The worst thing Matt and I ever did was that one day, we pretended to go to school but instead went off fishing by ourselves. By the time we got back home, Mom was frantic. She thought someone had kidnapped us. Even the police were there. But, until the day I die, I'll never forget the profound look of hurt and anger in my father's eyes when we came walking up with our fishing poles."

"Oh my gosh, Brad, I bet your parents were beside themselves."

"Yeah, it was really awful. We were pretty ashamed of ourselves for a long time after that. Anyway, Matt and I have always been very close. I still remember the day he left for college; what a miserable day that was. We got up early that morning and packed all his stuff in my father's car and then took a walk downtown and had breakfast together. When we got back to the house, the entire family drove to Schenectady, which is about two hours from Cooperstown. After we dropped Matt's belongings off in his dorm room at Union College, we stayed overnight in a hotel nearby. When my mom, my dad, and I got ready to leave the next morning, Matt and I were both pretty upset. We had a real hard time saying goodbye."

"Is Matt still working in Boston?"

"He's continued to work for the same bank, but he recently got promoted. He's now running their commercial loan department. My dad keeps on trying to convince him to come home and run the bank in Cooperstown once he retires."

After dessert arrives, Julie asks Brad to continue.

"When I was about ten years old, our family went through some really hard times. As I mentioned, my father was the president of the local bank. One day he came home looking really shaken up. I don't ever remember him looking quite that way before. It was the only time I'd ever seen my mother cry, and it really frightened me. Anyway, the next day in the paper was this story about him being accused of stealing a large sum of money from the bank. It wasn't until about three months later, at about the time my father was scheduled to go on trial, that it was discovered that my dad's best friend, Jim Tate, the vice president, had actually taken the money and had tried to frame my father. The whole town rejected our family until the investigation was completed and Mr. Tate was convicted. In an odd way, my father has never been quite the same since then. He's much more serious. I miss his quick wit and laughter. Mr. Tate ended up going to prison for a while, and I know that really upset my father. Even though he was betrayed by his best friend, he still hated to see Jim Tate's family get hurt."

"That's horrible, Brad! I can't believe that happened to your family."

"It was pretty bad. Matt and I were deeply hurt when the other children shunned us. For close to a year after that, he and I chose to play by ourselves. It brought us a lot closer together. Even through high school, we stayed best friends."

"When did you start running?"

"I was in the eighth grade at the time, and Matt was a sophomore in high school. He decided to try out for the cross-country team, and one day I went along with him to one of the practices."

"I understand that you were quite a track athlete at one time."

Brad's lack of comment piques Julie's interest.

"Sandy told me you were quite talented in high school and that you ended up having some sort of national ranking when you were at Princeton."

"I didn't realize that Sandy was writing my biography, but if he is, I recommend that he spice it up a little. I'm just a little too boring for the book to make any money."

Julie smiles. "You don't have to be so modest. You know I'll get it out of you anyway."

Surprised by the comment, Brad laughs. "Okay, okay, you win. For me, high school was the happiest time of my life. I felt so free back then, and competing in running was more fun than anything I'd ever done. During my junior year, I was in the best shape of my life. My mile times kept falling, and all of a sudden I had a national ranking. It really surprised me."

"Now, see, that wasn't so hard."

Brad then looks into Julie's eyes and grins. At that moment, he begins to feel sleepy. Politely, he asks Julie if she's ready to leave, explaining that he could really use a good night's sleep after his long week. With a work schedule often tougher than Brad's, Julie understands completely. After dropping Brad off in front of his apartment, Julie rolls down her window and calls him back over to her car. She kisses him briefly. As he nears his front door, she calls out to him, saying, "Thanks, Brad."

Turning back toward Julie, Brad yells, "Thanks for what?"

"Thanks for a lovely evening."

After Brad closes his front door, he hears Julie rev her engine and squeal her tires as she leaves the parking lot. He chuckles to himself, amused by her aggressive behavior behind the wheel. In the living room, he picks up the remote and turns on the television, deciding to rest on the couch and watch the news before going to bed. Unintentionally, he falls fast asleep. Several hours later, a loud commercial pulls him from his sound slumber.

At first, Brad, in his somnolent state, is unsure what happened or what time it is. A quick glance at the clock brings makes him aware. He drags himself to the bathroom to wash his face and get ready for bed. The lukewarm water against his skin partially awakens him. Before settling in for the evening, he returns to the living room to watch a portion of the local news. On his sixteen-inch color television screen, the main female newscaster, Brenda McAlpine, presents the evening's top story: nursing home care reform in the state of Tennessee. Brad can't help but be somehow amused by the giant mass of bleached blond hair piled atop her head, likely requiring several hours each morning to get under control.

After the political career of the state's lieutenant governor, Mr. Alan Carter, is described, his picture is flashed onto the screen during the entire news story. Depicting Mr. Carter as "a selfless unyielding champion for the elderly," Ms. McAlpine goes on to outline the types of abuses that had been commonplace in Tennessee nursing homes before his administration. She then describes the sweeping legislation Mr. Carter has enacted and the dramatic differences it has made for nursing home residents.

Staring at the lieutenant governor's image on the television, Brad notes his receding reddish-brown hair, his ruddy complexion, and his rounded face. To Brad, his appearance is more reminiscent of a backwoods redneck than of a politician.

Next, there is live footage of an interview taped earlier with Mr. Carter. With Carter's raspy deep voice and his somewhat crude manner of speaking,

Brad somehow has doubts about the man's "selflessness." After listening to the story for several minutes, Brad points the remote at the television screen and the image instantly vanishes. Afterward, the living room becomes completely quiet and dark. Guiding himself to the bedroom by the faint light of a solitary bedside lamp, Brad is soon in bed. A few moments later, he is sound asleep.

Chapter 9

I t had been a typical balmy June day in Nashville, with the thermometer reaching well into the nineties by midafternoon. At 7:00 p.m. on this Thursday evening, while the blistering sun still stands high in the sky, the Utilization Review Committee for the AmericaHealth Corporation prepares to meet. Seated at the large boardroom-style table in Robert Altman's extravagant penthouse office are twelve physicians from a variety of subspecialties. Independent from the health insurance company, these doctors have agreed to serve on the committee to review cost expenditures related to the provision of health care. Dr. Edward Westmoreland has been appointed chairman of the committee, and Robert Altman serves as the liaison to the AmericaHealth Corporation.

As things get under way, Drs. Altman and Westmoreland take their places at each head of the table. Robert quickly recapitulates the discussion that he and Edward had two evenings previous, which focused on reducing the number of hospital days that patients are allowed following surgical procedures. He then makes general recommendations in that regard to the distinguished group. To conclude this portion of the meeting, Robert mentions that the actuarial data will be reviewed by Dr. Westmoreland and him to come up with specific guidelines for the committee to evaluate at the next month's meeting.

After that introduction, the more mundane portion of the meeting ensues. Physicians who have been contracted to AmericaHealth are required to submit formal proposals for certain expensive tests or procedures. The committee's job is to listen to those requests and approve or deny them. Sometimes, physicians may come in person and make special requests for their patients should their initial written request be denied. Beginning with the most straightforward cases, Edward addresses his colleagues: "Dr. Ferrell is asking permission to perform a right knee replacement on a patient who suffers from severe dysfunctional arthritis caused from a high school sports injury. The patient, apparently, can barely walk at this point. Other pertinent medical history is his weight of 270 pounds."

Edward circulates the patient's recent knee X-rays for each physician to evaluate. The orthopedic specialist on the committee then offers his opinion. "The patient absolutely needs the knee replaced, but until he loses some weight, there's a substantial risk that the replacement joint could break down."

Signaling their agreement to approve the procedure once the patient has lost a significant amount of weight, the committee moves on to the next case. Edward resumes: "Surgical correction of severe lower extremity varicose veins in a fifty-two-year-old white female has been proposed by Dr. Nichols."

Two large photographs are then distributed, which demonstrate large, serpentine-appearing purplish vessels all over the women's legs. As the physicians review the photographs, many of them grimace. Robert Altman directs a question at Edward, who holds the patient's medical records. "Is there any history of phlebitis, thrombosis, or clotting disorders?"

After he reviews the chart, Edward says, "No details are given related to that."

Robert Altman then declares, "Unless this woman has known phlebitis or a prior episode of deep-venous thrombosis, this constitutes cosmetic surgery. AmericaHealth does not pay for plastic surgery!"

The Utilization Review physicians have a mixed response to this case. They ask that the vote be delayed until such time that further history can be obtained.

Over the several hours, the committee evaluates nearly thirty patient histories, along with suggested medical treatments. To keep things on schedule, Edward moves swiftly through the list. He is relieved when only a few cases remain.

"A forty-one-year-old, mildly overweight woman with severe ulcerative disease of the stomach has been evaluated by Dr. Spencer, a general surgeon. Because of the severity of her disease, he has recommended ablating several of the nerves to the stomach as well as partially removing the stomach itself. It is notable that she has had progression of her ulcers despite aggressive treatment with multiple medications over the past six months. Her history indicates that she has had intermittent rectal bleeding and anemia, and recently, a single episode of regurgitating blood."

The committee hums with discussion for several minutes. Dr. Brice, a specialist in gastroenterology, opens the remarks. "We need to get this woman to surgery before she perforates! Why are we even debating this case?"

Countering Dr. Brice, Robert makes an observation. "She has not yet had a trial of the new, more potent agents that could potentially further decrease gastric hydrochloric acid production. Nexium and Prevacid have been extremely useful in situations like this one. Current literature speculates that these medicines might obviate transection of the vagus nerve and partial gastrectomy in select patients."

Red-faced, Dr. Brice forcefully states, "If she perforates, gets peritonitis, and dies, you'll wish you had approved this one!"

The outburst stirs a heated discussion. Opposing views are openly debated. To intervene and to try to keep the meeting from degenerating further, Edward stands and speaks loudly to get everyone's attention. "Gentlemen, gentlemen, please. Let us proceed to a vote on this issue. I would like a show of hands to approve the surgery."

After several members signal their agreement, Edward asks for those in favor of a trial of other medications prior to surgical intervention. By a narrow margin, they elect to wait on surgery, further angering Dr. Brice. Reluctantly, and after many more concerns are raised, the physician group agrees to continue. Edward once again takes the floor.

"Gentlemen, please look at insert three in your packet this evening. This describes the very complicated case of a patient of Dr. Vanderhaden's, whom many of you know is a top-notch ophthalmologist at Vanderbilt Hospital. This sixty-eight-year-old woman has diabetic retinal disease with substantial new blood vessel formation in the retina, dramatically reducing her vision. Additionally, she has what appears to be a melanoma of the right choroid and glaucoma in both eyes. To make matters worse, she also has a very unusual clotting disorder. Dr. Vanderhaden believes that to correct all of these problems without possibly causing this woman to become permanently blind, he'll need the assistance of a world-renowned retina specialist from Germany, along with the input of one of the Vanderbilt hematologists. He is petitioning the committee to approve the cost of the surgery as well as the fees required to bring over his European colleague."

Dr. James Steele, a pulmonary physician on the committee, offers his impression. "It sounds to me that Dr. Vanderhaden has thought through this woman's situation carefully. I applaud him for being willing, first of all, to take on such a difficult case, and second of all, to know when to ask for help. I'd like to propose that we bring the specialist over from Germany."

Given that this appears to be a relatively straightforward issue, Edward asks for a show of hands, and the committee votes eight to three to approve the surgery. Before the next item can be introduced, Robert Altman again interrupts.

"I'm not sure we've thought this one all the way through, gentlemen. We don't even know what this retina specialist's costs are. Can't we get dollar figures before we agree to this?"

The introverted, scholarly-appearing ophthalmologist who holds a position on the committee, Dr. Marvin Yablonski, politely gives his opinion. "From her history and her visual-field mapping, I would dare say that this case would be a challenge for the most experienced retina specialist. Frankly, Dr. Vanderhaden could have requested a whole team of surgeons from both this country and abroad to assist him."

Having gained confirmation, Edward approves the decision and turns his attention to the next item. Before getting two words out, he is again halted. This time, from a darkened corner near the front of the room, the corporate attorney for the AmericaHealth Corporation, Howard Morgan, interrupts, waving a binder in one hand. He stands up and moves directly behind Robert Altman as he reads from the large notebook. "In Article IV, paragraph 3, please note the following: 'In the case in which a noncontracted physician attempts to be designated as a provider of care temporarily for the AmericareHealth Corporation, the decision of the appropriateness of this said appointment shall be decided upon jointly by the Committee on Utilization Review *and* the chief executive officer. Should there be a discrepancy between these two forenamed authorities, then the acting C E O, at his or her discretion, may override the decision of the Committee on Utilization Review.' I believe that Dr. Altman, pursuant to this document, may forbid the payment of fees to this German physician if he so chooses."

Dead silence overtakes the room following Howard Morgan's brief interlude. Not even the experienced Edward Westmoreland knows what to say. After several long minutes have lapsed, Jim Steele again speaks up. "If the C E O can override our decisions, then what *possible role* do we play on this ridiculous committee?"

With a less than confident demeanor, Robert Altman responds calmly. "Jim, this is a unique situation. Normally, in the majority of the decisions this committee makes, I am not even a voting member. Only in a situation like this, where work is being performed by doctors not under contract, do I have any say at all. At this point, I am not even asking that we not pay for the specialist from Europe; I'm merely asking that we wait to determine what the exact fees are before making that final decision."

Still dissatisfied, Jim Steele remarks, "Well, I'm afraid I don't find your comments particularly conciliatory, Dr. Altman. What if it was your mother who needed the eye surgery?"

Doing his best to stay calm, Edward tries to appeal to Dr. Steele. "Come on, Jim, don't jump to conclusions. We're only asking for a couple of days to get an estimate of the cost."

"And what if the cost seems reasonable to the committee but not to Dr. Altman and his attorney? What then?"

Still fuming from the earlier discussion, Edwin Brice interrupts the meeting with an emotional outcry. "Altman, do you remember what it's like to take care of patients, or has your obsession with profits driven out all your compassion? I *refuse* to be a member of these unethical proceedings! My resignation from this committee is effective immediately!"

Leaping to his feet, he tosses his chair aside and takes several steps before turning back to face the physicians seated at the table. This time, his voice becomes even more hostile. "God save us from all of our shame. I know many of you accepted huge allocations of stock from AmericaHealth when they first came to town. They sold it to you at a sweet price to get you financially intertwined with them. Don't you see what they are doing to you? They're getting you to do their dirty work for them by cutting costs to keep their profits high. They want you to have enough money of your own at risk so you'll do almost anything to keep from losing your life's savings. You're selling your souls, my friends, and your patients are suffering because of it."

Storming out of the room, Edwin Brice slams the large six-paneled wooden door so forcefully that the entire office shakes. After his departure, the room becomes engulfed in an uneasy silence. The remaining health-care practitioners lean far back in their chairs, shell-shocked, contemplating their colleague's last words. Uncertain how to handle this turn of events, Edward, in a faltering voice, dismisses his colleagues, ending the meeting early.

Chapter 10

As mid-June rolls around, Brad Pierson relishes the fact that in just two weeks, he will begin his fourth and final year of residency training at Vanderbilt. Nevertheless, on this Friday morning, he has little time to celebrate, as he once again struggles to keep pace with the work before him. While he organizes a large stack of pathology cases to review, he hears his name being paged on the overhead speaker system. Picking up the nearest telephone, he is pleasantly surprised to hear Julie's voice on the other end of the line.

"Brad, I just had to call you this morning to tell you how excited I am."

Somewhat puzzled, Brad does not reply immediately. Eventually he says, "Excited? About what, Julie?"

"You mean to tell me you've forgotten about tomorrow night already? You know … the Swan Ball?"

Mentally stumbling at first, Brad manages a quick recovery. "Of course, of course I remember. How could I have forgotten that? My swan costume is currently at the dry cleaner's being pressed."

Despite laughing to herself, Julie feigns irritation: "Very funny. Anyway, what time should I be ready tomorrow night?"

"Didn't you say it started around seven o'clock? What if I came by about six thirty?"

"Sounds good. That should get us there in plenty of time. Uh-oh, looks like I've got to run. Call you tonight."

As Brad reaches around to hang up the wall phone, he sees his friend Sandy Starke lurking nearby with a mischievous grin on his face. "Well, hey, Bradley. Was that little Julie?"

By the sarcastic tone of Sandy's voice, Brad realizes that he's about to be given a hard time. He tries to dismiss Sandy by pretending to go back to work, but unfortunately that does not dissuade his friend.

"You know, Julie's an extremely nice woman. Not only that, but also she's very good-looking."

With his head down, Brad continues to work, trying to ignore his friend's commentary. Eventually, though, he replies, "Yes, Sandy, I know that she's a wonderful person. She is much better than I deserve."

"Well, what seems to be the problem?"

"I haven't noticed that there were any problems, aside from *you*."

Sensing that his antics are irritating to Brad, Sandy continues. "Sure, there's a problem. ... She's the perfect woman for you, Brad, and you and I both know it. When are you going to act like a real man and ask her to marry you?"

The last sentence distracts Brad, causing him to drop one of the glass-mounted tissue specimens, breaking it. "Now look at what you've made me do, Dr. Starke!"

"I didn't make you do that. You're just afraid of the *m* word."

After he looks up at Sandy, Brad laughs. "You're right. I guess I just don't have your amazing maturity."

"Well, if you ever need advice, you know my rates are quite affordable."

Irritated, Brad throws a wadded-up paper towel in Sandy's direction, striking him squarely on the forehead. "Now that's what I think of your advice!"

The following evening, Brad arrives on Julie's doorstep wearing a traditional black tuxedo and carrying a bouquet of red roses in one hand. He is surprised when her mom answers the door.

"Good evening, Mrs. Christensen. How are you?"

"Fine, Brad, but I hope you'll please call me Anna. Come on in. Julie's almost ready. Here, let me put those flowers in water."

Leading Brad into the living room, she offers him something to drink while she searches for a vase. Then, she excuses herself and runs upstairs to help

Julie finish up. A few minutes later, Brad hears Julie call from the staircase. "Brad, don't look until I get downstairs."

To respect Julie's wishes, Brad turns around until he is given permission to peek. Listening to the sound of Julie's high-heeled shoes slowly step down the wooden staircase, Brad can tell she's nearby when he hears the rustling of her dress.

"Okay, Brad, you can look now."

When Brad turns around, his jaw nearly falls open. Dressed in a flowing, floor-length, pastel green silk-and-chiffon gown with her long blonde hair worn up in a formal style, Julie is truly striking. As Brad stares into her eyes, which are a light olive tonight, he is speechless. Not having heard a word from her date since he arrived, Julie shyly asks, "Do I look all right?"

Searching awkwardly for the appropriate words, Brad blurts out, "Julie, oh my gosh … you look beautiful! Your dress is amazing."

Julie blushes slightly and then beams in response to the flattering comment. Standing patiently behind Julie, Anna proudly joins in the conversation while she continues to adjust her daughter's gown.

"Believe it or not, I found this dress several weeks ago when I was shopping for something else. The moment I saw it, I just knew it had been made for Julie. She nearly fainted when I first showed it to her."

After reminiscing for several minutes about her personal past experiences at the Swan Ball, Anna walks with Brad and Julie to the car. On the way, she holds up the back of Julie's dress to keep it from getting soiled. As they drive off, she waves and then tears up, sentimental about the occasion, wishing her husband were here to see his daughter look so grown up. When she sees Julie roll down her window to wave back, she yells, "You kids have a great time now!"

While Brad drives in the direction of Belle Meade, Julie excitedly discusses many of the events surrounding the Swan Ball. At the tall stone archway marking the entrance to Percy Warner Park, Brad turns right to join a narrow road that winds along the first tee of the adjacent golf course. Then, the sign to Cheekwood appears, and a hundred yards straight ahead lies a massive Georgian-style granite mansion rising from a hilltop. Never having visited the home or the surrounding botanical gardens before, Brad is stunned by its appearance.

"I never knew this place was back here; it's incredible. It looks more like a castle than a private home."

Aware of some of the history of the estate, Julie enjoys sharing it with Brad. "From what I remember, the house was built sometime in the 1920s, and apparently at the time it was the largest private residence not only in Nashville but in the entire state of Tennessee. The owners of the estate, Leslie and Mabel Cheek, traveled extensively to Europe while designing the house. They came up with the name Cheekwood by combining their last name with Mabel Cheek's maiden name, which was Wood. Inside the house are supposed to be some fabulous European antiques and furnishings, which I've been dying to see. In the center of a large reflecting pool on the back lawn is a hand-forged swan fountain, which is how the ball obtained its name." She pauses. "I've seen part of the house before, but they only open it up completely once a year for this charity event."

With a partially concealed smirk, Brad teases Julie. "Wow, thanks. I didn't know I was going to get my own privately guided tour."

Lightly tapping Brad on one shoulder in a sign of displeasure, Julie responds playfully. "And you better darned well appreciate it, too, Dr. Pierson."

Once they've reached the long circular driveway leading up to the front entrance of the home, Brad sees a group of valets awaiting the arriving vehicles. After he exchanges his car keys for a numbered parking ticket, Brad pauses for a moment in front of the mansion, holding Julie's hand. There, surrounded by a large crowd, the couple is awestruck by the ostentatious array of people and automobiles that arrive shortly thereafter. In among the camera flashes of reporters and the spotlights of camera crews, country music stars, in flamboyant, ridiculously priced gowns and tuxedos appear in exotic sports cars or chauffeur-driven luxury cars. As if in some kind of competition, each tries to have the most expensive and memorable garb, matched by an equally celebrated entrance. Other well-regarded but more conservative people are present, including politicians, local civic leaders, and professionals. Even the governor, Harrison Moorhouse, and his wife make a brief public appearance.

In the midst of all the excitement, Brad reaches for Julie's arm. The two slide quietly through the front doors in between groups of celebrities. Inside,

Julie leads Brad along the immense hallway adjacent to the foyer, where she points out many of the home's priceless paintings and sculptures.

After the couple has had a chance to look over many of the antiques, Julie leads Brad to a nonsuspended circular staircase with a wrought iron balustrade that was retrieved in one piece from Queen Charlotte's palace in Pew, England. Before Julie can finish her browsing, the ringing of handbells downstairs signals the beginning of dinner. The large gathering that has accumulated slowly moves in the direction of a large living room located at the back of the house. There, a long row of glass doors are open to the outdoors. Brad and Julie follow the other guests out onto the back lawn, where they see a bright spotlight centered on the large bronze-sculptured swan fountain. From its long beak, a stream of water gently arches to the pool below, making a pleasant trickling sound. Beside it are multiple, portable dinner tables, where the evening meal is being served by elegant candlelight.

Fortunately for the planners of the event, the weather has been cooperative. The evening air is warm but not too moist, and a faint moon is already showing well before sundown. Also helping to create the mood are the soothing strains of classical music that emanate from an experienced quartet. Tastefully appointed, many of the dining tables are topped with mountainous flower arrangements, and alongside the fountain is a semicircular table where formally dressed waiters serve a variety of beverages. Rising several feet from this table is a swan ice sculpture, an exact replica of the one adorning the center of the fountain.

Relieved to see a familiar face, Brad guides Julie to one of the dining tables, where an attending physician he knows from the Deaconess Hospital, Dr. Alan Richards, is seated.

"Alan, good evening. Would you mind if we joined you?"

Respectfully, the wiry, moderate-statured Alan Richards stands and motions to the couple, indicating two seats directly across from him. "Certainly, Brad. We'd love for you to sit with us. I don't remember if you've ever met my wife, Paula."

After saying hello to the polite but businesslike Paula Richards, Brad introduces Julie while the couple gets settled. Julie then speaks up.

"Dr. Richards, it's nice to meet you and your wife. Brad has told me many times how much he enjoys working with you."

Pleased by the compliment, Alan smiles. "I'm honored Brad feels that way, Julie. Working with him is a pleasure also; he's a very dedicated young man."

After dinner has been served, several people come by the table to visit Alan and Paula Richards. One of these formally dressed guests is Doctor Robert Altman, accompanied by his wife. By the way he addresses the Richardses, it is apparent that he knows them well. "Alan, Paula, this is quite the event, isn't it? Anne and I have been having a wonderful time."

Now standing, Alan Richards shakes Robert Altman's hand and then gives Anne Altman a brief hug. Glancing in Brad and Julie's direction, Alan introduces them to the Altmans.

"Robert, this is Dr. Brad Pierson, one of the senior pathology residents at Vanderbilt. And I'd like you to meet his young lady friend, Dr. Julie Christensen, who is a resident physician in the radiology department."

Barely acknowledging their presence, Robert resumes his conversation with Alan and Paula Richards. Anne Altman, embarrassed by her husband's behavior, walks around to the other side of the table to apologize to Brad and Julie. With genuine interest, she asks about their evening. As Anne Altman then begins to tell them about her and her husband's move from Boston to Nashville a little over a year ago, Brad can't help but be distracted by Alan and Robert's interaction. They have moved thirty feet away from the table to a private darkened location alongside a tall cluster of bushes. Robert seems to be doing most of the talking, and Alan's expression is quite tense. Brad notices Alan cross his arms and nervously shift his weight from one foot to the other as the conversation continues.

Several minutes pass, and then the two men reappear at the table, at which point Alan Richards abruptly announces that he and Paula need to leave. Robert and Anne Altman exchange pleasantries with Brad and Julie as they move along. The interaction between Robert Altman and Alan Richards leaves Brad with an odd feeling.

Having arrived home at a late hour after the Swan Ball, Brad struggles to get out of bed on the following Sunday morning. He hits the snooze button when his alarm goes off. On the second buzz, he gets out of bed and stumbles into the shower. He quickly eats breakfast then slips on a dress shirt and tie for morning church services. After reaching the back parking lot of the

Gothic-style West End United Methodist Church a few minutes late, Brad hurries toward the rear entrance. Inside the church, it is late enough that few bulletins remain to be given out. The only unoccupied seats are in the back of the sanctuary. Brad manages to find a spot next to a large family while the first hymn is being sung. The booming baroque music of the enormous organ, whose polished metal pipes rise nearly four stories to occupy the entire front of the vaulted room, seems to shake Brad's body with every note.

After the introductory prayer, the short, prematurely gray-haired, middle-aged senior minister, Dr. Andrew Henry, moves to the center of the chancel, behind a white-painted wooden altar. Dressed in a black velour robe with a purple cross emblazoned on the center of his chest, Dr. Henry, wearing wire-rimmed glasses, begins his sermon. First, he recites from memory several verses from the book of Mark and then he lays his Bible down on the podium before addressing the congregation.

Initially, he describes the historical background of Israel prior to the arrival of Jesus, with the Roman occupation of the Jews and the horrible conditions that the latter had been subjected to. Praying to God for a savior, the Jews asked for a powerful warrior who would come down from heaven with a legion of angels to destroy their captors. Instead, God sent his Son, Jesus, a humble man, to turn the hearts of both Jew and Roman alike. Failing to believe that Christ was their savior, some of the religious high priests conspired against him. They pushed the Roman prefect, Pontius Pilate, to sentence him to death. Dr. Henry points out that Jesus was betrayed not only by the very people he came to save but also by his own disciples. Simon Peter, the man who had pledged his life to Christ, denied Jesus three times on the night Jesus was arrested. Then, with his arms outstretched and his voice getting progressively louder, Dr. Henry proclaims, "Then, my Christian brothers and sisters, came the worst betrayal. Judas Iscariot, one of the Twelve disciples who had given a sacred vow of love to Jesus, sold him to the Jewish high priests for thirty silver coins. *This man* had lived with Christ for three years as a brother. *This man* had witnessed many of God's miracles. *This man*, who had been given unqualified love from the Son of God himself, *chose to betray him* and turn him over to be put to death. And not only that, my friends, but also remember that *there were no cameras* in those days. There were *no pictures* of Jesus to identify him to the Jewish guards. Judas, the betrayer, had arranged a signal with the soldiers to lead them to Christ. And how did he do it? He identified Christ for them by *kissing him on the cheek*!"

At that moment, Dr. Henry is so overcome with emotion that he can no longer speak. His arms fall to his side, and his chin drops to his chest. The congregation becomes completely silent. After a long pause, Dr. Henry lifts his head and, in a quiet voice, makes one final comment.

"The Son of God, you must remember, was human like you and me. He withstood human temptation, horrible beatings, and an excruciating death by crucifixion. However, he overcame all of these insurmountable obstacles to achieve his final victory. He delivered his Father's message to humankind, and he died to save us from our sins and grant us eternal salvation." He pauses for effect. "Would you, my friends, have the courage to stand up for what you believe in under such conditions? Could you possibly understand that a friend and loved one might betray you and turn you over to your enemies to be put to death for the sake of a few silver coins? Can you imagine a greed that powerful? In today's world, in which money plays such a dominant role, each of us will face temptations of one kind or another. How will you respond; obedience to the Lord or to the ways of the world?"

Closing his eyes, Dr. Henry bows his head for the final prayer. Following that, the organ postlude signals the end of the church services.

Anxious to get in a few words with his minister, Brad lags behind the large crowd. Nearly at the end of the line leading to the narthex, Brad patiently waits. Finally, once it is his turn, he reaches his hand out toward Dr. Henry's.

"Drew, that was quite a sermon; it was one of your best ever."

By their interaction, it is obvious that the two men are friends.

"Brad, as always, you are far too generous. I'm merely the humble deliverer of the Word. God does the rest." He pauses. "Now, getting on to a less enlightened subject, will you be able to make it to the youth basketball program next Saturday night?"

"No conflict has come up yet, so I think we're all set."

"Tell me, how is Julie getting along these days?"

"She's doing well, thanks. Because we both work pretty hard, we don't get to see each other as much as I'd like."

Before Brad has a chance to walk off, Drew Henry catches him by the shoulder and lowers his voice. "Brad, I know what kind of hours you are putting in. Are you holding up okay?"

With a pretense of being serious, Brad answers with a lightness in his voice. "Don't worry, Drew. I'm doing just fine. I've got you and God on my side. That is what you keep telling me, isn't it?" Smiling, Brad winks at Dr. Henry and then goes in search of his car.

Chapter 11

Finally the morning arrives that Tom and Tracy Kilpatrick have long dreaded. While Tom is downstairs preparing breakfast, Tracy painstakingly packs some clothing for her upcoming hospital stay. Standing over her suitcase that lies open on the bed, Tracy, no longer able to control her emotions, bursts into tears. She then slides facedown onto the bed and lies there until Tom comes searching for her. He crawls alongside her and strokes her back, the only thing he can think of to calm her.

Finally, at her husband's urging, Tracy forces herself to get up, her eyes now red and swollen. Tom helps gather her belongings and walks alongside her down the stairs. In the kitchen, Tracy is only able to drink a few sips of water, as per Dr. Greer's instructions. Then comes the agonizing moment when Tracy must get in the car to begin the journey to the hospital, where she is scheduled to undergo a hysterectomy. All the while she is walking to the car, she feels numb, as if somehow this is happening to someone else and this could not possibly be her life. On the drive, the miles go by in a blur, with one irrepressible thought running over and over in her mind: that she'll never be able to have a child of her own.

After parking in front of the patient-unloading area at the front of the Deaconess Hospital, Tom goes around to help Tracy out of their car. Tracy remains painfully silent on the short walk to the entrance. Once they are seated in the waiting area, Tom briefly glances at his wife's face, which is now almost ashen. Her skin is cool and moist; her expression, lifeless. After a short time,

Tracy seems a little better, and soon an admission clerk calls out her name. Halfway through the admission process, while one of the nurses is giving Tracy some specific instructions, Tom steps out of the room for an instant to gather himself. He does his best to suppress the painful thoughts that have come to haunt him. Several times over the past couple of weeks, he has awakened in a cold sweat, dreaming that his wife died during surgery. He knows that Tracy needs him to be strong now, so he must push aside those fears for her sake.

After the check-in is completed, Tom and Tracy travel to the hospital room that has been assigned to them on the second floor. A nurse soon comes in to go over some final details and answer any questions. She leaves a gown behind for Tracy to put on before she goes to the operating room. Seeking privacy, Tracy walks to the bathroom to change. A few minutes lapse. Tom is startled when he hears his wife call out to him in a barely audible voice. He hurries across the room and sees Tracy's face partially visible behind the nearly closed bathroom door.

"Tom?"

"Yes, Tracy? What is it, sweetie?"

"Tom … you won't hate me will you?"

Confounded, Tom tries to think of what his wife could be upset about. "Tracy, what are you talking about?"

"You know, Tom, I can't have our children anymore."

Pushing the door open, Tom grabs his wife around the waist and holds her tightly while kissing her. "Tracy, I love you more than anything else in this world. You need to understand that. No matter what happens, you and I were meant to be together forever."

With a fiercely felt love in her eyes, Tracy looks up at her husband and says nothing else while she clings to him. Not long afterward, Dr. John Greer lightly taps on the door and enters, wearing a kelly-green surgical scrub suit. He stays with the Kilpatricks a long time, again reviewing the procedure and offering encouragement to them. After Dr. Greer leaves, Tracy finishes getting into the unflattering oversized hospital gown and then painstakingly hangs up her clothing in the tiny closet. Resigning herself to her fate, she then goes across the room and takes a seat in the wheelchair that was brought for her. Tom pulls up a chair beside her and reads to her from the Bible while they wait, hoping to distract her.

A young man dressed in a hospital uniform appears several minutes later at the door to transport Tracy to the surgical holding area. On the short journey, Tom walks alongside his wife, holding her hand.

Once Tracy is actually in the operating room, things proceed relatively smoothly. The anesthesiologist has no trouble getting her to sleep. Dr. Greer appears in the room shortly thereafter, scrubbed and gowned. The surgical procedure gets under way. Forty minutes later, and without a single complication, John Greer has nearly completed the hysterectomy. As he removes Tracy's uterus and reaches across to place it in the sterile container on the instrument table, he halts momentarily. The visual reality of what is happening catches him off guard. Knowing what impact this will have on the young couple, he can only begin to imagine the extent of their emotional burden. He instructs the scrub nurse to call for the pathologist and asks for a sterile towel to blot his forehead dry.

Shortly thereafter, Alan Richards enters the room, dressed in surgical attire. Surprised by his presence, John Greer says, "Alan, I didn't know that you were covering the operating rooms today."

Alan Richards responds, "I have taken a special interest in this case, so I came to collect the specimen personally."

Jonh Greer says; "I'm certain one of your colleagues would have brought the specimen to you."

This time Alan Richards's response is somewhat curt, "John, the Kilpatricks are depending on me to get it right, and that is what I want to do."

Alan Richards then leaves with the surgical specimen and heads back to the pathology department. One of the pathology technologists follows Alan Richards into the cutting room, where the sample will be dissected and mounted onto glass tissue slides. Kristin, the technologist, asks, "What can I do to help?" Alan Richards abruptly dismisses her, "Kristin, I don't think I'll be needing you, please close the door on the way out." Hurt, but not willing to show her emotions, Kristin returns to her other tasks.

Meanwhile, back in the waiting room, Tom Kilpatrick is growing more anxious by the minute. He goes up to the volunteer seated at the help desk and asks how his wife is doing. The volunteer calls into the room and relays the information to Tom, "Dr. Greer isn't in the operating room right now." Tom abruptly cuts her off.

"Dr. Greer *isn't* in the operating room right now? *Where is he? What's wrong?*"

The woman, startled by Tom's outburst, calmly continues. "Dr. Greer has already completed the surgery. He's on his way out to talk with you."

Not recognizing quite how rude his behavior has been, Tom darts out of the room to go in search of Dr. Greer. In doing so, he nearly knocks the physician over as the latter rounds the corner. When Tom sees the calm, almost happy look in John Greer's eyes, his tensions instantly melt. The words he hears next give him further relief.

"Tom, Tracy's just fine. She came through the surgery without a single problem. She'll be in the recovery unit for about an hour or so. In a few minutes, I'll take you back there to see her."

His eyes welling up with tears, Tom firmly grasps one of John Greer's shoulders.

"Dr. Greer, thank you. Thank you so much. Tracy and I ... we owe you a lot."

Once Tracy is completely over the effects of anesthesia the following day, one thing becomes perfectly obvious to Tom: his wife's body made it through the procedure perfectly fine, but her mind has suffered a devastating blow. For weeks following the hysterectomy, Tracy has no interest in any of her normal activities. Because of that, Tom has to contact her employer at the university to request an extended leave from her job. Almost every night when Tom arrives home from work, he finds Tracy alone in the nursery with the lights off, staring at the shiny white crib.

On a Tuesday afternoon in late June, Professor William Lockwood begins another lecture on Russian literature in Calhoun Hall. Over the past several weeks, he has had intermittent blurred vision in his left eye. Up until now, he has ignored it, pledging to see an eye doctor at the next convenient moment. Today, the blurriness is somewhat worse than usual. About halfway through the hour-long class, while scrolling the notes across the blackboard, he suddenly experiences a horrifying episode of complete blindness in his left eye. His distress becomes immediately obvious to his class. Yelling out, he flings his glasses aside and grabs the left half of his face. The long white piece of chalk he'd been holding in his right hand slips and falls to the floor, breaking in two. Obviously concerned, his students clamor around him, trying to assist in any way possible. Pushing them aside, William Lockwood stumbles out of the room and toward his office with one hand still covering his left eye.

At his office, his secretary, Francine Chase, is seated at her desk. After she gets one glimpse of her boss's contorted face, she jumps up out of her chair. William is frantic as he tries to explain what's happening.

"Francine, I need to go the emergency room right now! *I can't see anything out of my left eye!*"

Reacting quickly, Francine grabs William by the arm and guides him down the hallway in the direction of the staircases. After hurrying down the five flights to the ground floor, they immediately locate Francine's car in front of the building and speed across the campus toward the Vanderbilt Hospital emergency room. After she drops William off in front, Francine searches for a parking spot.

By the time William enters the emergency department, his anxiety has peaked and he has lost control of his emotions. He tries to walk directly toward one of the doctors he sees standing at a desk inside the department, but he is stopped by a check-in clerk.

"I'm sorry, sir. I'll need to see your identification and insurance information before I can let you see a doctor."

In a burst of anger, William yells loudly at the woman, "I'm Professor William Lockwood, and I've gone blind in my left eye. I need to see a doctor right now!"

From across the room, one of the nurses observes the interaction. Anxious to be of help, she walks over, places one arm around William, and leads him into an exam room, where she tries to calm him down. After obtaining a cursory history and doing a physical exam, she runs out of the room to get one of the physicians. Several minutes later, she reemerges with a thin, well-dressed woman in her early fifties, Dr. Joyce Crenshaw. Quickly confirming the nurse's evaluation, Dr. Crenshaw locates a handheld ophthalmoscope and flashes a bright light into both of William's eyes. She then completes a thorough physical exam and sits down at the tiny desk in the corner of the room to use the telephone.

"Hello, Radiology? I need a stat MRI scan of the brain with attention to the orbits. Patient's name is William Lockwood, a forty-eight-year-old white male with near complete visual loss of the left eye. Can you do him right now? … Excellent. I'll send him by wheelchair." After she hangs up, Dr. Crenshaw sits directly across from William to review her clinical impression.

"Professor Lockwood, you've still got some vision in that left eye, but it's minimal. Obviously we need to figure out what's going on in a hurry. The best way to do that is to perform an MRI scan, where you go into a tunnel. Very detailed images of the brain and the eye can be obtained. The scan will take about twenty minutes. You'll get some contrast material in the vein of one of your arms while you're doing that. In the meantime, I'm going to page one of the neurosurgeons to come by and look at you, and I'll need to call your insurance company to get approval for a possible hospitalization. Who are you insured with?"

"I recently switched insurance companies to AmericaHealth."

"Okay, I'll get right on it. I'll see you back here as soon as your MRI's been done." Thirty minutes later, while William is being wheeled back from radiology, the chairman of neurosurgery, Dr. Aaron Goodman, along with several of his resident physicians in training, awaits the patient's arrival in the emergency room. After introducing William to the gray-and-curly-haired Dr. Goodman, Dr. Crenshaw pulls up William's MRI scan on a computer screen outside William's room. After subjecting William to a brief but thorough physical exam, Aaron Goodman, along with the other physicians, stands beside Dr. Crenshaw to review the findings. Intermittently pointing to the gray-and-black images, Aaron Goodman explains his interpretation. He then walks directly to his new patient and sits down beside him.

"Mr. Lockwood, after carefully reviewing your MRI pictures and examining you, I'm relatively certain as to your diagnosis. You have a tumor growing near, and pressing on, the large nerve that transmits vision from your left eye to your brain, the optic nerve. Some tumors that appear in this location are benign, meaning that they're not cancerous, but some can actually be malignant.

Because of your near complete blindness, we need to operate immediately to try to save the optic nerve. The only thing holding us up is an approval from your health insurance company. While we're awaiting an answer from them, I'm going to get my surgical team assembled and reserve an operating room. Do you have any questions?"

Overwhelmed by the news and fighting to remain calm, William mounts the courage to ask Dr. Goodman several things.

"What are the chances this is cancer?"

"I'd say that, in this location, about 50 percent end up being malignant."

"How long do you think the surgery will take?"

"Depending on what we find, perhaps as long as six hours."

Now, with his heart racing, William raises his worst fear. "Is it possible that I'll lose my eye?"

Trying his best to reassure William, Aaron Goodman answers slowly and confidently. "Right now, William, I think it's unlikely that we'll actually have to sacrifice the eye, but I can't say for sure until I'm in the operating room. More often than not, these tumors are able to be resected without that being necessary."

Choked up after that last reply, William nods and thanks Dr. Goodman.

While Dr. Crenshaw obtains the appropriate blood work, chest X-ray, and EKG on William Lockwood prior to surgery, Aaron Goodman walks to a private conference room to contact William's insurance company, AmericaHealth. After reaching the main operator, he is transferred to a nurse whose job is to begin the approval process. All the while, his beeper continually goes off, and multiple doctors and nurses come in and out of the room to pass along crucial messages to him.

"Utilization Review, this is Ms. Jordan."

"Ms. Jordan, this is Dr. Aaron Goodman, the chairman of neurosurgery at Vanderbilt. I've got a Mr. William Lockwood here in the emergency room who needs urgent surgery. I'm calling to get permission to proceed."

"Just a minute, Dr. Goodman, while I pull up Mr. Lockwood's file on my computer."

"Ms. Jordan, I don't mean to hurry you, but we're dealing with an emergency situation."

"Okay, here he comes. Born in 1969?"

"Yeah, that's him."

"What kind of surgery does he need?"

"He's got a tumor of the left optic nerve causing near complete blindness."

"Has he had it before?"

Losing control, Aaron angrily yells into the phone, "Ms. Jordan, this is an emergency!"

Offended, Ms. Jordan snaps back, "You'll have to answer all these questions before I can help you. That's company policy."

"Get me your supervisor!"

"What?"

"You heard me!"

After a prolonged pause, a man answers the phone, identifying himself as Dr. Petersen, the physician in charge of the Utilization Review Department for AmericaHealth. Once he has heard the history and the proposed surgery, he puts Dr. Goodman on hold again after explaining that in cases like this, he has to consult with his supervisor, the chief executive officer, Dr. Robert Altman. Again, after being on hold awhile, Aaron Goodman hears the line being transferred. Then he hears Robert Altman pick up.

"Dr. Goodman? This is Dr. Robert Altman. I believe we've met once before. Thank you for your patience." He pauses. "I've heard about Mr. Lockwood. How may I help you?"

His patience strained, Dr. Goodman does his best to remain civil. "Professor Lockwood needs urgent surgery, Dr. Altman. This looks like an atypical glioma of the left optic nerve just proximal to the optic chiasm. If I have any chance to save his vision, and possibly his eye, I must act now! What else could you possibly need to know?"

Smug, Robert Altman knows that he wields the power in this situation. "Do you remember our conversation from six months ago?"

"I beg your pardon."

"Do you remember our conversation from *six* months ago?"

"Please inform me how this has any bearing on this patient's dire needs."

"You turned down the contract I offered you to be an AmericaHealth provider."

"I've got a blind professor of Russian literature in the emergency room, and you want to debate contract negotiations with me from half a year ago?"

"You should have taken the deal."

Now, nearly yelling into the phone, Dr. Goodman gives in. "I couldn't have even covered my overhead with the contract you sent me! I wanted to take care of your patients, but when I tried to negotiate with you, you never even returned my calls." He pauses. "Now let's get back to the situation at hand. I've got an operating room tied up, and two of my staff neurosurgeons are standing by to assist me with this case right now! Are you going to let us take care of this man or not?"

With little hesitation, Robert Altman truly enjoys his answer. "No."

"No! What do you mean, no? Nowhere on the East Coast will you find a group of neurosurgeons more experienced with this type of tumor. Who could you possibly send this man to?"

"AmericaHealth has contracted all of its neurosurgery in the Nashville area with a group in Clarkesville."

"*Clarkesville? Clarkesville?* Those guys aren't even board-certified, and one of them is partially retired. They've never even seen a case like this, and they sure wouldn't know how to handle it."

"Well, Dr. Goodman, that's who'll be doing the surgery. Please get Mr. Lockwood in an ambulance and send him on his way. I'll call Dr. Jerold Torguson right now, and I'll make sure he's ready to go."

Now mustering as much humility as he can under the circumstances, Aaron Goodman, one of the world's leading experts on optic nerve tumors, pleads with Robert Altman. "Now listen, Altman. Please let me help this man. My colleagues and I will do the case for free if you'll just agree to pay for Mr. Lockwood's hospital bill at Vanderbilt. ... That seems fair to me."

Savoring his authority, Robert's response is crisp: "You should have taken the offer I made you six months ago. You really ticked me off. The answer is still no. Please, get the ambulance for Mr. Lockwood."

"Altman, you're a real jerk. You'd let one of your patients suffer because of your petty feelings? If this case goes bad, I'll volunteer to stand as an expert witness for the attorney that'll sue your pants off. *Do you hear me?*" With that Aaron Goodman slams down the phone.

Meanwhile, back in the emergency room, William Lockwood stares up at the clock, anxiously anticipating Dr. Goodman's return. While he was undergoing his battery of tests, Francine Chase had agreed to pick up William's five-year-old daughter, Cynthia, from school. When the door pops open, William expects to see Aaron Goodman, but instead Cynthia runs in, her long blonde hair bouncing up and down. Her shrill cry nearly breaks William's heart.

"Daddy! Daddy! Are you hurt, Daddy?"

Crawling into her father's lap, she wraps both arms around her father's neck and kisses him multiple times on the cheek. Reluctant to show his emotions to his daughter, William tries to act strong.

"Cynthia, sweetheart, Daddy's got a problem with one of his eyes, and a nice doctor, Dr. Goodman, is going to help him. Everything will be just fine, angel."

From across the room, Francine Chase now enters, and William expresses his heartfelt thanks for getting Cynthia to the hospital safely. Looking into his daughter's eyes, William is well aware of the impact all this has on her, because it was less than a year ago that her mother, the woman whom William loved with all his heart, died of metastatic breast cancer.

Not far behind Francine is Aaron Goodman. His dour expression leads William to believe that something is amiss. For Cynthia's sake, he does his best to remain calm as he looks into Dr. Goodman's dark brown eyes and asks what the status of the surgery is.

"Mr. Lockwood, we've got a problem. AmericaHealth refuses to allow me to operate on you. I even volunteered to waive my surgical fees, but even after I spoke to the head of the company, a doctor by the name of Robert Altman, the answer was still no. He's instructed me to send you to Clarkesville to be operated on."

His world crumbling around him, William can barely cope with the stress he's under. He speaks quickly and frantically: "But … I trust you, Dr. Goodman. I want you to do the surgery. Isn't there any other way? Please help me."

"I'm afraid my hands are tied, William. I did everything I could think of to convince them that you should be operated on at Vanderbilt, but nothing I said could change their minds. I offered to do your case at no charge, but the hospital bill would be in the tens of thousands. It looks like we're stuck."

Eventually William resigns himself to the situation and agrees to get in the ambulance that will transport him to Clarkesville Community Hospital. Out of a great loyalty and a genuine concern, Francine volunteers to take Cynthia home and look after her until William is strong enough to be discharged from the hospital. To make matters worse, Francine is forced to tear the crying youngster away from her father as he is lifted onto the ambulance gurney.

Chapter 12

As the ambulance pulls away from the Vanderbilt Hospital emergency room, William Lockwood presses his face up against the back window to watch the image of his daughter and secretary grow increasingly smaller and eventually fade from sight. He hears Cynthia's voice call out to him one final time, and he sees her run several steps toward the moving vehicle before Francine Chase pulls her back. When he witnesses his tiny daughter so upset, he fights back his tears. It is not until several miles later that William is able pull himself away from the glass. On turning around, he is surprised at how stark the interior of the emergency vehicle is. Glistening steel completely encases most of the close, cramped compartment. Built into the walls are metal pull drawers of all sizes containing keylocks while the center of the vehicle is occupied by a gurney. Because of his almost paralytic fear of what might happen to him, William finds it difficult to make himself strike up a conversation with the lone paramedic riding with him, Keith Scarborough. Sensing William's anxiety, the moderately tall, muscular paramedic desperately tries to cheer up his patient during the journey by sharing stories of his wife and three young children and showing William photographs of them. An eternity seems to pass during the trip, giving William time to reflect on his situation. Several painful thoughts run through his mind, over and over again: *Am I ever going to see my Cynthia again? What happens if I have a serious cancer and die? Who will take care of her? Dear God, I can't bear it.*

His emotions lead him to the sense of utter helplessness. William's despondence is partially assuaged by the paramedic, who makes the initial preparations for surgery. First, while still in transit, an intravenous line is started, and then William is asked to sign several of the preliminary surgical permits. Struggling, with only his right eye to focus with, William tries to read the small print of the documents.

After long stretches of highway miles, the vehicle suddenly slows and makes a sharp turn. To keep from falling over, William grabs onto one of the steel bars that traverses the ceiling. Then the ambulance comes to a halt, and shortly thereafter the back doors are flung open. Awkward because of his visual difficulties and emotional stress, William needs to be assisted to a waiting wheelchair. Keith Scarborough has formed a bond with his patient and refuses to let anyone else wheel William inside the hospital. In one of the paramedic's hands is a CD containing William's MRI scan.

As William crosses the parking lot, the warm, humid air brushes against his face. He savors the fresh air, wondering if this will be his last opportunity to experience it. In sharp contrast to the bustling activity of the huge Vanderbilt Hospital complex, the tiny, four-story, white brick Clarkesville Community Hospital is almost painfully still. Architecturally, the hospital is a series of unimaginative box-shaped buildings designed in an institutional style from the 1960s. On their way into the hospital, Keith and William first pass through the emergency room, which is surprisingly quiet. Next, they come to a set of double doors, over which is posted a red sign with "Surgical Area" inscribed in white letters. William passes through the doors and reaches his final destination, the preoperative holding area. Just inside the entrance, he sees a short, bald obese man wearing pale blue surgical attire and sitting on the corner of a metal desk, reading a newspaper. Getting up when his new patient arrives, Dr. Jerold Torguson introduces himself, sits down across from William, and begins to describe the upcoming surgical procedure in great detail. Although he realizes the need to listen carefully to the discussion, William can't help but be fascinated by Dr. Torguson's eccentric personality and small chubby fingers.

Recognizing the time urgency, Dr. Torguson hurries to a nearby computer and quickly reviews William's MRI scan. While he is doing that, two nurses appear. They push William to the operating room while an anesthesiologist walks alongside him, describing the risks of general anesthesia. On entering the operating room, William notes the drab pastel green color of the wall tiles and the giant operating microscope covered by a large sheet of clear sterile plastic wrapping. Dr. Torguson catches up to William within the surgical suite and hands him the final consent form. William reads the form slowly and carefully. Possible complications such as permanent blindness, stroke, and death are listed. Seated in the wheelchair with the clipboard in his lap, William finds that his right eye lingers a long time on the word *death* until the nurses encourage him to sign the document.

Before being helped onto the cold, hard stainless steel operating room table, William hears a snap as the cap is taken off a syringe by the male anesthesiologist standing beside him. The sedative medicine feels warm as it infuses into the vein of William's left arm. Next, a breathing apparatus is placed over his face. William notes the sweet taste of the anesthetic gas before he goes to sleep. Looking up, William sees Dr. Torguson and two scrub nurses standing over him—his last memory.

Once William has successfully attained the anesthesia-induced suspended state somewhere between life and death, the more barbaric part of the procedure begins. One of the nurses turns William's head to the right and carefully uses an electric razor to strip the hair from the left side of his scalp. A conventional razor is then used to finish shaving the hair, including most of the left eyebrow. Then, long green draping is pulled across William's body from head to toe, leaving only his left eye and left temple exposed. While Dr. Torguson is assisted in acquiring his surgical gown and gloves, a nurse paints the entire surgical field on William's head with the brown sterilizing agent Betadine. From one corner of the room, Jerold audibly tests the conference call linkup with Vanderbilt Hospital. Because AmericaHealth would not approve him to operate on William, Dr. Goodman has agreed to guide Dr. Torguson through the procedure.

"Dr. Goodman, are you there?"

Seated in his office at Vanderbilt Hospital, Aaron Goodman communicates with Jerold via his desk telephone. From a small speaker embedded in the wall of the operating room, his voice booms. "Right here, Jerry."

"Thank you for making yourself available to help me with this case."

"No problem. To begin with, I would recommend a lateral temporal approach coming in adjacent to the orbit. That will give you maximal exposure."

Following Goodman's advice Dr. Torguson makes an elliptical skin incision with a self-cauterizing scalpel. As the skin is opened, the site of the left eye socket is exposed.

"Aaron, I'm about to enter the orbit. Everything has gone smoothly so far."

Two hefty male nurses precisely position the large operating microscope over William's eye. Jerold carefully surveys the orbital area. Very gently, using a small electric handheld saw similar to a dentist's drill, Jerold removes the bony side of the eye socket in one piece, and afterwards adjusts his microscope. For the first time, he can now see the tumor, which arises from the inner surface of the optic nerve. In contrast to the white meningeal coverings of the nerve, the tumor is dark gray and appears to contain two lobes.

"Aaron, good news. The tumor appears to be confined to the nerve itself. There is no extension to the optic chiasm. It is dumbbell shaped and seems to rise from a focal point on the medial aspect of the optic nerve. It encases the nerve at that site."

"Hmm, this doesn't sound like a typical glioma. We may be dealing with a different sort of tumor, possibly a meningioma or a vascular sarcoma."

"Visually, it doesn't have some of the usual characteristics of either tumor."

"Let's begin by dissecting the tumor away from the optic nerve in the hope that we don't have to sacrifice the nerve. The pathologist, during the case, should be able to give us the histology and grade, which will give us the crucial data we need. By the way, how good are your pathologists down there?"

"Excellent. They're on standby right now."

Using a rounded, toothpick-sized instrument shaped somewhat like a spoon, Jerold begins to dissect the tumor away from the optic nerve. With the help of the operating microscope, the tiny instrument is guided into place. The outer layers of the tumor are gently peeled away one by one from the side of the large nerve. In order to precisely stop the bleeding from tiny tumor vessels, a laser is utilized. A brief pulse of red light causes a puffing sound as the blood flow is halted. For several hours, instruments barely visible to the human eye are guided beneath the microscope into the operative field to painstakingly strip away the tumor.

After the fifth hour, Jerold pauses and looks over at the clock on the wall; it is now almost 9:00 p.m. He then glances at the instrument table and at the steel specimen container, which now contains approximately three quarters of the tumor. Pulling his eyes away from the microscope, he asks the nurse to blot the beads of perspiration from his forehead. Then, he temporarily closes his eyes to give them a rest from their arduous chore. To relieve some of the muscle cramping in his neck, he stretches his arms and slowly turns his head from side to side. Jerold then gives instructions to summon the surgical pathologist to review the specimen while he completes his dissection. From the speakerphone, Aaron Goodman announces his presence. "How's it going, Jerry?"

"I've completed the majority of the dissection. No major problems so far."

Resuming the case, Jerold realizes that discerning between cancerous tentacles and true optic nerve fibers is becoming quite difficult. He probes deep down into the tumor at the junction with the optic nerve. Without warning, a slip of his tired right hand results in sudden brisk blood flow that fills the entire orbital cavity. Panicked, Jerold screams for a suction device. The operating room, which had been nearly silent, now becomes loud with Jerold's shouting.

"Aaron, I can't believe it, but I may have severed the ophthalmic artery! I've got blood all over the field!"

"Can you identify the vessel?"

"I can't see! I can't see! I may have cut into the optic nerve!"

Alarm is evident in the nursing staff as Jerold struggles to identify the source of the bleeding. In sharp contrast to his calm and pleasant demeanor earlier in the case, Jerold is now frantic and agitated and begins to throw instruments. Hissing loudly, the suction apparatus drowns out Jerold's groans.

"Aaron, the bleeding *is* from the ophthalmic artery. I need some help!"

"Jerold, get your partner in there *now*. You're going to need help repairing that kind of damage."

"He's out of town."

"You mean you took this case on *without backup?* What were you thinking? I'm on my way!"

Aaron dashes from his office and tracks down Dr. Chip Newberry, his chief resident in Neurosurgery, who happens to still be in the hospital. After a brief discussion, the two physicians make a straight path to the Vanderbilt helipad. Running down four flights of poorly illuminated, half-century-old staircases of the Medical Center North Complex, they burst outdoors and sprint toward the main entrance of the new Vanderbilt hospital. Along the way, they dodge a series of ambulances, passenger cars, and pedestrians. After they reach the front doors, they dash straight across the nearly deserted lobby and hop on one of the elevators at the back of the room. Aaron punches the fifth-floor button, and the elevator careens upward at a high rate of speed. When the bell sounds, signaling the desired floor, the men exit, running down the hall and turning to the left. At the end of the hallway, they come across a large brown-painted metal door. Aaron inserts his magnetic identification card into a wall-mounted slot, and the door automatically opens, leading them out onto a flight deck, where two helicopters sit.

As they step outside, the sky is deeply black and cloudless. The flashing red-and-white lights coming from the underside of one of the helicopters are nearly blinding. The terrific force of wind from the helicopter thrusts the physicians' long white lab coats backward, while grains of sand pelt their faces, causing them to cover their eyes. The roar of the rotor blades strains their ears as they climb aboard. After hovering briefly on takeoff, the helicopter, painted black-and-gold to signify Vanderbilt's colors, quickly accelerates on a southerly course. Out a side window, Aaron watches the city lights and urban landscapes fly beneath him during the trip.

Precious minutes later, they touch down in the front parking lot of the quiet country Clarkesville Community Hospital. While running inside, they turn back and wave to express their gratitude to the pilot. A surgical nurse, awaiting them at the main entrance, guides them to William Lockwood's location. After grabbing surgical caps, face masks, and shoe covers, the two men hurry to the operating room. Dr. Goodman goes directly to Dr. Torguson and stands beside him to survey the situation, while Dr. Newberry washes his hands. Soon, the two Vanderbilt physicians are surgically garbed and standing across the table from each other. A wave of relief overcomes both Jerold and the staff in the room. Dr. Torguson has already initiated microsurgical repair of the ophthalmic artery.

Growling angrily, Aaron Goodman, with barely a hint of tact, excuses Jerold from the case. Once Aaron Goodman and Chip Newberry have focused in on the surgical field with the two-headed operating microscope, they quickly go to work.

"Chip, let's begin by repairing the artery, and then we can direct our attention to the optic nerve. ... Good grief, Jerold, that's one big tear!"

After Jerold Torguson steps away from the surgical table, he removes his gloves and gown and sits hunched over on a rolling stool in the corner of the room. Humiliation is evident in both his posture and expression as he watches the two other neurosurgeons work together in precise, well-coordinated teamwork. Forty minutes pass. Aaron and Chip celebrate the successful repair of the ophthalmic artery. One of the doors of the operating room quietly opens, and the surgical pathologist, Dr. Berger, walks in with a large tray of slides and a two-headed microscope on a rolling cart. After they exchange introductions, Aaron leaves the operating table and reviews the tumor's histologic appearance with the pathologist while Chip Newberry continues the case. Dr. Berger uses an arrow within the microscopic field to point out the pertinent findings. Behind Aaron, Jerold listens carefully, awaiting his turn to look at the tumor.

Dr. Berger says, "Dr. Goodman, Dr. Torguson, Dr. Newberry, although not typical, this has the appearance of an angioblastic meningioma. Fortunately, it looks well encapsulated, with only a few malignant features. The nuclear and cellular grade are both Grade 1, consistent with a well-differentiated lesion."

"How unusual," Aaron interjects.

"I'll say. I've only seen one case of this before in my lifetime, and that was almost twenty years ago. When the permanent slides come out in twenty-four hours, I'll be a little more comfortable with the final diagnosis."

Aaron then returns to the operating table, at which point Chip Newberry takes an opportunity to review the slides. Turning back toward the pathologist, Aaron expresses his appreciation.

"Dr. Berger, it's been a pleasure working with you. Thank you for coming in at such a late hour and for your diligent efforts."

After the two men are back together at the operating table, Aaron makes a comment to Chip Newberry. "What a miracle! Professor Lockwood won't lose his eye after all, and the cure rate with this tumor is outstanding. Now comes the hard part—the repair of the optic nerve where Dr. Torguson accidentally lacerated it. It looks like it's going to be a big job!"

At Dr. Goodman's request, a new set of instruments is brought into the room to assist with the next step of the surgery. With sutures as fine as a spiderweb, the tiny individual nerve fibers of the large gash of the optic nerve are reapproximated and stitched together. Tedious repair work goes on throughout most of the night.

Six hours have already gone by. It is now nearly 3:30 a.m. At the completion of the nerve repair, Aaron analyzes the remnants of the tumor. He and Chip slowly strip away the remaining cancerous tissue over the next ninety minutes. They next undertake a final inspection of the artery and nerve repair. Both physicians are satisfied with the outcome. Next, they restore the bone flap to its original position and suture the skin back together. Aaron steps back and surveys the room at the completion of the case. Dr. Torguson is nowhere to be found. One of the nurses mentions that several hours ago, he departed to the doctors' lounge to take a nap. As Aaron Goodman pulls off his bloody gloves and gown, he feels suddenly exhausted. Patting Chip on the back, he compliments him on doing a superb job. It is now 5:00 a.m. After thanking the surgical staff, Aaron walks alongside William as he is rolled to the recovery unit. He insists on taking William back to Vanderbilt by helicopter once his condition has stabilized.

It is not until later that morning that William regains consciousness. He awakens to find a large bandage covering his left eye and layers of gauze wrapped around his head. After emerging from his deep sleep, William looks around with his right eye, wondering where he is. His small room is well lit and packed full of electronic monitoring devices. Two large sliding-glass doors make up the far wall. His movement gets the attention of his nurse, who rushes in with a big smile.

"We've been waiting for you to wake up, Mr. Lockwood."

Still groggy, William's speech is initially slurred. "Where am I?"

"You're at Vanderbilt in the Neuro Intensive Care Unit."

"Vanderbilt? What am I doing here?"

"It's a long story. I'll let Dr. Goodman tell you when he gets here."

"Dr. Goodman? What do you mean? He didn't do my surgery."

Ten minutes later, an enthusiastic but fatigued Aaron Goodman comes into the room. He performs a cursory examination of William's right eye and then uses surgical scissors to cut away the bandages from his face. After inspecting the wound, he does more extensive testing of the left eye. He asks William to cover his right eye and describe the vision out of the left eye.

"I can see shapes, but everything is blurry. I can't see much on the right side of the room."

"Is everything normal in terms of color?"

"The color seems the same in both eyes."

"Excellent! That's enough for today. Let's put a fresh bandage on there."

William blurts out, "What happened with the operation, and how did I get here? I'm terribly confused."

With a broad grin, Aaron responds, "Let's save that for a little later on. Right now, I have a little surprise for you."

While William's nurse places a new bandage on, Aaron Goodman steps out momentarily. On his return, he asks William if he's ready. William nods. From behind Dr. Goodman, Cynthia's head pops out. She runs to her father and crawls up into the bed beside him. After laying her head on his chest, she reaches her arms across his abdomen.

"Daddy! Daddy! You're safe. Oh, Daddy, I was so scared. Are you okay, Daddy?"

Tears stream quietly down William's right cheek. He wipes them away quickly to keep from upsetting his daughter. Now that he has made it through the surgery successfully, the full realization of his own fear of dying strikes him. Instantly, those held-back emotions that were pent up within him come flowing forth. Choking his emotions back, he gently rubs his daughter's back. A sense of relief passes over him.

"Cynthia, I love you, honey. Daddy will never, ever leave you. He will always be there to take care of you, sweetie."

Aaron leaves the newly reunited family alone. He decides that when William is stronger, he will explain what happened at the time of the surgery and also discuss the possibility of permanent partial blindness in the left eye. The extensive nerve repair that he and Dr. Newberry performed on the optic nerve may or may not be adequate to restore vision. The next six weeks will be crucial in determining William's progress.

Chuckling to himself, Aaron remembers the phone call he made to Robert Altman after completing the all-night case. He told Robert of Dr. Torguson's significant mistake and the reason why William was at Vanderbilt Hospital. Robert's voice had stammered as he sucked in every ounce of his pride and agreed to cover all charges for the case, including Dr. Goodman's operating fees, with no discount. He even offered to pay for a suite at Vanderbilt Hospital so that Cynthia could stay with her father. Several expensive floral arrangements subsequently arrived from AmericaHealth with Robert Altman's name on the cards, all in an obvious attempt to avoid a potentially damaging public lawsuit. Aaron recalls that not once in their conversation did Robert ever ask him how William was doing or how successful the surgery had been.

Chapter 13

On a warm summer evening at the Nashville International Airport, steam rises from the concrete runways, creating optical distortions for the pilots as they try to land the large passenger jets. Standing in front of one of the large plate-glass windows that overlooks the tarmac, Brad Pierson patiently waits. As one of the planes touches down, he sees a cloud of black rubberized dust fly from one of the rear wheels. The distance is too far for him to hear the loud screeching sound made by that tire as the 300-ton aircraft lands. Initially hurtling down the runway at over 150 miles per hour, the jet is slowed by the huge wing-mounted turbines, which have been thrown in reverse, producing a deafening roar. Once halted, the giant, gleaming aluminum aircraft turns and slowly taxis toward the terminal.

It is Fourth of July weekend, so hordes of people have already gathered at the gate area to welcome their out-of-town guests. After a seemingly endless number of strangers emerge, Brad finally sees the familiar faces of his mother and father. It has been nearly six months since he's seen them, and he can barely contain his excitement. Dressed casually but conservatively, his father wears a pair of gold-rimmed reading glasses on the end of his nose. Tucked under one arm is the *Wall Street Journal*. By contrast, his mother carries a white canvas bag filled with reading materials and crossword puzzles for the trip. On seeing her son, Jean Pierson's eyes light up. Hurrying to him, she gives him a giant hug and a kiss on the cheek.

"It's great to see you, Brad! We've missed you terribly."

By this time, David Pierson has caught up to his wife. He pats his son warmly on the back. The usually stoic Brad is quite animated because of the occasion. "Thanks for coming all the way down to Nashville to see me. I'm sorry it's been so long since I've been able to get home."

Following their meal, Brad finds it difficult to say good night to his parents after having been away from them for so long. Grudgingly, he leaves them in the lobby of the hotel where they're staying, knowing that he needs to get to bed early because of his work schedule.

After arriving home that evening, Brad makes a brief phone call.

"Julie? I hope I'm not calling too late. ... Yeah, they made it just fine. They're staying at the Plaza Hotel. ... Absolutely, having them here really makes me homesick; I've really missed them."

"I'm so glad they arrived safely, Brad. I get a little nervous whenever my mom flies anywhere. ... Are we still on for tomorrow night? ... Good. What about Saturday? Do you think they'll want to go down to Franklin and have dinner with my mom on the Fourth?"

"Are you kidding? I know my parents would love to come."

The following evening, Brad and Julie walk hand in hand through the main entrance of the Vanderbilt Plaza Hotel. In a sitting area on the far side of the lobby, Brad's parents have made themselves at home in a set of matching, floral-upholstered Queen Anne chairs. As soon as David Pierson sees the couple, he gets up and walks in their direction. With a warm smile, he introduces himself to Julie.

"Julie, it is certainly a pleasure to finally meet you. As you can imagine, Brad has told us many wonderful things about you. Please come over and meet my wife, Jean."

By this time, Jean Pierson is also standing.

"Hi, Mrs. Pierson. I'm so delighted you could come to Nashville for a visit."

While warmly hugging Julie, Jean Pierson smiles. She says, "Julie, please call me Jean. Brad's father and I have really looked forward to meeting you; I only wish it had been sooner."

"Thanks, Jean. I'm happy you were able to come for a visit. I know you don't get to see Brad very often, so I am grateful you're willing to share some of your time with me."

Julie's gracious manner immediately puts Brad's parents at ease. Interrupting the conversation, Brad points out they need to leave if they want to make it to the restaurant in time for their dinner reservation. From the hotel, they travel several miles along West End Avenue in the direction of downtown. This places them at one of Nashville's best-known restaurants, Arthur's, in the Union Station Hotel. When they pull up in front of the Romanesque stone building, Brad mentions that back in the early 1900s, this served as an actual terminal for the Louisville and Nashville Railroad Company. Before going inside, David Pierson takes a moment to glance up at the tall clock tower and take note of the intricate stonework around the windows and front dormers. Within the hotel's lobby is a massive domed ceiling with stained glass that showers the lobby with brilliant color. Alongside the reception desk is the sign for Arthur's. On entering, they are immediately impressed by the atmosphere, due in part to the elegant furnishings. The interior contains dark walnut-paneled walls, several oversized white marble fireplaces, and antique crystal chandeliers.

After being seated, their waiter, or "Captain," as the waiters are called in this former railroad station, recites the menu by memory. Over the next two hours, while multiple courses of food are being served, Brad's parents and Julie have an opportunity to get acquainted with one another. At one point in the conversation, while Mrs. Pierson describes her career as a high school English teacher, Julie takes note of how youthful Jean appears. Only a few wrinkles exist around her animated mahogany-colored eyes, and there is barely a touch of gray in her hair. Within her confident, direct personality, Julie can see reflections of Brad. A quieter individual than his wife, David Pierson is certainly polite, but Julie senses that he is a private man. She finds his calm demeanor soothing and can't help but notice how much Brad looks like him, including the deep blue color of his eyes.

Brad's parents politely ask Julie about herself, and she reflects on growing up in middle Tennessee and how much it has changed in the past twenty years. She then talks about her family. Instead of her being sorrowful, Brad is happy to see that tonight, Julie manages to be joyous when describing her father. Toward the end of the meal, Brad changes subjects and discusses some of the activities for the following day.

"What would you think about taking a drive down to Franklin tomorrow afternoon and spending some time with Julie's mom, Anna? She's asked us if we'd like to have a Fourth of July dinner with her."

Obviously delighted, Jean Pierson says, "Julie, tell your mom we'd love to come and meet her. That's very generous of her to invite us to her home."

The following afternoon, Brad and his parents arrive at Julie's house in Nashville around one o'clock. For their drive south toward Franklin, Brad chooses a scenic route for the sake of his parents. Still a narrow two-lane rural road, Granny White Pike cuts a winding path through the countryside and hills of southwestern Nashville. In this part of town, some of the original farmhouses still exist, but they are overshadowed by newer developments with large homes shoehorned in beside one another.

Approximately ten miles from Nashville, they emerge from the narrow part of the roadway with its heavily shaded tree cover to enter a suburb known as Brentwood. Half a century ago, this well-to-do community was a sleepy farming village with vegetable crops dominating the landscape. Now that it is quite heavily developed, businesses and extravagant homes have taken the place of pastures and farmland. Only a few true working agricultural and horse farms can still be seen in Brentwood, with the majority of the larger properties having been bought up by country music stars and turned into estates. Simple wooden fences that once lined the roadways have been replaced by mile after mile of expensive wrought iron fence work. Large mansions, sitting off in the distance behind tall gates, have taken the place of modest farmhouses.

After leaving Brentwood, Brad turns onto a small highway, Franklin Road, to continue their southerly journey. After the horse farms have long disap-peared from view, rows of emerald-green vegetable crops in rich dark brown soil appear along either side of the highway. It is not long before they reach downtown Franklin, where Julie mentions to Brad's parents that the fifteen-block center of town was recently restored to its original late-1700s appearance.

After passing through the center of town, they continue on toward Julie's childhood home. In a few miles, the small city blends with rural countryside, and when a large field covered with yellow daisies appears off to the right, Brad recognizes that Anna Christensen's property is not far ahead. Her familiar wooden mailbox then comes into view along the highway. Brad turns left onto the dirt road beside it. The first several hundred yards of her long driveway are heavily blanketed by the limbs of tall trees. When the leafy green canopy eventually disappears from overhead, fields dotted with mature corn can be seen basking in the bright Tennessee sun. The tall ears gently wave back and forth in the light afternoon breeze. While they are traveling along the country road, a cloud of light brown dust is churned up, giving Brad's white car a reddish hue. Not far ahead, a farm-style house with wood siding comes into view.

Just before reaching the house, they see Julie's mom, Anna, open the front screen door and step out onto the porch. Waving to her guests, she walks toward the garage to meet them. Worn up, her hair is a faint gray color with blond highlights, and her clothing is casual. After Brad is parked and gets out of the car, he gives Anna a big hug while thanking her for her invitation. With her Southern graciousness, Anna wastes little time in welcoming David and Jean Pierson to her home and inquiring about their trip. Smiling broadly, she then hugs Julie and exclaims how great it is to see her "baby daughter."

Once inside, Anna leads the Piersons to a screened-in porch at the back of her home. On the way, Jean comments on the many tasteful decorations and antiques in Anna's home and says that her recently renovated kitchen looks fabulous. Off to one side of the porch is a small buffet table, where two glass pitchers rest on a silver tray. One contains water, and the other holds amber-colored iced tea. After offering two comfortable wooden rocking chairs to David and Jean, Anna sits down between Brad and Julie on a small fabric-covered sofa. As the families chat and get to know one another, Julie talks about her mother's new career in interior design and describes some of her recent projects. Then, walking to the study, she retrieves a photo album that contains pictures of some of her mother's most recent jobs. To the Piersons' delight, some of Nashville's elite entertainers and politicians are instantly recognizable.

After looking over the photographs, Brad asks if he could show his parents some of the farm. Not wishing to go herself, Anna decides to offer the services of her close friend and farmhand, Jimmy Hill.

"I hope you won't mind, but I have a few things left to do before I can serve dinner. ... Would it be acceptable if I asked Mr. Hill to take you out on the farm? He was out doing some repair work on the barn this afternoon. Let me give him a call."

Going back into the kitchen, Anna calls out to the barn on an intercom system. Luckily she is able to locate Mr. Hill immediately. A moment later, a balding man in his midfifties, wearing blue denim overalls and a white T-shirt, steps out of the unpainted horse barn located approximately two hundred yards from the back of the house. As soon as he is outside in the midday sun, he pulls out a red baseball cap to protect his shining white scalp.

It doesn't take Mr. Hill long to reach the screened porch. After a polite knock, he steps in. From a pocket in his overalls, he pulls out a fresh handkerchief and wipes the perspiration from his neck and face. Noticing his warmth, Anna welcomes him with a tall glass of iced tea. As soon as Mr. Hill sees Julie, his entire face is drawn into a generous smile.

"Hey, Miss Julie, I've sure missed seein' you o'er the past month or so. Down here visitin' your mama?"

"You bet, Jimmy. I don't get to see enough of her these days."

Walking over to Jimmy, Julie wraps her arms around him. Having known him since childhood, she regards him as a member of the family. After her father's death, Jimmy's devotion to the farm, as well as to Julie's mother, has been a godsend.

"Jimmy, how come you always look so good? The only thing I can figure is that Mrs. Hill must be taking awfully good care of you. ... And by the way, how's she getting along?"

Julie's comment causes Jimmy Hill to chuckle.

"Grace's gettin' along jus' fine, honey. It'd sure mean a lot to her if you came by for a visit while you're here."

"Tell Grace that I'll stop by tomorrow after church. She sure is a sweet woman, Jimmy."

Anna then introduces Mr. Hill to her guests.

"Jimmy, this is David and Jean Pierson, Brad's mother and father. They are down here visiting from New York State."

"Pleasure to meet you, ma'am, sir. Sure is hot down here, id'n it? You know, up until I'd met your son Brad here, I thought New York was jus' one big ol' city, but I believe he's gotten me straightened around on that one by now."

Next, Jimmy walks over to Brad and, with his large hand, gives him a firm handshake.

"Dr. Brad, sure am glad you brought your folks down to meet Ms. Anna and Julie. Hope they're havin' a good visit."

Politely interrupting, Anna asks, "Jimmy, do you have time to show Brad's parents some of the farm? I know it would be a real treat for them. ... If that's okay, I'll go and get my car keys."

Swelling with pride when faced with the chance to show off the land that he's devoted his life to, Jimmy jumps at it. With everyone loaded into Anna's Chevrolet Suburban, Jimmy starts off in the direction of the back side of the farm. Adjacent to the house are the series of flower gardens that were planted by John Christensen long before his death. Emotionally unable to let them wither away, Anna has rigorously maintained them over the years with the help of Jimmy Hill and a local gardener. Beyond the gardens, on a grass-covered hill, is a two-story, unpainted wooden horse barn that has weathered to a silver heather color. Surrounding the barn is a pasture. At the place where dozens of graceful horses once stood, in their place is only a small herd of slow-moving Hereford cattle. Thick reddish-brown hides of fur cover them from head to foot, except for the distinctive white of their bellies. One of the few things Anna couldn't take care of after being widowed were her husband's horses.

Farther out, among acres of vegetable crops, are giant irrigation rigs running the length of the fields. Mr. Hill points out his home on the far side of the huge estate, a one-story, ranch-style white house adorned with black shutters. Standing beside his home are giant tractors and combines that are used to cultivate Anna's farmlands. With the reputation of being a highly skilled farmer, Jimmy frequently has younger men from the area standing at his front door in the evening, humbly seeking his advice.

The drive affords Jimmy an opportunity to share some of his life's history with the Piersons. Apparently, at the age of six, his father died, and shortly thereafter, his mother went to work for the Christensen family doing housework. When John and Anna found out that he and his mother were living in squalor in a run-down trailer park, they insisted on building a small cottage on their property for them.

"Doc had jus' started his medical practice at the time, and he was sure gone a lot. He and the missus practically raised me, what with me being at their house all the time and all. They treated me like I was one o' their own.

I loved to watch ol' Doc in the gardens in his spare time; he really loved those flowers o' his. I used to help him raise those flowers when I was a young'un. ... When I got old enough, he surprised me and Mama and offered to pay for me to go off to agriculture school. That was so I'd learn a trade and all. ... He was one fine Christian man, that Doc was. Good Lord, I miss him so bad at times. ... I could have left here a hundred times over, but Ms. Anna and Julie and Lauren, well, they're my family."

When they get back to the house, everyone thanks Jimmy profusely for the time he spent with them. Before he leaves, Julie hugs Mr. Hill a second time and tells him she'll be over later to visit his wife. After handing Anna's keys to Julie, Jimmy waves goodbye and walks in the direction of his gray pickup truck parked in the driveway. Brad notes that on the driver's door of his truck is a large dent, partially filled in with a white epoxy, prompting him to ask about it.

"What happened to your truck, Jimmy?"

"'Bout six months ago, when I was out pullin' up stumps on the back side o' the property, my chain broke and I ran smack into a tree. ... I jus' hadn't had a chance to git it fixed yet."

"You didn't get hurt, I hope."

Smiling, Jimmy pulls out his handkerchief to wipe his neck a final time. "Wasn't hurt a bit. You know it takes more than a tree to get ol' Jimmy Hill."

While her guests were away, Anna was busily preparing a Southern-style Fourth of July meal. Carefully organized across the kitchen countertops are serving platters overflowing with food. In addition to barbecued chicken, grilled steaks, and mounds of potato salad, there is coleslaw and honey baked beans. On a cooling rack beside the oven are four steaming homemade pies. Freshly sliced watermelon, stacked in a large bowl, adorns the center of the dining table. The table itself has been meticulously prepared, with freshly polished sterling silverware and crisply folded cloth napkins laid atop a starched white linen tablecloth.

As Jean and David enter the room, their eyes grow wide in disbelief at all the wonderful food. Jean blurts out, "Oh, Anna, this is so beautiful. Thank you very much."

Smiling, Anna takes off her apron, walks over to Julie, and places one arm around her daughter's waist. "I don't get to do much entertaining anymore, and I wanted you to enjoy yourselves while you're here. I've become very fond of Brad, and it was my hope that we'd all have a nice holiday meal together."

Insisting that her mom sit down, Julie gathers a plate of Anna's favorite foods and places it before her. After everyone has had a chance to sample their meals, Julie mentions that she has five tickets to the fireworks display at Riverfront Park in downtown Nashville. In sharp contrast to Brad's enthusiasm, Anna initially resists the invitation.

"Oh, Julie, I don't know. You know how crazy traffic is downtown, especially on the Fourth of July."

Reluctantly, after much persuasion on her daughter's part, Anna gives in, with the understanding that she prefers not to stay very late. Following dinner, Brad volunteers to clear the table and do the dishes, and Julie agrees to help. Anna invites David and Jean to make themselves more comfortable in the living room.

Once her guests have gotten settled on the sofa, Anna sits down in a nearby upholstered chair. When Anna asks how their visit has been so far, Jean Pierson immediately bubbles over, saying how much she likes Nashville and the surrounding area. She expresses her own surprise at how beautiful the state of Tennessee is and comments on how friendly the people are. David quietly agrees, and then, because of a personal interest in U.S. history, he asks Anna about this part of the state. Discussing the Civil War, Anna mentions the horrible Battle of Franklin in which over eight thousand Union and Confederate soldiers lost their lives in a single day. She suggests that while Jean and David are in Nashville, they consider a visit to two particular places that have unique historical significance. One of these is the Hermitage, Andrew Jackson's former home and estate on the outskirts of Nashville, and the other is the Carnton Plantation, located not far from downtown Franklin, which served as headquarters and a hospital for Confederate soldiers during the Civil War period. The conversation then drifts toward comical stories about raising their children, and it's not long before they are all sharing a laugh together. Curious to see how their parents are interacting, Julie and Brad take a break from their kitchen duties and sneak to the doorway leading to the living room. They are happy that they seem to be getting along so well.

On the way to Riverfront Park, Brad bypasses the scenic country roads for the sake of time and heads straight for the highway, Interstate 65. Thirty minutes later, after taking one highway interchange onto Interstate 40, they arrive in downtown Nashville. Exiting on Broadway, they end up in a traffic jam. It is nearly an hour before they reach the river. Then, up ahead, Riverfront Park comes into view with its semicircular row of national and state flags hanging from tall aluminum poles. A blockade has been set up at the entrance, and Brad relinquishes his tickets to one of the policemen, who directs them to a parking spot facing the river. After they get situated, Julie points to the large number of motorboats, yachts, and sailboats anchored in the middle of the river. Many of the boat owners are enjoying an evening picnic while awaiting the fireworks. Along the shoreline, Brad notices several large passenger boats enter and leave Riverfront Park on a regular basis and inquires about them. Julie informs him that they are Cumberland River taxis that shuttle people back and forth from downtown to the Opryland Amusement Park and Hotel Complex further downriver.

As dusk approaches, Brad rolls down his car window to catch some of the evening breeze. The fresh air is accompanied by the loud synchronized chirping of hundreds of crickets from the grassy lawns nearby. Just after sundown, cannon fire suddenly thunders through the downtown area, beginning the fireworks display. After several booming rounds, a small platform in the center of Riverfront Park lights up. Standing in the middle of the stage is a young woman dressed in a floor-length gown composed entirely of red, white, and blue sequins. The minute she begins to sing "The Star-Spangled Banner," there is immediate silence. When the words "and the home of the brave" exit her lips, the crowd cheers loudly, and the boat owners honk their horns in appreciation. Seconds later, the fireworks resume. Loud cannon blasts bring brilliant colors that light up the sky and reflect in the river below. Excited oohs and ahs accompany each display.

Two-thirds of the way through the fireworks display, Brad wisely decides to leave early. Making a surprisingly easy escape, they are soon moving quickly along Broadway in the direction of the Vanderbilt Plaza Hotel. On their arrival, they walk together as a group to the hotel lobby, where Anna hugs David and Jean Pierson before saying good night.

"Julie and I have certainly enjoyed your visit with us. I hope you can both come back sometime soon, and please, feel free to stay with me on your next trip if you'd like. ... I want you to know how much I think of Brad; he's a fine young man ... Have a safe trip back home."

Julie also hugs the Piersons and tells them how much she has enjoyed meeting them. As Brad prepares to walk Julie and Anna back to the car, he mentions to his parents that he'll return to the hotel after driving Anna back to Franklin. Inside the car, Julie tries to convince Brad not to make the long drive.

"Brad, I'm going to stay with Mom tonight, anyway. Please just drop us off at my house, and I can drive from there. You need to spend time with your mom and dad before they leave."

"But Julie, traffic is heavy. I'll worry about you and Anna if I don't take you myself."

At that point, Anna Christensen interrupts. "Julie is right, Brad. We'll be fine on the trip home. Julie's a good driver, and you need some more time with your family."

With great hesitation, Brad relinquishes and goes only as far as Julie's house. To verify their safety, he escorts them inside and looks around briefly. He thanks Anna for the wonderful meal and for being so nice to his parents. As he steps out onto the front porch, Julie follows him, closing the front door behind her. She tells Brad how much she enjoyed their weekend together and then reaches up to kiss him. Quietly, Brad says good night to Julie. He waits to drive off until he sees that she's safely inside. Once he returns to his parents' hotel room, the three of them reminisce until nearly midnight. As Brad gets up to leave, his father walks him out.

"Your mom and I really like Julie and Anna. Julie's a terrific young woman, Brad. I'm glad we got an opportunity to meet her. ... Thanks for inviting us to come down this weekend. We've had a nice visit."

Looking beyond his father into the room, he waves at his mother and yells, "Mom, I love you! See you in the morning."

On the slow-paced drive home, Brad reflects pleasantly on the weekend. He already begins to miss his parents even before they are gone. His long and arduous education has prevented them from seeing each other as often as he would have liked. He consoles himself with the thought that one day, when he is established as a physician, his workload will level off, and he'll get to spend more time with them.

Chapter 14

On a Wednesday evening in July, Tom Kilpatrick arrives home from work somewhat earlier than usual. In one hand he carries a slender crystal vase containing a dozen plush red roses, and in the other is a legal-size envelope overflowing with papers. It has now been nearly a month since Tracy's hysterectomy. He tries to counter his wife's all too familiar melancholy expression by telling her he loves her. His heart sinks, however, when the flowers seem to have no impact. Covering his disappointment, he gives Tracy a big hug and takes a seat beside her at the kitchen table. He then asks if she would care to go out to dinner. She responds in almost a monotone. "Sure, honey. Whatever you want to do is fine with me."

A quick glance at her husband's face and Tracy realizes that her reaction has unintentionally caused hurt, so she attempts an apology. "You're sweet to try and cheer me up, Tom. I'm sorry if I've been so depressed lately. The surgery, well, you know ... I'm just having a hard time."

After sliding one arm around his wife's shoulder, Tom whispers softly in her ear: "Aren't you curious why I'm home early today?"

Her husband's gleeful tone and enigmatic smile brings only silence from the confused Tracy. A moment later, while staring into his wife's eyes, Tom places the envelope he's carried home with him directly in front of her. Timidly, she picks at the folded documents until Tom reaches over and opens the envelope directly in front of her. The top sheet is a cover letter addressed to the couple and dated July 12.

Dear Mr. and Mrs. Kilpatrick,

It is with great pleasure that I send this letter, notifying you that an opportunity has arisen to become the adopting parents of a newly born baby girl, given up unexpectedly by her teenaged mother at birth. I phoned Mr. Kilpatrick at the office this week, and he affirmed your interest in pursuing an adoption. Please contact me as soon as possible at my office number listed above if you wish to proceed, as we have many fine couples awaiting a child. A copy of your initial application is enclosed so that any necessary corrections may be made prior to the formal adoption process. I look forward to hearing from you in the very near future.

My sincerest congratulations,

Nancy P. Matherly, President, Christian Adoption Agency of Central Tennessee

As if frozen in her current position, the still unspeaking Tracy reads the letter over and over again. Then, tears pour forth from her eyes, causing the black ink to run on the embossed white stationery paper. After Tom helps blot his wife's eyes dry, he again detects a confused look and explains, "Remember when the first in vitro fertilization didn't work and we decided we might want to adopt? After we sent in all the applications and went through all the interviews, I stayed in contact with several of the agencies, just in case."

A big smile now crosses Tracy's face. Throwing her arms around her husband's neck, she cries out, "Tom, I love you. You're the greatest!"

After hugging him, she leans back in her chair. Her voice takes on an excited quality. "How soon can we see our new baby?"

On the same evening Tom and Tracy Kilpatrick receive their welcome news, Dr. Robert Altman and Dr. Alan Richards get together for a scheduled meeting at AmericaHealth's downtown headquarters. It is nearly 8:00 p.m., and the two men are just getting settled into Robert's plush penthouse office. With little in the way of any social interaction, the men quickly get down to business. Robert is initially distracted by the rustling of papers as Alan searches for his outline. In his truncated Philadelphia accent, Robert begins: "On the DNA testing capabilities you and I discussed, how far along are we?"

While responding, Alan Richards rubs the bridge of his nose with one index finger. "At this point, we have the ability to screen for a dozen or so major genetic disorders. The FDA is about to release six or seven more in the near future, and I've requested them as soon as they're available."

"What have you received so far?"

"For hereditary types of cancers, we'll be able to identify women at risk of developing breast cancer with the P53, BRCA1, and BRCA2 breast cancer gene probes. The familial adenocarcinoma syndrome gene has recently been isolated, as has the autosomal dominant rectal cancer gene."

With a suppressed grin, Robert excitedly begins to ask several questions. "How accurate are these genetic probes?"

"Extremely, with an 85 to 90 percent clinical correlation rate."

"What other tests do we have?"

"Ten days ago, the DNA screening kits for cardiovascular disorders arrived. Patients with familial hypercholesterolemia and hypertriglyceridemia are now able to be identified, as are pediatric patients at risk for juvenile diabetes. In terms of genetically transmitted psychiatric disorders, we have the ability to detect patients predisposed to schizophrenia, depression, and bipolar disorders. And finally, just this morning, I received the assessment tests for hereditary alcoholism and sickle cell anemia."

Leaning way back in his chair, Robert Altman laces his fingers together behind his neck. "Can we legally refuse insurance to potential clients based on this?"

After glancing at his notes, Alan Richards meets Robert's gaze. "At your recommendation, I just met with our corporate attorney, Howard Morgan, about this very issue. He indicates there is currently no state or national legislation that prohibits us from denying insurance to people based on the results of genetic screening. Not only that, but for people who are currently insured with AmericaHealth it is possible to terminate them or demand substantially higher premiums because of their elevated risk status."

Again a smile appears on Robert's face. "Excellent. How soon can we get started?"

"With your permission, I'll get things going right away." Turning the page of his typewritten outline, Robert then moves on to the next agenda item. "Where are we on the issue of cost containment of blood work and other laboratory studies?"

"As of June 21, comprehensive memos were sent to all AmericaHealth physician providers. Along with the letter were details about which lab work would and would not be covered by our insurance plan. For the expensive lab tests that AmericaHealth agrees to pay for, the primary care physician must order the test and specific forms for approval must be filled out. Additionally, *all* outpatient blood work, regardless of cost, must be drawn in one of *our* labs."

"But we only have two labs in town, one on Whitebridge Road and the other on Twenty-First Avenue South. Isn't that inconvenient for our patients?"

"That's the whole idea. You specifically asked me for measures to keep costs down. The more inconvenient it is to have blood drawn, the less likely it will be for patients or doctors to ask for certain tests. Additionally, by having only two facilities in town, we save a small fortune on equipment, office staff, and building costs."

With a look of surprise, Robert pauses momentarily and then blurts out, "Alan, you're a genius! One of the best decisions I ever made was to have you as our pathology advisor." Looking down at his desk momentarily, Robert asks one final question: "What about the other matter?"

"It was taken care of this afternoon. Don't worry about it."

The meeting between Doctors Altman and Richards continues for another forty minutes, at which point both men decide to call it an evening.

As mid-July rolls around, William Lockwood is now three weeks out from his surgery. This morning, he is sitting in the small, crowded waiting room of Aaron Goodman's office in the Vanderbilt Hospital complex. After one of the nurses calls his name, William puts down his magazine and walks to an examination room where Dr. Goodman is already waiting. Obviously delighted to see him, Dr. Goodman pats William on the back before giving him a thorough examination. Inspection of the surgical wound reveals that it has healed well. Dr. Goodman is pleased that some of the vision has returned in the left eye and is hopeful for a full recovery, based on William's progress.

On leaving the hospital, William leisurely strolls across the campus in the direction of his office. This will be his first day back at work since the day of his surgery. Yesterday he phoned his secretary, Francine, and asked her to gather his mail and fall teaching schedule for them to go over this morning. His eyes are still extremely sensitive to sunlight; on his short walk to Calhoun Hall, he puts on a pair of dark sunglasses. With much of his vision still intact, there is newfound delight in everything he sees. Somehow the trees appear taller and fuller, the buildings more ornate, and the grass—even the grass!—more beautiful.

As he makes his final step up to the fifth floor of the Calhoun Hall classroom building, he sees his name spelled out in gold lettering on his office door just ahead. With his hand on the doorknob, he pauses and stares intently at those letters. To him, it seemed this day would never come, the day he would actually return to work. Seated at her desk in William's outer office, Francine Chase stands to hug him on his arrival. Both shed joyful tears at William's return. William thanks his secretary again for looking after Cynthia during his illness. Next, the two walk together into William's office. William blurts out a surprised "Wow!" when he sees how neatly Francine has organized it.

For the next couple of hours, William and Francine go over the extensive number of phone messages and the pile of mail that has come in. They then review the upcoming departmental meetings and put together a preliminary lecture schedule for the fall semester. Just before finishing, Francine excuses herself, explaining that she needs to make a phone call.

After a long lapse, William goes in search of her, feeling that something must be wrong for her to be away so long. Still preoccupied in thought as he opens his office door, he nearly falls over when a large group yells, "Welcome back!" He is stunned to see the large collection of friends, college-level professors, and past and present students all crowded into his outer office and the hallway beyond. Standing proudly in the center, Francine holds a large cake with chocolate frosting and candles on top. Overwhelmed by the outpouring of affection in his honor, William can barely get out the words, "Thank you all."

Chapter 15

Outside the white, wooden Evangelical Baptist Church of Smyrna this Sunday morning there is somewhat of a commotion as the congregation gathers around its newly reunited member, Butch Kennedy. The church-goers are shielded from the piercing mid-July sun by the arching, densely foliated limbs of several mature white oak trees at the front of the property. This is a special occasion, as it is the first sermon Butch has attended since his heart attack nearly two months ago. Hovering near the entrance to the church, some of the men affectionately slap Butch on the back and praise him for how good he looks while Elinor's friends pull her aside and ask how she is holding up. The pastor is chagrined at being upstaged, as Butch garners most of the attention this morning. In the midst of the celebration, one of the elderly ladies, wearing a purple velour dress and a matching hat with long peacock feathers drooping over her face, walks up to Butch. Around her thin legs are sagging light-colored stockings. Because of her short stature, she stands on her toes, peering through thick eyeglasses as she looks up at Butch's face.

"You don't look sick, young Mr. Kennedy. Where have you been?"

The congregation breaks into laughter at the statement, and Butch, not knowing how to respond, is dumbfounded. Standing tall next to their husband and father respectively, Elinor, David, and Suzie are thrilled to witness Butch's return to one of his normal activities.

Instead of driving home after the services, the church members stream to the backside of the property where a luncheon in Butch's name is about to get under way. On long tables covered by white cotton tablecloths sits a smorgasbord of home-cooked foods in covered-dishes. A line of people holding empty plates has already formed. Today, Butch feels the best he has in a long time, and he falls easily into animated storytelling.

After the midday meal, the Kennedy family returns home. Butch hurriedly loosens his gold-colored tie and changes out of his suit. He emerges from his bedroom in an old, faded, maroon football jersey and white cotton fleece shorts. Calling for David, he walks down the stairs with the football that he has kept since his days as a college fullback. He instructs his son to get out of his "fancy clothes" and asks that he meet him out in the backyard in a few minutes. While strolling through the kitchen on his way outside, he encounters Elinor, who follows him closely and pleads with him. "Butch, honey, you know you shouldn't be throwing that football around. Dr. Peters said you need to be taking it easy for a while. Come on now and just sit down with me out back. We'll have a nice afternoon. I'll even make you some homemade lemonade … Please, Butch."

As always, Butch listens intently to his wife, whose opinion he has come to respect. While contemplating what she said, he continues to toss the football in the air with one hand.

"All right, sweetie, you're right. I'll jus' throw a few with David and quit. I'll be fine; don't you worry."

Elinor and Suzie, still in their long Sunday dresses, sit near the shaded back of the house on folding lawn chairs while the men play for a while. Despite a slow and easy start, Butch's throws are remarkably precise. Each time, he manages to place the football directly in David's hands, even when his son runs in a complex pattern. Elinor keeps an anxious eye every moment. After twenty minutes, Butch announces he has had enough and walks toward his wife and daughter. David sprints by him on one side, racing him to the back of the house.

Suddenly, a horrific chest pain strikes Butch, a pain that squeezes the breath out of him. Looking up at his family, he catches a glimpse of Elinor jumping up out of her chair and screaming and another of David running back toward him before he feels his face hit the soft, grass-covered earth below. Those are his last memories before his mind goes completely blank.

David quickly reaches his father, who is now lying face down. As he turns Butch onto his back, David notices that in addition to being unconscious, Butch's breathing is quite shallow and his face is blue. After checking his father's pulse, David begins chest compressions and yells to Suzie to call 9-1-1. Visibly flustered, Elinor runs to her husband's side and in a nervous voice yells out, "Butch! Butch! Wake up! Stop playing games with us. Now stop this nonsense and get up. ... David, tell your father to stand up and go back into the house. ... Dear Lord, help me!"

She now falls to her knees at her husband's side and stares at his closed eyes and his expressionless look. She visually inspects the graying temples of his closely trimmed hair and each detail of his face. Tears fall uncontrollably from her eyes, landing on her silent husband's lips and neck. David continues cardiopulmonary resuscitation until the ambulance arrives.

Soon, Butch is being raced toward the Deaconess Hospital. On their entry into the emergency department, one of the paramedics yells out, "Heart attack in room four. Patient critical!"

As Butch is wheeled in by gurney, Dr. James Sterling breaks away from a simpler matter and runs to help. While another doctor continues lifesaving measures, Dr. Sterling looks over the electrocardiograph and oxygen saturation monitors before assessing his new patient. Just completed, a twelve-lead EKG is dropped into Dr. Sterling's hands. An extensive anterior-wall heart attack is present, along with an irregular heart rhythm, punctuated by multiple premature ventricular beats.

While yelling out orders for specific pharmacological drips to be given to correct the dangerous rhythm, Dr. Sterling takes over the chest compressions and can now see his new patient's face. Momentarily stunned, he says aloud, "Butch Kennedy?" Turning to the paramedics, he asks this man's name, and they confirm his worst fears. Following their first encounter, Dr. Sterling had stayed in contact with Butch and his family and had followed his progress through the cardiac rehabilitation program. It brought him great personal satisfaction to see Butch make such long strides during his recovery. At one point, Butch even made a special trip to the emergency room to thank Dr. Sterling in person for saving his life. He and Butch had become friends in the process, a relationship that Jim Sterling cherished. With great despair, he observes his friend and patient lying before him in an unconscious state. Attempting to correct the aberrant heartbeats, he starts a lidocaine drip, and because of Butch's low blood pressure, he begins dopamine and dobutamine. Dr. Sterling requests the placement of an urgent page to Dr. Peters.

Suddenly, Butch's heart rhythm degenerates into an extremely dangerous ventricular tachycardia, at which point his heart beats rapidly and uncontrollably. A full code is called, setting off a blue light outside the room. From all over the emergency department, doctors and nurses come running. While Jim Sterling reaches for an endotracheal tube to insert into Butch's airway, another doctor assumes the duty of compressing the chest to manually pump the heart. Increasing the dose of lidocaine does not restore the heart to a normal rhythm, so a second medicine is begun. Ninety long seconds pass and still the abnormal beats continue. In frank desperation, Dr. Sterling calls for the electronic defibrillator and instructs the nurse to set it on 250 joules. Dr. Sterling rubs the paddles together to spread the contact gel evenly across the paddles' surfaces. Dr. Sterling then yells, "Charge!" and a brief high-pitched sound signals the device's readiness. As he places the handheld metal paddles on Butch's chest, Dr. Sterling yells, *"Clear,"* and everyone steps back away from the bed. With the discharge of the electric current, Butch's entire body stiffens and then relaxes.

After the electronic shock, the pattern of Butch's heartbeat becomes nearly normal. As a result, the medical staff in the room sound a cheer. However, the normal rhythm lasts but a minute or two before relapsing into ventricular tachycardia. The defibrillator is once again in Jim Sterling's hands, and he again calls quick commands in sequence: "Three hundred joules. … Charge … Clear!" This time there is no effect on the tracing. As Dr. Sterling prepares to give a third shock, Butch's heart falls into asystole, a pattern in which his heart stops beating altogether, and the EKG monitor shows a straight line. With his right hand balled up into a fist, Dr. Sterling strikes the center of Butch's chest firmly, trying to jump-start his heart, and then resumes hand-over-hand chest compressions. He shouts out for multiple medicines to be given through the large-bore venous line in the jugular vein of Butch's neck. Dr. Peters arrives at that moment. Tossing his lab coat aside, he assumes command of the resuscitation attempt. Several new pharmacological measures are undertaken, followed by the installation of a temporary pacemaker. Exasperation strikes everyone in the room when nothing seems to make a difference; Butch's heart simply refuses to resume beating. Forty-five minutes have now elapsed since the code was begun. With great hesitation, Dr. Peters instructs everyone to discontinue their efforts and pronounces Butch deceased at 3:38 p.m.

Silently, the despondent staff leaves the room with their chins down. Jim Sterling lags behind and stares at Butch's lifeless body for several seconds. He thinks to himself, *I'll never get used to this, death looking me in the face. Why does such a fine man have to die when there are so many criminals walking around that we can't build prisons fast enough to house them all? Dear God, where is the justice in all of this?*

Walking to Butch's bedside, he humanely closes the lids of his lost patient's eyes before the family arrives. He then takes over from one of the nurse technicians the responsibility of removing the endotracheal tube from Butch's mouth and the intravenous lines from his arm and neck. A burdensome sadness fills him as he takes one final look at Butch. He dreads the task that lies before him.

Together, Jim Sterling and Leonard Peters walk with grim expressions to a private conference room where the Kennedy family is already seated. With their eyes fixed on the floor, the two physicians enter and sit across from Elinor and the children. Elinor's eyes are swollen, and her makeup is smeared from crying. Trembling all over, she holds her children's hands as she faces the two men. Fear is also evident in the eyes of David and Suzie.

With great effort, Dr. Peters speaks calmly and professionally, fighting back his own emotions. "Elinor, David, Suzie ... I'm very sorry. Butch sustained a heart attack so severe that his heart just plain failed. Nothing we did could get his heart to start working again. Dr. Sterling made an incredible effort to bring Butch back. ... We all did. ... I can assure you that he felt no pain—"

Before Dr. Peters can finish his sentence, Elinor begins to wail loudly. On either side of her, David and Suzie hold onto her as she rocks back and forth in her chair. With his mother still crying loudly, David whispers, "Can we see my dad?"

Without a word, Jim Sterling stands up and escorts the family to room number 4 within the emergency department. Upon leaving, he closes the door to give the family some privacy. Elinor nearly faints when she sees her husband's still body; David barely gets her to a chair before she falls to the floor. Sitting beside the bed with tears flowing freely, she reaches for one of her husband's hands and tries to warm it, saying, "It's all right, honey, you're just catching a little cold. I'll tell the doctors you need to stay home from work." Turning to her daughter, she says, "Suzie, get your father a blanket. He's cold."

Suzie, also crying, reaches one arm around her mother.

"Mama, Daddy's gone. You've got to accept that. David and I love you, and we'll always be with you."

In an angry tone, Elinor now directs her voice at Butch's body: "Butch, you come back to me. You can't leave me. … Butch, honey, I love you. … Don't you leave me. I can't make it without you."

The pace of the work in the emergency room picks up dramatically, with critically ill people lining the halls. Dr. Sterling throws himself back into the midst of it and tries to push the thought of Butch's death from his mind. An hour or so later, while sitting at a desk doing paperwork, he feels a light tapping on his shoulder. Turning around, he sees David Kennedy, who asks for a moment of his time. They walk to a private corner, where David tries to speak, his voice frequently faltering.

"Dr. Sterling … I want you to know how much … Mama and Suzie and I … how much we thank you for what you did for Daddy. … We know you did everything … everything you could to save him, and we thank you."

Pausing, he strives to force back his pain.

"Mama and I … Mama and I, we talked about it, and … we think we want to have an autopsy on Daddy … to see … to see what actually caused him to die."

With his hand resting on David's shoulder, Dr. Sterling replies, "David, I'm real sorry about what happened to your father. Over the past couple of months, I got to know your father pretty well—he was a wonderful man, full of honor and integrity. … His death is a terrible loss. …I consider it a personal tragedy… In terms of an autopsy, if you and your mom wish us to perform one, I'll be happy to arrange it. Let me get the appropriate paperwork together, and I'll bring it to you. … God bless you, David."

Because his mother is too devastated to function adequately, David takes charge of the situation, including signing all forms and choosing a funeral home. When he returns to her, a hospital-appointed grief counselor is with her. In her current state of shock, Elinor gains little from the thirty-minute session, but the specially trained psychologist promises to contact her at home in several days to make an appointment. Elinor now relates to her children the desire "to go on home, where I can have some time by myself."

Before leaving the hospital, she asks if she can see her husband one last time. Along with Suzie and David, she goes again to Butch's room. Using one hand, she draws back the white sheet covering Butch's face to take a final look. At that moment, her mind is flooded with all her memories of them together: their first date, the day he proposed to her, the day the letter came from Kuwait announcing his war injury. Sobbing uncontrollably, she again falls to her knees, clenching tightly the bed rail of her husband's hospital gurney. Suzie places her hands on top of her mother's and sits down beside her, with her own tears streaming. With tender gentleness, she eases her mother's fingers away from the metal railing, and then she and David help her out of the room. Once Elinor's children have assisted her to the car, the Kennedy family begins the seemingly long drive home.

Every sixth weekend, the Vanderbilt pathology residents are assigned to an autopsy rotation at one of the community-based hospitals in Nashville. This afternoon, Sunday, Brad Pierson is knee-deep in responsibilities at the morgue at the Deaconess Hospital, where he has worked almost nonstop since his arrival the morning before. Luckily for him, the pace slowed long enough on Saturday night for him to go home and get in a few hours of sleep in his own bed.

Tired and achy from the many hours on his feet, he prepares to begin the anatomic dissection of his current case, a twenty-nine-year-old woman, the apparent victim of domestic violence. Standing within the cold, cramped windowless room, Brad notices that the pale skin of the victim's youthful body is lit by yellow incandescent lighting from ceiling-mounted lamps. Around the tiny room, three policemen stand guard, waiting for Brad to retrieve the three

.38-caliber slugs from her chest and abdomen. Within their possession is the perpetrator's handgun, the alleged murder weapon; the evidence is needed to make a ballistics match.

Before beginning, Brad puts on a fresh gown, two pairs of surgical gloves, a face mask, and plastic goggles. As he picks up the long razor-sharp scalpel, he questions the observers as to whether they are adequately prepared mentally for what is about to occur. One of the three blue-clad officers steps forward, explaining that he has witnessed several procedures. He volunteers to stay. The other two men, already queasy, gladly scurry from the room.

Positioning the surgical knife, Brad surveys the cold lily-white body and the three circular puncture wounds in the skin. The flaccid muscle tone indicates that rigor mortis has already come and gone. He studies the woman's face, noticing that she is the same age as he. This catches him off guard, causing him to drop the scalpel onto the table below. With resolve, he picks up the instrument and makes an incision lateral to one of the entry wounds in the chest and then uses a tiny saw to cut through several ribs. He positions a metal retractor to hold the ribs apart and inserts a long-handled ringed forceps to retrieve the first bullet.

He then repeats the procedure around the second bullet hole in the chest, but this time, the search takes more effort. Eventually, Brad spots a shiny reflection within one of the spinal vertebral bodies. In order to extract the slug without damaging it, he utilizes a drill to bore holes around it in the bone.

Gingerly, Brad next opens the abdominal cavity, where the third bullet appears to have sheared off the major artery supplying blood flow to the abdomen and lower extremities, the abdominal aorta. Somehow the bullet ended up lodged in the lower portion of the left lobe of the liver. Into the microphone beside the table, Brad lists the cause of death as "gunshot wound to the abdomen resulting in transsection of the abdominal aorta with massive blood loss and hemoperitoneum."

A metal clank is heard as the final lead slug is released by the forceps and drops into a metal basin. Because this particular autopsy was requested by the police department and not by the family for "cause of death only," Brad stops there. Requesting silk sutures on curved needles, Brad neatly stitches together the wounds he just created. He specifies that the woman's body be returned to the refrigerated storage area in the morgue until the officers have completed their investigation.

As Brad finishes the dictation of this forensics case, he is confronted by the tragic loss of this young woman's life and the abhorrent manner in which it was taken. Preoccupied by that thought, he finds himself mentally stumbling for the words to finish the report.

With all homicide cases, reams of documents, including a death certificate, must be completed immediately. Just after the final form has been signed, the pathology technician assigned to the morgue summons Brad to yet another case. Walking into the dissection area, Brad sees a long, blue cotton sheet draped over a tall human outline on the long steel table. Without some of the callousness that comes from years of experience, Brad has yet to get used to dealing with the spookiness of lifeless human corpses. He is happy that Ernie, the technician, is in the room with him. He pulls back the covering over the right foot and reads the manila paperboard tag attached to the right great toe. The black hand-printed name on the tag identifies the body as belonging to Randall Butch Kennedy. Ernie conveys to Brad that the arterial and venous blood has already been siphoned away from the body, so it is safe to proceed.

The initial step in an autopsy is to survey the body carefully and identify any obvious abnormalities. Beginning at the head, Brad slowly pulls the sheet back, noting the purple hue of Butch's skin, a sign that any remaining blood beneath the skin has been stripped of its oxygen. He also observes the recent puncture wounds in the neck and arm where the venous lines were placed during the resuscitation effort. Ernie then helps Brad turn the body on one side so he can undertake a cursory review of the back. He then methodically inspects and counts the fingers and toes and examines the surfaces of the palms and soles. So far, Brad's autopsy notes only contain the words, "Muscular-appearing middle-aged black male. No obvious trauma. No fractured bones. Intravenous line sites in left external jugular and right antecubital veins."

Brad then steps back from the table momentarily. Because of the frigid temperature, his plastic protective eyewear has fogged. He searches for a fresh towel to clean the goggles with. Then he carefully reads the instructions for the pathologic analysis, which state, "Likely cause of death—myocardial infarction. Family requests complete review of the body, with exception of the face, brain, and extremities."

Leaning over the still body, Brad picks up a fresh scalpel and makes his first incision in the skin overlying the sternal breast bone. Next, he uses a handheld electric saw to cut through the bone, exposing the contents of the chest cavity. A chest retractor holds the ribs apart.

Initially, Brad examines the shining blue-gray surface of both the right and left lung, the texture of which is firmer than normal following death. Reaching a gloved hand inside the chest, Brad first removes the left lung and places the boggy organ onto a hanging scale to be weighed. Into his notebook, Brad records a description of the left lung and its weight. Then he repeats the procedure for the right lung. He then places the two organs into their own separate containers for further analysis once the gross dissection has been completed.

His attention turns next to the heart, which sits alone in the chest now that the lungs have been removed. Encasing the heart is its dense fibrous cover, the pericardium. Exiting the upper portion of the heart is the body's largest blood vessel, the thoracic aorta. After Brad cuts across this vessel, he grasps the oblong-shaped muscular heart with both hands and slides it onto the scale. The remaining structures he then inspects carefully. After this, he opens the thoracic aorta, revealing minimal to moderate atherosclerotic plaquing.

Following removal of the chest retractors, Brad opens the abdominal cavity and again performs a thorough analysis. He removes and weighs the liver, spleen, gallbladder, and kidneys but leaves the remaining organs, including the bowel, as they are unlikely to produce evidence of the cause of death.

With the dissection completed, Brad moves to the next step, which is much more tedious. He walks to the preparatory room, where he evaluates tissue samples in-depth and then sections them to make permanent slides.

Under the thick gown and wearing two pairs of gloves, Brad begins to perspire as he begins his analysis of the heart. He first removes the thick covering of the heart and then lifts it from its metal specimen container and notes a large bluish discoloration, resembling a bruise, overlying the reddish-brown muscle of the main pumping chamber, the left ventricle. Manual palpation of this area reveals it to be soft and spongy, in sharp contrast to the normally firm texture of heart muscle.

With a large surgical knife, Brad carefully opens the left ventricle, confirming the cause of death. An extensive heart attack caused a large portion of muscle to die, resulting in a large blood clot. Continuing onward, Brad notes that the chamber is normal in size and anatomical configuration, with slight reduction in volume due to a moderate thickening of its muscle walls.

Brad then opens the three other chambers, the right and left atria and the right ventricle. There are no major pathologic abnormalities, with the exception of a slight muscle enlargement in the walls of the right ventricle. His attention is then focused on the four heart valves. After a thorough inspection, he determines that all appear to be in perfect condition.

Before proceeding further, Brad retrieves a digital camera and takes photographs of the heart and the other organs to document each of his findings. He then prints two sets of photographs. The first set goes into the patient's permanent hospital records, and the second goes into his own personal autopsy notebook.

The major arteries delivering blood to the heart, the coronary vessels, are studied next. Brad first opens the largest of the principal arteries, the left anterior descending. He discovers a mesh metal stent in one portion of the artery. At that site, the central portion of the vessel is wide open, which is consistent with Butch's previous angioplasty and stent placement. Approximately one centimeter beyond the stent is a large fibrinous clot that completely obstructs the large artery. This is the obvious cause of extensive damage to the heart musculature and the likely cause of death. He then analyzes the remainder of the heart vessels. A second artery exhibits a stent and scarring in one area, in keeping with Butch's other atherectomy site.

Brad allows himself a momentary break before continuing. An external inspection of the liver, kidneys, and spleen reveals them to be heavy and filled with venous blood, which supports the theory of a sudden heart failure. Microscopically, each organ demonstrates abnormalities characteristic of the sudden severe loss of oxygenated blood, as in the case of a massive heart attack. Having firmly established the cause of death with more than ample evidence, Brad places a page to the attending pathologist on call, who must review all of the day's autopsies with him before he can sign the cases out and go home. The phone rings within several minutes. Brad hears Dr. Alan Richards's voice on the other end.

"Alan, this is Brad Pierson. Listen, I've finished most of the cases that came in over the weekend. Is this a convenient time for you to go over them with me?"

"I've been expecting your call, Brad. I should be there in about fifteen minutes."

Replacing the receiver, Brad carefully completes his log and places the photographs into both sets of records. After finishing his notes, he begins the lengthy dictations. In the middle of reciting Butch Kennedy's case, Alan Richards walks in.

"Good afternoon, Brad. By the looks of things, you must have been pretty busy out here this weekend."

"I'm afraid so. At times it's been a little crazy, but I think I've gotten almost everything done."

"Well, let's get you out of here as soon as possible. I'll go change clothes, and then we'll look things over."

A few minutes later, Dr. Alan Richards appears from his office wearing a light green surgical scrub suit and knee-high rubber wading boots. Initially, the history of each case is presented by Brad, followed by a thorough analysis of the anatomic and pathologic findings. After going stepwise through his notes and photographs with his attending physician, Brad withdraws the bodies from the refrigeration unit to demonstrate the pertinent abnormalities. Finally, the organs from each case are inspected and analyzed by Alan Richards with Brad's help. Currently undergoing preservation and staining that will take one full day, the organ samples will then be mounted in paraffin wax and precisely sectioned. Alan Richards will be able to study them on Tuesday morning and will then send them to Vanderbilt by courier for Brad to review that afternoon.

After the two physicians have finished their discussion, Brad once again sits at the Dictaphone to complete the findings of the gross autopsy. He will add the microscopic details once the tissue slides are available. With that chore behind him, Brad snaps closed his hardbound notebook containing his personal autopsy notes. In block letters across of the front of the light blue cloth-covered volume is written, "Autopsy Book III – Bradley T. Pierson, MD."

As Brad reaches down to tuck the notebook away in his briefcase, Alan Richards walks over and asks if he may look at it. Flipping through the pages, Dr. Richards occasionally pauses to read some of the narrative. He is visibly impressed by the detailed descriptions and the pages of photographs precisely arranged. Lifting his head, he says, "Brad, this is outstanding. Have you done this for all of your autopsy cases?"

"I started doing this just after I began the residency program three years ago. It seemed to make sense for me to keep some record of my work to refer to at a later date."

"I wish all the residents had your compulsiveness. I'm very impressed."

"I hope this doesn't sound bad, but if you don't need me anymore, Alan, I'd like to go on home and get some sleep. I was here until about 3:00 a.m. last night."

"Go ahead, Brad. And by the way, you did a nice job this weekend."

"Thanks, Alan. I'll give you a call later in the week, after we've both had a chance to look over the slides from these cases."

In Smyrna that evening, the Kennedy family sits quietly in their darkened living room. With sundown approaching, the fading afternoon sunlight casts long shadows across the still room. Only the hazy outlines of the furniture and of the three occupants are visible. In one corner, David sits in an armchair with his gaze locked on a dark-brown reclining chair in the middle of the room. This was his father's favorite chair, the chair Butch rested in after a hard day at the plant, the place he sat to watch weekend football games. No one dares go near that chair, afraid of somehow violating their loved one's memory.

Feeling suffocated, David reaches into his pocket for his car keys and mentions that he is going for a drive. Elinor, as if in a daze, cannot respond, but Suzie asks him to please drive carefully. As the back door opens and the tired hinges creak loudly, he is startled by the words, "I love you, honey. You come back to me soon," coming from his mother. On the outskirts of town, he pulls into a fast-food restaurant and picks up a light meal. Not far from the restaurant, he turns onto a winding dirt road, and a half mile later, he pulls off to the side. Reaching for his sandwich, he takes one bite before realizing he's lost his appetite. He wraps up the food and pushes it aside. Now alone, he no longer feels the need to put up a brave front. He allows himself to cry.

Two days later, Butch's funeral takes place at the Evangelical Baptist Church of Smyrna late in the morning. The long wooden pews are completely filled with the mournful faces of family and friends. Solemn, the pastor stands tall at the front of the church with an open Bible in his hands. Just as he clears his throat to begin speaking, the double doors at the back of the sanctuary open and the entire several-hundred-member staff of the Nissan plant tries to crowd their way in. Unsuccessful in their attempt, some are forced to stand outside. The windows of the church are opened to allow Butch's former coworkers to hear the eulogy. Even the highest corporate executives are there to pay their final tribute to Butch.

Wearing a long black dress and a black lace veil covering her face, Elinor turns around when she hears the commotion and is overwhelmed when she sees so many familiar faces from the factory. The church service is followed by a brief graveside ceremony. The streets alongside the funeral home are overflowing with cars. With her face buried in one of Butch's cloth handkerchiefs, Elinor cries silently throughout the morning. The only sound she makes is a brief outcry of pain when her husband's casket is lowered into the dark brown Tennessee earth. Following the burial, a group of managers from Butch's workplace humbly go up to Elinor. Each man shares a personal story with her about her husband: how he saved this man's life or fought to save another's job, or how he just cared about his fellow worker. A box is presented to her with the framed awards and family photographs Butch kept in his office. The men then walk Elinor to her car and follow her home in their own vehicles.

Over the ensuing weeks, not a day goes by that at least two or three friends, neighbors, or church members drop by to see Elinor and the children. They show up on the front porch with an arm full of groceries, a cooked meal, or a loving word. It is obvious that Smyrna sincerely misses Mr. Randall Butch Kennedy.

Chapter 16

With August's arrival, Brad is now one month into his fourth and final year of the residency program at Vanderbilt Hospital. Besides being closer to finishing his formal training, he has discovered that the advancement in rank has ushered in a whole new set of responsibilities. He and Sandy Starke have been nominated by the attending physicians and the other residents to act as chief residents for the year. As such, their duties include assigning other residents to various rotations, making up call schedules, and arranging for formal lectures for the residency program.

This morning, Brad and Sandy are sitting together in the compact residents' office at their tiny cubicles where they are putting the finishing touches on the call rosters. Using a pencil, Sandy jots names on the master calendar beside various dates, while Brad takes note of the assignments. Toward the end of the process, Brad voices a concern.

"Sandy, what are you doing? We can't assign the holiday call yet; we're supposed to hold a lottery for that."

In a snappy tone, Sandy responds, "Listen, you and I are in charge, aren't we? That guy Ron Blackman has gone out of his way to be a real jerk, and since it's up to me, he gets to cover Christmas this year."

Laughing, Brad says, "Yeah, he's a real pain, but I think we need to be fair about the whole thing. Why don't you erase his name until after the lottery's been held?"

"All right, you win! I'll change it just for you. Instead of giving him Christmas, I'll give him Christmas *and New Year's!* How's that for being flexible?"

Brad chuckles again, saying, "Oh brother, why did I bother saying anything?"

After finishing up with Sandy that morning, Brad leaves to begin his first senior rotation at Saint Thomas Hospital, a privately run Catholic hospital with a formal Vanderbilt affiliation. His involvement will be primarily with surgical pathology cases, but he will also perform all the functions of a typical community-based pathologist. In addition to performing an occasional autopsy, he will be involved in surgical pathology, preparing and analyzing tissue samples, and performing outpatient tissue biopsies. With such a variety of tasks, he relishes the opportunity, hoping it will help to enhance his level of expertise.

Brad's first week in the new department proceeds relatively smoothly. As a plus, he finds he has a lot in common with many of the attending pathologists. They quickly recognize his disciplined work ethic and his solid fund of knowledge. This is the first time he has been given this degree of personal autonomy as a physician, and he finds the experience extremely satisfying.

For now, Sandy Starke stays on as the chief resident at Vanderbilt. He has been assigned to run the autopsy service, which is a full-time job at this academic institution. In addition, his responsibilities include the teaching of second-year medical students who rotate through the morgue. Generally, Sandy is quite reserved, but at times, his biting quick wit gets him in trouble with some of the attending pathologists.

Hectic wouldn't begin to describe Sandy's first week at Vanderbilt. After one day on the job, one of the second-year female residents went into preterm labor, requiring him to fulfill her duties as well as his own. With a shift in manpower, the end of the week was somewhat calmer, but he still logged in close to seventy hours in just five days. Luckily, Joanie, despite being extremely busy herself, managed to make several trips to Sandy's apartment to leave meals and fresh clothing for him.

This weekend, Brad and Julie, along with Sandy and Joanie, have planned a Saturday excursion to Radnor Lake, a nature sanctuary located on the southwestern edge of Nashville. Their plan is to meet early that morning, bicycle out to the park, and once there, hike on the trails that run alongside the lake. The two women have agreed to put together a picnic lunch for the outing.

With her bike stowed in the trunk of her car, Julie arrives at Brad's apartment early that morning. From there, she and Brad bicycle the short distance to Sandy's home. When they arrive, they find that the front door is cracked open. They can hear Joanie scolding Sandy for being cranky after his difficult week.

"Come on now, Sandy, it's Saturday. Stop worrying about the problems at work. It's a beautiful day. Once you're outside, you'll forget all about it."

Looking outside through the open door, Joanie waves to Julie and Brad and then walks out to say hello. She laughs when she gets to them, saying, "He's just having a rough start, but I think he'll be fine."

Coming out behind her, Sandy shuts and locks his front door. He grumbles a little bit on his way out, and in a sarcastic tone he addresses his coworker.

"Well, how is cushy private practice going, Dr. Pierson? I hope they didn't make you work past four o'clock this week. ... Personally, I can barely remember sleeping in my own bed even once."

Unable to pass up the opportunity, Brad goads his friend on. "Not only did I leave early from Saint Thomas every day, but also the secretaries served me homemade bonbons right after my afternoon massage."

Incensed by Brad's teasing, Sandy tries to knock Brad to the ground, at which point Joanie intervenes.

"All right, men, we've got a long bike ride ahead of us. We need to get going so we can enjoy our day off."

Their southerly fifteen-mile bicycle trip begins by crossing the bustling Hillsborough Village. Cutting through this busy downtown shopping area, the two couples end up on a moderately trafficked street, Belmont Boulevard. Winding through densely shaded older neighborhoods, this road, after three or four miles, takes them right past David Lipscomb College near Green Hills. Continuing onward through residential developments for another thirty minutes, they eventually intersect Granny White Pike, a winding two-lane country road. After being on Granny White for less than a mile, they see the street sign for Otter Creek Road, which signals the turn-in point to the state-operated wildlife preserve.

Just as the couples turn onto Otter Creek Road, a child darts out in front of Brad's bicycle. Swerving to miss the young boy, Brad careens into the woods and crashes to the ground, covering himself in a fine mist of brown soil. The mother, after grasping hold of her infant, chases after Brad and apologizes profusely. Never one to miss anything, Sandy laughs uncontrollably at Brad's misfortune. As he dusts himself off, Brad makes a comment with obvious irritation in his voice. "Don't you want to know if I'm hurt, or would that somehow interrupt your fun?"

"Ha-ha-ha. Hey, Brad, are you hurt or anything? Ha-ha-ha."

Unwilling to let Sandy bother him, Brad good-naturedly shrugs the incident off, retrieving his bike from the base of a nearby tree.

Near the park entrance is a ranger's station, where the four adventurers park and lock their bikes. From there, they load their food into two small knapsacks and then go inside to procure a map of the trails that encircle the lake. On one wall of the ranger's station is a plaque describing the park's origin, which attracts Brad's attention, prompting him to read it aloud.

"Radnor Lake's history began back in the early 1900s when the Louisville and Nashville Railroad dammed Otter Creek to provide water for the steam-powered locomotive engines of the day. It was not until the early 1970s that the park was actually created, at a time when several building contractors became interested in the land. To block a proposed residential housing development, the only option for the City of Nashville was to buy the land outright for the asking price of 3.5 million dollars. State and federal funds fell five hundred thousand dollars short of that mark, and in just three weeks, the citizens of Nashville raised the rest of the money to preserve the pristine wilderness. The one-thousand-acre natural area is a cherished place for the local inhabitants and has been dubbed 'Nashville's Walden.' An extensive number of rare birds and mammals call the area home."

After Brad finishes, the couples comment on how fortunate they are to have this pristine recreational area. Soon thereafter, they get under way. The first half-mile of their walk consists of winding dirt trails through thick foliage that lead them to the original dam site on the southern shore of the lake. A restored historic cabin sits on an incline adjacent to the edge of the lake.

A half-dozen wooden rocking chairs on the front porch make the cabin an excellent spot for lunch. Julie announces that she is famished.

After the main course of sandwiches and chips has disappeared, their dessert, consisting of marshmallows, is removed from the knapsack. Content after filling his stomach, Sandy is on the prowl for mischief. His teasing is initially directed at Julie.

"Julie, did I ever tell you that while we were in medical school together, Brad told me that he thought radiologists weren't *real* doctors?"

With her faint green eyes filled with indignation, Julie responds crisply, not recognizing that she's fallen for Sandy's ploy. "Oh, and I suppose working with dead people and chunks of tissue cut out of the living constitutes *real* medicine?"

Brad quickly intervenes. "Julie, don't believe anything Sandy's saying. You know I never said anything like that; he's just trying to get you riled up." Turning to Sandy's fiancée, he says, "Joanie, Sandy once said that if you two ever had children, it would be only logical if you were the one to stay home. He feels that 'dabbling with paints' is not nearly as important as *his* career."

Jumping up from her seat, Joanie pulls her wavy brown hair back away from her face and takes up a standing position directly in front of Sandy, who is still seated. She intentionally steps on the tips of his toes in the process.

"*Dabbling in paints?* You told me my work was very meaningful." Reaching for the marshmallow sack, she pulls out a handful and pelts Sandy with them, saying, "Take that, you nerd!"

Collecting ammunition, Sandy fires several of the soft white projectiles at Brad. Soon the entire group is involved and marshmallows are flying in all directions. The play ceases when so much dirt has gotten stuck to the white spongy confections that they are simply disgusting. A truce is accompanied by laughter from everyone. Joanie, with her shining brown eyes still ablaze, asks, "Did you really say that about my painting?"

In an overtly dramatic manner, Sandy gets down on his knees and reaches for one of Joanie's hands, which he kisses while saying, "If those words ever crossed my lips, it was in a moment of extreme stupidity on my part. I only can beg for your forgiveness."

The romantic gesture sways Joanie's heart, and her anger fades. So taken is Julie by Sandy's apology that she sighs audibly. With a mischievous grin, Brad then kneels down. Imitating Sandy, he reaches for Julie's left hand.

"Oh, Princess, even though I did not slur the name of radiologists, please forgive me anyway."

Rolling her eyes, Julie gently pushes Brad away. "Okay, wiseguy. Get out of here."

With harmony restored to the group, they gather around the trail map they'd gotten at the ranger's station. Their bicycle ride had been more taxing than anticipated, and because of the humidity and heat, they opt for a five-mile loop instead of some of the longer trails. Their journey begins along the Ganier Ridge Trail, a steep path that winds deeply through the nearby Overton Hills. Sandy, still physically exhausted from work, huffs and groans, while Joanie, thanks to her frequent aerobics classes, looks fresh and is barely perspiring throughout most of the hike. The two couples eventually emerge from the heavily shaded trail onto a clearing on top of one of the hills, from which there is a clear view of Radnor Lake below. The shoreline of the several-mile-long lake is shrouded by a humid mist, and the water's surface is gently rippled by a solitary canoe traversing the center of the lake. Scattered across the water's edge are hundreds of geese, wood ducks, and mallards, accompanied by their offspring.

Temporarily leaving the group, Sandy climbs atop a large boulder nearby to get a better look at the lake. A moment later, they hear a loud yell, followed by the sound of something crashing into the underbrush nearby. Brad rushes over to Sandy and pulls him up unharmed out of the dense bushes, asking him what happened.

"From out of nowhere, a giant owl swooped down and screeched at me and scared me to death."

Brad quickly glances up and sees a brown barred owl in flight, one of the few diurnal species in the area. While he helps Sandy up, he laughs loudly, barely able to get his words out.

"I can see what scared you, Sandy. That must be one of those man-eating owls."

Obviously embarrassed, Sandy dusts himself off.

"Ha-ha, very funny. I'm just so sure you wouldn't have been startled either."

Laughing again, Brad says, "Oh no, I clearly run for cover anytime I see anything larger than a chickadee."

Angered, but unable to come up with a quick response, Sandy merely pops Brad on the head with his baseball cap before moving along.

As they leave the hill's summit, the foursome begin their descent to the lakeside trail a half mile below, which will take them back to the park's entrance. On the return trip, Joanie is forced to pull Sandy along by one arm to keep him from lagging behind. When they reach the ranger's station, Sandy runs to the soft drink vending machine and hugs it to absorb the cold, after which he quickly downs two of its carbonated beverages. Before they pedal home, the couples take a momentary break on the shaded outdoor wooden deck of the ranger's facility to enjoy the light afternoon breeze.

Toward the middle of August, the second-year Vanderbilt medical students who are formally being taught pathology begin to rotate through the morgue. As chief resident, Sandy is expected to present an early morning lecture to the students, followed by the medical case history of the deceased patient scheduled to undergo an autopsy that day. Three times a week, he is involved in the supervision and instruction of the students. The interactions with the physicians-to-be is enjoyable for Sandy, but at times, the monotony of the whole situation bores him.

Several weeks into the rotation, Sandy decides to add some flavor to the dull process. Wandering the halls of the hospital, he comes across one of the senior housekeeping men, whom he enlists in his game. Once they've reached the morgue, he instructs the man to take off his shirt, shoes, and socks and climb up on the steel dissecting table in the middle of the room. Sandy then waits a few minutes, and escorts the medical students into the room. The housekeeper lies remarkably still. Under the bright lights, his skin looks unusually pale. Sandy begins.

"This homeless person was found on the streets this morning. Our job is to determine a cause of death."

Asking the group to surround the body, he encourages them to make any comments on the body before the dissection is begun. After the young students study the man carefully, one of the women comments, "How come the body is still so warm?"

Looking down at her name tag, Sandy responds, "Let's see, Amy … good observation. He was just brought in an hour ago. His body hasn't had a chance to cool off."

One of the male students pipes up. "The scar in the middle of his sternal area indicates that he has probably had cardiac bypass surgery, leading to the conclusion that his death may be due to a cardiac event, such as an arrhythmia or myocardial infarction."

"Excellent."

At that moment, the man begins to rigidly lift the upper half of his body several inches off the table. Some of the students panic and run to the corners of the room. In a nonchalant manner, Sandy walks to the housekeeper and gently pushes his chest back to the table, saying, "Rigor mortis is just now setting in. Don't worry, that was just an unusual muscle contraction."

After a few more minutes of discussion, the students regain their confidence and move closer to the body. One of the man's hands then closes, grasping tightly the tail of the lab coat of one of the nearby male students. Visibly distressed, the student asks for Sandy's help. As Sandy wrestles the hand away, all of a sudden the housekeeper's eyes open wide and stare around the room. The students scream loudly and run from the morgue, with Sandy doubled over in laughter.

That afternoon, while Brad is sitting at his microscope in the reading room at Saint Thomas Hospital, the phone beside him rings. One of the secretaries informs him that Dr. Robert Collins is on the line. Brad quickly picks up.

"Good afternoon, Dr. Collins. How are you?"

"Brad, could you please be in my office this evening at six o'clock?"

"Yes, sir. Is there a problem?"

"There is, and although it does not involve you directly, it will affect you. Do you think you can make it?"

"Yes, sir, I'll be there."

The controlled anger in Dr. Collins's voice is quite evident to Brad, who is uncertain what to make of the incident.

Later that day, just before the appointed time, Brad, with an uneasy feeling, knocks on Dr. Collins's office door. Hearing a snappy, "Come in," he steps inside to see Sandy Starke and Dr. Collins awaiting him. Judging by the crimson color on his chairman's face, Brad knows that things are not good.

"Thank you for coming, Brad. Please be seated next to Dr. Starke."

Without speaking, Brad sits down. Robert Collins, with great restraint, summarizes the incident at the Vanderbilt morgue that morning. He relates the phone calls that he received that afternoon from the irate parents of several of the medical students, followed by a stinging call from the dean of the medical school, Dr. John Chapman. Without raising his voice or directly expressing his anger, he speaks to Sandy.

"Dr. Starke, your work is exemplary, and already, before completing your residency, you are a very good pathologist. What possessed you to do such a thing?"

With his head hung low and his gaze at the floor, Sandy is too embarrassed to look his chairman in the eye. "I have no excuse, Dr. Collins. I take direct responsibility for my actions and ask you to please forgive me for a very immature and harmful prank on my part. Please let me contact each of the students directly and ask for their forgiveness. Tell me what else I can do."

"The news I am about to share with you is not completely bad. Because of your singular record up until now, I am not inclined to dismiss you from the residency program. However, you will be stripped of the duties of chief resident for a period of sixty days, after which time you and I will meet again to decide your future. For the time being, Brad will assume the autopsy service at Vanderbilt beginning tomorrow, and you will fulfill his duties at Saint Thomas Hospital."

Directing his attention to Brad, Dr. Collins continues. "I am sorry that you are suffering some of the consequences of Dr. Starke's inappropriate actions, Brad. There are times that being chief resident can be difficult. For now, you will have to shoulder all the responsibilities yourself. Is that acceptable to you?"

"I'm willing to help any way I can, Dr. Collins. I'll pick up my things from Saint Thomas tonight, and I can be here first thing in the morning."

"Thank you for your flexibility, Brad. I promise to make it up to you somehow. Now, if you gentlemen will excuse me."

Once Brad and Sandy are outside Dr. Collins's office and safely back in the residents' room, Sandy begins to shake. "I thought I was going to get fired."

"What were you thinking when you pulled that stunt, Sandy?"

"I don't know, Brad. It was really a pretty bad idea. I hope Dr. Collins doesn't stay mad at me very long."

"Don't worry, Sandy. He's a fair man. Just try not to do anything else stupid for a while."

"You're right. I guess the best thing is just to lie low for a few months. But Brad, you should have been there; it was really funny."

"*Sandy!*"

"Okay, okay, I'm sorry, already."

Now at home with her two-month-old adopted baby daughter, Tracy Kilpatrick has become quite contented. Electing to take a six-week leave of absence from her job, she is debating whether to retire altogether until the baby is older. With a fresh coat of pink paint on the walls, the nursery has become Tracy's favorite place to spend time with her daughter. She and Tom agreed on a name for her, Angel, somehow feeling that it fit the circumstances.

This morning, Tracy takes Angel for a walk in her stroller across the Peabody campus. They eventually end up in Tracy's workplace, where her coworkers gather around her and share in her excitement. Angel is having a good morning and is content and animated as the other women in the office hold and rock her. On the way home, Tracy takes her time, walking the perimeter of the shaded campus. She enjoys the newness of motherhood and talks excitedly to her baby as she points at squirrels and birds. Tom has easily fallen into the role of proud parent. For the first time in his life, he has had some difficulty concentrating at work. As he reaches for the framed picture of Tracy and Angel on the corner of his desk, his mind drifts, thinking of the time this evening that he will spend with his family. It had been a long time since he'd seen Tracy smile. It is a relief to see her happy again.

Elinor Kennedy continues to struggle with the loss of her husband, but she has set a new goal for herself. In Butch's memory, she has established cholesterol checks and blood pressure screening at her church in Smyrna. Her persistence in negotiations with one of the local chemistry labs has resulted in a substantial discount on the cost of cholesterol tests. She has also been able to convince several of the nurses who attend the Smyrna Evangelical Baptist Church to assist her at the back of the sanctuary on Sunday mornings after the worship services.

Another of her goals has been to establish a fully equipped exercise facility at Butch's former workplace. She has had several meetings with the board of directors of the Nissan plant, resulting in the establishment of a trust fund to pay for the gymnasium. The executives in charge have agreed to match dollar for dollar all money that is donated and allow workers scheduled time off during the day to work out. Elinor has convinced many of the employees to donate funds. And with aggressive campaigning, she has managed to get Butch's picture on local billboards and on milk cartons free of charge to raise money for the project. Ultimately, she hopes to have aerobics classes and enough treadmills and exercise bicycles to accommodate the large workforce. These endeavors have allowed Elinor to stave off some of her grief, knowing that she is trying to prevent someone else from experiencing Butch's tragedy.

About two weeks after taking over Sandy's position at Vanderbilt, Brad finally feels that things are under control. After a particularly long and stressful day, he is slumped down on his couch at home when the phone rings. He instantly recognizes his brother's voice on the other end of the line.

"Hey, little brother, how are things down in Nashville?"

"Matt, it's great to hear from you. How've you been? I've been missing you."

"Doing great, Brad. How are things with you? … I hope they're not still working you to death. Too bad you didn't have enough sense to follow me into business."

"Yeah, I know, you keep telling me that. At least I can say that, at this point, there seems to be light at the end of the tunnel. … What about you? Do you think you'll be able to come visit anytime soon?"

"Good question, which brings me to the purpose of my call. I've been offered a job with a large brokerage firm out in Seattle. It's a great offer, and

I'd get to manage some individual portfolios, which is just the kind of experience I've been looking for."

"Wow. Have you told Mom and Dad yet?"

"Not yet. I'm still trying to decide what to do."

"Have you been out there for an interview?"

"Yeah, twice, and I really liked it."

"What about Seattle? Did you like the city?"

"It was surprisingly nice, and there seemed to be a lot to do. I really enjoyed my stay out there, but I'm concerned that it's a long way from home."

"I'll say. Do you think you could handle being that far away from everyone? It's been pretty hard on me."

"Here's the way I've got it figured: I've never traveled much, and I thought I'd spend a couple of years out there to get a little more experience and see a different part of the country, and then head back toward New York. You know, Dad still talks to me about taking over the bank when he retires, but I'm not quite ready to settle down yet. What do you think?"

"Sounds like a great plan to me, if you feel that this is the right job for you. Good luck on telling Mom and Dad."

"Thanks a lot."

"I'm just kidding. They're smart people, Matt; they'll understand once they get over the initial blow. Just tell Dad first and let him get used to it before you break it to Mom. I think she'll be a little emotional about seeing another child move so far away."

"You're probably right, Brad; wish me luck."

"Now, when is this all going to happen?"

"The offer is good immediately. They asked if I could be out there within thirty days, which is cutting it a little close with my current job."

"Wow, that's quick. Just be sure on your way west that you stop over in Nashville for a couple of days."

"I wouldn't miss it for the world."

"I'd better get going, Matt. I'll call you in a couple of days to see what you've decided. Oh, by the way, I know what I'll be getting you for Christmas this year."

"Christmas? What are you talking about?"

"I've had my eye on a couple of really nice umbrellas lately."

"Yuck-yuck. Talk to you soon, Brad. Good night."

As Brad replaces the phone on the coffee table, he is instantly both happy and sad. At times like these, he wishes he were closer to home to make the transition easier for Matt and his parents. Walking into his bedroom, he picks up a framed family photograph from the top of his dresser. Before going to bed, he stands there a long time staring into the faces of his mother and father, as well as those of Matt and his sister, Kristin. He misses them terribly.

Chapter 17

A day in late August brings with it faint shades of early morning sunlight that stream in through the windows of Robert Altman's penthouse office at AmericaHealth's downtown headquarters. Seated at his long mahogany desk, Robert sifts through multiple documents prior to an 8:00 a.m. meeting. He calls for his secretary, Victoria Jamison, to locate other bits of information as he scans what is before him. Having arrived earlier than usual this morning, he is almost ready for the much anticipated appointment.

Just prior to the meeting, Ms. Jamison informs him that his guest has arrived. Shortly thereafter, Robert's large office doors open and Dr. John Oates, the senior member of the Vanderbilt Adult Medical Group, is escorted in. Besides being a full-tenured professor of internal medicine, Dr. Oates also maintains an active research lab at the university.

With the changing health-care climate, Dr. Oates and his fifteen associates in internal medicine have been forced to change their practice patterns. While maintaining a strong tie with Vanderbilt Hospital, the group has recently branched out into private practice on a part-time basis. The group is considered to be one of the best-trained, most astute collections of internists not only in the state of Tennessee but also in the southeastern United States. All members have obtained board certification in internal medicine and at least one other subspecialty, including advanced training in cardiology, endocrinology, gastroenterology, and pulmonary medicine. Not all members were trained at Vanderbilt. Diplomas from Harvard, Stanford, Duke, and Cornell also line their offices. These men, with their strong clinical and research interests, are considered to be a powerful influence on health care in the Southeast.

With the group's powerful name and sterling reputation, nearly all health maintenance organizations and insurance companies that do business in central Tennessee are anxious to contract with them for physician services. It is considered a powerful marketing tool to be able to announce that these men are a part of one's team of doctors. Robert Altman has been particularly anxious about this meeting with Dr. Oates and has spent weeks preparing for it.

Ironically, John Oates, despite his world-renowned status, remains a soft-spoken man of surprising humility. As he enters Robert's office, the contrast between the two men is readily apparent. Dr. Oates, now in his late sixties, is bald on top, and his remaining hair is a silvery gray. He wears a very conservative camel hair blazer and brown wool slacks. His speech is slow and deliberate, with the slightest of Southern accents. One might describe his mannerisms as exuding a gentlemanly politeness.

Standing to welcome Dr. Oates, Robert wears a modern double-breasted European-styled suit costing thousands of dollars. With a full head of thick and dark curly hair, exhibiting gray only at the temples, he appears at least two-and-a-half decades younger than Dr. Oates. He speaks quickly and at times abruptly.

Robert initially thanks John Oates for making time to meet with him and offers him a beverage before they begin their business discussions. Once settled, Robert sits several feet behind his desk and leans backward in his reclining chair with his legs crossed. John Oates, by contrast, sits straight up with his feet planted firmly on the floor. The meeting begins with Robert flattering Dr. Oates and his group, telling Dr. Oates how impressed he is with their work. He goes on to say that he hopes their group will consider seeing patients insured by his health insurance company. Reaching into his briefcase, John Oates retrieves the contract Robert sent to him and asks, "Would this be an appropriate time to get things under way, Robert?"

"Certainly, John. Please go ahead."

"Beginning with the proposed fee schedule, I see that you have offered us a capitated-type arrangement for payment of physicians' services. We currently don't have that type of arrangement with any other company. ... Is that an absolute requirement?"

"Right now, all of our physician providers are capitated."

"Could you please discuss with me what such an arrangement would entail?"

"I'm happy to go through it, John. Let's turn to page four of the packet I sent to you. First of all, I am prepared to send to you all of AmericaHealth's internal medicine patients who reside in the Nashville area. That would essentially amount to an exclusive contract with our insurance company. I would then ask you for a copy of your current fee schedule, including such things as office history and physicals, inpatient consultations, cardiac catheterizations, and so forth. After reviewing your prices, we will then come back to you with a specific offer."

"Could you please give me a general idea of what your offer might be like?"

"Utilizing large amounts of data about health-care costs from Medicare as well as from the insurance industry as a whole, we are able to very accurately predict how much it would cost for all of our patients to receive comprehensive internal medicine care in one year. Once we have that yearly figure, we can divide it by twelve to arrive at a monthly capitated fee schedule."

"It does seem very scientific, doesn't it?"

"Absolutely, it is completely nonbiased information. After we've arrived at that monthly figure for physician provider fees, you and I will need to negotiate a discount off that number. AmericaHealth will then send you a check at the end of each month reflecting that discounted amount. That is how our calculation system works. This guarantees you a fixed amount of money every month for taking care of our patients. ... Sounds good, doesn't it?"

"I guess it all depends on exactly what your discount turns out to be."

"We are currently asking for a 30 percent discount for specialty physicians such as surgeons and radiologists and a 20 percent discount for primary care physicians such as yourself. However, because we're very interested in having you see our patients, I'm prepared to offer you a 10 percent discount."

"Forgive me for asking an obvious question, but what happens if the number of patients we are seeing from AmericaHealth takes a sudden increase? Our monthly payments would be fixed, but our workload would be drastically higher. That could potentially put us in a situation where we might actually lose money taking care of your patients."

"We are willing to renegotiate the capitated payment every six months."

"Would there be any back compensation if we were to take a loss in the prior six months?"

"I can't guarantee that, John, but I certainly would make that recommendation to our Compensation Committee."

"Robert, as you are aware, internists are not well paid under today's health-care guidelines. We have a very high overhead, and we have a lot of sick patients. Not only that, but also our jobs are very labor-intensive. In the current economic climate, we are lucky to maintain a 15 to 20 percent profit margin on the patients who have insurance. That does not include those on Medicaid and indigent patients we take care of on whom we lose money. With some of the changes in recent Medicare reimbursements, we also either break even or lose money on some things we do. With your 10 percent discount, that allows us to potentially make a 5 to 10 percent profit, which is certainly better than losing money, but it is not really comparable to other private insurers."

"With our huge patient base, that 10 percent profit may be substantial enough to warrant your consideration."

"Why don't we proceed with actual numbers over the next several weeks, Robert? I will present your offer to my colleagues at our next large group meeting, which is in mid-September."

"I can have dollar amounts to you by next week at the latest."

With his brow furrowed, John Oates shifts in his chair and makes a comment, his voice exhibiting obvious concern: "I have more serious reservations about other things contained in the tentative contractual agreement you supplied to me. Could we please turn to page eleven and review what is meant by the two so-called 'gag clauses'?"

"John, before I undertake a lengthy discussion of these clauses, I first wish to make you understand that one of our goals is to maintain a profitable corporation. To that end, we are asking doctors to help us with two separate issues. The first, as we have discussed, is financial responsibility. The second is to maintain a good image of our corporation in the minds of the people we insure. With that in mind, let us begin with the first of the pair of gag clauses.

This part of the contract specifies that if you agree to become a provider of physician services with AmericaHealth, then you will *not* be able to openly discuss certain tests or procedures with the patient unless *we* give you specific approval to do so."

Again looking up, John Oates lets his mouth fall open in surprise. "Could you please enlighten me as to which tests and procedures I wouldn't be allowed to talk about?"

"These would fall into the category of outrageously expensive items such as M R I scans, certain blood tests, and specific elective surgical procedures."

"So what you're telling me is that if I *feel* that one of my patients needs a head M R I scan to rule out a stroke, I *can't order that test*? And not only that, but also I wouldn't even be able to tell my patient that an M R I scan is an option?"

"That's right. A C T scan of the head is almost as good as an M R I scan in that situation—and it costs half as much."

"That is certainly a matter of intense academic debate at the present time. But what if I were looking for, say, an unusual brain tumor, in which case a C T scan would clearly be inferior?"

"You still cannot mention the M R I to the patient as an option, but you could call one of our Utilization Review nurses to ask for approval for the study."

"You mean that in an emergency situation, I'd have to drop what I'm doing and call one of your nurses to ask permission to order a scan?"

Robert then blushes slightly and adjusts his chair so that he is now sitting straight up. Getting a bit flustered, he cannot look John Oates directly in the eyes as he answers. "I'm afraid so, Dr. Oates."

At this point in the discussion, John Oates's reserved exterior is visibly altered. He is indignant over the very concept that an insurance company could forbid him from obtaining readily available well-established tests because they have been deemed too costly. Even worse, he cannot even enter into a dialogue with a trusted patient about the existence of such tests. His voice takes on an uncharacteristically angry tone as he pursues further inquiries. "What happens if your nurse says no to my request for the study?"

"You then have at your disposal the option of petitioning our physician-based Grievance Committee."

"How long would *that* take?"

"The committee meets once a week."

"You mean, if I've got a critically ill patient who might need an emergency intervention, *I may have to wait a week for an answer?*"

Again appearing embarrassed, Robert looks down at his desk as he speaks. "That is our current policy, Dr. Oates."

"What happens if one of my partners misses a major diagnosis because you wouldn't allow us to order or discuss a certain test?"

"Dr. Oates, as you are well aware, the doctor is ultimately responsible for the well-being of the patient he has been charged with taking care of. You might decide to get the study and then request for us to pay for it at a later date if an emergency arises. ... However, I cannot offer any guarantees that we would extend payment."

"What you're telling me is that if I order a test that your insurance company doesn't agree to pay for to save a patient's life, *the patient might be responsible for the bill?*"

"Yes."

"And if I don't order that test and the patient dies, *I'm responsible?*"

"I'm afraid so."

His anger growing with each minute, John Oates begins to speak louder and faster. "What happens if I tell one of my patients about one of your so-called forbidden tests?"

"You would be at risk of immediate termination of your contract with us and a possible financial penalty."

A long silence then ensues as John Oates struggles to regain some of his composure. His face and neck are now flushed. With his right hand, he reaches up to loosen his tie and unbutton his shirt collar to release some of the heat produced by his strongly felt emotions. On the floor below, his right foot is tapping loudly. Many of Dr. Oates's associates would be shocked by his appearance. In his over thirty years of practice, not one of them has ever seen him even approach the point of losing his temper. With great effort, he tries to control his voice as he poses another question. "Robert, if you would, please explain the second gag clause."

Quite aware that the negotiations are going poorly, Robert's voice takes on a defeated tone while he attempts to appeal to his colleague's intellect. "John, before we go any further, I just want to remind you that we're trying to run a profitable business here." He shifts awkwardly in his chair before continuing … "Our second clause specifies that if you are overheard criticizing, or reported by one of our insured clients as having criticized or said something unpleasant about, our insurance company, then we can discontinue your contract with us immediately and assign your patients to another doctor. We can also exercise the option of suing you for any damages that might result from what was said."

"You've got to be kidding! You mean that you could interrupt a sacred doctor-patient relationship in the middle of medical management because you don't like something I said?"

"I'm afraid so."

Rising from his chair, John Oates slowly and precisely folds his glasses and tucks them in his shirt pocket. With one hand, he tosses his copy of the contract onto the middle of Robert's desk, causing many of the pages to fly up into the air. Then, crossing his arms, he makes a final statement, his voice exhibiting great resolve.

"I don't believe I'll be needing those figures after all, Dr. Altman. It has become quite clear to me that your organization is much more interested in making money than offering my patients the care they need. I am, and have always been, of the opposite mind-set. My patients are more sacred to me than any amount of money. I am not certain how it is that you sleep at night, Dr. Altman, knowing that you are destroying people's lives. Good day!"

John Oates then turns and walks quietly out of Robert's office, exhibiting no obvious hurry. Still seated, Robert remains still as he contemplates Dr. Oates's words. In the back of his mind, he has always been aware that many of the company's policies have hurt the very people who have turned to them for help. Unknowingly, he'd suppressed those thoughts in his quest to become a success in the cold corporate world. He wonders to himself how he let it happen.

From one of his desk drawers, he pulls out a picture of his wife, Anne, and a photograph from his childhood of his family together in Philadelphia.

Robert reflects on his childhood in the 1970s in urban Philadelphia. His father, Abraham, fled Eastern Europe in 1964 at the time of the Soviet Union's control of Hungary and arrived with his wife in the United States with only a few dollars to his name. After Abraham Altman had saved all the money he and his wife had earned doing manual labor for many years after their arrival, he opened a delicatessen in downtown Philadelphia.

In near tenement-style conditions, Robert and his family lived in a cramped two-bedroom apartment above his father's business. Being the youngest of three boys, Robert had to share a bed with one of his older brothers. Money was very tight, as every penny was spent to keep his father's business going. Food was also sparse. Robert vividly recalls going down to the deli with his father and looking at all the beautiful meats displayed in the case and hanging in the cooler and thinking how ironic it was that his own family could rarely afford any of it. He recalls the day when he was six years old that his mother took him shopping for his first set of new clothes.

With a remarkable endurance for hard work and an unquestionable honesty, Abraham eventually grew his business, becoming quite successful. Long after their family was able to leave the inner city and move to a nice home in the suburbs of Philadelphia, Robert's father still put in very long hours, by force of habit.

Anxious to afford their children the opportunities they themselves never had, Robert's parents strongly encouraged their three sons to study hard in school. At times, Robert felt that his father was an oppressive taskmaster, but over the years, he came to realize that it was out of his love for him that his father pushed him so hard. When the time came for Robert to apply to college, his father came into his bedroom one night while he was reading and said to him, "I am so proud of my son Robert, who has become a great scholar. I want you to go to the best school you can, my son. Our family will find a way to pay for it. … This is what your father wishes to do for you, Robert."

Having excelled academically in high school, Robert was accepted for admission by many prestigious universities. In order to stay close to his family, he chose to attend the University of Pennsylvania, the Ivy League's representative in Philadelphia. His next step was medical school at Harvard University. Graduation Day from medical school was another very special moment for Robert. His father, in failing health, rose to the occasion, his chest swelled with pride over his son's achievements. Tears of joy ran down his mother's face as she clung to Robert during the ceremony. Life could not have been sweeter.

Following medical school, Robert was offered a three-year residency position in internal medicine at the prestigious Brigham and Women's Hospital in Boston. Because of his remarkable education, he was heavily sought after by several very prominent groups of internists in the Boston area once he completed all his training. Within just a few years, he established a highly successful medical practice. He was praised by patients and colleagues alike for his remarkable caring manner and his enviable skills as a physician. While in the Boston area, he met his future wife, Anne. After dating less than two years, they were married. Life was wonderfully pleasant for Robert during those years. Robert reflects on why he decided to leave his medical practice. The work suited him. Honestly enjoying patient care, he had a natural way with people. After ten years in practice, his career radically changed direction, and he accepted an administrative job with AmericaHealth. Because of the financial deprivation of his childhood, the multimillion-dollar contract that AmericaHealth offered him was impossible to turn down. The material security of the salary offer they made him overshadowed his desire to continue direct patient care.

With his tenacity and drive, Robert rose swiftly through the corporate ranks. After only three years with the company, he was asked to become their chief executive officer. His confidence had grown dramatically while at AmericaHealth, but on the day he was offered the position of CEO, he was truly shocked.

The mission set forth for Robert by the board of directors has been to trim costs in an effort to make the health insurance company more profitable. On a daily basis, a barrage of commands lands on his head from both his superiors within the company and the executive committee representing the interests of the stockholders. The pressures of the job have been enormous. Indeed, many of the edicts contained within the contract he and John Oates discussed today came directly from the men who are Robert's bosses. The considerable annual salary and stock options only partly fill the void of Robert's existence. Within his heart is the knowledge that patients suffer because of his company's negligence. He also recognizes that dedicated healers, fine people such as Dr. Oates, are hurt very badly by the way his company does business.

At the very moment Robert is thinking this, the phone rings, startling him. Ms. Jamison, his secretary, informs him that Everett Halstead, the president of AmericaHealth, is on the line.

"Good afternoon, Everett. ... We just finished. ... No, Dr. Oates wasn't interested; there were some problems with the contract. ... Yes, I do have another group in mind, but they're not board-certified and not anywhere near the caliber of John Oates and his associates. ... I'd recommend we modify the contract so we could get the very best people, like John Oates. The quality of patient care needs to be a priority."

Initially enthusiastic, Robert's voice reflects the defeat he feels. "Come on, Everett, be reasonable. Why don't we think this thing over for a few days? We don't have to act immediately."

Robert's best attempts to effect a positive change are subjugated, and he is ordered to hire the other group of internists. Despite their substantially inferior training and practice habits, they were chosen based upon their price. Reflecting on his long-term life plans, Robert sits for a long time with his hand on the phone before placing a call to the other physician group. While pondering many thoughts, his mind drifts to his wife, Anne. He can picture her face and hear her supportive voice asking him to quit his job at AmericaHealth on many occasions because of the stress and long hours.

From his center drawer, he withdraws his personal financial ledger. With his annual salary plus exercised options on company stock, he will earn 110 million dollars this year. Of that amount, he has already saved 30 million dollars, adding to his already large bank account.

"You don't need to do this anymore. You can quit at any time ... do something you like. See patients. Make a difference in someone's life. ... Get your soul back before it's too late."

As Robert dials Everett Halstead's private office number, a feeling of euphoria strikes him. Realizing that in just a few seconds he will resign from his job and begin his life anew, he is flooded with a sense of great relief. For whatever reason, before the call goes through, his strength becomes fleeting, and he puts the receiver down. For a long time, he sits at his desk with his head down, contemplating his own weakness. Unable to give up the intoxicating money and power, he despises himself.

Chapter 18

It is now September, and the signs of fall's arrival are everywhere. Despite the searing heat of the late afternoons, there is a slight chill in the early morning air. Dawn brings with it the first rays of sunlight to highlight the glistening emerald-colored lawns, and a refreshing breeze that washes away some of summer's stifling heat and humidity. The Vanderbilt campus stirs again with activity as the autumn-semester students return. Across the university this morning, birds call out to one another from the treetops as fledgling chicks prepare to leave their mothers' nests. With a whistle in his voice and a briefcase swinging in one hand, William Lockwood returns to teaching, his life's passion.

Eight weeks have passed since William's surgery. The vision in his left eye miraculously continues to improve. While standing before his new class of students, he feels a renewed sense of satisfaction. His brush with death has left him with a newfound appreciation for even the simplest things in life. Cynthia, his daughter, will begin first grade in just a few days. It wasn't until recently that she began to sleep through the night. Up until then, the fear of possibly losing her other parent to cancer had given her terrible nightmares. Because of his concern for his daughter, William installed an intercom in her bedroom to listen to her at night. Upon hearing her cry or awaken, he would rise from his bed and go into her room to hold her and sing to her until she drifted back to sleep.

Having completed his stint as chief resident at Vanderbilt, Brad returns to Saint Thomas Hospital to finish up the rotation he had begun two months prior. He and Sandy Starke met recently with Dr. Collins at the end of Sandy's sixty-day probation period. Sandy has managed to be an ideal resident physician since the suspension and has not gotten into any more trouble. As such, the privileges of chief resident have been restored to him. He will now return to Vanderbilt to run the surgical pathology division. After the long and unpredictable hours of the autopsy service at Vanderbilt, Brad is perfectly content with his new assignment. The variety of tasks at Saint Thomas Hospital is much more appealing and less gruesome than doing the postmortem examination of four to five patients each day.

With Friday's approach, Brad grimaces to himself, knowing that he will be on call this weekend at the Deaconess Hospital. Because of a fluke in the call schedule, he has somehow ended up being responsible for covering the morgue. This task is his least favorite. After spending the past two months at Vanderbilt doing daily autopsies, he is almost nauseated at the thought of having to do this on his weekend, as well.

Lying motionless in his comfortable bed, Brad peacefully awakens on Saturday morning. It is so rare for him to get the chance to rest his mind and body that he finds it pleasant to let his eyes drift along the walls and ceiling of his bedroom as the light peeks around the edges of the window blinds. But it is only for a brief moment, because without warning, the unpleasant sound of his pager tells him the hectic outside world is searching for him. As he checks the digital screen of his beeper, he recognizes the phone number of the morgue at the Deaconess Hospital. He calls in to inform the on-duty clerk that he'll be about forty-five minutes, and then he reluctantly makes his way to the shower. With warm water streaming across his face, he ponders the first case, which is apparently a forensics case, meaning that the county coroner and police will be involved.

With keys dangling from one hand, Brad stands in the middle of his living room with the phone against his ear, hoping to catch Julie before she leaves for work. After he mentions to her that he has already been called in, she sighs loudly in sympathy. If their schedules permit, they will meet for dinner. Brad hurries along. Once he reaches the pathology department, Kim, the young female technologist who will assist him over the weekend, informs him that his first case is ready. She explains that the woman lost her life in a house fire and that the police are concerned about the circumstances. The Davidson County coroner has been notified and requests that Brad contact him once the analysis of the body is under way.

After he slips his arms through the sleeves of the long cobalt-blue cloth gown, Brad begins to read the woman's chart. He ties the long strings of the garment around his waist. He first takes note of her name, Mrs. Vickie Kimbrell, whose age, according to the record, is forty-two. Prior to putting on gloves, face mask, and protective goggles, he finishes reading the chart. According to the record, she died early this morning in a house fire in her first-floor bedroom only three feet from an open window. Luckily, the firemen had arrived on the scene quickly and were able to douse the fire before there was substantial damage to the house. The police questioned her husband, who was apparently at work at the time of the incident.

As is customary, Brad begins by first closely inspecting the body. Over much of the pearly white skin are dark blotches, soot-colored stains from the fire, but the skin itself is not burned. Her long bleached-blonde hair has been heavily singed and is now a charcoal color. Brad is relieved to see that the body is completely intact. Before beginning the dissection, he takes a complete set of photographs as documentation. Kim, the technologist, then pulls back the long blue sheet covering the body.

Two hours later, Brad strips the bloodstained rubber gloves from his hands as he finishes his analysis. He contacts the attending physician on call with him this weekend, Dr. Anthony Bertolucci, to review the case prior to the coroner's arrival. Not long afterward, Dr. Bertolucci appears. Brad readies himself to go over the crucial information with his colleague.

"Good morning, Tony. It looks like our call has gotten off to an early start. ... Let me tell you a little bit about this woman. Her death was supposedly the result of a house fire, but there's evidence that she may have been dead before the fire started."

Pointing to a page in the patient's file, Brad continues. "Look at the chemical analysis of the red blood cells from the lung tissue. There are normal quantities of oxygen and carbon dioxide bound to the hemoglobin. If she had really died in the fire from smoke inhalation, the carbon monoxide levels would have been off the scale."

Next, Brad goes to the body to demonstrate that there is a lot of ash in the nasal cavities but none in the trachea or lungs, again supporting the theory that her death occurred before the fire started. Brad, pulling another piece of paper from her chart, continues his discussion.

"The most convincing evidence is the serum toxicology screen. She had massive quantities of alcohol and the sleeping pill flurazepam in her bloodstream, more than enough to kill her."

Looking up from the paper, Tony Bertolucci peers through his wire-rimmed eyeglasses and asks, "Any other substantial findings, Brad?"

"She has an old facial fracture of the zygomatic bone that is at least three or four years old and several healed rib fractures. Otherwise, the autopsy was unremarkable."

"What do you make of the broken bones?"

"Either she's been in several car accidents, or she's been repeatedly beaten."

Nodding, Dr. Bertolucci compliments Brad on his compulsive and thorough evaluation of the case. He then asks Brad's opinion on how Mrs. Kimbrell died.

"I would have to say that there are two possible causes for her death: suicide or murder."

"Tell me what makes you think that, Brad."

"She was lying facedown only a few feet from an open window when the police found her. We have established that she probably died from an overdose prior to the beginning of the fire. It's possible that she was drugged and the fire was set in the hopes that her body would be burned beyond the point of recognition. Or alternatively, she committed suicide and the fire started accidentally."

"Excellent analysis. I wonder what the police will come up with."

"I'm curious myself, but in the meantime, I've sent for her medical record chart to see if there is a history of domestic violence. I've also asked for the police records for the same purpose."

Once the case is finally completed, Brad and Tony Bertolucci take a break, go to the hospital cafeteria, and chat over a couple of soft drinks. In contrast to his usual upbeat manner, Brad is unusually reserved. Tony Bertolucci takes note of that immediately.

"Brad, are you okay?"

"I'm afraid the Kimbrell autopsy shook me a little. Do these cases ever get to you?"

"All the time. When I was a resident, I often had nightmares about the people I saw in the morgue. A case like this would stay with me for months. It gets better as you get older and more experienced, but there are just some things that you'll never get used to."

"I guess not."

On Sunday evening, Brad is still hard at work at the Deaconess Hospital, reviewing the dictation from each case and finishing up final paperwork. Dr. Bertolucci has already signed off on most of the cases. Because there are no secretaries available, Brad begins to file the completed documents. Standing in front of the tall bank of drab-olive-colored metal filing cabinets in the pathology office, he places each person's record in the correct alphabetical order. He breathes a sigh of relief as the final case, Vickie Kimbrell, is about to reach its resting place. As the tips of the index and middle fingers of his right hand walk along the plastic file tabs, his hand suddenly stops. It is rare for Brad to recognize a name in this large collection of patients. His eyes linger momentarily on the name "Randall Kennedy."

As he stares at the black bold-printed letters of the name, Brad instantly pictures several images from Butch's autopsy. He remembers Elinor, David, and Suzie Kennedy sitting in the waiting area outside the pathology department while the autopsy was being completed. Elinor's eyes were swollen and red, and the children appeared overwhelmed with grief. Brad had never had the opportunity to speak with them directly, but Alan Richards said that they took the news badly.

After placing Mrs. Kimbrell's folder in the appropriate location, Brad, curious, decides to take a look at Butch Kennedy's autopsy report. As he pries open the manila folder, the photographic images of Butch's lifeless body startle him. Despite being knee-deep in autopsies all weekend, Brad finds that the pictures of death overwhelm his senses. Turning the pages slowly, he looks at the photographs of the internal organs. While holding Butch's file out in front of his body, Brad walks slowly to a desk across the room as he reads. To him, the precise, machine-printed block lettering that forms the words on the starched white stationery paper seem a cold way to summarize another human's life. The Latin-derived complicated medical terminology used to describe the individual pieces of this man's body cannot possibly do justice to the living, breathing man that was Butch Kennedy. How can one take into account the intricate components of the soul that defined that person? How can these words begin to capture the essence of the man who saved another's life in a confusing war or who was a father and a friend and a husband? How can this impersonal decription possibly say anything about the goodness of his heart or his kind personality? In the end, to Brad, the sterile text seems so removed as to be almost arcane.

As Brad continues to follow the pathologic diagnoses, he ponders the nature of the man named Butch Kennedy. Despite his imaginings, each word sent to his brain through his eyes is carefully sifted. One paragraph in particular fails to make sense to him, so he stops to reread it.

"Heart weight – 425 grams. Dimensions – 21.5 centimeters in length by 16.5 centimeters transverse by 14.3 centimeters anterior to posterior. External pericardium – normal. No evidence of pericardial effusion. A 4.5-centimeter area of extensive necrosis on the anterior wall of left ventricle, site of acute transmural myocardial infarct (see arrow on photograph). On sectioning, there is severe dilated cardiomyopathy of both atria and ventricles. Chamber thickness right ventricle – 5 millimeters. Chamber thickness left ventricle – 1.2 centimeters. Endocardium – normal. Valves and valve leaflets – connective tissue thinning, moderate."

Returning to a single sentence, he reads again: "On sectioning, there is severe dilated cardiomyopathy of both atria and ventricles."

Lifting his head from the written text, Brad's mind returns to the day of Butch's autopsy. He can visualize how the heart appeared as it was removed from the body. He remembers holding the muscular organ in his left hand over the sink in the morgue, using his right hand to direct a stream of water from the faucet to rinse the blood off its surface. His next image is of the scalpel slowly cutting through the outer muscle layer and the appearance of the right and left ventricles. His thoughts pause there, after he has confirmed his suspicion. He thinks to himself, *Yes, I'm absolutely certain. The wall of the left ventricle was very thickened, not thin and enlarged.*

Sifting rapidly through the pathology report, Brad searches for the photographs he had taken of the heart. Again he thinks to himself, *These aren't the pictures I shot. This doesn't even look like Butch's heart. I wonder what happened.*

Concerned, Brad drops the chart as he attempts to recall other details about the case. Several minutes of concentrated thoughts bombard his brain. Then, he feels relief as the obvious solution to the dilemma comes to him. From beneath the desk, he retrieves his briefcase and pulls out the blue hardbound notebook that serves as his personal autopsy journal.

With a burning sense of curiosity, Brad rifles through the pages of the book. Near the front of the volume, he stops when the name Randall Kennedy appears at the top of one of the pages. He quickly reads and rereads his notes, until his suspicions are confirmed by the photographs. Butch's heart was clearly thick and strong, as Brad remembered it. To compare the two sets of photographs, he opens the permanent autopsy file and lays it beside his notebook. It is obvious that the pictures show two completely different hearts. Having taken and filed the set of photos himself, Brad wonders how a discrepancy this serious could have occurred. Slapping the file closed, Brad ponders the situation. After a short deliberation, he decides to photocopy Butch's hospital pathology record and take it home for further study. On the following afternoon, Monday, he will try to schedule an appointment to see Alan Richards to go over the mistake with him.

Not long after Brad arrives at Saint Thomas Hospital the following morning, he phones Dr. Richards's secretary to set up a meeting for late in the afternoon. He then settles into a busy day of reading cases, collecting surgical specimens, and preparing tissue samples for histological analysis. Five o'clock rolls around in a hurry, at which time Brad scampers out of the department and is soon on his way across town in the direction of the Deaconess Hospital. Upon his arrival thirty minutes later, Alan Richards is waiting for him.

"Good afternoon, Brad. Come on in and tell me what I can do for you."

"Thanks, Alan. I just had a couple of questions about a case, if you have time."

"Sure. Let's see what you've got."

Convinced that the mistake is a relatively straightforward one, Brad feels certain that he and Dr. Richards can sort it out quickly.

"I ran across a mistake in an autopsy that you and I did back in July, and I wanted to go over it with you."

Alan Richards's brow furrows as he responds, "A mistake? That would certainly be odd."

Confident and collected, Brad explains his concerns. "Yesterday, when I was doing some filing out here, I happened to come across a folder belonging to a fellow by the name of Randall Kennedy. He was a middle-aged black fellow who died of a myocardial infarct. I found some discrepancies that I wanted to go over with you."

"I vaguely recall his case. Tell me what your questions are, and I'll try to help."

"Would it be all right if I showed you what I mean?"

"Absolutely. Let's take a look."

Walking to the long row of filing cabinets in the main reading room, Brad withdraws the original report of Butch's autopsy. After he returns, he places the file in the middle of the desk in front of Dr. Richards. While standing beside his attending physician, Brad turns to the pathological review of the heart. He then withdraws his personal autopsy notebook from his briefcase and places it beside the other document. He then compares the two sets of descriptive texts and photographs. After the review, Alan says, "There is a substantial disagreement between your notebook and the file autopsy reading. ... Why don't we get out the slides from the case and see what they tell us?"

Getting up out of his chair, Alan Richards walks to the next room, where he locates the fixed-glass-mounted tissue samples. He brings them back to his office. As Brad slides the sections from the heart into place under the microscope and adjusts the focus, Brad is startled by what he sees. The heart *does* appear dilated, and the valve leaflets *do* look thin.

Confronted by what possibly cannot be real, Brad pulls his eyes away from the microscope and reaches for one of the slides. In disbelief, he reads the eight-digit code on the slide and then checks it against the autopsy report.

He repeats the comparison because of his certainty that this cannot be Butch Kennedy's heart. Again the numbers match. His voice exhibits the anxiety he feels.

"Alan, there must be a mistake. I remember looking at this heart as if it were yesterday. These can't be Butch Kennedy's slides."

Very calmly, in a soothing voice, Alan reassures Brad. "Now, Brad, remember that was a really tough day for you. We did eight or nine cases that weekend. Perhaps you were just tired. I've made such errors myself."

"I don't mean to sound disrespectful, Alan, but something still seems wrong to me."

"We've reviewed the file and the slides. What else is there? I remember the autopsy in great detail myself, and these findings are very consistent with my recollections. You must have transposed your notes and photos from another case that weekend. That's all there is to it."

Confused, but not knowing what else to do, Brad gathers his things and thanks Alan Richards on his way out. All the way home, his mind is preoccupied by the disparities in the case. He is so distracted he misses several familiar exits, making his drive home much longer than usual.

Back at his apartment, Brad's certainty of the error grows. Seeking direction, he asks the advice of two of the people closest to him, Sandy and Julie. To both, Brad's anxiety arising from the situation is so out of character for him that it is taken quite seriously. They also acknowledge his remarkable memory for both visual and factual information. After both phone calls, Brad's confidence has increased even more. The events of the autopsy play over again and again in his mind, with the same outcome. To resolve the situation, he decides to seek the counsel of his chairman, Dr. Robert Collins.

The following morning, scarcely before Brad is awake, his mind already clamors with thoughts. Prior to leaving for work, he is on the phone with Dr. Collins's secretary. The soonest she can work him in is 4:00 p.m. that day.

Arriving ten minutes early for the appointment, Brad sits impatiently outside Dr. Collins's office. After what seems like an eternity, the door finally opens and Robert Collins steps out of his office.

Politely thanking his chairman for taking time to meet with him, Brad explains why he is there. "Dr. Collins, I have some serious concerns about a postmortem exam I was involved in out at the Deaconess Hospital a couple of months ago. I need your advice about what to do."

"What seems to be the problem, Brad?"

Brad explains. Then he pulls out the photocopy of the permanent autopsy report along with his personal notes and photographs. After reading the two sets of documents, Robert Collins lifts his head and asks, "Did you discuss the possible error with Dr. Richards?"

"Yes, sir, I certainly did. We even sat down and reviewed the slides together. They showed a heart with severe dilated cardiomyopathy."

"Hmm ... Brad, I think I only have one possible way of resolving the situation. You and I and Alan need to sit down together to look at the permanent sections and the original autopsy report. I'll set it up for tomorrow afternoon. And by the way, please bring your notes back for us to look at."

Twenty-four hours later, all three men are gathered in Robert Collins's office at Vanderbilt Hospital. After some low-key conversation to ease some of the obvious tension, Dr. Collins initiates the more formal nature of the meeting.

"Alan, thanks for your willingness to appear on such short notice. As you are aware from our phone conversation yesterday, Brad has some concerns about an autopsy the two of you performed some months ago. I understand you have both reviewed the report and slides, and there are some possible inconsistencies in the findings."

Although he is not entirely happy with the situation, Alan Richards is surprisingly pleasant. "That's absolutely correct, Robert. Brad and I went over everything thoroughly, and there was a substantial disagreement between his notes and the actual autopsy report. As I mentioned to Brad, my recollections of the case match the report and photographs from Mr. Kennedy's file exactly."

Dr. Collins then asks for Alan's permission to review the permanent tissue sections. Each slide is methodically placed onto the microscope and scrutinized carefully. Just as Dr. Collins completes his analysis, Alan Richards comments, "Now that you've had the opportunity to look things over, Robert, you'll notice that the slides and photographs match the autopsy report. I think all that happened was that Brad accidently mixed up two cases."

Barely changing his placid expression, Robert Collins looks toward Brad and asks, "Brad, how confident are you of your memories?"

"Very certain. I don't recall seeing any dilation."

With a momentary pause to gather his thoughts, Robert's face displays the dilemma that he feels.

"Alan, Brad, I must confess to you my uncertainty about how best to handle this matter. Alan, you and I have worked together for over twenty years, and I have a great deal of respect for your professional abilities. However, Brad is a very astute young pathologist, and his concern has me quite baffled. … I know of no other way to handle this situation except to have the body exhumed and for me to look at the heart myself."

Completely surprised, Alan's mouth hangs wide open. He stares blankly at Robert Collins as he struggles to gather up a response.

"Robert, Mr. Kennedy died of a heart attack. That seems perfectly clear. I'm not certain what there is to be gained by retrieving his body from the gravesite."

Confident of his decision, Robert Collins responds calmly. "Alan, we are physicians first and pathologists second. We have to give our very best when it comes to the well-being of the patient or their family. A mistake in an autopsy may not seem of great magnitude, but it is my opinion that it should be addressed."

As the conference breaks up, Brad is anxious to move things along as quickly as possible. Walking to his tiny desk in the resident physician's workroom, he calls the Deaconess Hospital to obtain Elinor Kennedy's phone number from their computer database. Luckily, he reaches her on his first attempt. Not wishing to upset her, he downplays the controversy over some of the autopsy findings. Before he can adequately finish explaining why the body needs to be exhumed, Elinor begins to cry loudly on the other end of the phone.

Brad says: "I didn't mean to upset you, Mrs. Kennedy. Please forgive me. Why don't I call back another time?"

"Didn't … didn't anyone tell you what happened to my Butch?"

"I'm sorry, Mrs. Kennedy, didn't anyone tell me what?"

Brad can hear Elinor Kennedy begin to cry again as she tries to form the words of her next sentence. "The funeral home called me. … They called me the day before … before my sweet Butch was going to be buried. They told me that he had … that he had been cremated by mistake!"

After Elinor struggles to get those last words out, she breaks down. All Brad can hear is her loud sobbing. No amount of soothing on Brad's part can halt her tears of anguish. With his own heart sinking, the only thing Brad can say is, "I'm sorry, Mrs. Kennedy. I'm so sorry. I had no idea. ... Please forgive me. Please forgive me for upsetting you."

Long after his conversation with Mrs. Kennedy, Brad sits at his desk, still holding the telephone receiver in his left hand. With his eyes closed and his chin down, he gently taps the phone against the side of his head. He is numb with confusion and emotionally stunned by the news he just received from Elinor Kennedy. When he conveys the information to Dr. Collins by phone, Dr. Collins's surprise is quite evident.

"What? The body was cremated? I'll have to be certain that this was reported to the State Board. ... Brad, I'll be honest, I'm not certain what to do from here."

"Dr. Collins, something is wrong here. I don't know how to explain it, but something bothers me about all this. Alan Richards was too calm about a discrepancy this big; could he have something to do with all of this?"

Robert Collins pauses a long time before speaking. His voice is quieter and more certain this time. "There's nothing else we can do, Brad. The man did, indeed, die of a heart attack. The medical records at the Deaconess Hospital and your own notes reflect that. We have an unresolved data conflict on a man who is known to be dead, and we have no way to determine exactly what happened. I'm recommending we halt any further action on this case."

"Yes, sir. I suppose there is no other solution. I'll notify Dr. Richards of your decision."

Seemingly stunned by the news, Alan Richards is quite taken aback as Brad describes the course of events to him. After the phone conversation, Brad tucks his autopsy notebook away, trying to accept the fact that he'll likely never know the truth about what happened to Butch Kennedy.

Chapter 19

Shrouded between towering glass and concrete high-rises, the streets of downtown Nashville are extraordinarily dark on this early morning. Even the moonlight struggles to find a path between the tall buildings. The only reprieve from the darkness comes from the tall, silvery aluminum streetlamps, whose yellow beams cast long indigo shadows. A light breeze whisks along the sidewalks and gutters, and carries with it discarded paper, autumn leaves, and small clouds of dust. Unexpectedly, the stark silence is interrupted by the loud distinctive throttle of a sports car engine. At first, the sound is seemingly far away, but just a moment later the roar approaches and becomes deafeningly loud. The body of a perfectly sculpted black Porsche 911 becomes visible as it flies along the pavement. The piercingly bright LED headlights illuminate the bodies of several homeless people as they sleep on the cold, hard steps of many of the buildings. As he passes them by, Robert Altman barely takes notice of these frail and desperate human beings.

Accelerating rapidly, Robert causes his tires to screech as he pulls into the entrance ramp of AmericaHealth's corporate headquarters. The all-night security guard in the illuminated glass booth recognizes his car and raises the white-and-orange-painted metal barrier to allow him entry to the parking garage. After tediously winding up four stories, Robert stops briefly and reaches for the glove box to withdraw a handheld transmitter. The metal garage door opens before him, giving him access to a secure parking area large enough for only a dozen cars. Driving forward, Robert sees the door close quickly behind him. As soon as he steps from his car, an array of wall-mounted security cameras focus in his direction. Slamming his car door shut, Robert steps onto a private elevator accessible by key and four-digit pass code. He ascends twenty-one stories and is taken directly into his office. Once inside, Robert snaps on the lights, stripping the room of its blackness. Over the intercom, the twenty-four-hour security officer verifies Robert's identity, having seen the movement of his elevator on his computer screen. Before getting started, Robert pulls off his suit jacket and folds it neatly over a chair, and places his briefcase in the middle of the desk. After removing a stack of paperwork, he carefully organizes it on the left-hand side of his desk. Next, he walks to one corner of the room and lifts up a hanging tapestry, exposing a wall safe where a second set of documents are stowed. With that accomplished, Robert settles into his chair and begins to work.

Two hours pass without interruption. As Robert puts the finishing touches on a series of documents, he reaches for a telephone-style dictating machine on one corner of his desk.

"Ms. Jamison, I'll need this memo transcribed immediately. Please date it with today's date, September nineteenth. Address the letter to Everett Halstead, president of the AmericaHealth Corporation, with a carbon copy to each member of the board of directors. First paragraph: 'Mr. Halstead, I'd like to review with you and the board of directors a method by which we may further reduce expenditures on patient care and protect our profits.'" He pauses. "'Besides limiting patients' access to certain types of health care, we may improve our bottom line by reducing the amount of money we are paying our physicians. As you are well aware, we currently maintain a capitated arrangement with all physicians who are contracted to provide services for the AmericaHealth Corporation. Under this agreement, each physician is paid a fixed monthly dollar amount for all of our patients he or she takes care of, regardless of how much time is spent or how many procedures are performed on those patients. This type of arrangement has given us the ability to precisely regulate physician fees. This contrasts sharply with the more traditional health-care plans, in which physicians are paid a certain fee for each specific service or procedure that is rendered.

"'When our health-care plan has been introduced in new markets, the reimbursement for primary care physicians has been intentionally set substantially higher than our local competitors'. This has several advantages.'" Again he pauses. "'First of all, it has given us a jump-start in a given geographical area because more physicians are willing to accept our patients into their practices if they're getting paid more. Secondly, with more of our patients being enrolled in our health-care plan, we have access to more and more specialty-trained physicians, which makes our plan more enticing to both individuals and companies in search of health-care companies. Finally, by initially offering higher compensation to the physicians in a given area, we directly undermine our competition, thereby forcing many companies out of the region we just entered.'" After pausing a moment, he continues, saying, "Final paragraph: 'There are several ways by which we may reduce physician fees. In Nashville, as in many of our cities, our health insurance company has had excellent penetration of a large number of physician practices. Many doctors' practices are made up of between 30 percent and 50 percent of our patients. As you may have surmised, this makes those physicians economically dependent upon our corporation to make ends meet. Once we have extinguished enough of our competition, we can substantially reduce payments toward capitated physicians to cut our costs. The physicians have absolutely no recourse but to accept our fee cuts, because otherwise we could threaten to take away our patients from them, thereby potentially causing them financial ruin. The exact method by which I recommend we implement such a plan, and the specific dollar figures, will be discussed at our corporate meeting this afternoon. It is my feeling that this is a viable method by which we may accelerate our profitability and fuel the growth of our corporation.' ... That's all, Ms. Jamison. Please close the letter, 'Most assuredly, Robert Altman, MD.' After I've signed the memo, please fax a copy to Everett Halstead and make up ten originals for me to carry to our meeting."

As soon as Robert finishes his dictation, he says to his secretary, "Victoria, could you please send for Susan Hamilton and Brian Sanders? I'm ready for them now. ... And would you please be sure that the corporate limo is waiting for me downstairs? I'll be leaving for my meeting in Boston in about thirty minutes."

This morning Robert and two of his highest-ranking executives will meet briefly to discuss pressing business matters. Only a few minutes pass before Ms. Jamison announces the arrival of Susan and Brian. As Robert stands to welcome his associates, he looks out one of the windows at the far side of his office to take note of the daylight, which is just beginning to creep across the waters of the Cumberland River below. He gestures for his guests to take a seat at the conference table while he gathers his notes.

"Good morning, Susan and Brian. ... Thank you for agreeing to meet me on such short notice. I want to go over a few critical items I'll be presenting this afternoon to the company's senior officials when I reach the Boston area. ... To begin with, let me review with you some of the policies I've drafted in regard to cost-containment issues. There are multiple areas where we'll be trimming expenditures, so let me give you an idea with just a few examples. A series of mandates would initially call for limiting specific highly expensive medical and surgical procedures. I will propose to AmericaHealth's board of directors that we hold down the cost of patient care by the elimination of payment for all heart transplants and heart-lung transplants regardless of circumstances. Their life span is already substantially reduced, so it's hard for me to justify that kind of capital expenditure on the situation. We will, however, continue to pay for kidney transplants in suitable candidates. Bone marrow transplants will be paid for only when the strict criteria are met. Knee and hip replacements will be scrutinized carefully to be sure the appropriate patient criteria are being met before we agree to cover the costs of such expensive surgical procedures. Another area where our costs are extremely high is MRI, CT and PET scans. We have got to find a way to cut down on the numbers of these being done! ... Susan, in my absence, I want you to draft a memo to all participating doctors letting them know that they will have to ask permission for an MRI, CT or PET scan and mention that a specific form will have to be filled out in advance. ... Please also begin working on those forms for me to implement as soon as possible. The document needs to contain vital information, including patient medical record number, a brief history, and the clinical indication for the scan.

"One other major problem is pharmaceuticals. They're killing us on drugs! The pharmaceutical companies are just gouging us. We've got to revise our drug formulary. Brian, be sure you do a comprehensive overview of this matter while I'm gone. I want us to move to as many generic drugs as possible, and I want the physicians to provide written justification for all expensive medications they've prescribed, telling us *why* they're indicated for the particular patient. ... In drugs that cost above ten dollars a pill, prescriptions need to be held to a maximum of ten pills per prescription. Also, we'll need to sharply increase the patient's copay on all medications. That, in and of itself, should cut down on demand.

"The final issue is psychiatry. We spend way too much money on mentally ill patients and their doctors. I am in the process of bringing to Nashville several foreign-trained psychiatrists from Korea and eastern Europe who are willing to work for a fraction of what our U.S.-trained psychiatrists are charging us. I've gotten them temporary work visas until they can obtain U.S. citizenship."

Frowning, Brian Sanders politely interrupts his boss. "But Dr. Altman, do you think these foreign doctors can honestly be of help to our patients? Their command of the English language may not be sufficient to communicate effectively."

Irritation is evident in Robert's expression and tone as he responds to the question. "Brian, since you're not a trained physician yourself, your understanding of this situation may be somewhat limited. ... Psychiatry is more about holding hands and prescribing pills than it is about true medicine. One doesn't need to speak perfect English to get the job done. Besides, if it were up to me, we'd stop paying for psychiatric care altogether, so these drastic cuts seem perfectly legitimate. I want both of you to begin working on getting these doctors into the local health-care system and verifying their Tennessee licenses and DEA numbers so that they can begin practicing as soon as they arrive. My secretary has all of their information for you to get started on."

Robert then lays his papers facedown on the table and asks if there are any further items to be discussed before he leaves for Boston. A look of dread and fear appears on Susan Hamilton's face as she pulls several documents from her binder. In search of support, her eyes dart briefly to meet Brian's before she starts. As she begins speaking, she reaches up to pull several strands of her straight brown hair away from her face. Beneath the table, she nervously taps one of her feet. Looking at her notes instead of matching gazes with Robert, she asks his advice regarding several incidents that require his immediate attention. The strain in her voice is obvious.

"I'm sorry to take up your valuable time, Dr. Altman, but I need your help in making a decision on two pressing issues. The first is a request for reimbursement of services rendered by a physician not currently under contract with AmericaHealth, Dr. Harrison Griffith. Dr. Griffith is a cardiologist who was in the intensive care unit at Saint Thomas Hospital two weeks ago, on September 3, when one of our patients went into cardiopulmonary arrest. He successfully resuscitated the patient and now asks for payment of emergency services."

"Did the patient live?"

"I beg your pardon?"

"Did the patient *live*, Ms. Hamilton?"

Somewhat flustered by the odd question and by Robert Altman's hostility, Susan flushes as she attempts to answer his question. "Yes, sir, he certainly did."

"Is he still alive right now?"

"As far as I know, he is."

"Well, then we may have to pay the doctor since he kept one of our patients alive. How much is the bill he sent us?"

"Seven hundred dollars. ... He says he was there several hours stabilizing the patient."

"Which doctor is under contract with us to handle just such an emergency?"

Looking down at her notes, Susan mentions the name of Dr. Howard Parker.

Snarling, Robert asks, "And *why* wasn't Dr. Parker called?"

"He was, but he was in his office at the time seeing patients, two miles from the hospital."

Smiling, Robert Altman's stern brown eyes show some sign of relenting. He lightly taps his fingers on the tabletop as he contemplates the incident. "Send Dr. Griffith a nice letter denying his request for payment. Tell him that he should have waited for Dr. Parker to arrive."

Stunned, Susan searches for words to formulate her question. "But, Dr. Altman, Dr. Parker was *two miles* away when the patient coded."

"Are you questioning my judgment, Ms. Hamilton?"

As Robert stares over at her, Susan drops her gaze to the tabletop and answers quietly, "No, sir."

After a short lapse, Robert asks her to present the second matter as he checks the time on his wristwatch. Fumbling with her pen, Susan attempts to regain her composure. To compensate for her distress, her voice assumes an inappropriate upbeat tone. "The second matter is a bit more complicated and requires an immediate intervention. One hour ago, Dr. Horace Altmeir, one of our psychiatrists, called in to get permission to hospitalize a schizophrenic patient who is threatening to commit suicide. ... He's in the patient's home right now trying to calm her."

"Do you have the woman's medical file, Ms. Hamilton?"

"Yes, sir, right here."

"Then please let me have it."

With one hand, Susan slides the chart across the table to Robert. Without picking up the folder, he opens it and quickly reads the contents.

"I see that this woman has been hospitalized ten times this past year for psychiatric breakdowns. ... It appears that her condition is not improving."

Leaning forward and placing both elbows on the edge of the table, Susan makes an impassioned plea. "But Dr. Altman, her psychiatrist feels certain that she's likely to kill herself if she's not brought in right away."

"Does she have any next of kin?"

Barely audible, Susan whispers her response. "Not that I'm aware of."

"Who pays her insurance premiums?"

"I believe the state of Tennessee does. She's disabled."

"How much have her medicines and admissions cost us this year?"

Susan quickly scans her notes and comes up with the figure of fifty-three thousand dollars.

Robert continues his questions. "How much has the state paid us this year for her insurance premiums?"

"It should be in the range of three-hundred dollars a month, or about thirty-six hundred dollars."

Stopping to digest the information, Robert again taps his fingers on the tabletop. As he speaks, his expression is cold and calculating. "Do not return Dr. Altmeir's phone call."

Even more shocked, Susan quickly asks, "I'm sorry, Dr. Altman, what did you say?"

"If Altmeir calls again, give him a verbal denial, but *do not, under any circumstances,* send him anything in writing. Listen, we've taken a huge loss on this woman. She is of no use to society, and she's using up precious health-care dollars that could be better spent on a patient who has some remote possibility of recovering from their illness."

"But, Dr. Altman, what happens if she kills herself?"

"I thought you told me she had no family."

"What do you mean?"

"Well, then there is no one who can sue us over her death. … Just don't issue a denial letter, or else the psychiatrist or the state could potentially press charges against us."

Swallowing loudly, Susan is unable to comprehend what was just said. With an obvious look of confusion on her face, she sits still in her chair, struggling to make some sense of the situation. Because of her failure to respond, Robert gives her a final order.

"I don't want anyone talking to Altmeir except you. Just stall him, and if it comes to court, it will be his word against ours. We would deny that we ever said the patient could not be admitted. We'd make him look responsible for the whole matter."

As the last word falls from Robert's lips, his secretary, Victoria Jamison, again appears at the door and informs him that the corporate limousine awaits him in front of the building. Walking quickly to his desk, Robert snatches his briefcase and then rushes out of the room, leaving Susan Hamilton and Brian Sanders still seated at the long table.

After Robert's departure, Brian turns to Susan and instructs her to follow him down two flights to his office so that they can complete their part of the meeting. Brian carries on very little in the way of conversation on their short walk and only nods at his secretary as he passes her on the way into his office. After he closes his outer office door and is certain that he and Susan are alone, his taut expressionless face relaxes and his rigidly held shoulders begin to slump. Despite being a relatively young man, Brian has a severely receded hairline. Large beads of sweat soon appear on the pale skin of his scalp, appearing shiny in the brightly lit room. As he turns toward Susan, she reads a look of controlled panic in his eyes.

"Susan, I had no idea things were getting this bad. This is just horrible."

Sensing she has found an ally, Susan lets her guard down. "Brian, I'm so glad you feel the same way I do. I was really starting to get nervous. I need to get out of here; I can't work for a company with this kind of morality. It's sickening!"

"I agree with you. We both need to make a move as soon as possible. I can't possibly live with what's going on here."

Moving closer to her coworker, Susan lowers her voice. "I've been looking for a job for six months. With my family here, I really need to stay in the Nashville area."

Brian also lowers his voice to just above a whisper as the two continue their private conversation. "I've had a couple of offers over the past few months. Now may be the time to act on them."

Over the next thirty minutes, the two become resolute in their decision; they decide to help one another find a position with another company as soon as possible and then resign at the same time. Also, they agree to secretly begin copying company policies and memos and store them in a secure off-premises location in case they need to protect themselves at a future date. Closing their notebooks in unison, they stand and straighten their clothing. Susan smooths her hair, and Brian takes out a handkerchief to blot his forehead dry a second time. Both try to restore their face to the mask of cold professionalism expected in the corporate world. As Susan places her hand on the rounded brass doorknob of Brian's office door, she turns briefly to him and whispers, "Thanks."

Within her eyes, Brian can see a look of profound gratitude.

Meanwhile, Robert has nearly reached the private airstrip that runs alongside Nashville International Airport. As the stretch, black Lincoln Towncar gently decelerates along Interstate 40, Robert peers through the heavily tinted windows to note the approach of the exit just up ahead. He tucks away last-minute notations and snaps his briefcase shut. After a series of turns, the car picks up speed across a wide expanse of black tarmac and then stops abruptly beside a fifteen-passenger, executive-style jet.

Ready for immediate departure, the jet's loud turbines are running wide open. The captain stands in wait beside an open hatch door. Making the transition from automobile to aircraft, Robert feels the gusts from the plane ruffling his precisely combed hair. He barely acknowledges the presence of either the chauffeur or the pilot as he swiftly boards the plane. After his luggage is stowed aboard, the pilot, Jack Carmichael, quickly climbs into the cockpit. Even before Robert is completely settled, the plane taxies into position and begins its takeoff, Robert is in the air within five minutes of his arrival at the airport. Over the private phone adjacent to his tufted leather seat, he summons the pilot.

"Jack, it is imperative that we arrive in Boston on time."

Without lifting his eyes from the cockpit gauges, Jack Carmichael responds, "Yes, sir. I'll do my best."

The plane glides smooth and easily upward, guided by Jack Carmichael's capable hands. His resume includes being a veteran of the Iraq War and working for two decades in commercial aviation. As if designed purely for the pilot's pleasure, the sky is clear, and the flight is seamless. No uncooperative updrafts or turbulence threaten to alter the voyage. At the cruising altitude of twenty thousand feet, the silver-bodied Beechcraft jet floats above an increasingly thick cover of white, billowing cumulus clouds as it travels further northward.

In the lavish passenger compartment, Robert scarcely notices the journey as he takes an opportunity to eat for the first time that day. Once the steward brings him a chef-prepared breakfast, he focuses on getting himself intellectually and emotionally prepared for the upcoming meeting. He reviews and re-reviews the data he'll present in just ninety minutes or so. The top corporate officers come together every six months in Boston to review the company's profitability, marketing trends, and strategic policies. As chief executive officer, Robert is not only responsible for organizing this complex meeting but is also expected to show the board of directors how well he has managed the corporation. He must demonstrate past successes, explain failures, and define the future goals of the health insurance company. Knowing what information is at his fingertips, Robert grows increasingly confident during the flight.

The landing into Boston's Logan Airport is just as smooth as the takeoff from Nashville. Robert makes a swift transfer to a running limousine. Once again, he doesn't deem it necessary to either acknowledge or thank his pilot as he dashes down the steps of the plane and gets into the car. The only sound that reaches Jack Carmichael's ears is the loud clank of Robert's expensive leather shoes against the aluminum steps of the airplane as he departs. Three minutes pass as the limousine driver speedily transfers Robert to a private boat dock on the northern side of the airport. There, a fifty-foot fiberglass yacht with engines running and captain aboard await Robert's arrival.

Once out in the open air, Robert immediately senses his proximity to the ocean. His sinuses become permeated with the thick smell of ocean brine intermixed with the pungent aroma of the boat's diesel fumes. As opposed to the warm humid air of Nashville, the heavily moisture-laden air is cold and damp and sends a chill down Robert's spine. All around him are echoing raucous cries of seagulls, partially drowned out by the loud engine sounds of the boat. With two steps, he is across the tiny wooden bridge between dock and boat. The very instant he is seated in the cabin below, the low-pitched drone of the motors becomes a deafening roar as the yacht hurtles across Boston Harbor. Aware of the urgency, the captain dares not waste precious seconds.

Just across the harbor, the looming skyscrapers of downtown Boston meet the waters of the Atlantic Ocean. The skyline's reflections are made imperfect by the slight rippling of the water's surface. Soon, the vessel slows, and the ride, which had been a hard, choppy one, becomes a slow bobbing. Their destination becomes clear as they approach land.

Up ahead lies a newcomer to the Boston Harbor. Just three decades old, a fifteen-story, colonial-style brick complex, the Boston Harbor Hotel, has been shoehorned into a space between long-standing architectural monuments. The gateway to this landmark begins with a private marina, in which resides an exact replica of John Rowe's clipper ship that started the infamous Boston Tea Party. Seated on a concrete embankment on the back side of the hotel is a twenty-five-foot brick rotunda capped by a circular copper roof. Lined by windows on all sides, the structure somehow gives a defining presence to the hotel. The true entrance to the building lies twenty yards beyond the rotunda and consists of an elaborate recessed archway composed entirely of glass and brick. In keeping with the historical nature of the city of Boston, the area in which the hotel rests has been named Rowes Wharf.

Before the boat is even adequately secured, Robert impatiently jumps onto the dock and walks quickly in the direction of the hotel. Not far behind him, a crewman ambles along carrying his luggage. Once inside the hotel, Robert barely breaks stride as he is guided by one of the corporate secretaries directly to the second-floor conference room. Two bellmen stand in wait beneath the arched entryway to transport Robert's luggage to his private suite.

Right arm extended, Robert forcefully pushes open one of the tall wooden doors leading to the conference room. From an elongated mahogany table in the center of the room, the heads of the seven highest-ranking officials of the AmericaHealth Corporation turn in unison in Robert's direction as he enters. Pausing briefly, Robert hands his computer to one of the secretaries and then takes his position at the head of the table. From his inside jacket pocket, he retrieves a handheld laser pointer. Taking one long deep breath, he calls the meeting to order.

"Good afternoon, gentlemen. I hope your travels to the Boston area were as safe and uneventful as mine were. That is, with the exception of Mr. Halstead and Mr. Armistead, who reside locally, and whose major obstacle was to avoid colliding with the suicidal drivers of this city."

Everyone at the table chuckles, which helps to ease some of the tension.

"Forgive me for launching directly into the heart of this business meeting, but I know time is a precious commodity for everyone present."

Robert then nods his head slightly. A long, white projector screen glides silently down the far wall. Hesitating only momentarily, Robert introduces the first topic, the company's current financial status. Using a handheld remote, Robert dims the lights, and the page of the PowerPoint presentation comes into view.

"Our company's profitability for this past year has been quite impressive. From the graph, you'll notice we have achieved a 9–10 percent increase in gross revenue each year for the past five years. This is quite an achievement by any measure. We have further penetrated health-care markets in our traditional strongholds, the Northeast and the Southern states, and have managed to expand into two new geographical areas, Texas and California. I anticipate tremendous growth in both of these new sectors. ... I'm in the process of negotiating several large contracts in the Midwest and feel that this is a potentially large untapped market for our company."

Robert runs through a dozen or so more slides, while entertaining a variety of questions from the heads of the AmericaHealth Corporation. He then moves on to a discussion of the current fiscal year's financial figures, which piques everyone's interest.

"On this next slide, you'll see that our gross income for the first six months of this year was 100.1 billion dollars, compared with 92.42 billion dollars one year ago. Our net profit on that figure of 100.1 billion dollars is 5.3 billion dollars, meaning that for every dollar we receive in health-care premiums, we have managed to keep approximately 5.3 percent. We have labored long and hard for that 5.3 percent, and I'm proud we've been able to achieve a number that high. Projecting out to this coming year, our annual income should be well over 200 hundred billion dollars, with net revenues of 10.5 billion dollars, which is up 3.5 billion dollars from one year ago."

Robert's discussion is interrupted at that point by his associates, who politely applaud him for his achievements. After taking a sip of water, he continues.

"Obviously, gentlemen, up to this point we have been extremely successful. The numbers I have shown today clearly demonstrate that. The key issue I'd like to raise this afternoon is, how do we continue to sustain this type of growth in the increasingly competitive health-care arena? Over the past several months, I have put together a series of strategies that I feel may keep our company on track. As I mentioned earlier, we need to expand our horizons and take on new markets. Another of our goals must be to continue to seek out the most desirable clients, mainly young people with minimal health problems. First, we offer extremely attractive rates for young people who rarely use the health-care system, thereby luring them away from other health insurance companies. This approach has dramatically undermined our competition in many of the geographical areas we have entered. Our focus on younger insured clients means that our competitors are left with the oldest, sickest patients, who burn up more health-care dollars than they pay in insurance premiums. As our competition has faced financial difficulties, we have positioned ourselves to control more of the market share, which has further accelerated our growth. Ultimately, this could result in limited or no competition in certain geographical regions, allowing us to raise our rates, again to our advantage."

After a momentary pause to address several questions, Robert resumes.

"My third ploy for increasing AmericaHealth's financial strength is to reduce some of our capital expenditures. In order to accomplish that, I am recommending a three-part approach. First, we need to severely limit some of the most expensive medical procedures to only a very select group of patients. Second, certain procedures need to be eliminated altogether. And finally, we need to further cut our physician compensation."

On the screen appears some of the very same proposed restrictions that Robert discussed with Susan Hamilton and Brian Sanders earlier this morning in Nashville. At the same time, the memo that Robert dictated to Everett Halstead about reducing physician fees is distributed to each member. After the merits of each proposal have been evaluated, the AmericaHealth executives break for a late lunch.

One hour later, the meeting resumes, with Robert again at the helm.

"Let us begin with our second-to-last agenda item. If you gentlemen would please turn to page thirty-four of your outline. ... As many of you are aware, the federal government, as well as several state agencies, are drafting legislation that may have a serious negative impact on the way we presently do business. As a matter of fact, there is some suggestion that a number of our current policies may be deemed illegal over the next couple of years. If that were to occur, the government could be in a position to demand that we surrender to them some of our previously earned profits. As you recall, Bill Burns and I began to address this very issue some time ago. ... Bill, would you like to take over?"

From the opposite end of the table, William Burns, one of the senior officers, rises and begins to walk in Robert's direction. Once the men are side by side, the difference in their physical appearance is quite striking. The rotund, balding William Burns is substantially shorter than the trimmer and younger-appearing Robert Altman. This, despite the fact that the two men are nearly the same age. After getting everyone's attention, Bill Burns, with his deep gravelly voice, proceeds quickly.

"Two years ago, at this very meeting, it was decided to spin off some of our corporate profits into a separate holding company and move capital offshore to keep it out of the hands of the federal government. ... In the case of a sudden downturn in the health-care industry, the goal was to keep all of the company officers seated here today in good financial shape—even if AmericaHealth itself were to go bankrupt."

William Burns then flashes his first slide on the screen.

"Over the past twenty-four months, we have transferred 1.6 billion dollars to a series of numbered accounts in the Cayman Islands. The majority of this money has been used to purchase multiple resorts around the world, primarily in western Europe and Australia. We have also acquired a substantial portion of the smallest island making up the Cayman chain, Little Cayman. Following extensive negotiations with the Cayman Islands' government, Robert and I have obtained permits to build a midsize marina and four luxury hotels with approximately eight hundred rooms each. We are nearing completion of the first hotel and one of two golf courses that will wind through the resort areas."

The AmericaHealth executives temporarily interrupt Bill Burns with several questions about the details of the various projects. After answering, he returns to his presentation.

"The remainder of the money has been invested in several high-tech companies in this country, the amount of which you will find listed in your outline. As you'll notice on our next slide, our current asset value of our overseas properties and tech companies has nearly doubled in the past twenty-four months to 2.9 billion dollars, meaning that our economic future has been clearly secured."

At this point, the presentation is interrupted by applause for both Robert Altman and William Burns. After this brief interlude, Robert returns to the head of the table and resumes control of the meeting. Before speaking, he stiffens his back and straightens his suit jacket by tugging at the lapels.

"The final item on today's agenda will not be found in your outline, gentlemen. Please bear with me as I begin a lengthy and somewhat complicated discourse. … I believe that we are reaching a crossroads in the American health-care system. In the not-so-distant future, legislation *will be* enacted that will force us to spend more of the money we collect in health-care premiums directly on patient care. It has been hypothesized that we may be allowed to keep only 2 percent of all revenue for profit, which, as you realize, is a substantial drop from our current 5.3 percent. It could be devastating!"

This last bit of information brings dead silence to the room as each ear strains to hear Robert's next words.

"With such a potential cataclysm looming before us, I have taken several steps to avert what could be a disaster. What I'm about to say may not make complete sense to everyone when I first say it, so please give me time to explain. ... Recently, I have entered into preliminary discussions with several large insurance carriers who have expressed an interest in *purchasing* our company."

Frank disbelief would be the phrase used to describe the stunned expressions of the seated AmericaHealth executives as they try to understand what was just said. After a prolonged silence, a heated debate ensues, with everyone trying to speak simultaneously. After much deliberation, the company's vice-president, Paul Armistead, manages to yell above the other voices and get his question posed.

"*Robert,* besides upcoming legislation, why would we want to sell our company? We are all making a good living; we could ride out a few bad years."

Barely allowing Paul Armistead to finish, Robert says, "Price."

In unison, several voices use that identical word to ask a question: "*Price?*"

"That's right, *price.* Currently, AmericaHealth is valued at approximately 800 billion dollars. In preliminary negotiations, I have been offered *one trillion dollars* for the company, which, you must understand, may change depending upon the final agreement. As you'll recognize, that's a 200 billion dollar profit. According to our contract with AmericaHealth, 80 percent of the profits of a corporate sale would go to the stockholders and the other 20 percent to the senior corporate executives. That means that each person seated here today could walk away with roughly *5.71 billion dollars in the bank* if the deal goes through!"

The emotional roller coaster that Robert has taken his colleagues on, on this September day in Boston has just climaxed. Much calmer than everyone else in the room, the trim, silver-haired president of AmericaHealth, Everett Halstead, then addresses his chief executive officer, interrupting the excited conversation.

"Robert, that's quite a proposition you put together for us. I'm impressed, but let's not rush into anything. Why don't we set up another meeting in thirty days to discuss the particulars once we have a more concrete offer? ... In the meantime, let's get our team of attorneys to review what you've obtained so far."

As the discussions conclude, Robert is eventually left alone at the long conference table. Tired and achy after the long day, he slowly gathers his belongings and carefully organizes them in his hard-sided briefcase. For the first time in several weeks, he begins to relax as he realizes the difficult meeting is behind him. Enjoying not having to run off anywhere, he sits with his elbows resting on the table, staring out the three-story windows that make up one entire wall of the room. Despite sundown's approach, the sky is a rich blue and heavy winds cause whitecapping of the waves as they approach shore. Carefree seagulls effortlessly ride the updrafts just beyond reach of the windows. A few fishermen's boats pass by, anxious to reach landfall before dark. As he witnesses the simple beauty before him, Robert again searches his soul, seeking the repose that never comes. He ponders why money and power have so consumed him that he cannot make himself leave a job he so despises. Recognizing that he does not possess the strength to alter his path, he sits silently in the room until long after the sun has vanished below the horizon.

At seven thirty the following morning, Robert is already showered and stands on the concrete embankment beside the corporate yacht at the back of the hotel. The cool salt air bites at his neck and ears, and he shivers despite wearing a long, insulated poplin raincoat. Impatiently, he awaits the arrival of David Rowland, the chief financial officer, and William Burns, a senior officer of the AmericaHealth Corporation. Once they are all together, Robert signals the boat's captain. Within minutes, they are across Boston Harbor and aboard the corporate jet. The three men say little to each other as they settle in for their journey.

Their pilot, Jack Carmichael, exchanges information with the radar tower, and soon the powerful turbines have the small jet at cruising altitude. A due-southerly course is chosen for the three-hour flight. Twenty minutes pass. Baltimore is just below, with Washington, DC, up ahead. An hour later, Jack informs his passengers that Jacksonville is on the horizon, signaling a westward turn in order to sweep around Cuba's airspace as they approach the largest of the three bodies of land making up the Cayman Islands—Grand Cayman.

As the jet slowly loses altitude in preparation for landing, Robert packs away his notes and handheld Dictaphone and glances out the window of the aircraft. Beneath them, he notices a broad bay, the Northern Sound, on the western end of Grand Cayman Island. Here, the deep blue Caribbean waters change color to a pale aquamarine as they enter the shallow, white-sand-lined basin. As they begin their approach into the compact Owen Roberts Airport near the capital city of George Town, Robert hears the mechanical whine of the landing gear drop and then lock into position. A long, pearl-white Rolls Royce limousine awaits their arrival. The three AmericaHealth executives are soon on their way to the Bank of the Caymans, where they have an appointment with the president, Arthur Smithfield.

Left over from the days when this island was a British colony, Arthur Smithfield truly exemplifies the English gentry. Despite the balmy climate, he insists on wearing a traditional three-piece dark wool suit and handcrafted English leather wingtip shoes, polished to an impressive shine. A resident of Grand Cayman for over four decades, Arthur's platinum-colored hair belies his age. With etiquette and an English accent befitting a nobleman, he welcomes his three American guests, whom he knows well.

"Dr. Altman, Mr. Rowland, Mr. Burns, what a great pleasure it is to have your company once again on our humble island. Your phone call of several days ago alerting us to your visit was certainly much appreciated. Please come and make yourself at home in my office."

Bowing his head slightly, Arthur extends his left arm in the direction of his office and walks several steps behind his three clients. An assortment of iced beverages, neatly arranged on a sterling silver tray, await the three men in Arthur's office. Once his guests are comfortably seated, Arthur Smithfield takes his place behind his desk. Robert wastes little time in getting the meeting under way.

"Arthur, thank you for your time this afternoon. I just wanted to take a few minutes to review our holdings and our accounts with you."

Again, with his unfaltering perfect speech, Arthur answers, "I am most anxious to honor your request, Robert. Give me direction as to where you might wish to begin."

"Let's start off with our present account balances, and then we'll move on to current construction costs of our development on Little Cayman Island."

From the vest pocket of his suit, Arthur withdraws a tiny brass key on a chain. Opening his center desk drawer with the key, he removes a long ledger bound in dark blue leather, and after this he reaches for a thick pair of reading glasses. Across from him, Robert distributes to David Rowland and William Burns two large sets of documents in plastic binders marked "AmericaHealth Corporation – Confidential." He instructs them to turn to page five and then asks Arthur to read off their numbered accounts with current balances while he and his associates verify the accuracy of the numbers. After that has been accomplished, the men go over the activity on the construction project, reviewing its progress to date. Robert then tries to wrap things up.

"Arthur, thank you. David, Bill, do you have any more questions before we adjourn?"

David Rowland, having looked carefully through the financial statements in his booklet while many of the discussions were ongoing, says, "Robert, these account numbers on page thirty don't have a designation. What exactly are they used for?"

Robert quickly leafs through the loosely bound booklet and pauses before answering. Out of the corner of his eye, he sees Arthur shift uncomfortably in his chair.

"David, those are accounts that were set up to cushion the company in case of a severe financial loss. They remain secret and away from the United States so that capital can be quickly brought in during an emergency. As we discussed yesterday, we are trying to keep as much money offshore as possible to keep the Feds from getting a hold of it. That's all."

Nervously biting his lower lip, William Burns inserts his opinion. "I agree with David, Robert. We need to have a method of tracking and accounting for this money by using some type of nomenclature to describe what these accounts represent."

Remaining unruffled, Robert stares at Arthur while he speaks. "Well, Bill, David, you have certainly made a fine point. ... Arthur, before my departure later this week, let's schedule an appointment to work on that very issue."

With the conclusion of the meeting, Robert sends his colleagues off to their hotel. Little encouragement is required for David Rowland and William Burns to leave early; their ties are loosened, and they've already removed their jackets. Usually having little time for recreation, they plan to take advantage of the opportunity to play some golf while they are in the Caymans.

Robert stays behind with Arthur Smithfield to go over several other business matters. A luncheon is brought in to them while they work. This private get-together is much more intensive. Arthur quietly closes and locks his door and instructs his secretary to hold all calls. Two hours later, the two men emerge from Arthur's office and walk together in the direction of the safety deposit boxes. Inside the brightly illuminated vault made of polished stainless steel, Arthur runs his index finger along a particular row of boxes to locate the one that is of interest to Robert. Again reaching into his vest pocket, he retrieves this time a silver key and inserts it into one of a pair of locks. He then excuses himself, asking Robert to call him when he finishes.

At Arthur's instruction, the security guard closes and locks the sliding door composed of metal bars and turns his back while Robert looks over his belongings. Pulling out a second silver key, Robert places it into the lock beside the first. The metal door then swings open, revealing a large brass box, which is withdrawn and placed upon a marble-topped table in the center of the vault. After opening the long lid backward, Robert first sees several leather-bound ledgers. He scrutinizes these carefully and makes multiple entries as he reads. Beneath the ledgers lie big stacks of European and U.S. currency in large denominations, arranged beside generously sized velvet bags containing gold coins. After finishing his notations and evaluating things carefully, Robert asks the guard to summon Mr. Smithfield.

After his departure from the bank, Robert settles into his oceanfront suite at the Westin Resort Complex located along Seven Mile Beach north of George Town. After spreading out on a long sofa in the living room, he places a call to his wife, Anne, at their home in Nashville. After explaining that his meeting in Boston went well, he mentions that over the next couple of days, he'll be inspecting the construction site on Little Cayman Island. Then, uncharacteristic for Robert Altman, his voice takes on an excited, carefree quality.

"Anne, I just wanted to let you know that I've sent the corporate jet to Nashville to pick you up tomorrow morning. It's been six months since I've had any time off, and I miss you terribly. I thought we'd spend a few days down here on Grand Cayman together. I promise that I won't even think about work."

Anne bubbles over with excitement at the unexpected offer. Remarkably, she remains devoted to her husband, sincerely believing that he is trying to improve health care by helping the patients who are insured by his company.

"Oh, Robert, I just can't believe it! You work way too hard. You need some time off. You know I'd love to spend a few days alone with you *anywhere*. I'll pack my things right now. I love you, and I can't wait until I'm with you tomorrow."

Chapter 20

Despite his best efforts, Brad finds it difficult to stop thinking about Butch Kennedy's case. Frequently, he awakens at night plagued with memories of Butch's autopsy. A recurring image haunts him in his dreams; he is standing over Butch's lifeless body, while in his hands is Butch's beating heart. Even at work, he often catches himself pondering the inconsistencies of the findings. After several weeks go by, Brad can no longer contain his curiosity. Late one Sunday evening, when he is certain to be the only one there, he drives out to the Deaconess Hospital and cautiously enters the pathology department.

After verifying that he's alone, he walks to the large metal cabinets containing the tissue slides and searches for Butch's samples. A few minutes later, he is relieved when he discovers what he's searching for. Glancing around, he then walks to the reading room to analyze the slides at one of the microscopes. As the dark-red striated muscle of the heart comes into focus, Brad is hoping this time the findings will make sense. Once again, however, the heart is severely enlarged. In frustration, Brad pulls his eyes from the microscope. As he puts the slides back in their storage place, one of the secretaries walks in. Trying not to arouse suspicion, he calmly greets her and chats with her in a very nonchalant manner, explaining that he's preparing a talk for the following morning and has some last-minute details to attend to. She readily accepts his story. Once Brad wishes her good night, she quickly goes to work on a lengthy report due the following day.

Still confounded after his review of the heart samples, Brad is determined to continue his investigation. Later that week, he returns to the Deaconess Hospital in search of Butch Kennedy's angiogram that was done at the time of his initial cardiac catheterization. The films demonstrate the obvious narrowing of the coronary arteries with a seemingly normal heart size. Unfortunately, the status of the individual chamber dimensions is not clearly depicted on the X-rays. His next step is to take a trip to the medical records department, where he requests Butch's hospital chart, which luckily has not yet gone to electronic archive despite the fact that this is a "deceased file."

Patiently and systematically, Brad reviews the data entries, beginning with the paramedic's notes from when Butch had his first heart attack at the Nissan plant. He carefully sifts through each page, all the way to when Butch sustained his second and final heart attack on that Sunday afternoon. Again he finds not a single helpful clue in the written material, with one exception: a note in the chart from Dr. Edward Westmoreland written just after Butch's first admission to the Deaconess Hospital. In his consultation, Edward Westmoreland makes reference to an echocardiogram he performed at Butch's bedside that displayed "severe dilated cardiomyopathy." His assessment, at the end of that dictated report, was that Butch was not a candidate for bypass surgery because of the enlargement of his heart.

Folding the record closed and placing it aside, Brad sits back in his chair and again questions his own memory. *Could I be wrong? Was I tired and did I somehow remember things incorrectly? ... But what about my autopsy journal? Why does it support my memory? The slides, though—the slides show a large baggy heart, just as Dr. Westmoreland describes. I don't understand it anymore; it's all too confusing!*

Fraught with intellectual conflict over the discovery of the echocardiogram report, Brad decides he can accomplish nothing further this evening. He returns the chart to the record room file clerk. Because of his mental preoccupation, Brad barely mumbles "Thanks" as he walks off. Along the dimly lit long gray hospital corridors leading to the parking area, Brad stares at the carpeted floor as he attempts to relive the autopsy in his mind. He can visualize the electric saw sending bone dust into the air as Butch's chest is opened and the bluish discoloration of the heart as the ribs are retracted. Even the moist coolness of the heart comes back to him as he remembers holding it in his hands. Then in slow motion comes the moment he sees the scalpel in his right hand opening the muscular wall of the left ventricle. He can see the shining sharp blade cut into the brown-red muscle. *Yes, yes, it was thick and strong,* he thinks to himself as the image becomes clear. At that instant, he smiles and looks up, again convinced of the accuracy of his memories.

Several days pass as Brad contemplates what to do next. His distraction is plainly obvious to Julie, who can barely maintain his attention when they're together. Concerned, she asks about his preoccupation. At first, he is reluctant to burden her with his quandary. One evening in particular, however, when they are at Julie's house for dinner, Brad is not at all himself. Julie corners him and eventually forces him to confess what is bothering him. Recounting his recent discovery in Butch's chart, Brad explains to Julie that he feels lost, uncertain how best to sort out the mystery surrounding Butch's death. Julie listens patiently, not once interrupting him. After hearing the new information, she encourages him to go and speak with Edward Westmoreland, who, she hopes, might shed some new light on the situation.

Relieved after sharing his concerns, Brad takes Julie's suggestion and makes a formal appointment to meet with Dr. Westmoreland. On the designated evening at six o'clock, Brad nervously stands outside the surgeon's office. From the doorway, he can barely see Edward, who is hidden behind several looming stacks of loosely organized charts and piles of paperwork on his desk. To make himself heard, Brad taps lightly on the open door. Looking up, the silver-haired Edward Westmoreland points to a chair beside his desk while he continues to work. After a few minutes, he puts his pen down and looks over at Brad. Seated stiffly, Brad appears self-conscious as he awaits an opportunity to explain the reason for his visit. While making small talk with Dr. Westmoreland, Brad can't help but stare at the many framed photographs hanging in his office. There are pictures that one would come to expect of an acclaimed academic physician, for example, of Edward standing with deans and presidents of Vanderbilt over the years at medical school graduation ceremonies. There are also pictures of him with some of the institution's most famous scientists and physicians. However, other images directly attest to Edward's profound political ties, namely, photographs of him with eminent state politicians and several past presidents of the United States.

Along one wall, Brad sees the framed faces of hundreds of men and women whom he does not recognize. They appear to be people from all walks of life, and most have smiles on their faces. Brad becomes unintentionally distracted by the images. At one point in the conversation, he asks Dr. Westmoreland who these people are. He is startled to learn that these are the patients upon whom Edward has performed heart transplants. Looking lovingly in the direction of the photos, Edward tells Brad that the majority are still alive and doing well. It becomes obvious to Brad that Dr. Westmoreland's pioneering work has saved most of these people's lives.

In contrast to Brad's rigid posture, Edward leans way back in his chair with his legs extended and his feet crossed at the ankles. One arm dangles loosely across the corner of his desk, while the other rests comfortably on the armrest of his chair. Pulling his silver-rimmed reading glasses from his nose, Edward comments, "Brad, I remember when you rotated on my service as a third-year student. You did a fine job, son. ... Now, tell me how you like pathology. From my perspective, the big drawback to that specialty is that you don't get to work with people. As I recall, you were very good with my patients."

"To be honest with you, Dr. Westmoreland, I do miss the patient contact, but pathology was the right choice for me. I find it very challenging, and I really enjoy the work."

"Well, that's the important thing. ... Now, what is it I can do for you, Brad?"

"I came by to ask about one of your patients who died several months ago. ... I ended up doing the autopsy on him out here at the Deaconess. He died of a heart attack, and I had a couple of questions. ... His name was Randall Kennedy. Does that name sound familiar?"

"Hmm. ... Is that the fellow who worked down in Smyrna at the car factory, the guy with the nickname Bert or Barney or something like that?"

"Yes, sir, that's him. He went by Butch."

"I remember that guy's case pretty well, Brad. Nice fellow. His death was a real shocker. Now, what would you like to ask me?"

"As I was saying, when he died, he ended up having a postmortem exam, and I was involved in the dissection. ... I was hoping to review a couple of the findings, if that's okay."

"Sure, no problem. Let me go get his chart to refresh my memory."

Getting up from his desk, Edward walks into the next room to hunt for the records. While he waits, Brad hears several filing cabinets open and close. As Edward walks back into the room, he holds the file open in both hands and reads from his notes. Sitting down at his desk, he slowly strokes his chin with the index finger and thumb of his left hand while digesting the contents of the chart. His expression remains solemn as he reads. After a brief lapse, Edward closes the record, places it face down on his desk, and removes his eyeglasses.

"All right, Dr. Pierson, I'm ready. Tell me what you've got."

Nervously, Brad clears his throat before speaking. "At autopsy, Mr. Kennedy's heart had some component of ventricular hypertrophy. ... I understand that at one point in your evaluation, there may have been found dilated cardiomyopathy. I'm trying to see if that is accurate."

Reaching up and scratching the side of his head, Edward's expression remains placid while he speaks. "I recall the echocardiogram well, Brad. Mr. Kennedy had severe four-chamber dilatation. That's the whole reason I couldn't do bypass surgery on him. The problem was, he needed the surgery. His disease was very severe, but he wouldn't have survived the procedure. Does that answer your question?"

To avoid offending Dr. Westmoreland, Brad carefully weighs his words. Somewhat intimidated, he casts his gaze at the floor. "Because of the differences in the heart at autopsy and the time of echocardiogram, do you think I could possibly look at the video that was made of Mr. Kennedy's heart?"

Looking briefly into Edward's steel-blue eyes, Brad is disappointed to discover that he cannot read any emotion. Just as matter-of-fact as before, Edward responds, "Brad, I'm afraid that an echocardiogram done that long ago is not likely to still be around. Given the fact that Mr. Kennedy died several months ago further lessens the chances. We generally discard the discs when we are informed of the death. ... Is there anything else I can help you with?"

"No, Dr. Westmoreland. Thank you for taking the time to speak with me. I have no other questions."

As Brad is on his way out of the office, he turns and steals a final glimpse at Dr. Westmoreland. Again engrossed in the mountain of paperwork on his desk, Edward barely notices Brad's departure. On the way to his car, Brad remains convinced of the error, but he has exhausted all avenues of recourse. With the sullenness of defeat, he resigns himself to the possibility that he'll never know the truth about what happened.

Several weeks pass. Brad manages to nearly forget all about Butch Kennedy. The tension that had thrashed about deep within his stomach has receded over time. Brad's relaxed but confident manner gradually returns. His thoughts become focused on his work, and he prepares himself mentally for his fellowship year, which will begin at the end of his residency. He devotes his spare time to Julie, and their relationship continues to flourish. The couple gets out frequently with Sandy and Joanie, and on an exceptional weekend, when their call schedules permit, they all catch one of the Vanderbilt home football games together.

All seems well among Brad's and Julie's respective families, also. Brad's parents are planning another visit to Nashville around Thanksgiving, and Matt has broken the news to everyone about his move to Seattle. Brad was surprised how well his parents took it. On his way out west, Matt plans to stop over in Nashville for a visit. With winter's approach, Julie's mom, Anna, has just begun to slow down with her landscape architecture business. She recently told her daughters that she is contemplating a trip to Europe in the spring and asked if they might be interested in going with her. Sandy and Joanie have finally set a wedding date, and Joanie's mom is looking just a bit frantic as she helps put the final plans together.

To Dr. Goodman's astonishment, William Lockwood continues to show visual improvement in his left eye. William has also recently gotten other good news. He has been offered a promotion in rank from associate to full professor in the Vanderbilt English department, giving him a tenured status. His daughter, Cynthia, continues to progress along nicely in school. On nights and weekends, she and her dad are virtually inseparable.

As expected, Tracy Kilpatrick has decided to temporarily retire from her secretarial duties in the Vanderbilt history department so she can stay at home full time with her daughter, Angel. Parenting has enriched their lives so much, that Tracy and Tom have already begun the adoption process for a second child. With Tracy now off from work, Tom's burdens have eased and things at home are quite a bit smoother.

Now that life has been restored to its normal routine, Brad is more contented. He has just started a new assignment at Vanderbilt Hospital in surgical pathology, where he will stay for the next two months. One evening after work, Brad hurries home, hoping to get in a run before it gets too late. Nearly back at his apartment, he jogs across Blakemore Avenue with his soft-sided briefcase in one hand, dodging heavy traffic in both directions. Continuing on, he walks along Twenty-Fourth Avenue South for several blocks and then takes a couple of quick turns, which leads him to Convent Place. As his feet strike the tree-lined walkways of this tiny avenue, it is nearly seven o'clock.

Convent Place is a tiny dead-end street with several tasteful small apartment buildings and a few private residences. Because of its small size, it has a comfortable feel for Brad. Having lived here since starting medical school nearly eight years ago, he knows almost all of his neighbors by sight. As he vigorously strides along, Brad is focused on getting home in time to exercise. Halfway up the street, not far from his residence, he notices an unfamiliar tan-colored car parked on the left-hand side of the street, facing his direction. When he gets close to the vehicle, he recognizes the unmistakable shape of a Volvo sedan. Seconds later, a tall man appears from the shadows and jumps into the car. The bright headlights are then turned on, nearly blinding Brad, and then the car drives off at a high rate of speed.

Startled by the unusual behavior of the driver, Brad steps out into the street after the car has passed to see if he can identify the license plate number. Unfortunately, the vehicle is moving fast enough that it's quickly out of sight. Turning around, Brad resumes his walk home. As he gets closer to his apartment, he hears something rustling around in the bushes behind the building. Unclear about what is making the noise, Brads slides behind a tree and peers in the direction of the activity. He is barely able to make out the darkened outlines of two men lurking alongside the building. His heart begins to race and his breathing becomes more rapid as he realizes that he has stumbled upon a burglary in progress. He is bowled over when he sees a dim light on in *his* apartment. These people are stealing *from him! Brad immediately takes out his cell phone and dials 9-1-1 to summon the police emergently.*

Now panicked, Brad can hear his heart beating loudly in his chest. Competing emotions of fear and anger affect his judgment, causing him to move out from behind the large tree. He tells himself he absolutely must get a better look at the intruders before the police arrive. Several other cars are parked along the curb. Brad slinks down beside them as he painstakingly eases his way closer to his apartment.

On his hands and knees, he cautiously steals a glance from behind the chrome bumper of one of the automobiles. Right now, one of the men who was inside his apartment is climbing out his bedroom window. The three men he's seen so far are all dressed in tight black garments. Just as Brad gets a clear look at them, he feels a streak of pain coming from his right kneecap, caused from several tiny pebbles that have ground into his skin. Reflexively, he shifts positions. His movement attracts the attention of the driver of another unfamiliar car parked nearby. A deep male voice then yells from the window of the vehicle, and the three intruders run toward the street. One of the back doors is flung open, and two of the men jump into the backseat. Brad hears the engine roar to life. Now losing all fear, Brad stands and runs directly at the car at a full sprint, hoping to grab the final thief before he escapes. Too late in his attempt, Brad watches the third burglar makes it to the vehicle before he does. The car, with its lights off and one door still open, accelerates toward Brad, nearly running him down as he leaps out of the way. As his body strikes the sidewalk, all he can hear is the gut-wrenching sound of tearing steel. The streetlamp he was standing beside is nearly destroyed by the impact of the vehicle. The crash does not slow the car's progress for long, as Brad can hear it speed off down the street.

Jumping up, he chases after them, hoping to get their license plate number, but he is too far away. However, as the vehicle passes under the light of one of the streetlamps up ahead, he's able to see the color and model, a burgundy four-door Cadillac sedan, with a large fresh dent in the left front quarter panel. As the car careens around the corner and out of sight, Brad stops running and stands in the middle of the road while bending over to catch his breath.

Several minutes later, when the danger appears to be gone, he turns back toward home and dusts himself off. A quick survey of the damage reveals a tear in the right leg of his navy-colored wool slacks and dirt stains on his shirt sleeve. Anxious to see what the thieves stole, he runs toward his apartment. On the way, he hunts for his briefcase, which ended up in the middle of one of his neighbors' front lawn. When he reaches his front door, he tries the knob and finds it still locked. Fumbling for the keys in his right trouser pocket, he unlocks the door and pushes it wide open. Brad apprehensively gropes for the wall switch. Deciding not to move any further, he stands in the doorway for a long time and listens for any unusual sounds. Brad then looks around carefully. Luckily the living room is virtually undisturbed; neither the television nor the stereo were taken. The only thing ruffled is the sofa, the cushions of which have been thrown onto the floor.

Gaining confidence, Brad walks across the living room toward the kitchen. To his relief, this room is also nearly intact. Only a few drawers have been left wide open, and nothing obvious is missing. After a brief assessment, he thinks to himself, *Perhaps I startled them before they could take anything.*

When he reaches his bedroom at the back of the apartment, his growing quiescence is shattered. Piles of books, torn from the bookshelves, are strewn all over the floor. The filing cabinet has been ransacked, and files lie open all over his desk, with their contents tousled and strewn throughout the room. The lock on his desk has been forcefully pried open and the drawers rifled through. On further inspection, he sees that the only things left untouched are the clothing closet and the bathroom. Again, the telephone and other electronic equipment have been left behind.

At the back of the room, both windows have been left wide open. A warm breeze lofts in, billowing the curtains. Now more calm, Brad feels his racing heart slow. He then walks to the windows but doesn't touch them in case fingerprints may have been left behind. Minutes later, the room is engulfed by the flashing blue lights of an arriving police car. Brad first hears a car door open and then static-riddled conversation on a policeman's two-way radio. Leaving the bedroom, Brad hurries outside to meet the officer.

After the front door is unlatched and opened, Brad steps out into the darkness. The night air is warm and damp, causing him to sweat. At about that time, a second patrol car arrives in front. Because of the commotion, many of the neighbors have begun to congregate outside Brad's apartment. Two male officers, dressed in starched blue uniforms, meet Brad in the parking lot and begin asking questions. One man jots notes on a small, spiral-bound notepad while the other assumes charge of the inquiry. Brad gives a description of the darkly dressed intruders and of the two cars. He mentions he was unable to get the license plate number of either the Volvo or the Cadillac, or a description of the drivers. Halfway through his narration, Brad is interrupted by the voice of the precinct sergeant over one of the men's radios. He questions where they are and what their status is. One of the men responds through a small, black plastic transmitter clipped to his left shirt sleeve.

"Arrived 328 Convent Place— no visible signs of intruders. Place is quiet—apartment resident on-site. Just beginning investigation."

Turning back toward Brad after he updates his sergeant, the officer asks Brad to continue. Completely unexpectedly, Brad begins to shake all over from the combination of fear and anger. In his mind, he has begun to mentally entertain a variety of scenarios, imagining what could have occurred if the men had guns or other weapons. His voice wavers and he begins to feel dizzy. To support himself, he leans back against the warm hood of one of the police cars.

By this time, nearly all the occupants of the two apartment buildings are out in the parking area, loosely encircling Brad and the two policemen. Their curiosity builds. Several members of the crowd begin firing off questions. The officers briefly detail the situation and then ask everyone to stay calm and return to their homes. Most everyone moves along, with the exception of a young couple that knows Brad well; they stay with him to offer support. While the police are getting organized, Brad and the couple quietly chat. The senior of the two officers, a fellow by the name of James Nesmith, returns shortly thereafter and asks Brad if he's ready to go inside to collect evidence. The younger officer stays behind to take statements from anyone who might have witnessed anything.

Brad accompanies Officer Nesmith through his home and points out what has been misplaced. Charcoal-colored powder is sprinkled in several key areas and then gently brushed off to reveal any fingerprints. No traces are found, except for Brad's prints. It is concluded that the men must have worn gloves. Brad is asked if anything is missing. At this time, he is unable to identify anything that is gone. Not until he can carefully sort through his books, files, and desk will he be able to clearly define his losses.

A preliminary assessment is written down on a set of carbon-copy forms attached to a clipboard. After each officer has signed his name, the form is then handed to Brad for review. Once Brad feels that the documents are accurate, Officer Nesmith asks him for his signature and then hands him his card. He asks Brad to phone him after he's had an opportunity to further inventory his belongings. With genuine gratitude, Brad walks the men to their cars and thanks them profusely. Now with their cars' blue lights turned off, he watches the policemen drive off slowly along the seemingly desolate street and gives them a wave as they round the corner.

Turning back toward his apartment, Brad feels a lonely uneasiness. He can't help but wonder what the men were after and what would happen if they were to return now that the police have departed. As soon as he's through the front door, he hurriedly closes it and locks it and then drags a large chair to block the entrance. In the bedroom, after closing the windows, he locks them and then yanks the curtains closed. Next, he turns on every light in the apartment, giving Brad a minor sense of security. He then slumps down on the couch to decide his next step.

Reaching for the phone, he elects not to call his parents for fear of worrying them. He pushes the familiar seven digits of Sandy Starke's cell phone number. After four or five rings, his voicemail picks up. Brad hangs up without leaving a message. Instead, he immediately turns around and pages Sandy on his beeper twice in close sequence to get his attention. Not more than ninety seconds pass before Sandy is on the other end of the phone. His voice is cheerful but a bit antagonistic.

"Hey, Brad, what's the emergency? Do you need some advice on cooking dinner or something?"

"Listen, Sandy, where are you? I need your help right away."

Sandy is caught off guard by the uncharacteristically frightened tone in his friend's voice. "Brad, what's wrong?"

"When I got home tonight, I found a few guys breaking into my apartment. I scared them off and then called the police. The police just left. ... Do you think you can swing by here?"

"Good grief, are you all right? You didn't get hurt, did you?"

"No, Sandy, I'm fine. I just need some company, and I don't want to upset Julie just yet."

"I'll be right over. I'm at Joanie's; we're almost finished with dinner. See you in a minute."

After putting the phone down, Brad is so immensely preoccupied by what has happened that he leaves his hand on the receiver. Seconds later, while he's staring blankly into the middle of the room, the phone begins to ring. The vibration and the noise startle him. By impulse, he unintentionally answers and hears Julie's pleasant, animated voice rattling off her day's activities. At first, Brad dares not interrupt her. Because of his unusual silence, she senses that something is bothering him. Once he speaks, the pain in his voice is obvious. Julie tries to pry information out of him. Despite his best efforts, he is eventually worn down by her persuasive, loving concern, so he tells her about the robbery. In frank disbelief, she cries out and insists on driving over that very instant. Before Brad can mount an effective argument, he hears only a dial tone on the other end of the line. He knows she's already on her way.

Within fifteen minutes, Brad is surrounded by his closest friends. Sandy arrives first, with Joanie tagging along. Hesitantly answering the door, Brad is hugged warmly by his two friends, who have brought along some dinner for him on a covered plate. For the first time that night, Brad begins to feel less agitated. At that moment, he realizes he is starving. The meal is graciously accepted. After eating two mouthfuls, he hears a knock at the front door. This time Sandy answers the door. A panic-stricken Julie runs directly to Brad. She grabs him and then looks him over carefully, bemoaning the damage to his nice clothing. After assuring herself he is not seriously injured, she allows Brad to resume eating his meal.

Between bites, Brad talks about the car that nearly struck him and the thieves who crept out of his bedroom window. Still quite shaken up, he admits to being afraid to sleep in his apartment that night. Julie and Sandy both offer him a place to stay. Brad elects to spend the night at Sandy's apartment, both to minimize Julie's burden and out of a concern for her safety. Determined to help in any way possible, Julie begins gathering some of Brad's belongings for him. She cries aloud on entering the bedroom when she sees how badly torn apart the room is.

Brad decides not to begin cleaning up the mess in his apartment until the arrival of daylight the following morning. Prior to going with Sandy Starke, Brad walks Julie to her car and does his best to reassure her. Her reluctance to leave him is apparent; he has to continually convince her he'll be fine.

Even though Sandy's couch is comfortable, Brad's sleep is fitful. His subconscious continues to conjure up unpleasant nightmares. Long before dawn's arrival, he is awake, lying on his back, staring at the ceiling. Famished, his stomach forces him to get up. He quietly searches the kitchen for a snack. He downs a large glass of his host's orange juice then returns to the sofa, assembles his clothing, and packs away the sheets and blankets. Still fearful, he waits for Sandy to rise before he dares to return home.

Thirty minutes later, with Sandy accompanying him, Brad timidly unlocks and pushes open his front door and notices that all the lights are still on. Together, the two men walk through the apartment and are relieved when no surprises await them. Sandy stays a few minutes to verify Brad's safety and then promises to call him in a couple of hours. Once the front door is double bolted, Brad eats a quick breakfast and then calls Dr. Collins to inform him of his disaster and to ask permission to take the day off from work. Next, he showers before beginning the arduous task of returning the huge mound of books back to their places on the shelves and sorting through the scattered files.

After meticulously inspecting all of the disheveled paperwork, notebooks, and texts, Brad makes a mental checklist of what's missing. Strangely enough, his credit card statements and checkbooks are undisturbed. Some of the files relating to patient care are gone, as are the first two of his hardbound autopsy journals. Worried, he slides his hand into his briefcase, in search of his third and most recent autopsy notebook. He's relieved when he feels the familiar rough texture of the clothbound journal. Because of the oddness of the things missing, Brad feels profoundly uneasy.

With his inventory completed, Brad locates Officer Nesmith's card in his wallet and places a call to the police station. After being on hold awhile, he hears James Nesmith's familiar voice. He shares with him which items were stolen. After a brief discussion, Brad also explains his theory: that somehow the whole incident must have revolved around something related to his work at the hospital because of what was taken. This intrigues Mr. Nesmith, who explores some of the possibilities. The phone call ends after an appointment is set up at Brad's apartment for that evening to review the evidence further.

Laying down the phone for just a second, Brad recognizes his next task, something he dreads. He dials by memory the phone number to his father's private line at the bank in Cooperstown. While waiting, Brad tries to come up with a way to cushion what he has to say. Never meaning to underestimate his father's strength, Brad finds himself marveling over the calm manner in which his father handles the news.

"Brad, why didn't you call sooner? I'm relieved you're safe. Why don't you check into a hotel for a few days until the whole thing blows over? I'll be happy to pay the bill. Now, listen to me, please don't call your mother. Let me break it to her gently. She'll be worried sick about you. Brad, I need to get down there to look in on you this weekend. I'm concerned about what's happened. I'll make airline reservations for Friday night for your mom and me."

"Dad, that's an amazing offer, but it's really not necessary. I'm really okay right now."

"Not that I'm doubting you, son, but can you pick us up at the airport on Friday night?"

"I sure can."

"I'll call you back later today with our flight number and arrival time."

"You're incredible, dad. I'll look forward to seeing you in a couple of days."

"Be careful, Brad—go check into that hotel!"

"I'll think about it. Thanks for everything."

After speaking with his father, Brad begins to feel a lot calmer. He stretches out on the living room sofa. It is unclear to him if his relaxation arises from feeling safe or from his plain fatigue after having slept only a few hours the night before. After resting for just a few minutes, he anxiously gets up to check all the windows and doors again. Next, he drags a chair to block the front door by wedging it under the doorknob and moves a dresser in front of the bedroom windows. With a newfound sense of security, he crawls in bed for a welcome nap.

Several hours later, Brad awakens in a peaceful state. Instead of getting up right away, he lies in bed for a while, allowing his dreams to slowly drift away. He then begins to wonder what time it is and whether it's time to go to work. Still somnolent, he turns his alarm clock toward him to read the time. As he reads the number, he becomes quite confused. "Why am I in bed at 6:00 p.m.?" Then, with the horror of what happened the night before flooding his mind, he is instantly alert. Leaping to his feet, he once again turns on lights all over his apartment. With his heart pounding, he calls Sandy to ask if he can stay with him again that night, explaining his anxiety over the situation.

Brad manages to sleep relatively well on Sandy's couch. After he wakes up, he thanks Sandy for his hospitality and walks home to shower. Now, thirty-six hours since the robbery, Brad is just beginning to feel like himself again, with his emotions nearly back under his control. In the past, he had found himself complaining at times about the monotony of his life as a resident physician. In contrast, this morning, while on the way to work, he is grateful for the routine.

After arriving at the hospital, Brad first picks up his mail and then goes by the pathology department to drop some things off at his desk before surveying the day's schedule. As he enters the residents' office area, he is surprised to see his chairman standing in the middle of the room. Initially, Dr. Collins's back is to him. Brad decides he must be there to console him over his recent bad experience. However, as Brad gets closer and Robert Collins turns around, Brad is bewildered by the doctor's expression, one of severe displeasure. Before Brad can get a word out, Dr. Collins tersely addresses him.

"Brad, would you please come with me to my office? We've got something to discuss."

Dumbfounded, Brad walks a half stride behind his chairman on the way to his office. Inside, Dr. Alan Richards is seated. He barely looks over as Brad enters the room. After Brad sits down, Dr. Collins walks behind his desk, where he remains standing, his arms tightly crossed. Stealing a glance to his left, Brad notices that Alan Richards's face and neck are scarlet colored and that he grimaces while clenching his teeth. Robert Collins then addresses Brad.

"Brad, I'm terribly sorry about the recent burglary of your home. I know the incident has been very difficult for you. Unfortunately, we have a serious problem facing us at this very instant. I understand that you have continued your investigation into the Kennedy case despite my specific instructions that you refrain from doing so."

"Yes, sir, but I gave that up weeks ago."

Still quite calm, Dr. Collins continues. "Brad, Dr. Richards informs me that you recently borrowed Mr. Kennedy's slides from the Deaconess Hospital without permission. I understand that you also checked out his X-ray jacket and hospital records and even questioned the surgeon in charge of the case, Dr. Westmoreland. Dr. Richards received a phone call from Dr. Westmoreland to ask about the problems with the case. All of your actions have caused quite a stir out at the Deaconess and have cast a poor light on Dr. Richards. To make matters worse, the family somehow got wind of your inquiry. Mrs. Kennedy has made a call to the CEO of the Deaconess Hospital, demanding an explanation of what's going on."

Stunned by Dr. Collins's words, Brad feels terribly humiliated. An unpleasant warmth creeps through his neck and face as he flushes, and he feels sticky perspiration break out over his chest and back. He stammers while trying to explain.

"I'm sorry, Dr. Collins, Dr. Richards. I had no idea my actions would cause this kind of trouble. Please, let me reassure you that I meant no harm to anyone. I still feel that something is amiss with the autopsy slides and report and some inconsistencies are present in Mr. Kennedy's hospital records." Containing himself as long as possible, Alan Richards points to a document on the corner of Dr. Collins's desk, while yelling out, "You see this paper? This is from the *state medical board!* The Kennedy family has filed a legal complaint against me and has asked for a formal inquiry into the case. Not only that, but it's also likely that your actions have prompted a lawsuit over a very straightforward autopsy! I spent yesterday afternoon in my attorney's office trying to figure out how to deal with this mess. *Nice work, Dr. Pierson!*"

Robert Collins's head snaps toward Alan Richards at his outburst. "Alan, that's enough. We're trying to keep this meeting as professional as possible."

"Okay, Robert, I'll keep my voice down, but let's discuss what you and I talked about before Dr. Pierson arrived."

Looking disheartened, Robert Collins now sits down. His shoulders slump as he looks directly at his desktop. It is obvious he is about to say something that causes him great consternation. Brad can see a profound struggle going on within the chairman. After a long silence, Robert Collins begins speaking slowly and softly.

"Dr. Pierson. Brad. ... I'm afraid this matter has gotten out of our hands, and there have been serious ramifications stemming from your actions. I'm afraid some disciplinary measures are required in an instance like this. ... Earlier this morning, Dr. Richards asked for your resignation from the residency program, effective immediately."

As Robert Collins's words echo in Brad's ears, a cascade of thoughts rush through his mind. *I'm going to lose my position! I'll never be able to practice medicine! My life is about to be destroyed!*

Recognizing the tremendous impact his words have had upon Brad, Robert Collins pauses briefly before continuing. Brad struggles to force back his own emotions and strains to pay careful attention to Dr. Collins's next words.

"I must confess that I can see Alan's reason for asking for me to dismiss you, Brad. However, my perspective is very different from Dr. Richards's. I will recommend a six-month suspension to the Residency Review Committee, during which time you will be stripped of all clinical responsibilities. On your return to duties, you will not be allowed to return to the Deaconess Hospital under any circumstances for a period of one year."

Alan Richards makes a brief grumbling noise, which is quickly dismissed by Robert Collins. Now partially appeased, Alan gets up and leaves the room. Brad remains seated, still shell-shocked by what has occurred. Displaying some of the kindness that makes up his remarkable character, Robert Collins seeks to console his resident physician.

"Brad, I'm terribly sorry. You know how fond of you I am, but this had to happen. Too many things have gone wrong over too short a time span. My hands are tied. I'll be sure that any trace of this incident is expunged from your permanent record so that it can't possibly harm you. I did my best for you, son, but I'm afraid that your accessing Mr. Kennedy's records without the family's permission is illegal and legal action against you may be forthcoming. I hope you can respect my decision."

Fighting back tears, Brad, in a defeated tone, musters several words of thanks. As he slowly moves in the direction of the door, Dr. Collins walks beside him. In a show of support, he lays one hand on Brad's shoulder while reassuring him that everything will eventually work out. It is obvious that neither man is happy with the outcome.

Chapter 21

After the meeting with Dr. Collins and Dr. Richards, Brad feels emotionally numb. Horribly confused, he walks to the residents' office area and sits at his desk, putting his face down on his folded arms. Several of the younger physicians come in and stand in the center of the room, chatting nervously while trying not to stare at Brad. They are confounded by his appearance; he is a role model to them, someone of enduring confidence and strength. The defeated man they see before them is barely recognizable, only a shell of the person they know so well.

In his usual boisterous manner, Sandy Starke comes stumbling into the room, teasing one of the junior residents who walks beside him. As he catches a glimpse of Brad, he stops his loud chatter in midsentence and walks in his friend's direction. Gently placing one hand on Brad's back, he stoops over in an effort to get a look at his face. After noting his pained expression, he looks over toward the center of the room and waves everyone else out. He then turns back toward his friend.

"What's going on, Bradley? You look really beaten up. Are you still upset over the break-in?"

Without lifting his head, Brad begins to speak. Because of his physical position, the words are muffled against the desktop. Sandy strains to hear him. As Brad explains what happened in a depressed monotone, Sandy gasps loudly in disbelief. When Brad reaches the part about his six-month dismissal, Sandy nearly falls over.

Instantly, Sandy is furious. While yelling loudly, he paces the interior of the small room. "That jerk Richards! He's such a big baby! I'm going to drive out to his office right now and pop him in the head! What in the world is firing you going to accomplish?"

Touched by Sandy's strong sentiments, Brad gets up out of his chair, walks toward him, and grabs him by the shoulders. While shaking him gently, he looks directly into his eyes.

"Sandy, I agree with you: this doesn't make any sense. Come on, calm down and help me figure out what to do. I need you to give me a hand sorting this mess out."

Sandy relaxes as he recognizes the wisdom of his friend's words. "Okay, okay, maybe you're right. What are we going to do first?"

"Well, one thing's for sure: I need to get out of here. Can you help me pack up my stuff? I can't stay around here much longer."

"Whatever you say, Brad. Let me go get some boxes. I'll be right back."

After Sandy leaves, Brad begins emptying his desk and filing cabinets. After a couple of minutes, he feels the soft touch of a woman's hand on his shoulder. One of the second-year residents who is close to him, Helen Wong, is standing behind him. As Brad turns around, he sees the worried look on her face. Standing on her toes, she reaches up to hug him.

"Brad, I don't know what's going on, but we all care about you. Can you tell me about it? We all want to help."

"Helen, something's happened with one of my cases that I don't quite understand. I tried to pursue it and got myself in some trouble. I'm afraid I've been dismissed from the program for six months. That's all I know right now."

"You've got to be kidding. They kicked you out of the program? Are they crazy? You're the best resident in the place. ... Oh my gosh, Brad!"

With a look of anguish, Helen buries her face in her petite hands. Ironically, Brad finds himself trying to console her while attempting to adjust to his own shock.

"You're sweet to care about me, Helen, but right now, I just need to get out of here. I'll call you later this week."

With that, Brad returns to his desk and continues sorting. Just as he finishes packing up his belongings into a series of cardboard boxes, the remainder of the pathology residents come in and offer to help him carry things out. When the final carton is stowed away in the back of Brad's car, Sandy leans over to close the trunk lid. He then pats Brad on the shoulder.

"I'll call you tonight, Brad. We need to come up with some kind of strategy to get this thing straightened out. We can do it; I know we can."

With a look of gratitude, Brad forces himself to smile. "Sandy, you're a great friend. I don't know what I'd do without you. ... I'm not going to take this abuse if I can help it. Just be careful. You saw what happened to me."

Consumed with a pervasive sense of failure, Brad gets into his car, but he does not drive off right away. Inside the parked car, he weighs his emotions. Fifty feet in front of him lies the towering red brick Vanderbilt Hospital complex. Brad's eyes scan every detail of the buildings he has gotten to know so well over the past eight years. His mind desperately searches for comfort in their familiarity. He pictures the day he arrived in Nashville long ago and recalls how overwhelming the medical center seemed to him then. Now it is a second home to him, a place where a large part of his life has been spent. The memory of medical school graduation then comes back to him, which took place in the courtyard between the hospital and the student building, Light Hall. What a great day that was!

Instead of soothing him, these recollections seem to cause him further conflict. It is time for him to get away. He reaches for the car's ignition switch. After arriving at his apartment, he pulls off his tie and changes into comfortable shorts and a short-sleeved shirt. It is a warm afternoon. Brad plans to spend the majority of it outdoors.

Hurriedly, he unloads the boxes from his car and stacks them in a far corner of the living room. Then, feeling suffocated, Brad desperately seeks to find some open space. Reaching for his keys, he drives in the direction of Interstate 40. By now, the pressure of the situation causes him to drive much more aggressively than he normally would. He does not let up on the accelerator pedal until the sign for Stewart's Ferry Pike appears on the shoulder of the highway. Brad feels somewhat relieved when he reaches the exit ramp.

After several miles of winding hilly roads, Brads makes a sharp turn to the left down a narrow tree-lined entranceway. Two hundred yards later, the shimmering water of a large lake appears, reflecting the brilliant reds and yellows of autumn foliage on its surface. Barely parked, Brad hops out of his car and briskly walks down a winding path by the water's edge. The dirt walkway plunges initially into a dense thicket of trees and underbrush. As Brad inhales air ripe with tree sap and pine pollen, he can feel his pulse slow and his anxiety fade. Twenty yards later, he emerges onto a series of tall rocky cliffs overlooking Percy Priest Lake, which stretches for miles into the distance.

With near complete solitude, Brad is finally able to relax. He takes a seat on one of the large granite outcroppings and stares down at the water's surface fifty feet below. With his feet dangling and the warm sun on his cheeks, his mind can finally go idle. He spends several hours skipping stones and climbing around the rugged shoreline. As the afternoon wanes, Brad has gained some perspective on his temporary career loss. By the time he is back at the parking lot, he finds that some of his confidence has been restored. Within him, he has an odd sense that somehow everything will eventually work itself out.

Heavy afternoon traffic engulfs Brad on his commute back home. By the time he reaches his apartment building, the memories of the robbery and the subsequent events once again gnaw at his intellect. Momentarily agitated, Brad desperately needs to be out in the open air again. Without first going inside his apartment, he jogs off in the direction of Hillsborough Elementary School, two blocks away, where the large campus affords him a pleasant diversion. After walking the periphery of the grounds, he sits down to watch some of the young children play. Their joyous laughter distracts Brad, calming him. As the school day comes to a conclusion and the baseball field and swings eventually become silent and empty, Brad sets off on a long walk in the surrounding neighborhood.

With dusk's arrival, he cuts his wandering short to get home before nightfall. As he winds across familiar streets and dark alleyways, the bright colors of the waning sun contrast against the darkened profiles of trees. He spends the remainder of his journey trying to decide how to break the news to Julie and his parents.

Julie was right. I should have given up on the Butch Kennedy thing long ago. ... Now look what's happened. She'll think I'm a failure. I don't know how I'm going to face her. ... And then, what about

Mom and Dad? How are they going to react when I tell them I've lost my residency position? … I hope they'll understand; I've always wanted them to be proud of me.

With that last thought, a startling realization comes to Brad. He abruptly stops walking.

Oh my gosh! My parents! They're flying into town tomorrow night! I forgot all about it! I better call them as soon as I get home and get their flight numbers. … I guess I'll just tell them the bad news this weekend in person.

Once he reaches the driveway leading to his apartment building, Brad grabs for the keys in his shorts pocket. By this point there is a chill in the night air. The door to his home is just ahead and soon he will be warm! His focus is instantly snapped when a car across the parking lot turns on its bright headlights. They shine directly into his eyes, startling him. Without any warning, the car then revs its engine loudly and launches itself directly at Brad. Responding instinctively, he throws himself out of its path and drops behind a parked car. Then he hears the explosive sound of shattering glass and ripping steel as the car he is hiding behind is struck forceably. Without looking back, he lunges forward to an upright position and sprints off at full force.

Frantic, Brad gets off the street and runs through nearby private residential areas, trying to take shortcuts to stay ahead of his pursuers. He reaches Twenty-Fourth Avenue South in a matter of seconds and leaps across it in several strides. Behind him, he can hear the sound of a car trying to catch him as it accelerates through the surrounding neighborhoods. Using his knowledge of the local area to his advantage, he weaves in and out of the backyards and tiny parks, staying away from any main roads. No matter what he does, however, the loud reverberations of a gunned car engine are never far behind. At one point in his flight, Brad catches a glimpse of the vehicle behind him. His heart sinks as he recognizes the long burgundy Cadillac. His thoughts race: *Who are these guys, and what do they want? Oh God, I need your help!*

Finally, after leaping over wooden fences and dodging trees and dogs for mile after mile, he hears a reassuring silence around him. Against his writhing chest is the warm glint of perspiration. He allows himself a short respite. Nearby is a tiny, completely darkened, one-story home. There, he reclines in the shadows against the house to ascertain his location. Up ahead, he can see where West End Avenue arches across the in-town expressway, I-440. Before leaving his secure hiding place, he plots a course that believes will lead him to safety. Unfortunately, it involves the risk of being seen as he crosses several main roads.

Slinking along in the darkness, he inches his way alongside a series of houses prior to reaching West End Avenue. Once again, he carefully surveys his surroundings before making a move. When things look clear, he slides down a grassy embankment on his hands and knees and lands on the sidewalk beside the large roadway. From there, he crawls forward and crouches between two parked cars. He waits cautiously until there's a break in the fast-moving traffic coming from both directions. Nervously, he hopes he's gauged his speed well enough in relation to that of the passing automobiles and trucks. Finally there is an opening. Hesitating only a fraction of a second, Brad gives it his best thrust forward. The oncoming headlights distract him, causing his heart to pound fiercely out of both fear and physical effort. Astonishingly, several seconds later, there he is on the other side of West End Avenue, unharmed. Barely slowing once across, he continues to sprint in the direction of cover.

Once safely tucked away in the cluster of office complexes and small residences in this heavily tree-laden part of Nashville, Brad feels more protected. He slows to a moderate-paced jog. Without wishing to be readily spotted, he stays in the shadows and away from the streets as much as possible. Deviating very little from his original plan, he meanders toward his final destination.

Atop a hillcrest several miles later, Brad pauses briefly to rest. Beneath him lies the open, well-lit Centennial Park. In the middle of the grounds stands the full-scale reproduction of the Parthenon, appearing majestic with broad beams of light projected on it from all sides.

Bent over, Brad slides quickly down the grassy hillside. He then stays hidden beneath a clump of bushes at the periphery of the park while looking around to make sure he is safe. As he approaches West End Avenue, the air becomes heavy-laden with the aroma of fried food. Not having eaten anything since this morning, Brad is shaky and weak, and the smell is overwhelming. Crawling behind bushes and dashing between trees, Brad reaches the fast-food restaurant in a few minutes. He peers from side to side for a few minutes before moving from his hiding place. Hesitantly, he walks along the back side of the building and slips in a side entry door. Lucky for him, tonight McDonald's is quite busy. Having left his cell phone in the car, he travels unnoticed toward the pay phones, quickly dialing 9-1-1. Two rings connect him with a female dispatcher. As calmly as he can, he describes the events that have taken place and asks that a patrol car meet him at the backside of the Parthenon, where he says he'll stay until the police arrive. He also informs the dispatcher of the break-in at his apartment two days ago, when he first saw the burgundy Cadillac, and mentions James Nesmith's name as the officer at the scene. In the woman's professional but empathetic voice, Brad finds security. She tries hard to convince him that he'll be safe very soon, but Brad is still horribly shaken up.

Certain that it will take at least ten minutes for the police to arrive, Brad goes to the bathroom to clean up. Looking in the mirror, he sees the obvious evidence of his physical effort. His shirt is darkly discolored with sweat, and his hands and knees are badly dirt-stained. First, he pulls off his shirt, and then he washes his chest and arms thoroughly, using paper towels to dry himself. Then, he uses the wall-mounted hand dryer to dry his shirt. The warm air feels so good against his cold body that he kneels under it to let it run over his head and chest. During this time of drying himself off, several customers come in and out of the bathroom, each giving him a curious stare, but noone gathers the mental strength to ask him what he is doing. Feeling more present-able and certainly warmer, he returns to the dining area. At the counter, he orders a light meal to go and then stands with his sacked-up food by the exit for several minutes. Fear weighs heavily upon him, making him reluctant to leave the safe enclave and step back out into the uncertain darkness.

After opening the door, Brad plunges into the open air, quickly seeking refuge behind dense foliage on his way back toward the park. Only a few yards away from the restaurant, Brad realizes he's made a serious time miscalcula-tion. Two black-and-white police cars drive swiftly right past him. He now runs, trying unsuccessfully to catch them. The vehicles pull up alongside the Parthenon, leaving their headlights on.

Brad is about fifty yards behind when two uniformed police officers appear from each car. As he approaches them, he slows to a walk. After hours of fear and pursuit, he finally begins to feel he'll be rescued from this horrifying misery. As he gets closer, he actually begins to smile as he approaches his rescuers. Before they have seen him, he is startled when he sees the men draw their guns. Stunned, he slides behind a tree and listens. The most senior member of the group, a tall blond-haired man, instructs the three other policemen to fan out and then yells commands to them.

"Remember, this fellow Pierson's armed. He just shot a clerk during a liquor store robbery. *If necessary, use your weapons.*"

A gong goes off in Brad's head as he hears these words that make no sense, causing his knees to buckle beneath him. He braces his fall to make as little noise as possible, but the paper sack containing his food strikes the ground. Fortunately, the sound is not heard by the policemen, who continue to look straight ahead. In sheer astonishment, Brad lies on the warm, moist ground trying to understand what just happened.

How could the police think I'm dangerous? I'm the victim here! What's going on?

Not making a single sound, Brad runs in a stooped-over position to a nearby office building and slides around the corner. From there, he sprints off, hopelessly confused and utterly exhausted. Anguishing thoughts plague him.

Why are both the police and criminals after me? What is this all about?

Assuming that the police have set up a perimeter to arrest him, he utilizes residential areas as much as possible to stay hidden and runs in a random path away from Centennial Park. Following many hours of intense effort, his thigh muscles begin to cry out in fatigue. Mentally preoccupied, Brad is not as careful as usual. A mile or so into his flight, he manages to trip on a large tree root, sending him facedown onto a grassy lawn. He lies there motionless for a while, wondering if he has the strength to get up. Then, a piercing pain in his left leg announces itself. From a moderate-sized abrasion over his shin, warm blood slowly oozes out.

Rolling over, Brad forces himself to a sitting position. He compresses his wound for several minutes to slow the blood flow. Then, for the sake of survival, he concentrates hard to clear his mind and come up with a plan of action. Downtown, because of its crowds and its distance from his current location, would potentially offer him safety from his would-be captors. Again, and hopefully for the final time, he sets off in search of a safe haven.

Initially, things go smoothly. Brad detects no sign of either the men driving the Cadillac or the police. He continues his trek until he reaches the intersection with Interstate-40, where most of the secondary streets dead-end. His limited options become clear: he can place himself in full view by traveling across one of the bridges that cross over the highway, or he can take his chances by crossing the expressway itself. With two such unpleasant choices, Brad decides he'd rather dodge fast-paced traffic. Climbing down a concrete embankment, Brad waits until there are very few cars in sight. He quickly crosses the eastbound lanes and hides behind a pillar until an opening arises in the westbound traffic.

Once across, Brad formulates a plan to make a mile dash along back alleyways and come out on one of the principal downtown streets, Broadway, which should be relatively busy this time of night. There, he'll try to blend in with the crowds and use a pay phone to call one of his friends.

Approximately two blocks from the center of downtown, Brad climbs atop a flat-roofed building using fire emergency stairs to look around. Just ahead, he sees a three-story, pink neon guitar attached to the front of a building identifying Hard Rock Café's location. Deciding this is as good a choice as any, Brad scours the area from his perch and then climbs down to the street level. Once on the sidewalk, he slows to a fast-paced walk to avoid drawing attention to himself. It is now almost nine o'clock. The temperature continues to plummet, sending Brad into a hard shiver. The loss of his McDonald's food earlier was a tough one. He is completely starved.

Twenty feet ahead, Brad can see people going through the double doors on their way into and out of the casual eatery. He is nearly safe! However, off to the right, something nags at Brad's peripheral vision. He sees a police car trolling the area. To avoid detection, he steps inside and peers through the glass of the door. Within minutes a second police car drives by very slowly with two policemen carefully surveying the crowd. Maintaining a constant vigil from just inside the doorway of the restaurant, he waits to step outside back into the darkness until half an hour has lapsed from the passing of the second police car. Unbeknownst to him, his assailants have a police monitor in their car and have been monitoring police radio communications. The police initially set up a perimeter around Centennial Park and the surrounding area in their search for Brad. When that didn't yield results, their best guess was that Brad fled to the downtown area. The men, who have been in pursuit of Brad, followed the police's lead and are now scouring the area where Brad is located. As he leaves the protection of the restaurant, he tries to maintain protective covering by hiding in the crowds of people walking on the sidewalks outside of the Hard Rock Café. He then mentally composes an escape route away from downtown Nashville. A short distance later, only moments from the time he left the restaurant, he is horrified when he hears a man yell, "*There he is!*" and recognizes the hated burgundy car. In sheer anguish, he almost throws himself to the pavement, thinking, *How can this keep happening to me? I can't possibly go one more step!* Brad's mood quickly turns from fear to rage. An overweight man climbs from the backseat of the Cadillac. Brad dashes directly at the car and slams the door against the man's head. The attacker falls to the ground. Brad, kicking him in the chest and abdomen, shouts, "Leave me alone. Just leave me alone!"

Two men from the other side of the car jump out and run toward Brad. Recognizing he is in imminent danger, Brad chooses to flee and turns back in the direction of the restaurant. One block farther down Broadway while running at top speed, Brad turns onto a narrow one-way cross street, the cobblestone-paved Commerce Street.

Tall, Victorian-style, turn-of-the-century warehouses line the darkened narrow avenue on both sides. Brad is forced to leap over garbage cans and dodge oncoming traffic during his escape. Up ahead, he can see where Commerce Street dead-ends along the Cumberland River. Still at a full sprint, he recognizes he is running out of options.

Are they behind me? Where are they? I can't see them! After a split-second of indecision, he presses on toward the river. As he turns the corner onto First Avenue North at a full sprint, Brad's sugar level quickly drops and his stamina wanes. To his dismay, he hears the recognizable drone of a Cadillac engine at his heels as he arrives in a wide-open area. Again he struggles with his choices.

A dive in the cold Cumberland River will only hasten his demise, but he hasn't the strength to fight off several attackers who likely have weapons. Without faltering, he dashes across the wide street and onto a dirt path beside the river, searching for yet another escape route.

With tires squealing and voices yelling at him from behind, Brad begins to lose faith. Then, just up ahead, he sees a familiar circular row of flags, and he remembers Julie's comment about water taxis that leave Riverfront Park every few minutes. Scaring him nearly to death, gunfire erupts from the car, and bullets zip through the air by his head, narrowly missing him. Beside the bank of the river, he sees a boat preparing to leave the dock. His calf muscles cringe as he pushes hard one final time. If he misses the boat, he'll have to jump into the river to save himself. Flying down four flights of steps next to the river's edge, Brad takes one final desperate leap, which lands him in the back of the thirty-five-foot fiberglass craft. As he glances toward land, he sees three men dressed in suits standing on the pier, staring in his direction. His peace is short-lived, because moments later he feels someone from behind grab him firmly by his shoulder. He reels around to discover an overweight, bearded ticket collector. "Now what was that all about, sonny? We're sold out here! Wasn't you willin' to wait for the next one? Now what are you doin' on my boat!"

Brad, bending over and grasping his knees to catch his breath, pleads with the man while trying to think quickly.

"You don't understand. It's a matter of life and death! My sister called me at home an hour ago and told me that my mother had just had a stroke at a concert at Opryland. My car broke down five miles up West End, and I couldn't find a taxi. I ran all the way to get to you. You're my only hope!"

Immediately, the man's expression softens, and he gruffly apologizes. With regret in his voice, he explains to Brad that he'll have to collect the admission fee, or he could lose his job. Then, in a surprising turn of events, the man walks him below to the sheltered cabin and throws a blanket over him. He then acts as a spokesman for the bewildered young Brad.

"Folks, this poor young fellow's mama just had a big ol' stroke out at the Opryland, and he's ridin' with us just to git to her. He's just as cold and sweaty as he can be. Is anyone willin' to give up their seat for him? I sure know he'd be mighty grateful."

Congruent with the tenderhearted people of this part of Tennessee, a dozen of the passengers stand to offer their seats. One man then surrenders his worn sweatshirt, and another offers a Nashville Sounds baseball cap to keep Brad warm. An older woman comes to him and offers a sandwich she'd saved for later and tells him she'll pray for his mother. Meanwhile, Brad is feeling guilty about having taken advantage of people's generosity under a false pretense. Understandably, the truth would be a little harder to explain—and even Brad himself is not exactly certain what the truth is at the present moment. In any event, the outpouring of love has deeply touched him.

Not naïve, Brad recognizes that his safety is transient; the men seeking him will know exactly where this boat ends up, and Brad is confident they will be waiting for him on arrival. The cap and oversized sweatshirt will provide a partial disguise when he needs to blend in with the large group of passengers who get off at the first stop, the Opryland Amusement Park and Concert Hall. He is hopeful the men may not spot him. If all goes well, they may look for him at the second stop, Opryland Hotel, which will give him some time to escape.

Knowing for the moment that he is out of harm's way, Brad settles in to enjoy the twenty-minute ride as much as he possibly can. His frozen limbs are beginning to warm up with the combination of the heat of the enclosed cabin and the blanket draped over him. The sandwich Brad eats barely makes a dent in his ravenous appetite. He flags down the steward to ask what sort of food they carry. Soft drinks and crackers are not much of a meal, but to Brad it is a feast.

After he has finished eating, Brad begins to scour the shoreline, trying to find some landmark to identify the position of the boat. According to his watch, it is now 10:30 p.m. They've been under way for just over ten minutes. Off to the right are the bright headlights of cars traveling along a major road. Brad decides that must be Briley Parkway since they're about five miles from Opryland. A few minutes later, the captain announces the first stop, which is coming up soon, and instructs the crew to prepare for docking. With that, Brad again thanks his fellow passengers for their gifts and jots down the names of the woman and the two men who donated items to him. If he is still alive after all this, he promises himself that he'll return their generosity.

Along the shallow silt-packed shoreline lies a large, well-lit concrete embankment. As the motor slows and the boat comes to a standstill, Brad gets ready.

He waits for several small groups of people to depart before making his exit. Then, after thanking the bearded ticket seller, he finds his way to the center of a large crowd. While climbing several flights of stairs, Brad tries to stay in the middle of the group. He dares not look around, but up ahead he can see the back entrance of the Opryland Concert Hall. Pulling the baseball cap down over his face, he keeps his head ducked and pulls a twenty-dollar bill from his wallet. The group quickly disperses at the ticket booths. Brad hurriedly purchases the cheapest seat and rushes toward the turnstiles.

For the first time, he glances around at his surroundings. Across the courtyard, he recognizes two of the men who were standing by the boat dock at Riverfront Park. They have already spotted him and are moving in his direction. Nervously, he drops his ticket as he runs toward the concert hall. Weaving through the crowds in the foyer, he runs the entire length of the back hallway. A backward glance confirms that the men are not far behind.

Bursting through a side exit door, he immediately comes upon a tall chain-link fence surrounding the Opryland amusement park complex. With one leap, he lands halfway up the fence with his fingers spread and his toes pointed. He then vaults his body up and over the top in a single motion and scales down the opposite side of the fence. As soon as his feet hit the soft dirt, he's off at a full sprint. The park closes early at this time of year. There's not a single soul to be seen as Brad dashes past the stationary rides and empty food courts.

Perhaps only minutes ahead of his pursuers, Brad begins to hunt for an obscure hiding place. As he reaches the crest of a short hill, he comes across a ride that resembles a log flume. Two water-filled tracks from a tall incline look as if they convey fiberglass logs containing passengers to a large pool below. From there, the logs pass under a wide concrete bridge just above the water's surface. With the water to the flume turned off, nearly four dozen empty logs lie floating in the pond beside the bridge.

With a quick hop, Brad is over the fence that encloses the ride. He then runs alongside the man-made pond almost all the way to the bridge. Leaning over, he manages to grab hold of one of the logs. He jumps in. Using his cupped hands, he paddles several feet to get underneath the bridge, and then he slinks down inside the fiberglass craft. He uses the other logs around him to maintain his position and keep him from drifting. Once he is settled, he strains to hear any sound. He quiets his heavy breathing by pulling his sweat-shirt over his nose and mouth.

Not long after this, Brad can hear several men speaking loudly nearby. Their footsteps get closer and closer, causing Brad's heart to pound loudly. Then, to Brad's horror, they are standing directly over him on the bridge. He can discern part of their conversation. One fellow's name is Dave, and his accent smacks of Manhattan or upper New Jersey, and the other, whose name is not mentioned, has a rural Southern accent. Judging by what they've said, they are carrying guns and do not plan to let Brad live if they find him. Unfortunately, they fail to divulge why they are after him.

While the men are overhead, Brad rigidifies his body and holds his breath, hoping not to call attention to himself. It seems like an eternity until they move on. Brad begins to feel some relief when their voices trail off and can no longer be heard. After having to stay completely still for such a long period of time, Brad's muscles begin to tremble when he allows himself to relax. Knowing he'll have to stay in his current hiding place until morning, Brad searches for a way to secure the position of his floating log. Not long afterward, he locates a short piece of rope, which he uses to anchor his boat to the bridge overhead. He then curls up and wraps his sweatshirt over his knees. That night, underneath the clammy dark bridge, he sleeps only intermittently, a few minutes at a time.

The long night cannot end soon enough. When the park finally opens the following morning, Brad decides it's safe to leave his hiding place. Initially, workers noisily warm up the rides, and then Brad can hear the voices of park visitors. As he begins to move, he notices that his back and legs are terribly stiff and cramped. Moderate effort is required to arrive at a sitting position. With both hands, he releases his rope and then pushes against the rough concrete undersurface of the bridge to move his tiny craft out into the open. Accustomed to the cave-like quarters, he strains his eyes in the bright morning sunlight. Then, reaching up, Brad grasps the edge of the bridge and pulls himself to a standing position in the fiberglass log. Struggling to maintain his balance on the tiny boat, which threatens to tip, he manages to get both feet on the side of the bridge. Then, he takes a single step over the railing and calmly walks in the direction of the entrance.

Still quite apprehensive, Brad scours the area around him at all times and stays near the more populated walkways and attractions. When he sees the sign announcing the upcoming exit, he ducks into a small souvenir shop to use their pay phone. After reaching a taxi company and instructing them to meet him at the entrance to the park in thirty minutes, he turns his attention to the clothing section of the store. The staid woman at the cash register locks her eyes on Brad and follows his every movement, undoubtedly because of his rough appearance. He selects a complete attire of Opryland paraphernalia: oversized sweatpants, a sweatshirt, and a cap. To allay the clerk's fears, he pays in cash. The new outfit serves two purposes. First, his current clothing is badly soiled, and second, the men following him know exactly what he was wearing the night before.

A quick trip to the bathroom gives Brad an opportunity to change. The next order of business is breakfast. The clothing purchase has left Brad cash poor, but luckily there is a bank fast-teller machine in the vicinity. He withdraws a sizable amount to get him through the next several days. At one of the open-air cafés, he hurriedly consumes two Danishes and a fruit drink and then walks toward the exit. Standing behind some large shrubs by the front gates, Brad sees his cab waiting for him. It is quite a distance to the parking lot, and he's afraid to be out in the open that long. The question of whether the taxi driver will wait for him causes Brad a great deal of consternation. He turns his head back and forth quickly, in search of an appropriate opportunity. At that moment, two long yellow buses full of elementary schoolchildren pull up, and Brad makes his move. Running bent over between long rows of second graders who stare at him, he safely reaches the cab. In minutes, he's away, with the driver grumbling about his tardiness. After specifying his destination, Brad slumps down in the backseat and peers in all directions through the rear windshield. Having decided to get as far away from the Briley Parkway area as possible, Brad discovers that the trip ends up being a relatively lengthy one. After a series of highway interchanges, Brad sees the sign for Brentwood. Shortly thereafter, he is in front of a large Holiday Inn, situated adjacent to Interstate 65.

The receptionist at the front desk gives him the once-over because of his tourist-style clothing and lack of luggage. Brad fights hard not to be nervous under the close scrutiny. Aware that any credit card transactions could provide his location, he asks if he may pay for the room in cash. This again raises eyebrows. Brad's hand shakes slightly when he signs a false name to the registration card.

Once inside his room, he is better able to relax. He does, however, secure both locks and push a dresser in front of the door. Next, he reaches into the middle drawer of the small wooden desk to pull out a phone directory. Aware that his pursuers may have tapped the phones of his close friends and family, he struggles to come up with someone whom he can safely contact. Flipping through the listings for Franklin, he turns to the page containing last names beginning with the letter *H*. With his right index finger, he runs down several columns until he finds the desired entry.

Anxiously, he barely breathes as he dials the number. After a seemingly endless series of rings, he hears the affable, slow-talking voice that he is very familiar with on the other end of the line. So grateful is he to finally find a friend that he blurts out his first few words.

"Mr. Hill?"

"Yes, sir, it is."

"Jimmy, this is Brad Pierson—"

Before Brad can finish his sentence, Jimmy exclaims loudly, interrupting him, "Dr. Brad, *where'a you been, son?* Julie and Ms. Christensen, they'a been worried jus' sick about you. Where in the goodness are ya?"

"It's a long story, Jimmy, and I can't tell you much of it right now. I desperately need your help, though."

"Whatever you say, Dr. Brad. Tell me what I can do."

"First of all, don't tell anyone you've heard from me. The people after me might try to hurt Julie or her mom if they think they know where I am. Understand?"

"Whaddya you mean, the people *after you?*"

"I'm sorry, Jimmy, I can't explain right now. But just don't tell anyone you've spoken to me."

"Whatever you say."

"The next thing is, do you still have your gray pickup truck?"

"Sure do, Dr. Brad."

"Do you know where the Holiday Inn in Brentwood is, Jimmy?"

"The one over by Route 65?"

"That's it."

"Yeah, I know exactly where it's at."

"I'd like you to pull up in front of the hotel at eight o'clock tonight with the back end of your truck almost up against the front of the building. Leave the tailgate down for me, and if you have one, put a cover over the bed. I'll come around the side of the building in the dark and crawl in back. When I'm safely inside, I'll knock on the cab behind you."

"All right, I think I got it. I'll be seein' you at eight o'clock."

"God bless you, Jimmy. … Listen, I'd better get off the phone now. I don't want to get caught. If anything happens to me, mention the name Butch Kennedy to Julie."

"But Brad, what's wrong with me a comin' after ya right now? I'm scared over this whole thing, I don't mind tellin' ya."

"I don't want anyone to get hurt, Jimmy, and I think this is the best way. See you tonight, I hope."

As soon as Jimmy Hill hangs up, Brad calls another number known to him by heart. It is his pastor, Drew Henry—his private line at the church. After speaking a few muffled sentences to Dr. Henry, Brad lays the phone down. Completely exhausted, he sets the alarm for 6:00 p.m. before crawling into bed for a nap. Because of his sleepiness, he jots down a description of the men following him and the unit numbers of the police cars at Centennial Park, concerned that he might forget them later. This being the first time he's rested in nearly two days, the pillow feels incredibly soft as his face lands on it. Within seconds, he's sound asleep.

Meanwhile, Julie is pacing back and forth in Sandy Starke's apartment. She, Sandy, and Joanie are beside themselves and in a panic, not knowing where Brad is. They take turns on the phone calling the police, as well as every emergency room in town, trying to determine Brad's whereabouts. Julie is especially distraught over the fact that Mr. and Mrs. Pierson called her last evening when they were unable to reach Brad to give him their flight numbers for their arrival tonight. Sandy does his best to calm the teary-eyed Julie, but it is obvious that he's also quite upset.

Several hours later, Brad thinks he's dreaming when he hears the alarm clock buzzing beside the hotel bed. A huge amount of effort is required to pull himself from the intoxicating sleep. Feeling almost hungover, he rolls over and falls out of bed, crashing to the floor. First crawling and then standing, he staggers toward the bathroom. He hopes a shower will clear his mind. After getting cleaned up, he looks at his watch, noting the time as 6:30 p.m.

Cautiously, he pulls back one corner of the curtains and peers out the eighth-story window of his hotel room at the darkened grounds and highway below. No sign of either the burgundy Cadillac or Jimmy Hill's truck yet. Now he waits.

Just before eight o'clock, Brad sees Jimmy Hill's familiar truck arrive, with white epoxy filling the dent on one side. He watches Jimmy park in the front parking lot off to the left side of the building and turn his lights off. Now comes the frightening part—how will he get downstairs? Should he risk the stairs, or is the elevator safer? Are they waiting for him? Taking a chance, he calls housekeeping and asks for a rollaway bed to be brought to his room. Aware that a male housekeeper will have to perform that task, he hopes to convince the housekeeper to allow him to ride back down the service elevator with him.

When he hears a knock at the door, he asks the man to identify himself. After the bed is set up, Brad travels downstairs with the housekeeper, without any incident.

From the lobby, Brad walks calmly down a short hallway and to the left, where he sees an exit sign. Hunched over, he pushes the glass door open and looks both ways. On his hands and knees, huddled close against the building, he crawls around the corner and slides into the back of Jimmy's truck. With his right hand, he painstakingly pulls the steel tailgate closed as quietly as possible and then knocks on the back of the cab several times. The engine starts. He is relieved when he feels the vehicle slowly pick up speed.

Chapter 22

Very relieved that he might finally be safe, Brad barely notices the bits of straw and gravel that grind into his knees and elbows as he crawls along the cool steel bed of Jimmy's pickup. After reaching the back side of the cab, he stops and tries to attain a partially upright position with his legs extended. The tough, dark-colored nylon bed cover overhead prevents him from sitting up all the way, forcing him to lean on one elbow. With his heart still pounding out of fear, he listens carefully to every sound around him, hoping his pursuers are not awaiting him. Unfortunately, much of the background noise is drowned out by the truck's transmission, located just beneath him, as it loudly shifts gears. When things finally become quieter, it seems that all that Brad can hear in the tight compartment is his own loud breathing.

After several miles pass and nothing unusual occurs, Brad's intense anxiety gradually begins to wane. At that time, he begins to pay attention to the journey. Despite knowing their ultimate destination, he is confused by the route that Jimmy Hill is taking. Initially, it is obvious they are traveling at highway speeds, and judging by the sound of rushing cars and the loud diesel engines of tractor trailers, traffic is quite heavy. Because of the heavy dust in the back of the pickup and the pungent aroma of car and truck exhaust, Brad begins to cough. He pulls his sweatshirt over his nose and mouth to filter the air. Fifteen minutes pass. Jimmy Hill slows to get on what seems like an exit ramp. After a brief stop, they begin moving again, picking up enough speed that Brad judges them to be on a highway again.

After a short distance, the vehicle again slows and comes to a complete stop, at which point Jimmy takes a sharp turn to the left. This causes Brad to slide across the bed to the right, but fortunately he braces himself before hitting the side wall. Traveling slower now, as if on secondary roads, Jimmy stops three additional times but continues on in the same direction. Because of the amount of traffic noise around them, Brad is convinced they are somewhere in the middle of Nashville. All of a sudden, they take a quick turn to the right. Given Brad's recent experience, he firmly grasps the steel floor to avoid being tossed around. After another turn, the truck stops and then slowly backs up.

When the vehicle comes to a complete halt, Brad again scrutinizes the background noise for any sounds that might give him a clue as to their location. Unfortunately, it is painfully quiet, with only an occasional passing car to disrupt the silence. To Brad's surprise, Jimmy does not get out of the cab right away, which sends his imagination running wild. Convinced that either the police or the men in the Cadillac have somehow discovered Jimmy and waylaid him, Brad quietly searches the back of the pickup for a weapon. Patting the dusty floor, he comes across a crowbar, which he grabs and holds tightly. Then, he positions himself into a tight ball, so that he can forcefully strike the first person who comes into view. The next sound is the creaking of rusty hinges as the driver's-side door is opened. Beside the truck, Brad can discern the sound of two men walking. He then hears the latch on the tailgate being released. Gripping the crowbar with all his might, he holds his breath and waits. As the steel gate falls open, only a faint amount of light is visible. Brad squints to make out any possible human outlines. Fully expecting to see one of the faces of the men he saw stalking him by the shore of the Cumberland River, he lunges forward. Then, shockingly, he sees only the familiar smile of his pastor, Dr. Andrew Henry. Managing to stop the forward thrust of the heavy crowbar and his body in time to miss Dr. Henry, he ends up falling to the ground at Jimmy Hill's feet. Somewhat bewildered by Brad's actions, the stoic Jimmy Hill reaches out one hand to help him up.

"Dr. Brad, what in the goodness is goin' on? Remember, we're the folks tryin' to help you."

Brushing himself off, Brad can't help but laugh as all of his tension melts away in the company of his two close friends. "I'm sorry, Jimmy, but after what I've gone through over the past few days, I've gotten a little paranoid. I was afraid somehow we'd been caught."

Not saying a word, Dr. Henry nudges both men inside the back entrance of the West End United Methodist Church and pulls the door tightly closed behind them. Concern is evident in his eyes as he speaks quietly. "Brad, given what's happened to you, I think it's wise to get you out of sight. We probably also need to get Jimmy's truck out of here before it's spotted."

Recognizing the merit of Dr. Henry's words, Jimmy prepares to leave, but Brad stops him before he gets far. With heartfelt gratitude, Brad grabs Jimmy around the shoulders and squeezes him tightly.

"Thanks for saving my life, Jimmy! I sure hope this won't put you in any danger."

Profoundly humble, Jimmy Hill responds casually, as if being thanked for something inconsequential. "Nothin' to it, Dr. Brad. Happy to help. Jus' glad you're safe 'n' sound."

Before turning back toward Dr. Henry, Brad makes one further request. "You've got to somehow get word to Julie and her mom that I'm safe, Jimmy, but you better not use the telephone. I'm not certain if they're being monitored, and these guys mean business."

Nodding, Jimmy Hill walks on and waves goodbye, saying over his shoulder, "Whatever you say, Dr. Brad."

Before Brad has a chance to say anything else, Drew Henry pulls him by one arm, leading him into the basement of the church. To guide them, he carries a long, blue-colored aluminum flashlight. As they meander along a seemingly endless series of dark corridors directly beneath the church sanctuary building, Dr. Henry rarely pauses, knowing the way by heart. It's not long until they've reached their destination. Drew Henry points the broad flashlight beam at a darkened recess at the end of a hallway. There, on one wall, is a narrow door. Reaching into his slacks pocket, the pastor retrieves a worn brass-colored key. After sliding it into the lock, he turns the tarnished brown doorknob. On the inside wall, he reaches for the switch, and a suspended ceiling light comes on, bathing the room in a dim yellow light. Apologetic, he explains the living quarters: "I'm sorry there's nothing else available, Brad. I know this is a little bit run down, but it belonged to our gardener, who retired several years ago.

Since then, it's been used for storage and has fallen into disrepair. Only a small part of the original living area is still available. Even so, I feel that the safest place for you right now is somewhere hidden in the church."

As Brad steps inside the room, he notes the sparse furnishings. Against the far wall is a twin bed mattress, without a box spring, on a metal frame. Nearby is a tiny wooden desk along with a wobbly brass lamp with a torn yellow shade that has seen better days. Beside the desk is a wooden chair and a short three-drawer chest. Off in one corner of the room is a door leading to a tiny bathroom, containing a compact shower, a sink, and a toilet. Thankful to be out of harm's way for the moment, Brad is overjoyed at the humble surroundings.

"Thanks, Drew. It's just perfect."

Excusing himself, Dr. Henry steps out for a few minutes and then returns with his arms full. On top of a stack of freshly washed bed linens is a silver tray containing dinner. Brad hurries to be of assistance. After reaching for the tray, he helps stack the blankets, sheets, and towels on top of the bed. At Brad's request, Dr. Henry says the blessing and then stays with Brad while he eats his dinner. Between bites of a chicken salad sandwich and salty potato chips, Brad relates all the events that have transpired over the past several days. Able to control his emotions for most of the story, Brad's voice falters temporarily when he relates the incident of the men chasing him at Opryland.

After Brad finishes his meal, he notices that Drew Henry has taken off his eyeglasses and is staring at the floor. When the pastor lifts his eyes, Brad is able to see within them a look of profound pain, an expression of this sensitive man's empathy for Brad's situation. How remarkably lucky Brad feels to have such a friend. Getting to his knees, Drew Henry asks Brad to pray with him before he leaves for the evening.

"Dearest God, we are so blessed to have Brad here today in one piece, and we know that you are responsible for that. We pray that you will continue to guide Brad to safety and that we might discover who it is who wishes him harm so that they might be captured quickly. We also ask that Brad's friends and family might be protected from the reach of these men. In Christ's name we pray, Amen."

After the prayer, Drew Henry stays a few minutes longer and then tells Brad he'll be back first thing in the morning. Closing the door behind his pastor, Brad's tenuous confidence shatters instantly, replaced with a fear of being left alone. He locks the door and pushes the chest, desk, and chair up against the door. Then he sits down on the bed. To distract himself, he goes in to inspect the bathroom. Despite Brad's moving the wall switch up and down several times, the light fails to come on. He then inspects the desk lamp, now sitting by itself in the middle of the room. The 60-watt light bulb looks new, and it shines brightly when tested. Brad temporarily removes the wooden chair from its position in front of the door and takes it to the bathroom. He stands on the chair to install the new light bulb in the bathroom.

As the light comes on, which barely illuminates the small room, Brad notices the green bacteria that rings the toilet and sink. He then pulls back the white shower curtain, noting it to be in good condition. On top of the toilet is a roll of paper towels and some scrubbing powder, which Brad uses to scrub the sink before he washes his face. After blotting his face dry with a soft cotton towel, he looks into the scratched and smudged surface of the mirror built into the medicine cabinet. He is surprised to see how haggard and drawn his face looks and how deeply recessed his bloodshot eyes appear. This catches him off guard, drawing him into a moment of self-pity.

"Almost killed, fired from my job, scared my girlfriend and my parents half to death. Hiding out under the church while I risk other people's lives. And to think I've managed to accomplish all this in such a short amount of time."

Wrenching out that last statement for the sake of levity, Brad actually starts to laugh, which dissolves quickly into fatigued tears. Physically and emotionally drained, he pulls his sweatshirt back on and makes up his bed. Finally able to lie down and rest, he finds that the fresh detergent smell of the sheets and blankets only partially covers the bitter mildewy smell of the thin, uncomfortable mattress. Fortunately, sleep comes quickly and is deep.

Little does Brad realize that while he lies there asleep, his parents are anxiously awaiting him at the baggage claim department at Nashville International Airport. Terribly upset that they haven't heard from him in two days, they sit patiently for ninety minutes before renting a car to get them to their hotel. Their call to Julie an hour later only hastens their worst fears. She relates to them the fact that she hasn't spoken to or seen Brad in the past two days, and is terribly concerned herself. Uncertain what to do, the Piersons first drive to

Brad's apartment and note his car parked in front, but their hearts sink when he doesn't come to the door. They peer in the front window and, not seeing anything, decide to leave. By the time they've returned to their hotel, they are surprised to see Sandy and Julie waiting for them in the lobby. Although they exchange hugs, little is said until they are back in their hotel room. Calm, but obviously upset, David Pierson begins the conversation.

"Sandy, Julie, thanks for coming to meet us. We just went by Brad's apartment and he wasn't there. Any ideas what's happened or where he might possibly be?"

His anxiety getting the better of him, Sandy continually paces back and forth, stopping only long enough to address the question. "I'm not sure where he is, Mr. Pierson. Julie and I have been looking for him for almost two days. He hasn't phoned either of us, and we've been really worried about him."

At this point, the teary Jean Pierson blurts out, "Has anyone called the police?"

Looking at one another, Sandy and Julie nod their heads to the affirmative. Sandy then says;

"After twenty-four hours went by, we called the police officer from the Hillsborough precinct, James Nesmith, who oversaw Brad's apartment break-in. We have been in constant contact with him."

Out of great concern for his son, David Pierson asks Sandy and Joanie for officer Nesmith's phone number. David Pierson's expression then takes on a dour quality. It is obvious that he is weighing several thoughts. Then, he methodically reaches for the telephone and dials the main number to the Hillsborough police station.

"Yes operator, this is David Pierson. I need to speak to officer James Nesmith about my son, Dr. Brad Pierson, who disappeared forty-eight hours ago...Yes, I'll hold...Mr. Nesmith, thank you for coming to the phone—this is Brad Pierson's father—my wife and I just flew in from upstate New York to look after Brad following his apartment robbery...Do you have any updates on his possible location?...No? How can we help?..Can you give me details on where you are with Brad's disappearance?"

It is nearly twenty minutes until David Pierson is off the phone. All the while, both Brad's mother and Julie, with worried looks, stare at him, straining to hear everything that's said. Muttering to himself, Sandy continues to circle the room. When the call is finally over, David Pierson looks visibly drained from all that's happened. He again consults everyone for their opinion.

"I'm not sure what else to do, but I can't just sit here. What if we call some of the people at the hospital to see if they know anything? … Sandy, you work with Brad. Who should I call?"

Before Sandy has a chance to open his mouth, David Pierson continues.

"I know Brad has spoken many times about the chairman of your department. I believe his name is Dr. Robert Collins. Let's see if I can reach him."

Picking up the phone, David is surprised by Julie's outburst.

"Mr. Pierson, there's something Sandy and I need to tell you before you call Dr. Collins."

Calmly, he puts the phone down. Both he and his wife stare intently at Julie while Sandy looks on.

"All right, Julie, go ahead. You sound like something's wrong."

By now, Julie's apprehension over Brad's disappearance has peaked. She beings speaking quickly in a high-pitched tone. "Brad was going to tell you something when you got in tonight. It has to do with his job."

"We're listening."

"There was this case Brad got involved in, an autopsy. Apparently, he got in some trouble over it and temporarily lost his job."

The shocking news causes Jean Pierson to blurt out, "*What?*"

This time, it is Sandy's turn to speak. "I'm sorry, Mrs. Pierson. We didn't want to tell you, but under the circumstances, we thought we'd better. Brad discovered a mistake in one of his cases, and you know how Brad is, he researches everything down to the finest detail. After Dr. Collins told him to leave this particular case alone, he continued to pursue it, and it caused quite a stir. Because of that, he's been suspended from the residency program for six months."

With a defeated look, David Pierson places the telephone back on the end table. "Well, I don't think there's anything else to be done tonight. The police said they'd send someone by in a little while to give us a briefing. How can I get ahold of you two during the day tomorrow? I know I'll need your help."

After Sandy and Julie write down their home and cell phone numbers, they hug Brad's parents at the door. It is obvious to them that the Piersons need some time alone to sort through what's happened.

On their way home, Sandy expresses concern about Julie.

"You can't stay alone tonight, Julie; I'm worried about you. I already called Joanie, and she said you can stay with her. Let's go by your house and pick up some of your things, and then I'll take you over to Joanie's."

Even though still quite upset, Julie agrees. "All right, I guess that makes sense, but if you hear anything about Brad, you've got to promise you'll call me right away."

When they arrive at Julie's house, Sandy is surprised to see Anna Christensen's Chevrolet Suburban sitting in the driveway with the lights on and the engine running. As Julie gets out of Sandy's car, Anna runs to her and, visibly distressed, will not say anything, asking only that she and Sandy ride with her to Franklin. Once they are inside her large vehicle, Anna insists that Sandy drive. She crawls into the front seat beside Julie. Her reluctance to speak begins to make Julie a little nervous as they travel south on Interstate 65.

"Mom, what is it? You're scaring me. Tell me what's going on."

Suspiciously looking at the cars around them, and then in the rearview mirror, Anna's response is curt. "I'll tell you when we get home."

On the other side of the city of Franklin, Anna directs Sandy to her driveway. Because it is pitch-black along the wooded road to Anna's home, Sandy turns on the high beams, the light of which attracts a host of grasshoppers, crickets, and tree frogs. Instructing Sandy to park in the garage, Anna nudges the two young people inside and hurriedly locks the door. She then turns on almost every light in the house, both upstairs and downstairs, and retrieves one of her late husband's shotguns, which she hands to Sandy. This seems to relax her. Then after walking Julie and Sandy to the living room, she calls Jimmy Hill on the telephone.

"I'm back safely, Jimmy."

"Pleased to hear that, Ms. Christensen. I'll be up shortly with the missus."

While all this is happening, Julie is a little stunned at her mother's unusual behavior. Once they are all seated, she voices her curiosity.

"Mother, what's going on? Why are you so secretive, and what's the gun for?"

Leaning forward, Anna reiterates the story Brad related to Jimmy Hill about what happened to him. Anna reassures her daughter that Brad is safely tucked away in the Methodist church, saying that there's nothing to be done tonight except to try to get some sleep. In contrast to Julie's frightened astonishment, Sandy is immediately angry, threatening to hunt down the men who tried to harm Brad. After everyone has calmed down, Anna suggests that Sandy and Julie stay for the night, but Sandy is extremely concerned about Joanie's safety, so he calls to check on her. After hearing her voice, he's somewhat relieved and mentions he'll be at her apartment in about thirty minutes. Anna offers to loan him her vehicle. Sandy leaves as soon as Jimmy Hill and his wife arrive.

The following morning, a sharp knock at Brad's door jars him awake. Up and off the bed in a single motion, he bounds swiftly across the room and crouches beside the door. Then, without moving any of the furniture aside, he asks who it is.

"It's Drew Henry. I've been out here awhile. Is everything okay in there, Brad?"

From the darkened hallway, Dr. Henry can hear Brad pushing furniture across the concrete floor inside the room. He then sees the door crack open and Brad look out suspiciously before he is allowed in.

"Sorry, Drew, I'm still a little shaken up. I hope I didn't worry you."

Proceeding forward with an understanding smile, Dr. Henry lays down a basket containing an assortment of sliced fruits and pastries. In his other hand are an assortment of Christian books and magazines. Brad notices that over his right shoulder is a cobalt-blue nylon knapsack, which appears to be stuffed full of something. Although famished, Brad's curiosity supersedes his hunger and he asks about the backpack. Without any hesitation, Drew Henry hands it to him, saying, "For you."

Still uncertain about the whole matter, Brad gingerly tugs at the zipper at the top of the bag. Atop a pile of neatly folded new clothing is an envelope, which Brad opens. Enclosed within is a folded handwritten note. Brad immediately recognizes Sandy Starke's handwriting.

"Hey buddy, we've been worried sick about you. I'm so glad you're safe! Anna Christensen got word to us last night that you are okay. I checked on your parents—they arrived safely last night and are staying at the Vanderbilt

Plaza Hotel. I went by to see them this morning and to let them know you're out of danger. They know not to tell the police or anyone else about you. Your parents, Julie, and I are working on a plan to help. Anyway, I figured you could use something to wear, but I was afraid to go by your apartment. Julie helped me guess at your sizes; I hope the clothes are a good fit. Glad you're safe, and let me know what I can do. Dr. Henry knows how to get word to me. – Sandy."

Confused, Brad puts the note down and glances over at Dr. Henry. Seeing his puzzled look, Dr. Henry explains. "I do rounds at Vanderbilt Hospital daily to check on members of the congregation. This morning, when I was in one of the patients' rooms, Sandy found me and handed me this bag."

Finding comfort in the knowledge that Sandy, Julie, and his parents are unharmed and that they know he is alive, Brad breathes a sigh of relief. His mood suddenly changes to impatience, and he reaches out to grab Dr. Henry by the elbow. In Brad's blue eyes, there is a look of controlled agitation, which is mirrored in his voice. "Drew, I've got to see Julie and my mom and dad! Please help me think of a way."

Looking at Brad, Drew Henry does his best to provide reassurance. "Don't worry, Brad, I'll come up with something. Just give me a little time to think about it."

The words give Brad an odd sense of peace about the whole matter, and he releases his grip. After Dr. Henry leaves, Brad again stacks the furniture in front of the door and then turns his attention to breakfast, which is still sitting untouched.

Despite the small selection of books and magazines that Drew Henry brought him, Brad spends much of the day trying to distract his thoughts by reading wonderful Christian novels and current news stories. Unfortunately, Brad spends much of the rest of the day worrying about his situation. After showering, he changes into his new garments and then begins pacing back and forth. Obsessed with wanting to see his parents and Julie, Brad feels as if he has been caged up for an eternity by the time Drew Henry knocks on his door later that afternoon.

To Brad's disappointment, Dr. Henry has not yet arrived on a plan for him to safely leave the church to make contact with his family. In fact, he tries to convince Brad that he may threaten everyone's safety if he is spotted in public. With anxiety clouding his judgment, Brad initially argues with Dr. Henry. As the debate goes on, Brad hears the distant echoes of a gas-powered lawn mower from somewhere near the church. The sound gives him an idea, and he abruptly stops talking. Then, after some reflection, he explains his plan and convinces Drew Henry to help him.

Two days later, Brad is up and showered long before dawn. Dressed in a uniform-style pair of khaki-colored work slacks and a matching shirt, Brad sits and waits patiently at the foot of the bed. As if on a precise schedule, he looks down at his watch when he hears the roar of commercial-sized lawn mowers and the intermittent high-pitched whine of lawn trimmers just outside the church building. A short time later, as the lawn service finishes their work and things begin to quiet down, Brad hears a knock at his door. Slipping on a baseball cap, he quietly opens the door to see Dr. Henry standing there alone. After they weave through the concrete corridors lined with water pipes and heating ducts, they eventually come out to the back loading dock area of the church.

As daylight first strikes Brad's eyes, he winces in discomfort, having gotten used to only the dim light and darkness over the past several days. Somewhat fearful, he turns and glances over at Dr. Henry before stepping outside. Drew Henry's unspoken reassurance gives him confidence. Putting on a pair of sunglasses, Brad walks directly to a large pickup truck parked beside the building. All around the vehicle are the lawn maintenance men, sipping water while trying to cool off before their next job. To avoid calling any attention to himself, Brad doesn't speak to the men but silently acknowledges them with a wave and a head nod. Then, without hesitation, Brad climbs into the backseat of the truck's extended cab, and the lawn crew, also dressed in tan-colored uniforms, follow right behind him. As they drive off, Brad glances back and makes a hesitant wave to Drew Henry, who is still standing on the loading dock. He then turns around to focus on their short journey ahead. From the church parking lot, they turn onto the busy West End Avenue and drive south just a few hundred feet, where they reach the rear entrance of the Vanderbilt undergraduate campus. Three-quarters of a mile later, after winding along narrow paved roads and dodging college students, they reach their destination. Brad initially helps the men unload the heavy lawnmowers, and afterward, he reaches for a rake and follows behind one of the crew members to spread the piled clippings as the grass is cut.

With his head down, Brad inches closer and closer to a bookstore on the edge of campus. Slowly and painstakingly, he proceeds toward the front entrance. Unexpectedly, a large group of boisterous students emerge from the store, startling him. Trying to remain calm, he weaves around them and ducks inside. Carefully stowing his rake just inside the bookstore's entrance, he walks quickly to the back of the store and takes the staircase down one level to the basement. There, after he looks to see if any of the salespeople are paying attention to him, he walks toward the bathrooms in the back of the room. Beyond the entrance to the men's room is a tall door, which is barely visible because of its location in the shadows. When he turns the doorknob, Brad is relieved that it's unlocked. He hurries inside and pulls the door closed behind him, and then he is off, jogging at a fast pace.

Several years earlier, while still in medical school, Brad happened upon a series of tunnels that run under the Vanderbilt campus. He had been in the older part of the hospital, in Medical Center North, at the time and noticed a long corridor beside the old radiation oncology department. Passing by it time after time, he noticed it was almost always deserted. One day, when he wasn't in a rush, he decided to explore. He was surprised by the elaborate underground passageways that went for miles and eventually ended up in the bookstore he has just left. Now, as he hurries along the passageways lit by dim fluorescent lights, he tries desperately to remember the way.

A quarter mile or so in, Brad becomes discouraged given the uncertainty of his location. All the dark, gray, musty hallways have begun to look alike. Then, a landmark appears, a small circular room that is almost dead center under the campus. Relieved at having gauged his course well, Brad gains confidence. From there, the rest of the way is straightforward, so he breaks into a run. Still anxious for his safety, he muffles his breathing so he can hear anyone who might be following him. Up ahead, he comes to a sharp turn and then an incline, where on one side of the hallway are stacked hospital beds and other unused medical equipment. This marks the end of the tunnels. Brad stops for a minute to survey things before proceeding.

After making certain that he is alone, he walks slowly but quietly forward. Just beyond the final turn is a doorway off to the right, which leads to a small storeroom. Glancing at his watch to verify the time, Brad pushes the door open and is surprised to find that the overhead lights are already on. Quickly scanning the room, which is stacked haphazardly with dusty metal desks and bookshelves, his heart sinks when Julie isn't there. Moving slowly through the room, he stops and checks the time again. The minutes pass incredibly slowly, and Brad begins to pace. After he looks at his watch multiple times while becoming increasingly anxious, the door behind him suddenly creaks open.

Ducking down, he hears the clicking sound of high-heeled, leather-soled shoes on the concrete floor. From behind a tall stack of cardboard boxes, Brad peers out. He nearly falls over backward when he sees two legs standing directly in front of him. Just before he hits the floor, he looks up to see Julie's olive-colored eyes staring down at him. In those eyes, he sees both pain and concern. Getting to his feet, he grabs Julie by the waist and swings her around.

"Julie! Julie!"

Ripping Brad's cap from his head, Julie places both hands on his cheeks and kisses him. Uncertain whether she'd find him alive, her emotions bubble over. In the midst of their kiss, Brad can feel warm salt-laden tears trickling down her cheeks. After putting her down, he carefully blots her moistened eyes with the sleeve of his rough-textured shirt. Julie then throws her arms around his neck and buries her face into his chest.

"I can't believe you're okay, Brad! I've been so worried; this has been a nightmare!"

After a long hug, Brad pulls the cloth cover from one of the desks to give them a place to sit down. Then he reaches for Julie's hand. As he describes what has happened to him over the past week, Brad cannot take his eyes from Julie's face. He goes over each detail of her eyelashes, her lips, and her tiny nose again and again as if he could never study them long enough. While Brad relates the chain of events, Julie's face grimaces in abject horror. Halfway through, she interrupts him.

"You mean they chased you all the way to Opryland and they had guns? It's a miracle you're alive."

"Yeah, I know. I can't believe any of this is happening to me. Why would anyone want to hurt me?"

Unnerved by the story, Julie stares at the floor, thinking. Several minutes lapse before she says anything.

"I may have an idea of somebody who can help us. My father's best friend was a man by the name of George Adams. Mr. Adams is a retired county sheriff and has stayed in contact with my mom since my dad's death. He now does private detective work. I'll call him and see if he has any advice for us."

A little nervous about the suggestion, Brad reminds Julie of his last encounter with the police.

"I understand your concerns, Brad, but Mr. Adams is a family friend. He and my parents knew each other when they were children. I don't know of a more ethical man than George Adams. I promise."

Anxiously looking at his watch, Brad stands up.

"Julie, I've got to get back. I'm supposed to meet the lawn crew in a few minutes."

As he pulls his hat back on, Julie asks, "What should I tell Mr. Adams?"

"Why don't you ask him if he could come to the church, to the eleven o'clock service this Sunday? Have him meet me in the men's bathroom off the hallway at the back of the sanctuary at the beginning of the sermon."

"Anything else?"

"No. For now, I think all I need is a chance to talk to him."

After helping Julie up, Brad hugs and kisses her a final time. He then opens the door to the storage area and peers side to side. Not seeing anyone nearby, Brad reaches for Julie's hand and pulls her out behind him. Apprehensive, Julie won't allow him to leave immediately.

"When will I get to see you again, Brad? I'm still real worried about you."

"I'm not certain about anything right now, Julie, but don't worry. I'll find a way for us to be together again soon. Promise me you'll be careful; I'm afraid they might try to hurt you."

"I'll be fine, Brad. I'm staying at Mom's for the time being. I feel so much better since I've gotten to see you!"

Reluctant to leave, Brad encourages Julie to return to the safety of her workplace. He waits until she safely reaches a crowded corridor before he sprints off. Back in the bookstore, he grabs his rake and hurries to meet the men he knows he has unintentionally kept waiting.

It is not until nightfall that he is once again safely in his hovel in the church basement, having traveled the remainder of the day with the lawn crew.

Sunday morning rolls around without further incident. George Adams, in his somewhat aged, bronze-colored Chevrolet sedan, arrives prior to the appointed time in the side parking lot of the West End United Methodist Church. Unassuming in appearance, George's receded hairline, gray handle-bar mustache, and moderate belly is more reminiscent of a local farmer than of a retired law enforcement official. He slides into the sanctuary unnoticed, and takes an end-pew seat toward the back of the room. After getting settled, George pulls out a pair of wire-rimmed, rectangular reading glasses and tries to blend in by pretending to study the paper bulletin. Two hymns and one prayer into the service, George glances toward a side exit door and quietly eases out. Having verified the location of the men's room on the way in, he now walks patiently in its direction. Before entering, he knocks twice. Not getting a response, he pushes the door open. A study of the room reveals two stalls, a urinal, and two unoccupied sinks. Because the bathroom is completely empty, George Adams merely waits. Several minutes pass. Self-conscious, he tries to keep himself busy by washing his hands. Then, clearing his throat, he says, "Julie Christensen sent me." A few moments later, the bathroom door partially opens and Brad emerges. He quickly closes the door behind him. George Adams then retrieves a wire-bound notepad and pencil from his suit jacket pocket. Brad walks directly to George.

"Mr. Adams?"

"Yes, sir, that'd be me. You must be Dr. Pierson."

The relief Brad feels to finally have someone who can help him is obvious in his voice. "Thanks for coming to meet with me, Mr. Adams. You have no idea what I've been through."

"You're welcome, Dr. Pierson, but it'd suit me just fine if you'd call me George."

"Okay, George. My first name is Brad."

"Well, let's get down to it, son. Anna Christensen tells me you're in a whole lotta trouble."

While Brad shares the recent chain of events, George Adams takes copious notes. He is particularly intrigued by the policemen's actions at Centennial Park.

"Are you sure that's what they said?"

"I heard them say to shoot me if I tried to run. They called me a dangerous criminal. I would've thought they were talking about someone else, except I heard them use my name. … It just doesn't make any sense. Why would they be after me?"

"I don't know, Brad, but this is more complex than I'd imagined. I'm going to need some help on this one. I'll find a way to get word to you in a coupla days. Just don't do anything until then. Understand me?"

"Yes, sir."

Before George leaves, he reaches into his coat pocket, pulls out a .38-caliber revolver and a box of shells, and hands them to Brad. With a deadpan look, he asks, "Ever shot one?"

"Never."

"Here's the safety. Now all you have to do is point and pull the trigger."

"Do you think I'll need it?"

"Hope not, but I'll feel better knowin' you got it."

Looking as if he had been handed a completely alien object, Brad, at first, isn't certain how to hold it. After stowing the gun away in his sweatpants pocket, he cautiously opens the door and hurries out. Then George Adams quietly returns to his seat, just as the sermon ends. He walks out with the congregation. After he leaves the church parking lot, he drives not toward his home in Franklin but in the direction of downtown Nashville. Several blocks from the Capitol Building, he enters a residential neighborhood and parks in front of a recently renovated, three-story Victorian home. As he climbs the steep front steps, he takes note of the security cameras, hung under the eaves of the front porch, that track his movements. The doorbell is a simple but pleasant three-toned chime that brings a man's voice over the intercom.

"Who is it?"

"George Adams."

"How do I know that's you, George?"

"Wes, I saved your butt in the Johnson case back in '08. Is this any way to treat an old friend?"

Still staring up at the video camera, George is caught off guard and jumps a little when the door loudly pops open. There, in the doorframe, with his head bent forward, is the substantial, six-foot-four-inch homeowner, Wesley Shiels, the bureau chief of the Nashville FBI. With a firm pat on the back and a big smile, he welcomes George inside. After he shuts and locks the door behind his guest, Wes Shiels leads him into the living room, where they run into Wes's wife, Karen, and their teenaged daughter, Stephanie, both of whom are still in their Sunday-morning dresses. Having known George for many years, Karen Shiels offers him a cup of coffee. Afterward, George and Wes retire to the study.

As they settle into a couple of comfortable upholstered chairs, George notices that Wes's black hair has taken on some gray at the temples since he last saw him, but the intensity of his brown eyes is unchanged. Originally from Illinois, Wes's Midwestern accent has taken on a bit of a Southern twang from his years in Nashville.

"George, what are you doing over here on a Sunday afternoon all dressed up? Are you still doing private detective work?"

Smiling, George enjoys the friendly bantering as he eases back into his chair and takes a sip of coffee. "Well, doggone it, Wes, if your guys down at the FBI didn't screw up so much, us private detectives could just take it easy, but I'll be danged if you don't need me to follow after you all the time."

The comment produces a grin on Wes's face, but his next question is asked more seriously. "What is it you're after, George? I get the feeling something's bothering you."

"Wes, I'll be honest with you. I've come across something that's over my head, and I could really use your help."

"Okay, George, tell me what you've got. I'll see if there's anything I can do."

In order not to miss anything, George reaches for his eyeglasses and carefully reads each entry in his notepad. He relates how Brad, in just a few days, was first burglarized and then fired from his job because of his pursuit of the Butch Kennedy autopsy case. He then describes the men in the Cadillac who hunted him and the police thinking he was an armed felon. Wes listens carefully and interrupts George occasionally to ask questions. His reaction, similar to George's when he first heard the story, is one of frank disbelief.

"Wow, that's quite a story. How reliable do you think the kid is, George?"

"As reliable as they come."

"He's lucky to be alive. Where's our young doctor now?"

"Dr. Pierson's holed up somewhere safe where I don't think anyone will find him for now. And as far as I can tell, there aren't any other obvious players right now. ... What do you think? Can you help me, Wes?"

Stroking his chin while lost in thought, Wesley Shiels takes a moment to reply. His conclusion is similar to the one that George arrived at.

"Seems pretty unlikely that all these things could have happened to one guy in such a short period of time without them somehow being related. I'll tell you what I can do, George. Why don't you come meet me in my office around ten o'clock tomorrow morning and we'll do a little digging. Fair enough?"

The last statement brings a smile to George's face. He reaches over and amicably pats his friend on the shoulder. "Thanks, Wes. I knew I could count on you."

Chapter 23

The following morning, George Adams, dressed casually in blue jeans and a blazer, appears in Wes Shiels's office right on schedule. More serious and businesslike today, Wes tosses a couple of manila files across the desk at George as he sits down.

"I've done a little checking on your fellow's story and was able to get ahold of the officers' log the night Pierson says he was in Centennial Park. It turns out two cars were dispatched from the Hillsborough precinct to the scene. Also a perimeter with multiple police cars was put in place. The senior officer in charge was Sergeant Bill O'Neill. I know him—he's a good man—but this report doesn't say anything about a Brad Pierson. It lists a convicted felon by the name of Lester Drury as the perpetrator of the liquor store shooting. In about an hour, what if we swing by and chat with Sergeant O'Neill?"

"Whatever you say, Wes. You're the boss."

Shortly thereafter, a phone call to the Hillsborough precinct is successful in locating Bill O'Neill, who agrees to meet George and Wes for coffee in a small café nearby. Quite gregarious, the young and muscular blond-headed Bill O'Neill is happy to cooperate in any way possible. His recollections of the incident, now over a week old, are accurate and match Brad's description completely. As they near the end of their conversation, Wes looks over at George and directs a question at the sergeant.

"Bill, do you remember who the shooter was supposed to have been in that liquor store heist?"

"The guy's name began with a *P*, something like Perkins or Peters."

Staring into Bill O'Neill's blue eyes to see if any reaction is triggered, Wes asks, "What about Pierson?"

"Yeah, that's it, Pierson. I was working the late shift that night and was filling out some routine paperwork when Captain Lefevre sent for me. He said there had been a liquor store shooting and that the perp had been spotted in Centennial Park. He said the guy had two previous felony convictions and wouldn't come easily because of the three-strike rule. He told me to take two cars and setup a perimeter around the area because of the armed robbery."

"Ever heard of a guy by the name of Lester Drury?"

Again, there is no emotion in Bill O'Neill's eyes. "Nope. Was he in on it, too?"

Acting very nonchalant, Wes thanks Sergeant O'Neill for his time and informs him that this is a confidential FBI investigation. He instructs him not to discuss the case with anyone else, including Captain Lefevre and any of the other officers who were on the scene that evening. After Wes hands him his card, he asks him to call if anyone mentions the incident or asks questions.

Back at the bureau office, Wes and George sit down to go over the findings of their interview, but they are interrupted before they can get very far. One of the junior agents, Michael Harris, knocks on Wes's door and walks in.

"Director Shiels, I have some information you might be interested in. Remember you told us to put a car on Pierson's parents to keep an eye on them?"

"Sure. What about it?"

"Well, we found another car watching them also."

This gets Wes's full attention. He sits straight up in his chair while staring at Agent Harris.

"We ran the license plate and found out that the car belongs to the governor's office."

Absorbed in the photographs, Wes's head snaps up. "*What?*"

"Yes, sir, it belongs to the state secret service agents assigned to protect the governor and lieutenant governor. We checked it twice." The shock on the faces of both Wes Shiels and George Adams is quite obvious, and the news causes Wes to drop the pictures. Completely stunned, Wes sits down and leans back in his reclining desk chair, contemplating the information.

"The governor's office? The state secret service office? The Hillsborough precinct commander?" Turning to Adams, Shiels asks, "Good grief, George, what is all this? What in the devil do all these people want with Pierson?"

After being silent for several minutes, Wes lifts his head and barks out several commands at Michael Harris. "Harris, go find Assistant Bureau Chief Trimble, and the two of you meet me in the conference room for an emergency meeting! We've got some kind of conspiracy going on here. George, you can come with me."

Ten minutes later, Wes, George, Michael Harris, and Assistant Bureau Chief Martin Trimble gather for an intensive briefing in the conference room at the main FBI headquarters. On a shiny whiteboard at the front of the room, Wes grabs a broad-tipped black marking pen to outline the events that have transpired so far. Before starting, he introduces George.

"Martin, Michael, this is George Adams, a retired sheriff from Franklin County who is now a private investigator. I've worked with him before. He got this whole thing started, so I'll turn the floor over to him."

Before George can get out a single word, Martin Trimble expresses his irritation. "Wes, this is a little irregular, to let some country cop in on our top-level meeting."

Angry, Wes raises his voice. "George uncovered this chain of events, Martin, so you can either zip it or leave. George, go ahead."

Crossing his arms and easing down into his chair, the mildly overweight, gray-headed Martin Trimble elects to stay. Because he is embarrassed, warm perspiration accumulates on his forehead. As George reads from his tiny notebook, Wes jots notes on the board, ending with the most recent events involving the secret service.

After that has been completed, Wes loudly addresses the whole group. "So here's what we've got. We've got a young doctor who is first burglarized and then chased, and an attempt is made on his life. And somehow the police are in on it. We've got a captain at the Hillsborough precinct who seems tied up in it, along with the governor's office and the state secret service. ... I'm not exactly certain what we've stumbled onto here, but I'm authorizing a full-scale investigation. Harris, take notes. I'm assigning Hendricks and Santorino to follow Pierson's parents. I want twenty-four-hour security on them until I bring them in for safekeeping in a day or two. Arnold and Everett will be assigned to pick up Pierson and bring him directly to me. Michael, you and Nelson are in charge of rounding up phone taps after I get a warrant from one of the judges. I also want you to put together the surveillance vans. … Martin, I'd like you to stay here and act as the communications interface and brief the other men on their assignments. George, come with me; we've got a couple of places to go."

In Wes's car, the two men take a short drive to Legislative Plaza, only a few blocks from the bureau office. After Wes parks in a space marked "Official of the Court Only," he and George get out and enter the federal district courthouse building. Very familiar with the building, the two men hurry up the concrete steps and walk past the massive, limestone Corinthian columns in front on their way into the marble-tiled lobby. At the far end of the darkened first floor, they climb up a circular staircase, their leather-soled shoes slapping loudly on the marble steps on their way up. Two flights above, they arrive in the plush decorated outer office of Judge Sydney Isaacson. There, seated at a small desk, is Isaacson's somewhat elderly, pleasant administrative assistant. Before Wes can say anything, she buzzes the interior office.

"Judge Isaacson? FBI Director Shiels is here to see you. … What? … Yes, sir, will do." The gravelly voiced petite woman then looks up at Wes and George. "He'll be a few minutes. Make yourselves at home."

Wes then winks at the woman. "Thanks, Harriett. You're the best."

After a short wait, the pair of broad, decorative, dark walnut doors swing open and the short-statured Sydney Isaacson emerges from his chambers. As the head of the Tennessee federal court, Judge Isaacson wields a great deal of power. Having been in court earlier today, he still wears his long black robe, which drapes over his thin frame. A short gray beard and pensive eyes give him the somewhat scholarly appearance that one expects of a federal court justice. Originally from the Northeast, his careful and precise manner of speaking belies his birthplace.

"Come in, Director Shiels. And who might be our guest today?" the judge asks, taking a seat behind his desk.

"Judge Isaacson, this is an associate of mine, George Adams. Mr. Adams is a retired Franklin County sheriff who works as a private investigator and is helping me out on a case."

As the men get settled in his office, Sydney Isaacson, with his hands folded before him on his desk, addresses George Adams. "Mr. Adams, it is certainly a pleasure to make your acquaintance. ... Now, gentlemen, what can I do for you?"

Summarizing the events quickly but thoroughly, Wes pauses whenever Judge Isaacson has a question. At one point before Wes can continue, the judge interrupts. "I'm gathering the reason you're here before me today is to request legal authorization to monitor the phones of the governor's office and the Hillsborough Police Department. Am I correct?"

"Yes, sir."

"Is there anything else?"

"We also need a warrant to gain access to the landline and cellphone records of Harry Lefevre, the secret service officers assigned to the governor and the lieutenant governor, and the police officers dispatched to the scene at Centennial Park the night Brad Pierson was to be arrested."

Sydney Isaacson readily agrees to the request much to director Shiels's delight. He then addresses Wes.

"Does that satisfy your needs for now?"

"Yes, sir. Thank you, Judge Isaacson. We appreciate your time, sir."

Back at the office, Wes assembles his team again. He instructs Michael Harris to put the phone line monitoring in place and set up two surveillance vans. Next, directing his attention to the two agents at the far end of the table, Wes calls out, "Arnold, Everett, what'd you do with Pierson?"

At first, Jim Arnold is hesitant to respond. "We, we went to the church, but he wouldn't let us in. He said he had a gun."

Wes's tone is sharp. "You mean you didn't get Pierson? Two trained FBI agents couldn't bring in one twenty-nine-year-old doctor who is living in a church basement? Did you do like I told you to do and call ahead so he knew you were coming?"

"Well, we thought we could handle it."

"Nice job. Meeting's over. George, let's go."

Twenty minutes later, with Drew Henry beside them, Wes and George stand outside Brad's door.

"Dr. Pierson, this is FBI Director Wesley Shiels. I've got Drew Henry and George Adams with me. Now please open the door. We're here to help you."

Shaken up, Brad says that Dr. Henry may enter by himself while the other men stay outside. After Drew Henry is inside safely and conveys to Brad that nothing is amiss, Wes and George are allowed in. Once Brad begins to relax, he listens to Wes Shiels's offer of protective custody. Before accepting, he looks over at Dr. Henry, who nods. Brad agrees, on one condition.

"I don't mean to sound ungrateful, Mr. Shiels, but I'd rather stay where I am, unless you can promise me that my girlfriend, Julie Christensen; my parents; and my friend Sandy will also be protected. From here, I can at least keep an eye on them."

"I don't think that'll be a problem, Brad. Now, why don't you get your stuff, and you can go with us right now."

Half an hour later, Brad, Wes, George, and Martin Trimble sit down in the conference room at FBI headquarters. Brad is initially distracted by all the highly technical electronic and video equipment scattered throughout the large room. As Wes asks him questions, Brad initially speaks slowly, trying to assess the men who are supposedly there to help him. After the last several days, Brad can't help but be suspicious. Soon, however, there is an odd quality to Wes's confident demeanor that allows Brad to trust him. Wes goes over Brad's personal recollections before sharing with him the new information that has been collected.

"Brad, what do you think the link is between everything that's happened to you?"

"I can't help but feel this whole thing is related to something at work. During the break-in at my apartment, all that was taken were my notes and files. There was this one case, Randall Kennedy, who died of a heart attack. My notes and photographs differed from the final pathology report at the Deaconess Hospital. When I researched the case, Dr. Alan Richards disagreed with me on the autopsy findings, and he got me suspended from work for six months. But why the burglars would want to kill me, that part I don't understand. And what about the police—why are they involved?"

Wes then discusses the outcome of his interview with Bill O'Neill and shows Brad the photos of the secret service watching his parents. Although previously unsettled, Brad suddenly displays an uncharacteristic anger and his face reddens.

"Who are these guys and why do they want to hurt my family? How can they do this to me? Can't you stop them? Why aren't you out there doing something about all of this?"

Sliding next to Brad, the fatherly George Adams reaches his arm around him. "We're here to help, Brad. And don't worry: we've got several men protecting your parents right now. At this very moment, we're sending some other men to protect Sandy Starke and Julie. We're not sure about every facet of what's happening, either; that's why we got you down here. Now give us some direction."

Now silent, Brad closes his eyes. After several minutes, he slowly opens them and looks over at Wesley Shiels.

"The case I was telling you about, Randall Kennedy; the day the guys in the Cadillac showed up was the the same day I got fired. Maybe there's a connection."

Wes and George exchange glances once they hear this information. George responds with a question: "How do we look into this, Brad?"

"The best way would be for us to get the slides from the autopsy itself."

"Got any suggestions?"

"We need to send someone in who won't look out of place, someone who's familiar with the layout of the pathology department so they can get in and out quickly and not arouse suspicion."

Several hours later while at his desk at the residents' office of Vanderbilt Hospital, Sandy Starke receives a letter-sized package hand-delivered to him by a FedEx courier. After he signs for it, Sandy lays it aside and continues to read. He is surprised when the deliveryman directs a comment toward him: "You might want to open that right away. It may be important."

Looking up at the uniformed middle-aged man, Sandy notices the stern look in his eyes. A bit taken aback by the unusual statement, he decides to unseal the large envelope. Inside is a one-paragraph written note. "From: FBI Director Wesley Shiels. Brad Pierson is with us and safe. Need autopsy slides, Randall Kennedy, Deaconess Hospital. Two agents in an unmarked car will pick you up from your home this evening at 6:00 p.m. Do not tell anyone. Come alone."

Stunned by the content of the note, Sandy turns around to ask the deliveryman a question but is surprised to find the room completely empty. Reading the note again, he has the same thoughts run through his mind over and over. *FBI? How'd the FBI get involved in all this? What's Brad gotten himself into?*

At precisely six o'clock that evening, a white van pulls up directly in front of Sandy Starke's residence. Having looked out every window of his apartment with binoculars for the past thirty minutes, Sandy immediately rushes outside when he sees the vehicle. As he approaches the van, the paneled windowless sliding door opens, and he is pulled inside by two men in their midforties dressed in surgical scrub suits. They identify themselves as FBI agents Michael Harris and David Nelson. Before the door is completely closed, though, the van careens off, causing Sandy to nearly fall over. Inside, Sandy is petrified by the high-caliber automatic weapons the men are carrying. He tries to speak but stammers. After a brief introduction, the two men are silent, except to give Sandy explicit instructions about what to do.

When the van arrives at Deaconess Hospital's loading dock, Sandy is initially quite nervous and shaking. To allay his fears, Michael Harris and David Nelson inform him that they will follow closely behind him. This helps to bolster Sandy's confidence. As they walk through the familiar hallways inside the hospital, Sandy talks to himself in an effort to keep up his bravery. At the pathology department, he musters the best front he is capable of putting up under the circumstances. He leisurely strolls past the main secretary's desk and stops to chat for a minute.

"Good evening, Myrna. What are you doing working so late?"

"Oh, hi, Dr. Starke. Just finishing up some typing for Dr. Lee; you know how he is about his reports. ... Hey, I didn't know you were on duty."

"I'm not. I just came out to use your library to look up a couple of things."

"Well, help yourself. No one else is around, so you should have the whole place to yourself. Call me if you need anything."

"Thanks, Myrna."

More relaxed after his conversation, Sandy immediately goes to work. He first proceeds to the main file log and flips through several pages before he locates the cases beginning with the letter *K*. Finding where Butch Kennedy's slides are supposedly kept, Sandy walks over to the large metal storage area on the other side of the department. Relieved that he is able to find them easily, he matches up the index number from the file log with that of the glass slides.

"Let's see, 99-342-088; yeah, that's it."

To double check, he takes several samples to the microscope to be certain there is no error. Then he takes only a few of the slides, as per the FBI's specific instruction, and drops them into his pants pocket. On the way out, he says good night to Myrna, with his palms sweating and his heart pounding. He quickly heads in the direction of the van and is relieved when the sliding side door is open. As he climbs into the van, his response to the two agents is succinct:

"You're in luck." The van lurches forward.

Inside the main FBI headquarters, there is a happy reunion between the two friends. After grabbing Brad by the shoulders and slapping him on the back, Sandy allows his usual sarcastic manner to take over.

"Why, you little devil, you. Here we were all worried about you, and you're down here eating doughnuts and swapping stories with these FBI types."

Not to be outdone, Brad grabs Sandy and puts him in a headlock, knocking him gently on the skull with his fist.

"Eating doughnuts? I'm down here trying to save the Western Hemisphere while you wander freely about in your cushy civilian job!"

Sandy then snaps Brad's grip on him. The two men wrestle briefly while laughing. Meanwhile, Butch Kennedy's slides have already been packaged and sealed and are about to leave by jet for Washington, DC. Their final destination is the lab of the well-regarded forensic pathologist Dr. Nelson Chang. They should be in his possession within two hours. A conference call has already been scheduled for when he performs his preliminary review. Complex analysis, including DNA testing, special staining, and electron microscopy, will take at least thirty-six hours. Dr. Chang has promised to give the case high priority.

Unbeknownst to Brad, while he and Sandy are catching up on what's happened, a field operative dressed in a bellman's uniform is standing outside David and Jean Pierson's door at the Vanderbilt Plaza Hotel. It was Wes's decision to move the Piersons, as he felt their lives might be in jeopardy. Along with the notification of Brad's continued safety, the note that the disguised agent delivers gives detailed instructions about their move, which will take place soon.

At 10:32 a.m. the following morning, a cab pulls up in front of the bell stand at the Vanderbilt Plaza Hotel. Brad's parents are observed walking out the front entrance and getting in the backseat of the taxi while their luggage is loaded in the trunk. As expected, the black Crown Victoria with Tennessee Secret Service plates is not far off. En route to the airport, FBI agents Hendricks and Harris note that the Crown Victoria closely tails the cab. As David and Jean Pierson board an American Airlines flight back to Cooperstown, New York, both the secret service agents and the FBI carefully monitor their entry onto the plane. Their flight takes off without delay. Once their plane is gone, both cars leave the airport.

In Wes's office, Brad listens to the radio communications and is relieved when his parents make it safely out of town. As he sits by the phone waiting for an opportunity to discuss Butch Kennedy's case with Dr. Chang he hears George Adams call to him from the next room.

"Brad, come on in here for a second. I've got somethin' I need to show you."

Curious about what George needs, Brad gets up and exchanges glances with Wes. As he comes around the corner, and as the sentence "Yeah, George, what do you want?" exits his mouth, he is nearly bowled over by what he sees.

With her arms wide open and tears streaming down her cheeks, Jean Pierson stands in the middle of the room, loudly yelling out her son's name. Beside her, Brad's father, David, smiles broadly when he sees Brad. Running to them, Brad grabs them both.

"Mom! Dad! I thought you were—"

Not allowing Brad to finish, George Adams explains, "The people who left were decoys, Brad. They've been set up to live at your parents' home in Cooperstown, just in case whoever's after you decides to take a shot at your family. We've got the house completely staked out. ... In the meantime, I don't mean to cut your welcomin's short, but we'd best be gettin' your mom and dad down to the safe house in Bellevue. We've got some people expectin' them soon."

Chapter 24

Apthe tissue samples, Dr. Nelson Chang is on the phone with the Nashville FBI headquarters. Gathered in the conference room, Wes, George, Brad, and Assistant Bureau Chief Martin Trimble anxiously await his conclusions. On one wall of the room is a complex audio and video linkup. Not only can they interact directly with Dr. Chang over the large television screen, they can also actually visualize what he is looking at under the microscope. Born in Hong Kong but educated in London, the forensic pathologist has a strongly British accent.

"Dr. Pierson, before we evaluate the slides themselves, could you please describe to me what your conclusions of the autopsy were and what you believe the cause of death to have been?"

"Certainly, Dr. Chang. When I opened the chest and removed the heart, there was a large bruised area on the anterior wall of the left ventricle, leading me to believe that the cause of death was a massive heart attack. The heart itself exhibited striking muscle hypertrophy of both ventricles, consistent with long-standing hypertension. The other organs displayed evidence of ischemia, consistent with a sudden massive loss of blood flow, again supporting a theory of a myocardial infarct."

"Excellent. Thank you, Dr. Pierson. That fills in some of the gaps for me. Let's first look at some of the samples of the liver and kidneys. Let's see, is that in focus for you?"

"Yes, sir."

"As we scan across this cross-section of liver, note the destruction of the primary tissue, the hepatocytes, just around the vascular bundle, the artery, and the vein. As Dr. Pierson is aware, this is called centrilobular necrosis and is consistent with an acute ischemic event such as a heart attack. Now, moving on to the sample of Mr. Kennedy's kidney, we note destruction of the kidney's filtering apparatus, termed acute tubular necrosis. This again fits our working diagnosis as to the cause of death. … However, let's now evaluate the heart. As opposed to what Dr. Pierson told us earlier, the muscle walls of the two main pumping chambers, the ventricles, are not thickened. If you'll look to where I'm pointing the arrow, you'll notice how thin the muscle is and how dilated the left ventricle appears. Now, direct your attention to the bottom of the field. There is a large blood clot in the wall of the left ventricle, which is the site of the heart damage caused by the heart attack. This is exactly how Brad described Mr. Kennedy's heart on initial inspection. These findings precisely match the typewritten pathology reports that were sent along with the specimens, but it differs from Dr. Pierson's account."

Temporarily losing faith in himself, Brad groans quietly. He begins to rethink the entire autopsy, until Dr. Chang resumes his discussion.

"But, now, gentlemen, we come to the DNA analysis. The liver, kidneys, lung, and bowel are an identical match and come from a male of African descent. The heart, however, belonged to a woman of northern European heritage, likely a Scandinavian country."

Certain all along that something was awry, Brad feels vindicated by Dr. Chang's conclusions. Joyous, he yells out, "Yes!" Not feeling Brad's elation, Wes Shiels and George Adams merely stare at the television screen, wondering how to tie this new bit of information to their ongoing investigation. Compelled to ask one further question, Brad wishes to challenge the expert's mind. "Based on your experience, Dr. Chang, what would you estimate Mr. Kennedy's height and weight to have been from the tissue samples we sent you?"

"Given the sheer sizes of the kidneys, liver, and spleen, and the degree of fat surrounding each organ, I would estimate him to have been a man of approximately five feet and nine inches to five feet and ten inches in height, and one-hundred-and-eighty to two hundred pounds in weight."

"Wow, Dr. Chang, you're amazing."

At this juncture, Wes interrupts. "Dr. Chang, I hate to oversimplify things, but what you're telling us is that someone substituted another heart for Mr. Kennedy's, presumably to cover something up?"

"That is how it appears, Director Shiels."

"Thank you very much for your expert opinion, Dr. Chang. Is there anything else you'd like to comment on?"

"I believe that about takes care of things as far as I'm concerned, Director Shiels."

"Thank you very much."

"No trouble whatsoever."

As soon as the audiovisual transmission is terminated, the reserved Martin Trimble immediately turns to Brad to ask several questions. "What's the name of the doctor you worked with on the Kennedy autopsy?"

"Alan Richards. Why?"

"Isn't he the same guy who got you fired?"

"Yes, that's right. But what are you saying?"

"Didn't you two disagree over the autopsy findings?"

"To be honest with you, I began to be suspicious of Alan Richards after I got fired—this new information makes him look guilty."

"I agree with you, Brad—there's certainly enough circumstantial evidence to warrant an investigation."

Having listened carefully to the conversation, Wes adds a comment: "Brad, Martin's right. We need to get surveillance going on your Dr. Richards; he's somehow tied to this entire operation. Harris, get a writ from Judge Isaacson for phone taps on this guy's home and office immediately."

An hour later, over lunch, Wes assembles his team in the conference room to review the new information that has come to light. After much discussion, he expresses one obvious fact: they still haven't identified many of the individuals involved in the conspiracy or their motivations. With help from George Adams, Martin Trimble, and several of the agents present, he devises a sting-type operation that hopefully will bring in more data. Each with his own specific assignment, the men go to work.

Later that afternoon, the plan is about to be set into motion. Using sophisticated, unique-frequency cellular telephones, the agents call in to Wes from their positions when they are fully prepared to move ahead. At 3:16 p.m., with everyone on precise time synchronization, Wes nods at George, who picks up the telephone in the middle of the conference table. He dials the seven digits of Captain Harry Lefevre's private line at the Hillsborough Police Precinct. A large, wall-mounted reel-to-reel tape begins to turn, recording the conversation as soon as Harry Lefevre picks up the phone. George speaks quickly, with his voice being disguised by the electronic equipment embedded in the telephone.

"Pierson's in room 527 at the Holiday Inn Vanderbilt."

"Who is this?"

"You know. Now take care of it right this time. I'll be in touch."

Harry Lefevre then puts the phone down. Brad, Wes, and George anxiously wait to see if he takes the bait. Hunched over in their chairs, they stare at the recording device, which continues to roll. At the moment they're about to give up hope and assume they've accidentally tipped off a savvy Harry Lefevre, they hear a dial tone on his phone. Six rings later, they hear a voice on the other end of the line.

"Yeah, whatcha got?"

"Same job. Don't screw it up this time. Holiday Inn Vanderbilt, room 527. Call me when it's done."

Not stopping to celebrate their initial success, Wes remains focused. He immediately calls Field Operative Bert Hendricks. "It's a go. Repeat, it's a go. They'll be paying you a visit. Get ready. Out."

With the first part of the operation under way, George looks over at Brad, who puts on a set of large black headphones with a microphone at the end of an adjustable mouthpiece. As Brad gets situated, he can see the tension and apprehension in everyone's eyes. When Wes nods his head, Brad makes his call and notes that according to the large digital clock on the wall, it is now 3:38 p.m. The call goes through quickly and is answered after the second ring.

"Pathology. This is JoAnne."

"Could I please speak with Dr. Richards?"

"May I tell him who's calling?"

"This is Brad Pierson, JoAnne. How've you been?"

"I've been good, Dr. Pierson. Just a minute. Let me see if I can find Dr. Richards for you."

After being on hold for a few minutes, Brad feels himself getting nervous. His hands begin to shake slightly, and he feels a cold sweat on the back of his neck. A glance at the clock tells him it is now 3:42 p.m. Then, on the other end comes Alan Richards's voice. Brad fights to stay focused.

"Hello, Brad … is that you?" Despite his best attempt to cover it up, the surprise in Alan Richards's voice is obvious.

"Alan, listen carefully. I need your help. You're not going to believe this, but someone's been trying to kill me."

Surprisingly, Alan remains quite collected. "Someone's *trying to kill you?* Brad, you've got to be kidding. Are you all right? … Listen, I want to help in any way possible. Tell me what to do."

"I'll need some money and a secluded place to hide out, and possibly a car."

"Tell me where you are, Brad. I'll come get you right now."

"I'd better get off now, Alan. I'll call again soon."

"I'll be waiting for your call."

The moment the conversation is over, Brad rips the headphones off his head and drops them onto the table. He stands up and paces around the table, his voice angry. "I could tell it in his voice that he knows all about this. He didn't even ask me who was trying to kill me or what it was all about. It's obvious he's involved!"

Looking over at Brad, neither Wes nor George knows what to say. To themselves, they silently agree with his sentiment. A phone call from Agent David Nelson temporarily disrupts the mood inside the room.

"Richards is making a move. We're in pursuit."

As Alan Richards leaves through the side exit of the Deaconess Hospital and gets into his car, he is photographed by David Nelson, who rides with Michael Harris. They loosely tail him as he makes a moderately high-speed run north on Interstate 24, and they temporarily lose him when he exits at Woodmont Avenue. Not leaving anything to chance, they have attached a tracking device to the rear fender of his car. He is picked up again as he gets on Twenty-First Avenue South near the Vanderbilt campus. He then drives somewhat recklessly in the direction of Green Hills, where he stops in front of a First American Bank office. Photographed on his way into and out of the bank, he stops again just a few hundred feet away to use a pay phone. The call is over before the agents have a chance to hone in on him with their eavesdropping equipment. Then, Alan leads them on a winding chase across Green Hills and over to Belle Meade, where he parks outside the clubhouse of the Belle Meade Country Club. From there, he walks directly to the restaurant.

Michael Harris and David Nelson scramble to get their cameras and electronic surveillance equipment in position. Standing in the shadows of two tall, densely foliated Japanese magnolias off to one side of the clubhouse, they get set up quickly. Unfortunately, the restaurant is crowded and the majority of the conversation is jumbled. They are, however, able to get a clear photograph of whom Dr. Richards is meeting with through one of the large plate-glass windows on the side of the building. Listening to the communications from the agents at the scene, Brad again looks over at the clock and notes the time to be 4:25 p.m.

After only a few minutes, Alan Richards is back in his car. Again he drives at dangerous speeds. This time, he leads Michael Harris and David Nelson to his home in Green Hills. They log their time in as 4:52 p.m., and then they sit and wait for his next move. Parked nearby is one of the FBI vans, where all calls into and out of Alan Richards's house are being monitored and recorded. While that is going on, Wes orders his men to evacuate the fourth, fifth, and sixth floors of the Vanderbilt Holiday Inn to minimize risk to any innocent guests or hotel employees.

For the next several hours at downtown FBI headquarters, things are relatively quiet. It's not until 11:08 p.m. that the next communiqué arrives from the stakeout at the Holiday Inn.

"Burgundy Cadillac just appeared. Dent in front left side. Three occupants."

Wes, who moments ago looked as if he'd nodded off, jumps into action. He switches on the series of video screens that line one wall, directly communicating with the men at the scene. Over the video linkup, enhanced with a special night vision lens, he, Brad, George, and Martin Trimble watch the car park in the hotel's back parking lot behind a large satellite dish. Wes then notifies the men inside the hotel: "Coming in back entrance, ground floor level. Get ready."

Once the intruders are inside, Wes switches to a second camera, located in the stairwell. On the screen, the three men, in dark skintight clothing and with masks over their faces, march quietly up the stairs.

"On second story. Moving up."

Wes now activates all cameras in the stairwells and watches the men climb to the fifth floor. Swiftly and silently, they ease down the hallway as a close-knit unit, checking room numbers as they go.

"Almost there."

When they reach room 527, the tallest of the three men withdraws a semiautomatic pistol with a silencer attached to it and shoots through the door handle and lock assembly. As he kicks the door open, the other two men also draw handguns.

Without turning on any lights, the first man enters the bedroom and fires half a dozen times at the person sleeping in the middle of the bed while the other two slide toward the bathroom and closet. After the room has been quickly searched, one of the men flips on the lights. The intruders are surprised to find the room empty. The comforter is peeled back, revealing that the mound in the center of the bed is a series of pillows. This panics the intruders.

"Somethin's wrong! Let's get outta here."

Hurriedly exiting through the doorway and rounding the corner in the direction of the staircase, they are suddenly blinded by large strobe lights surrounding them in all directions. Reaching up to cover their eyes, they cry out in pain and fall to the floor when they are struck in the abdomen by several rounds of rubber bullets. From both sides of the hallway, multiple FBI agents appear, each pointing automatic machine guns at the perpetrators as they move from behind tall metal and glass bulletproof shields. They kick the intruders' weapons out of their reach. Without a fight, the three men are rolled over onto their stomachs and handcuffed.

Ecstatic that this part of the operation has gone so well and without blood-shed, Wes yells into his microphone, "Great job, guys! Now come on home!"

Back at the bureau office, the pictures of Alan Richards have just been developed and are being intensely scrutinized at the conference table. The photographs move down the line one by one, from Wes to Brad. When he sees the photo of Alan getting into his car, Brad exclaims loudly, "That's the

Volvo that was outside my apartment the night it was robbed! How could I have been so stupid? He's been in on it all along."

Getting up out of his chair, Wes walks over to Brad and slides a picture in front of him taken of Alan Richards and the man he met with at the country club. With his index finger, he points to the other gentleman and asks if Brad can identify him. Able to recognize him instantly, Brad grimaces. "Oh my gosh, that's Edward Westmoreland! I can't believe he's involved in this, too."

George asks, "Who is Edward Westmoreland?"

"He's a heart surgeon who does some teaching at Vanderbilt, but he works mostly at Deaconess Hospital. He was a consultant on Butch Kennedy's case."

George looks up at Wes and comments, "This thing sure seems to have far-reaching tentacles, doesn't it?"

A little overwhelmed by this latest development, Brad merely stares at the photograph, focusing on the men's faces and wondering how they could be involved in something like this. His concentration is broken when Wes is summoned from the other room. It is the deep voice of the stocky muscular agent Jim Arnold. "Prisoners here in downstairs lockup, director Shiels."

Leaving George and Brad behind in the conference room, Wes accompanies Jim Arnold down one flight to the interrogation rooms. The three men from the crime scene have been split up. Each man now sits alone, handcuffed to a chair. Not surprisingly, all three men are confident and arrogant, especially the tallest of the three, who, based upon his actions at the Holiday Inn, is presumed to be in charge. Stubborn, none of them will answer any questions, asking only for their attorneys. Wes tries to break the silence of the tall man but is unsuccessful. By this time, the fingerprint analysis becomes available, and there is a positive match for two of the three perpetrators. A file is handed to Wes as he sits across from the presumed ringleader, a slender man in his midforties with shoulder length, greasy black hair.

"Let's see here, Willie Buck. You've got quite an interesting history, Mr. Buck. I see you're wanted for a double murder in New Orleans. You know, Willie, I could extradite you right now. And you know what, Louisiana still has the death penalty. What do you think about that?"

To Wes's disappointment, his prisoner remains mute, which angers him.

"Come on, Willie, who are you working for? They must be some pretty bad dudes if you're willing to risk lethal injection for them. Now's the time to make a deal, while I'm still in the mood."

Over the next two hours, Wes and Martin Trimble use alternating tactics of intimidation and threats to try to force Willie Buck to divulge any incriminating information. Despite their best efforts, he refuses to say anything. Finally, when Wes is nearly exhausted, he hears Willie's voice for the first time.

"Okay, I'm ready to make a statement."

Eagerly, Wes asks Martin to bring in a tape recorder.

"Okay, Willie, go ahead."

Leaning forward, Willie hesitates a moment and then purses his lips, as if contemplating something. "All right, here it is; quit harassin' me and get me my lawyer!"

Barely displaying the intense anger he feels, Wes stands up, slides on his suit jacket, and says, "The governor of Louisiana is a personal friend of mine; I'll send him your regards when I let him know you're here."

Out in the hallway, Jim Arnold catches up with Wes and asks if Brad should be brought down to see if he recognizes any of the men.

"Good idea, Jim. Listen, I'm going to step out for a minute. Tell Dr. Pierson I'll be right back."

Ten minutes later, Wes returns and discovers that Brad was able to make a positive identification of two of the three men. One he placed at the Opryland Amusement Park and the other at the scene of the crime when his home was robbed.

It is almost 2:00 a.m. Paul Everett asks if the prisoners should be allowed to call their attorneys. This evokes a blunt and hostile response from Wes: *"Are you kidding?"* If I let these guys talk to their lawyers, they're going to get word to their accomplices. ... Get a car ready to go. We're shipping them to Atlanta for holding."

Exhausted, Wes and George decide to call it a night. They agree to meet again at 8:00 a.m., now just five-and-a-half hours away. It is too late to get Brad back to the safe house, so makeshift sleeping quarters are arranged in Wes's office. As he gets settled on the lumpy couch, Brad feels remarkably protected, but he can't remember ever being so tired.

Still curled up at ten to eight the following morning, Brad barely flinches when Wes turns on his office light. After rolling over and nearly falling to the floor, he gets up and follows Wes, who directs him down the hall to a bathroom containing a shower. Twenty minutes later, with his hair still damp, Brad enters the conference room and sips on a cup of coffee to help himself wake up. Wes has already gotten started, outlining the chain of events that have transpired so far. Once Brad takes his place at the table, George Adams, who is seated beside him, winks at him. Wes then summarizes the situation.

"All right, we've confirmed Harry Lefevre's involvement and picked up three of the four men initially involved in the robbery and subsequent attempted murder of Dr. Pierson here. We've also got a pathologist and a heart surgeon somehow intimately entwined in this whole affair. They may be tied to the death of an automobile assembly worker who's had his autopsy data messed with. Not only that, but also we've got a missing connection of this bizarre case to the State Secret Service Agency and the governor's office. Two days ago, I asked Michael Harris to start putting together profiles on our current players. Michael, please brief everyone on what you've found out so far."

As usual, the slim Michael Harris is well-dressed in a double-breasted blue blazer and a pair of perfectly creased tan wool slacks. Even after working long days, the only thing unkempt about him is his dark facial hair, which hasn't been shaved in the past forty-eight hours. Standing up, he begins a PowerPoint presentation. The first page is a head-and-shoulders shot of Alan Richards.

"So far, Dr. Richards looks pretty clean. Forty-eight years old, married eighteen years, wife's an attorney. No children, nice house in Green Hills with standard thirty-year mortgage. Usual credit cards, good retirement account. Nothing out of the ordinary. I did, however, come across a few large deposits from a health insurance company by the name of AmericaHealth. Apparently, he works part-time for them doing some type of consulting work."

Wes Shiels then poses a question to Michael Harris: "Mike, what about any unusual trips, expensive cars, or gambling?"

"Couldn't find any of that."

"What about the wife's business?"

"Tax attorney, usual clients, nothing suspicious."

"How much are these checks for from that AmericaHealth company?"

"All told, in the range of 300 thousand dollars."

The last sentence gets Wes's attention. "Hmm, that's pretty good pay for a little consulting work, wouldn't you say? Anything else on our good Dr. Richards, Michael?"

"That's it."

"Why don't we move along? What about police chief Harry Lefevre?"

"On the surface, everything seems to fit pretty well. He owns a modest house in Hillsborough Hills and drives a Chevy Impala. Divorced three years ago with typical monthly alimony payments. Once I started digging, though, I came up with some pretty good stuff. Over on Hilton Head, the guy's got a half-million-dollar home and a brand-new Jaguar convertible stashed away. Unless police captains are paid a whole lot more than they used to be, this guy's dirty."

A wry smile now appears on Wes's face. "We gotcha, Harry. Now we just need to reel you in. Keep going, Michael. Tell me about Dr. Westmoreland."

"I've gotta tell you, this fellow's the blueblood of the bluebloods. Comes from big family money, way back, you know, high society and all that. Owns a 5 million dollar mansion in Belle Meade and has a nice beach house in Palm Beach, Florida, and a mountain place down in Asheville, North Carolina. From what I can figure out, he's a real big-shot surgeon. Trained at Harvard and Vanderbilt. Been married to the same woman for thirty years. Wife's also from a rich Nashville family. Three daughters: one's at Duke, another at Emory, and the third goes to a private high school in town. Lots and lots of money in several bank accounts and investment firms. Everything looked pretty legitimate, and I just about gave up until I went back a few years. Back in 2008, the guy almost went belly-up. Made some bad stock deals and lost himself several million bucks. He pulled out of it with some money that I can't quite get a trace on. Came out of a bank in Fort Lauderdale, Florida. I tried every which way to get a handle on it, but this bank has got really tough computer security."

"Anything else?"

"Oh yeah, one other thing. Westmoreland also works for this same AmericaHealth company, although he doesn't get paid by them. He's in charge of something called the Utilization Review Committee."

With the index finger of his right hand, Wes strokes his cheek. "Well, isn't that interesting? Our two doctors are tied to this same AmericaHealth outfit."

At that moment, an excited Paul Everett disrupts the meeting. As he walks in, he waves a compact disc in one hand. "This just came in. Take a listen. I got it off Harry Lefevre's office line."

Walking to a wall-mounted CD player, he turns it on and stands beside it while the disc plays.

"Buddy, this is Harry. Listen, the boys I sent out last night haven't come back. I'm nervous. Whaddya think we oughta do?"

"Harry, you idiot! I told you not to call me on this line. Now get off. I'll make arrangements for us to get together somewhere private soon. Stay at your office, and *don't make any more phone calls!*"

Martin Trimble can't contain his surprise.

"That wasn't Buddy Carter the lieutenant governor, was it?"

Smugly, Paul Everett responds, "One and the same."

"Holy smokes."

Several minutes lapse while Wes quietly digests the new data. Excitedly, the other men chat among themselves, trying to piece things together. Wes then pulls Brad and George aside and leads them to his office to run some of his theories past them. In the interim, he assigns two agents to begin gathering information on Buddy Carter and the AmericaHealth Corporation. Another meeting is set for two hours from now.

Back in Wesley Shiels's office, Brad can barely keep pace with everything that's happened so far. The caffeine in the coffee is unable to compensate for his recent sleep deprivation, and he finds himself a bit sluggish mentally. Uncertain how he managed to get in the middle of something so complex, he desperately wants to return to the mundane life he just left a few weeks ago, a life that was safe and comparatively carefree. For the first time, while Wes is talking, Brad has a hard time focusing. His mind drifts to Julie. More than a week has gone by since he last saw her, a week that feels more like a year. As he reflects on many of their wonderful times together, the pain he presently feels eases slightly. Unfortunately, his pleasant daydreams are ended abruptly by Wes's sharp voice. "*Brad*, are you with us here? George and I are trying to figure this out, and we need your help."

"Sorry, Wes. I don't know what happened. I was gone there for a minute."

"Do you have any thoughts for me?"

Thinking hard, Brad summarizes his own interpretation of what's happened. "Up to this point, we know that Alan Richards is tied to a falsified autopsy, which somehow revolves around Mr. Kennedy's heart. Dr. Westmoreland, the surgeon who consulted on Butch Kennedy's case, seems to have pulled himself out of near bankruptcy by uncertain means. Both men are linked to a health insurance company by the name of AmericaHealth, and a whole lot of money is involved. After I started asking questions about Mr. Kennedy's autopsy, I got fired and nearly killed, and somehow Alan Richards and a police chief are involved in that, too. The lieutenant governor seems to have a role in this and so does the state secret service following my parents. ... The problem is, I have no idea what the link between all these events is."

Wes then turns to George. "Have you got any ideas?"

Pulling off his eyeglasses, George massages the bridge of his nose before answering. "I think we ought to bring in Lefevre and shake him and see if anything falls out. Then, we should scare our two doctors and Buddy Carter and see where they lead us. Maybe we'll get lucky."

"Sounds reasonable. Let's figure out where to get started."

Over the next forty-five minutes, the three men bounce ideas off one another, which are presented to the entire team later in the morning. They decide to get all the mechanisms in place for a second sting operation, which is scheduled to take place twenty-four hours from now. Each man is given a specific task, beginning with Cooper Smith and David Nelson, who are to apprehend Captain Lefevre at his home early the following morning. That way, no one else at the Hillsborough precinct will be made aware of the operation. Until then, they are to follow Harry Lefevre and stake out his home overnight.

After the meeting concludes, Brad pulls Wes Shiels aside. "Wes, do you think you can arrange for me to see Julie and my parents? I'm really missing them."

Thinking a minute, Wes responds, "That shouldn't be too hard, Brad. We've got two men keeping an eye on Julie right now. We're close enough to wrapping this thing up that we need to bring her in for protective custody, anyway. As for your parents, they're safely tucked away in Bellevue. We can get you down there anytime."

"Thanks, Wes. I know you've got a lot going on. I'm sorry to trouble you."

"No problem. You've hung in there real well, Brad. You need to help me get things set up for tomorrow before you leave, though, and I may need you back here once everything gets under way."

"You bet."

Later that same day, Wes sets into motion a plan to bring in Julie for safe-keeping. This may present somewhat of a difficult challenge because she's been followed around the clock for over a week now, presumably for the purpose of leading the conspirators to Brad. Up to this point, she is the only one who appears to be in danger. For now, Sandy Starke and his fiancée, Joanie, will be closely monitored but will not require FBI protection.

On August 14 at 5:42 p.m., Agent Jim Arnold and Agent Paul Everett watch Julie leave the main entrance of Vanderbilt Hospital and walk a short distance to one of the parking decks, where they see her get into her red Honda Accord. Through their binoculars, they watch her course carefully. Initially getting onto Twenty-First Avenue South, she turns right at the second stoplight onto Blakemore Avenue. It is there that Jim Arnold takes note of a silver Buick Regal that pulls in close behind her.

At the intersection with West End Avenue, Julie turns left, with the Regal not far behind. Two miles up on the right, close to the intersection with Highway 100, Julie stops at an Exxon station. By this time, she has let down her long blonde hair and has on a pair of dark, aviator-style sunglasses. After walking to the adjoining convenience store to prepay for her gas, she fills her tank. Getting back in her car, she drives directly home. After picking up the mail, she goes inside. Farther up the block, the Regal finds a parking spot and waits.

As soon as the Regal is out of sight of the Exxon station, a white-paneled van emerges from the back parking area of the convenience store. Safely tucked away in the back of the van is Julie Christensen, along with two FBI agents. Wearing identical clothing, a blonde wig, and dark sunglasses, a female FBI operative built similar to Julie is now in her home, maintaining surveillance on the two men inside the Regal. Meanwhile, Julie is en route to Franklin to her mother's house, which has been heavily fortified by the FBI and the local sheriff's office. After it is verified that she has arrived safely, Wes intends to send Brad down there for temporary safekeeping.

Chapter 25

At 5:08 a.m. the following morning, it is barely dusk when FBI agents Cooper Smith and David Nelson leave their parked car one block away from Harry Lefevre's house. Wearing black, nylon-covered bulletproof vests under their jackets, the men, each carrying a shotgun, cautiously approach the house. Over their handheld radio, communication has just come in that the two other FBI agents working with them have secured the back of Harry's property. Then, they are informed that a surveillance van is precisely situated and operational one block away. When both men are in position on either side of the front door, the stocky African American Cooper Smith begins banging loudly on the door.

"This is the FBI, Captain Lefevre, open up!"

After a count of five, they kick the door open. Both men crouch as they enter. The house is still dark. The men travel together in their search, not speaking to one another, instead using hand gestures to signify their intended actions. First, they cross the living room off to the left of the front entrance. Ahead of them, they can see a small kitchen on the back side of the house. Their gazes meet; nothing yet. Then, the early morning silence is broken by the squeal of car tires and the sound of an explosion as Harry Lefevre's car barrels through his closed garage door, spraying wood fragments in all directions. As the men sprint back toward the front door, they see Harry's white Impala, nearly airborne, fly past them and speed down the street. Aware it's of no use, they don't bother firing their weapons at the car that is quickly out of range. They immediately make radio contact with the surveillance van, which is still in the vicinity. Harry Lefevre's car comes to a sudden screeching halt in a few hundred feet. To everyone's relief, the electronic cutoff switch the FBI installed on the car's fuel pump has worked. But Harry Lefevre is not willing to give up easily. Dressed in slippers, pajama bottoms, and a loose robe, he gets out of the car and makes a run for it. With Agents Smith and Nelson close behind on foot, Harry is quickly intercepted by the other set of agents from the surveillance van.

After being booked and fingerprinted at FBI headquarters, the unshaven police captain is put in one of the interrogation rooms with his arms handcuffed behind his back. Moving to within several inches of Harry, Wes straddles his chair, with his elbows resting on the seat back. It does not take long to ascertain that Harry's mood is confrontational.

"Captain Lefevre, I'm Bureau Chief Wesley Shiels."

"Mr. Shiels, *could you possibly tell me what this is all about?*"

Not acknowledging the question, Wes continues. "Why do you think you're down here, Harry?"

"I think you and your men have lost their minds. That's what I think. You do realize I'm a police captain, don't you?"

"Of course I do."

"Then, at the very least, could you remove these handcuffs and tell me why in the devil you've arrested me?"

"How about attempted murder?"

"What are you talking about?"

"Why'd you run, Harry?"

"*It's pretty damned obvious;* there were two guys standing on my front porch with shotguns."

"We're the FBI, Harry."

"And how was I supposed to know that—open the door and have somebody blow my head off before I get to ask who they are? What if they happened to be a coupla ex-cons that I put away who came back to get even? Did you ever stop to think about that?"

Already becoming tired of this discussion, Wes looks over at a tape recorder sitting on the table beside him and pushes the Play button. On the phone with Buddy Carter, the lieutenant governor, Harry's voice is unmistakable as he gives an update on where his men are with Brad Pierson's attempted abduction and possible murder. When Wes stops the tape, Harry's expression becomes more somber.

"Well, Harry, that sure sounds like you, doesn't it now? Want to tell me anything yet?"

"That's not my voice on that tape."

"The crime lab tells me different; they say it's an exact match."

"Your crime lab is mistaken."

"Before we go any further, Harry, do you want an attorney present?"

Not saying anything immediately, Harry rubs his wrists, which have been recently released from the handcuffs. Under his breath, he mumbles, "I guess so."

Wes then leans over, close to Harry's thin wrinkled face, and whispers, "Harry, I've got you on the attempted kidnapping and attempted murder of a Dr. Brad Pierson. I've also followed a money trail from a company called AmericaHealth to a private bank account overseas belonging to you. What did you do for them that was worth half a million? Now may be the time to come forward while I'm still willing to make you a deal."

Lifting his eyes from the floor, Harry meets Wes's gaze. "I guess now's about the time I need to call my lawyer."

Without saying another word, Wes gets up and walks out of the interrogation room, slamming the door behind him. Out in the hallway, he pours himself a cup of coffee. While in the midst of deliberating on how to handle Harry's situation, he is interrupted by Martin Trimble.

"Wes, we're ready for you now."

Gulping down his last sip of coffee, Wes straightens his tie and walks with Martin to the central operations room. There, Agent Paul Everett, George Adams, and several other male and female FBI operatives await his instructions to begin the second part of their sting operation. With nearly everything ready to go, confirmation of the direct telephone linkup to Anna Christensen's house is made in case instant communication with Brad is necessary.

As Wes takes his seat at a table in the middle of the room, he looks around at his staff, whose eyes are trained on him. After putting on his radio communications headset, he picks up a mechanical pencil to make one final check. Satisfied, he looks up at the clock and notes the time as 9:34 a.m. He then nods.

Three events take place nearly simultaneously. First is the arrival of an unmarked car at the main entrance of the Deaconess Hospital. From the front passenger seat, Agent Bert Hendricks emerges and opens the rear car door just behind him. Wearing dark sunglasses, he scouts the area and then helps Elinor Kennedy out of the backseat. After the door is closed, he taps lightly on the roof of the car, at which point his associate Victor Santorino drives off slowly. Elinor enters the hospital as Bert Hendricks, with radio backup, trails her from a distance.

While all this is going on, a second FBI vehicle, containing Sandy Starke and two other men, takes its position in one of the patient parking areas beside the Deaconess Hospital. Well before six o'clock this morning, they initiated their part of the operation, and now they await the outcome. The men, including Sandy, take shifts monitoring all exits with high-powered binoculars and other surveillance equipment. Meanwhile, back at FBI headquarters, Wes prepares to place a phone call to trigger the third event.

In the lobby of the Deaconess Hospital, Elinor Kennedy is quite nervous, which is only made worse by all the early morning activity. She tenuously tries to cross the large waiting area but is blocked at nearly every attempt by patients being wheeled in and out or by doctors and nurses hurrying in all directions. Doing her best, she presses on. She reaches a private corner where she refers to the small map given to her by the FBI to help guide her to the proper location. Farther along in the hospital it is much less congested, making it easier for Elinor to find her way. After verifying she has located the correct office, she turns the door handle, but before going in, she looks back and is relieved to find that Bert Hendricks is not far behind. Then she pushes the door open and walks directly across the nicely furnished, spacious waiting room toward the receptionist.

The woman's friendly smile helps relieve some of Elinor's tension.

"Is this Dr. Westmoreland's office?"

"Yes, ma'am, it sure is. Can I help you?"

"My name is Elinor Kennedy. I wanted to come by and see Dr. Westmoreland in person to thank him, to thank him for helping my husband … who passed away … several months ago."

Fighting back her emotions, Elinor refuses to cry in front of this young woman who is a stranger to her. From her pocketbook, she digs out a tissue to blot the corner of her eyes dry.

Surprisingly compassionate, the chunky red-haired secretary immediately gets up from behind her desk, guides Elinor to a chair, and then sits down beside her.

"Mrs. Kennedy, I'm so sorry. Is there anything I can do?"

Momentarily quiet, Elinor continues to rein in her emotions. She then looks over at the woman. "Please tell me your name."

"It's Stacy."

Elinor reaches over and pats her newfound friend on the hand. "Stacy, you're sweet. … You see, I lost my husband not long ago. Dr. Westmoreland had helped take care of him. He was so nice to Butch that I had to come by and thank him for what he did for us. … It would mean a lot for me to get to see him."

Nodding empathetically, Stacy gets up and walks back toward her desk. "He's busy seeing patients, but let me try to interrupt him for a minute. Can you wait right here? It shouldn't be long."

"I sure can. Thank you."

Not long afterward, Stacy returns and asks Elinor to follow her. She takes her down a short hallway and seats her in Edward's office, with an assurance that he should arrive momentarily. Barely noticing the antique furniture or the plush tapestry-style rugs, Elinor is lost in a temporary daydream, going over in her mind what Wes Shiels instructed her to say. She reminds herself it is imperative she remains calm and focused in order to be effective. Temporarily startled when Edward enters the room a few minutes later, she stands up and reaches out both of her hands to affectionately grasp his right hand.

"Dr. Westmoreland, thank you for seeing me without an appointment; I'm sorry to interrupt your busy day. … I don't know if you remember me or not. I'm Elinor Kennedy. My husband was Randall Kennedy; you saw him several times when he was here in the hospital. You were so good to us that I had to come by and thank you after Butch passed away."

His expression reflecting humility, Edward asks Elinor if she would care to sit down and talk a moment. "I'm awfully sorry about your husband, Mrs. Kennedy. I remember him quite well. He was a wonderful man, full of life."

"He was very impressed by you, Dr. Westmoreland, and that was a job, as not many people could impress Butch. ... I really came by to thank you for trying to help us when Butch had his first heart attack; you felt that surgery wouldn't help him, and you didn't put him through any unnecessary tests."

"You're certainly welcome, Mrs. Kennedy. I'm sorry there wasn't more I could do."

Edward's steel-blue eyes then soften. In them, Elinor can see a look of sincere pain over her loss. Before asking a question, Elinor pauses. Then she speaks in a hushed tone. "There is one thing I did want to ask you though, Dr. Westmoreland, if you have time."

"Yes, Mrs. Kennedy, what is it?"

"I don't know if you knew this happened, but my husband was accidentally cremated."

"No, ma'am, I wasn't aware of that. I'm terribly sorry."

Looking directly at Edward, Elinor leans over in his direction and again softens her voice. "That's what I wanted to ask you. ... Do you think that one of the doctors who was taking care of Butch when he died could have made a mistake and had his body cremated to cover it up?"

So unexpected was this question that Edward can't cover his surprise. From his relaxed position, he sits straight up in his chair and begins to shuffle papers on his desk. His eyes dart back and forth to Elinor's as he struggles to come up with a response.

"Absolutely not, Mrs. Kennedy! You're understandably upset over your husband's death and cremation, but I know the doctors and nurses who took care of your husband in the emergency room. They did everything they could, I can assure you of that."

By this time, Elinor is so calm she appears almost devoid of feelings. The thought that Edward might somehow have played a role in her husband's death gives her the strength to continue.

"Perhaps you're right, Dr. Westmoreland, but I've decided to hire an attorney to look into things, anyway. Would you be willing to help me?"

Again, Edward hesitates. Then he responds nervously, "I'm not sure I could be of much help to you, Mrs. Kennedy. You see, I wasn't even there when your husband died. Not only that, but also I am absolutely certain that everything was done appropriately."

Edward then stands and walks Elinor in the direction of the doorway.

"I hope you'll forgive me, Mrs. Kennedy, but I've got to get back to seeing patients. I'm terribly sorry over your husband's death."

As soon as Elinor is out in the waiting area, Edward turns around and quickly closes his door. Long afterward, Elinor stands in the hallway outside Edward's office, staring at the panels of the dark-stained wooden door. Then, turning around, she slowly walks away, thanking Stacy again on her way past the front desk.

As she travels along the broad hospital corridors lined with cheerful cranberry- and evergreen-colored wallpaper, Elinor wonders if anything she just did will be of any help. On reaching the lobby, she hears Bert Hendricks identify himself from behind her, and next she feels his comforting hand on her elbow as he guides her back to the car.

Although she is unaware of it at the moment, the question Elinor posed to herself is answered less than thirty minutes later. While Agents Hendricks and Santorino drive Elinor back home, one of the surveillance vans snaps a photograph of Edward Westmoreland leaving the Deaconess Hospital with a briefcase in his hand. Making a direct path for the doctors' parking lot, Edward climbs into his long black Mercedes sedan and hurriedly drives off. In a desire not to be seen, the FBI agents tailing Edward give him a lot of leeway and nearly lose him as he approaches the highway interchange. With help from a police helicopter overhead that has been loaned to them, the FBI tracks Edward all the way to downtown Nashville, where they are informed by radio communication that he has exited Highway 40. Because of the loud roar of the rotor blades, Agent Jim Arnold, in the van, has to yell into his radio to make himself heard by the police officer in the helicopter.

"Where is he now?"

"He got off on First Avenue South and is traveling east along the Cumberland River. ... Step on it. He's picking up speed."

"Anyone in the car with him?"

"From up here, I can't tell."

"Where's he headed?"

"Not sure, but he's right now passing the AT&T tower and is just beginning to slow."

At that moment, Wes, who has been monitoring all radio communications, orders the helicopter to drop back. He then interfaces directly with Jim Arnold. "Arnold, get up close and get ready. He's probably making his move."

"I'm almost there, I'm almost there. ... Okay, there, I see him now. He's turning into a parking garage under a high-rise."

"Which one?"

Bouncing around in the front seat because of the van's high speed, Jim Arnold frantically points his binoculars at Edward's car. "I can't see the sign yet. ... Looks like it begins with an a...Yeah, that's it Amer...AmericaHealth Corporation."

"Can you still see him?"

"No, he's outta sight."

"Get in there."

"Yes, sir."

After the van screeches to a halt in front of the building, Jim Arnold jumps out. The driver, Paul Everett, tries to find a vantage point. Running up the front steps, the mildly overweight, middle-aged, brown-haired Agent Arnold forces his way in front of several people to get through the turnstile-type glass doors. In the middle of the three-storied lobby, he stops and quickly scans the room in search of any clue that might lead him to Edward's location. He's discouraged to find the sparsely decorated lobby nearly empty. On the far wall, all four elevators are in motion, and beside them are several receptionists at a long desk. Frustrated, he kicks his heel on the highly polished black marble floor. As he does so, he notices something he hadn't observed before, a security guard sitting at a semicircular desk in one corner of the lobby.

Discreetly sliding his radio into his suit jacket pocket, he strolls casually across the room, avoiding several large modern brass sculptures. The gray-haired older gentleman sitting behind the multiple computer terminals doesn't notice him immediately, which gives Jim Arnold a chance to read the guard's name tag.

"Mr. James, are you the one who called us?"

Unaware that anyone was nearby, the man is caught off guard by the question, so much so that he almost falls backward while in his chair.

"Called who?"

"Called us about an elevator that wasn't working."

"You must be in the wrong place. All five of ours are workin' fine."

"Five? I only see four."

"Yeah, we got five. The big cheese upstairs, Dr. Altman, he's got his own private elevator."

"That's the one we were told wasn't working."

"No, no, take a look for yourself; someone just went up in it a few minutes ago."

Turning one of the computer screens to face Jim Arnold, the security guard shows the elevator's position as being in the penthouse.

"Unless it gets used, it stays down in the basement. That's how I know it's workin'. ... Now what'd you say your name was?"

"Hardcastle, Mike Hardcastle, I'm the manager of Otis Elevators here in town. We were told it was a major repair, so I wanted to come down here to check it out before sending my guys out. Every once in a while we get equipment failure. I wanted to be sure this wasn't that sort of case. ... Nice to meet you, Mr. James, but it sounds like a false alarm. Mind if I look around just the same?"

"Hey, no problem. Suit yourself."

Not far from the security desk is a door leading to the stairwell. Jim Arnold walks down one flight, where he locates a men's room and locks the door behind him. He wastes no time in calling his colleague Paul Everett, who is in the van.

"Everett, are you there?"

"Yeah, I'm right here."

"Focus in on the penthouse."

"Okay, okay. ... I see a couple of guys moving around. ... Oops, they're out of view. I can maybe get some photos, but audio's impossible at this distance."

With the largest zoom lens commercially available, Paul Everett tries to get a picture of the men in Robert's office, but the images are not terribly clear on account of the reflected glare off the windows. All that Agents Everett and Arnold can accomplish at this point is to follow Edward Westmoreland once he leaves the AmericaHealth building.

Meanwhile, at the present moment in Robert Altman's office, Edward accosts Robert and instigates a heated argument.

"Guess who paid me a visit at my office? *Well, I'll tell you: it was Elinor Kennedy.* ... Why didn't you tell me that her husband was cremated? What kind of stupid move was that? Are you trying to make us all look guilty?"

Not one to take criticism lightly, Robert yells back, "I had no choice—we had to cover our tracks on this one! When the family wanted an autopsy, there was no other option. What'd you want me to do, let them find out what happened if they ever saw the autopsy report? Don't be naïve. ... Besides, what exactly did the Kennedy woman want?"

Still extremely tense, Edward stands nearly toe to toe with Robert, staring him directly in the eyes. Robert asks, "How exactly did you handle it?"

"I stayed calm and pretended not to know anything. I can't tell if she believed me or not."

"Listen, Edward, you've got nothing to worry about. Everything's been taken care of. There's nothing for anyone to find, especially not anything that would tie this to you."

At the door on his way out, Edward turns back briefly. "There's only one thing I've got to say Robert: you'd better be right!"

Meanwhile, Wes Shiels and George Adams pore over the file that has been put together on the AmericaHealth Corporation. After glancing over the report, Wes makes several observations. "Let's see, the CEO's a guy by the name of Dr. Robert Altman. The company looks like it's in pretty good shape financially. ... Wow, would you look at that bottom line—201 billion dollars last year. They made more money than some small countries did. George, go get Harris."

A few minutes later, Michael Harris arrives.

"Hey, Chief, looking for me?"

"Yes. I need you to start running some stuff through the computer on this AmericaHealth company. I want all you can find; I want info on every officer in the company and every bit of financial data on them. Give me an analysis of the company's workings, and let me know if anything's out of the ordinary. Call Washington, if necessary, and take as many men as you need to help you. But I want it fast and I want it complete."

"Yes, sir."

After Michael Harris leaves the room, Wes jots down several notes to himself and then addresses Martin Trimble. "How we doin', Marty?"

"We're almost ready, Wes. Our two cars just called in. They should be in position within ninety seconds."

With the first two phases of the operation under way, Wes prepares to initiate the third. As he picks up the telephone to make an anonymous call, Paul Everett and Jim Arnold prepare to follow Edward Westmoreland as he exits the parking garage of the AmericaHealth Corporation. Wes's phone call goes through immediately, but it is not until six or seven rings later that there is an answer.

"Hello."

"Mr. Carter?"

"Yeah, this is Buddy Carter."

"Mr. Carter, I've got some bad news for you."

"Who is this?"

"Never mind that. I just wanted to let you know we've got some of your friends who'd like to say hello to you."

"Is this a crank call?"

"No, Buddy, but Harry Lefevre and three of his henchmen are out of business. And now we're comin' for you."

Before "Buddy" Ridgeway Carter slams the phone down, he yells defiantly, "You're outta your mind, whoever you are! *And it'll be me that'll be comin' for you, you piece of trash!*"

Back in the operations room at FBI headquarters, all phone conversations from the lieutenant governor's office are being transmitted with remarkable clarity. Something must have hit a chord, because Buddy Carter is soon back on the phone. When he is unable to reach Harry Lefevre on his private office line, he decides to try the main number at the Hillsborough Police Station. After identifying himself, he is immediately connected to Harry's secretary.

"No, sir, Captain Lefevre hasn't come in yet today. We got a little worried, so we sent a couple of men by his house a little while ago. .... They reported that the captain's garage door was destroyed and is in splinters. He was nowhere to be found. We're very upset."

Completely stunned, Buddy Carter slowly hangs up the telephone. For several minutes, he sits glued to his desk chair, staring at his folded hands on the desktop. Then, the field agents watching him through their binoculars see him get up and go to a wall safe, where he begins stuffing a series of objects into a duffel bag. From there, he leaves his office and is not seen again until he emerges outside. With his protruding gut bouncing up and down as he walks, he hurries toward his car, a brand-new gold Chrysler 300 four-door, and gets in, throwing his duffel bag in the back seat.

Communication is made to Wes: "He's making a move. We're on his tail."

Taking a meandering and, at times, haphazard course, Buddy Carter travels from the downtown governor's office toward the Hillsborough police precinct. Once there, he parks in back and knocks loudly on the back exit door. After a couple of minutes, Harry Lefevre's secretary, Alice, slowly opens the door and then greets Buddy Carter. Inside, he questions Alice, asking her if she's heard anything from her boss since they spoke on the phone.

"Why, yes. Funny you should come all the way down here, Mr. Carter. Not long after you called, some man called and told me Captain Lefevre was on a long trip and wouldn't be back anytime soon. It was a really strange phone call."

The ruddy complexion of the lieutenant governor's face becomes more reddened once he hears the news. Looking like he is in a hurry, he scurries out the back door in the direction of his car, using a handkerchief to blot nervous perspiration from his face and neck. Rattled by what's happened, he accelerates out of the alley behind the police station and nearly hits several moving cars as he makes a wild turn onto Twenty-First Avenue South in the direction of Interstate 40. Agents Cooper Smith and David Nelson have a hard time staying with him as he weaves in and out of traffic at high speeds.

In keeping with Wes's orders, the men merely follow him for now, hoping he'll lead them to other parties involved in the scandal.

Across town, Edward Westmoreland returns briefly to his workplace, where he picks up a stack of documents and then travels to his home in Belle Meade. At the same time, Sandy Starke and the two agents assigned to watch Alan Richards are still sitting outside Deaconess Hospital. It is now midafternoon, and Wes checks on them. After finding out that nothing has changed with their situation, he turns around and calls Cooper Smith to see where the lieutenant governor is.

"Now on Highway 40 heading west—about ten miles out of town."

"Stay on him!"

"Yes, sir."

Before this day was chosen to carry out the operation, Sandy Starke was instructed to check the work roster for the pathology department at Deaconess Hospital to be certain that Alan Richards would be working. Having a busy day, Dr. Richards has worked nonstop since his arrival early this morning. From one operating room or another, it seemed that every case coming in was an emergency and had to be processed immediately. He reviews and analyzes slide after slide. It is 3:00 p.m., but Alan has yet to have lunch. Finally, there is a lull, so he has an opportunity to sit down with something to eat. Putting his feet up on his desk, Alan Richards leans way back in his chair and tries to release some of his built-up stress. After everything stays quiet for a while, he goes to the sample preparation room and begins the arduous task of cleaning up. Two technologists help him label samples with patients' names and medical record numbers; they also place whole organ specimens in a preservative solution prior to being refrigerated.

On top of a rolling cart, Alan stacks the clear glass containers containing large specimens to take to the refrigerator. Going back and forth several times, he eventually finds there is little room in the refrigerator for anything else. By now, the day's pressures have caught up with Alan physically; he barely has the energy to move things around on the shelves to make more room. When he is almost finished, he happens across a large glass jar he hadn't noticed before. Turning the cold and moist clear container around, his eyes become fixated on it. He stands and stares at it for several seconds.

Floating in a formaldehyde-based preservative, the dark reddish-brown coloration of heart muscle is unmistakable. The label attached to the outside of the glass container reads, "Randall Kennedy, Date of Birth 9/18/68." In disbelief, Alan steps back and then turns his head from side to side to see if anyone else is around. Relieved to find he is alone, he grabs the jar with both hands and throws a white cotton hand towel over it before walking to his office. Horribly shaken up, he instinctively knows something is terribly wrong. While his mind desperately searches for an explanation, sweat begins pouring off his forehead.

What is this? This guy died months ago. The body was cremated. The heart should have been in there. ... What am I going to do with this thing?

Unable to come up with an immediate solution, Alan Richards closes his door and sits down at his desk. After resting his face in the palms of his hands for a short time, he pulls open the bottom file drawer of his desk, drops the glass jar containing the heart specimen inside, and then locks the drawer. Remarkably calm-appearing on the outside, he adjusts his tie and goes back to work as if nothing had happened. All that anyone can tell is that he acts and speaks a bit more mechanically than usual.

By now, Edward Westmoreland has been home for over an hour, and the two men who have been assigned to monitor him maintain a constant vigil from a spot near his sprawling estate. At over ninety miles an hour, Buddy Carter is still traveling west on Interstate 40, not having stopped once since he left the Hillsborough police precinct. He's reached the city of Jackson, Tennessee, nearly a hundred miles from Nashville. Wes, in constant communication, instructs his men to continue to pursue, but not apprehend.

In the main control room at FBI headquarters, there is currently a hubbub of activity. Several screens across one wall of the room are filled with ongoing surveillance footage. Between incoming written and voice communications, Wes intermittently looks up to see the different cameras pan Deaconess Hospital, Edward Westmoreland's house, and the lieutenant governor in flight. One wall contains a series of reel-to-reel recording devices, all of which are currently operating. While sipping on his coffee and giving out directives, Wes is interrupted by Michael Harris, who brings his initial evaluation of the AmericaHealth Corporation to his boss.

"Most everything looks routine so far, except I came across a series of patient accounts that struck me as a little unusual. Of the three thousand or so of these types of accounts, they've all been open for at least four years and all of them are private individual insurance policies. The odd thing is, despite being up-to-date on monthly premiums, none of the policies has had any activity. So far, not one of the insured clients has shown any use of the health-care system. No physicals, no routine office visits, no X-rays, no lab work, nothing."

"Is there any link between them?"

"Not that we've been able to establish so far."

"Go after home addresses, employment histories, criminal records, dates of birth, and immigration records; see what that turns up."

"Yes, sir."

With enough circumstantial evidence to support his request, Wes asks Judge Isaacson's permission to tap the phone lines at the AmericaHealth Corporation, including the office of the chief executive officer, Robert Altman. Very interested in Dr. Altman's possible role in the conspiracy, Wes listens in on Robert's phone lines for a couple of hours. After hearing only routine business discussions, Wes assigns another man to monitor and record Robert's phone calls and instructs him to report anything out of the ordinary immediately to him.

Chapter 26

After a long day of sitting in the hot sun, at 4:52 p.m. Sandy Starke finally sees through his binoculars some activity outside Deaconess Hospital. Alan Richards, with a cardboard box under one arm, exits the building and gets in his tan-colored Volvo. From a distance, Sandy and the two FBI agents follow him as he drives home. Interestingly, Sandy notices that Richards doesn't take the box inside. From a telephone inside his house, he makes only one call, to his wife, who is still at her office. He informs her that he'll be home late for dinner and says not to worry about him. Several minutes later, he reemerges with a briefcase and a second box, overflowing with loose papers. Getting back in his car, he drives approximately five miles and then stops at a large storage facility. He parks directly in front of a garage-sized locker and uses a key to open the padlock. Several trips back and forth to his car are required to stow away the boxes and several other items. After the sliding metal locker door is closed and locked, Dr. Richards is off again, traveling at surprisingly moderate speeds.

Enthralled by all of this, Sandy Starke is allowed to radio back to Wes Shiels, giving him Alan Richards's location as they track him. At times acting like an excited teenager, Sandy occasionally needs to be calmed down by the men who are with him. As if in no hurry, Alan returns to work, parks back in the doctors' parking lot, and returns to the pathology department. At that point, Sandy's enthusiasm bubbles over.

"Are we gonna arrest him now? Do you think he'll put up a fight? Wow, this is great!"

Quite patiently, Bert Hendricks tries to quell Sandy's excitement. "Well, actually, Sandy, we're going to sit here again for an hour or two, unless Director Shiels orders us to do something different. Now, you take the first watch while Victor and I fill out some paperwork. We probably shouldn't be letting you do this, but we really need to get these reports in."

At that moment, Wes receives an excited update from David Nelson: "Buddy Carter's pulling into Memphis International Airport, heading toward short-term parking."

In a split-second, Wes has to make a decision. "All right, it's time. Pick up the lieutenant governor before he's out of reach."

Forty seconds behind Buddy Carter, Cooper Smith and David Nelson park directly in front of the terminal and run in after him, scouring the first floor. Not able to locate him immediately, the two men begin running in numerous directions. A security guard who has noted their erratic behavior approaches David Nelson from behind. Before he reaches him, Agent Nelson sees the lieutenant governor emerge from the men's room and walk in the direction of an international flight bound for Paris. As he prepares to sprint off, he hears a command from behind him.

"You, right there, stop where you are!"

Heeding the command, David Nelson halts and slowly turns around to see two security guards approaching him. Out of the corner of his eye, he can see Buddy Carter check in and get on the boarding ramp. The men move him toward a private corner and, without asking any questions, pat him down. When it is discovered he has a firearm, they push him forcefully up against the wall.

Agent Nelson tries to explain. "I'm with the FBI! Look at my badge."

While one man stands behind him with a gun pushed up against the small of his back, the other takes David Nelson's shield and revolver away from him. They then look over the contents of his wallet, including his driver's license and other identification. Apologizing, the men return the belongings and ask how they can help. Turning around, David Nelson sees Cooper Smith down the hall, and he frantically waves his arms at him. Both men descend upon the Paris boarding gate at the same time, only to discover that the plane has already begun taxiing out onto the runway. As he looks up at the overhead signs, Cooper Smith yells a question at the security guards: "Where's the comptroller's office?"

Pointing above his head, one of the guards directs Smith toward a staircase. "Come on, I'll show you."

After climbing up three flights, the two FBI agents push open the door to the flight control room and wave their gold-colored shields at the men seated at the computer terminals.

"Who's in charge? We've got to stop the Paris flight."

After several questions are fired back and forth, the order is carried out. The large Boeing 747 stops in the middle of the runway. Before instructing the pilot to return to the terminal, the supervisor demands an explanation. He says he will not be fully satisfied until he speaks with Wes Shiels directly and gets an FBI written directive faxed from Nashville. Then, and only then, will he allow the jet to be brought back around.

It is quite a scene when Cooper Smith and David Nelson arrest Buddy Carter. Ranting and raving, he calls the agents a number of awful names and threatens to sue everyone involved, including the airline. After Buddy Carter is safely tucked away in the back seat of their car, with his wrists handcuffed behind him, Agents Smith and Nelson finally get some satisfaction when they contact Wes Shiels.

"We've got Buddy Carter, and we're on our way back home with him right now!"

Two hours have now elapsed since Alan Richards returned to the Deaconess Hospital. There has been no activity on his phone line. Wes decides that perhaps, since Buddy Carter's arrest will likely be publicized, this is the appropriate time to apprehend Dr. Richards. With Sandy as their guide, Agents Santorino and Hendricks quietly enter the hospital and proceed directly to Alan's office. Inside the pathology department, the overhead fluorescent lights are still on, but aside from several lab technicians, the place is deserted. After searching every room and finding nothing, Sandy takes the agents to the cafeteria and several of the physician lounges. Alan Richards is nowhere to be found. Bert Hendricks, deciding to make one final attempt to locate Dr. Richards, calls the hospital operator to have him paged overhead. Again, no response. The two FBI agents grab Sandy and run toward their car.

Squealing out of the parking lot, they decide to try Alan's house first. His wife, Paula, who answers the front door, tells them she doesn't know where he is and questions them as to what they are after. Not having time to answer her, they trigger the blue flashing light inside their car and scramble as quickly as possible to Alan's storage facility. When they arrive, the padlock is missing and the door is ajar. After swiftly raising the garage-style folding door, they are stunned when they discover the room has been completely cleaned out. Forlorn, they share the bad news with Wes, who instantly contacts the local police and sends photographs of Dr. Richards to them by fax. He also asks for their cooperation in searching the airports, railroad stations, bus terminals, and rental car agencies. Meanwhile, Wes orders one of his men to contact Alan's bank and credit card companies to freeze all assets. He also asks them to inform him of all transactions on his Visa or MasterCard.

While Wes is in the midst of coordinating these efforts, Agent Michael Harris approaches him. "I think I've got it figured out."

Disgusted with Alan's escape, Wes responds abruptly, "You figured *what* out?"

"Remember those accounts at AmericaHealth I was telling you about?"

"Of course."

"Remember also when you told me to start looking into Social Security numbers and birth dates? Well, I started digging around on a couple of them and came across some interesting stuff."

"Okay, keep going."

"The accounts appear to be falsified. I traced the names and Social Security numbers, and they don't match up. When I researched it further, I found out that the Social Security numbers have been recycled from people who've been dead at least twenty years."

Intrigued by the information, Wes looks over at Michael Harris. "Good work, Michael! It looks like you may have discovered some type of money-laundering operation for AmericaHealth. ... But what in the world do they need that kind of cash for?"

"Not only that, but also I found out that the money that was paid to keep up the monthly premiums for these accounts was wired to a series of banks but eventually ended up in this one particular bank in Fort Lauderdale, Florida."

"Fort Lauderdale?"

"Yeah, that's right. After I looked into it, I discovered that it's the same bank that's been cutting Edward Westmoreland's checks—the one with the tough computer security."

"Isn't that interesting? Any luck on getting into it yet?"

"I'm afraid not."

Digesting the information, Wes looks down at the tabletop. Because of all that has happened in such a short amount of time, he decides to call another short meeting to sort out some of the details. At the time they all sit down, there has been no word yet on Alan Richards's location. The lieutenant governor will soon be in their possession, and Edward Westmoreland and Robert Altman are still being followed. Aggravated over Alan's loss, Wes makes a snap decision.

"Have Pierson brought back in here from Franklin, and get Westmoreland down here. I want to see what he knows."

While Edward Westmoreland is being apprehended, George Adams remains in Wes's office, pondering the missing piece to the puzzle: the connection of this conspiracy to the AmericaHealth Corporation. As yet unable to ascertain the exact cause of Butch Kennedy's death, the attempted murder of Brad, and the money laundering, Wes, George, and Martin Trimble are at a loss. Theories are hashed and rehashed, but none of them seem terribly compelling.

After an hour or so, George Adams manages to come up with a fresh idea. He explains his plan, which rapidly gains the enthusiasm of Wes and Martin. On the board in his office, Wes maps out the possible chain of events in the plan's execution with suggestions from the other two men. Then, he briefs several field operatives, and a timeline is established for when to institute this new avenue of attack.

At roughly the same time Wes's meeting concludes, Agents Paul Everett and Jim Arnold arrive in front of Edward Westmoreland's house. Luckily, the tall wrought iron gates at the entrance to the driveway are open, making their entry smoother. With their badges draped down over the breast pocket of their blazers, they ring the front doorbell. A seemingly long period of time elapses without an answer. As they reach for the doorknob to see if it's locked, an older butler, in formal attire, pulls the door wide open. Not noticing their badges, he looks the two men over before speaking.

"How may I help you, gentlemen? And before you begin, let me please remind you that we don't allow salesmen in *this* neighborhood."

Tired, and a little irritable, Paul Everett taps on his gold shield with the index finger of his right hand.

"We're with the FBI, and we'd like a moment of Dr. Westmoreland's time. Is he at home?"

This gives the elderly gentleman a start. He mistakenly slams the door in the men's faces. To follow appropriate legal etiquette as much as possible, Jim Arnold presses the doorbell again. Less than a minute later, Patricia Westmoreland arrives at the front door. Dressed in riding clothes with her hair worn up, she looks remarkably youthful.

"I'm terribly sorry about Mr. Drummond. He's very excitable. ... I'm Patricia Westmoreland. Is there something I can help you with?"

"Mrs. Westmoreland, I'm Paul Everett, and this is my partner, Jim Arnold. We're with the FBI, and we'd like to speak with your husband right away."

Obviously taken aback by the request, Patricia escorts the men in and seats them in a large sitting room just off the high-ceilinged foyer.

"May I ask what this is about?"

Very politely, Paul Everett begins, doing his best not to alarm Patricia. "We need to verify some information with your husband, Mrs. Westmoreland."

"Just a minute. I'll go and see if I can locate him."

"Yes, ma'am. Thanks."

Upstairs, Patricia finds Edward in his study. From out in the hallway, she peers in through the cracked door to see him sitting at his desk, shredding reams of documents. His face is heavily shadowed from the dim light of his desk lamp, the only light on in the room. Nudging the door open, she notes a surprised look in his eyes when he sees her.

"Edward, there are two men downstairs. ... They say they're from the FBI."

Edward's head snaps in his wife's direction. "The FBI? Did they say what they wanted?"

Reaching for her husband's hand, Patricia begins to tremble. Her face is contorted, and her deep brown eyes mirror the fear that is welling up within her. "Edward ... do you know why they're here?"

Emotionally unable to lift his gaze to look into his wife's eyes, Edward gets up from his desk and kisses her on the cheek. Without answering her question, he adjusts his collar and straightens his back. Then he walks resolutely to his fate, down two flights of stairs to the foyer. On the way, he gathers all the strength he can muster, telling himself that things can't be nearly as bad as they appear.

Despite being quite shaken up, Edward appears calm when he arrives at the sitting room. After introducing himself to Paul Everett and Jim Arnold, he asks if they would care for a soft drink or a glass of water. Neither makes a request. While the three make small talk, Edward looks into the eyes of each agent, hoping he'll find a glimmer of compassion. Pleasantries soon vanish, and Jim Arnold gets down to the heart of the matter.

"Dr. Westmoreland, do you know why we're here?"

"No, Mr. Arnold. I'm afraid I have no idea whatsoever."

From inside his brown blazer jacket, Jim Arnold withdraws a set of folded papers and lays them unopened on the table in front of Edward. "This is an arrest warrant for you, accusing you of the manslaughter of one of your patients, Randall Kennedy, and of being an accomplice to the attempted homicide of a Dr. Brad Pierson."

The conversation causes a wave of warmth and perspiration to well up within Edward. It is clear that his stoic exterior is beginning to crumble.

"Attempted murder? Manslaughter? There's obviously been some kind of horrible mistake."

Paul Everett now pipes in. "All the same, Dr. Westmoreland, could we ask you to go down with us to FBI headquarters this evening?"

"Is that really necessary?"

"Yes, sir, I'm afraid it is."

"Can I at least say goodbye to my wife first?"

"Yes, sir, you may, but please ask her to come in here."

Edward sends Mr. Drummond in search of Patricia, who arrives several minutes later. He explains that the two FBI agents have asked him to go downtown with them to answer a few questions. Immediately, Patricia becomes quite agitated.

"Edward, what's this all about? What do you mean they want to ask you some questions? You don't have to go with them, do you? ... Edward, answer me!"

Looking dejected, Edward wraps his arms around his wife momentarily and then, without resistance, walks between the two men on the way to their car. Neither he nor the two FBI agents address Patricia's questions. Out of courtesy to Westmoreland's family, Jim Arnold does not handcuff Edward until he is inside the car. Before they drive off, Edward sees Patricia standing steadfastly on the front steps. Her bravery in the face of what's happening comes through in the strength of her voice.

"Edward, Edward ... I love you."

Longingly, he looks back at his home and his wife as he is driven away. In his heart, Edward knows that from this day forward, the life he has known will never be the same.

While Edward is in transit toward downtown Nashville, the lieutenant governor is just arriving at the main FBI headquarters. Greeted by a moderate-sized group of attorneys waving all kinds of legal documents, Wes Shiels can't even get within an arm's length of Buddy Carter. As soon as Mr. Carter is in the door, his lawyers order Wes to have his handcuffs removed and relinquish him to their custody. Saying that such actions might possibly be breaking federal statutes, Wes manages to keep Buddy Carter locked away for now. He knows, however, that with all the legal protection afforded his office, the lieutenant governor will probably never be questioned privately. To make matters worse, the press got wind that something was awry, so the front steps of the FBI building are awash in camera crews trying to peer in. It is at about that time that Wes's head begins pounding.

In the middle of trying to get the lieutenant governor's situation settled, Wes gets an urgent call from Ted McKenzie. Nearly out of breath, Agent McKenzie can barely be heard over the loud sounds of jet aircraft landing and taking off.

"Wes, I'm out here at the Nashville airport. I've got bad news; Alan Richards is nowhere to be found. The taxi company said a guy matching his description was driven to the airport about forty-five minutes ago, but we can't find him anywhere out here. We're checking with the major airlines, but we haven't come up with anything yet."

"Keep after it. Something's got to turn up!"

"Yes, sir."

Because of the furor in front of the building, Wes turns around and makes a call to Paul Everett, instructing him to bring Edward Westmoreland in through the rear entrance of the FBI headquarters. Fifteen minutes later, while Wes is trying to wrench a statement out of Buddy Carter, he is notified that Edward has now arrived and is in the back holding area. Because of the time pressure and high stakes of the operation, Wes decides to question Edward himself.

As he walks alone into the brightly lit but tiny interrogation room, Wes sees Edward, dressed in a plaid short-sleeved shirt and lightweight twill slacks, sitting quite casually with his legs crossed. By his posture and the placid look in his blue eyes, Wes can tell that he might have a difficult time getting any information. Taking a seat close to Edward, Wes introduces himself.

"Dr. Westmoreland, I'm FBI director Wesley Shiels."

Quite composed, Edward nods his head without saying anything.

"Would you mind if I asked you a few questions, Dr. Westmoreland?"

"Certainly, go ahead."

"Before we begin, I need to inform you that you're entitled to an attorney."

"It doesn't seem to me that a lawyer is necessary, Mr. Shiels. Please go ahead with your questions."

"Do you remember a former patient of yours by the name of Randall Kennedy?"

"I certainly do; he was quite a nice man."

"Did you know that he died of a heart attack?"

Yes, I did, one of the cardiologists at the Deaconess Hospital told me about it."

"Were you aware that there was a problem with his autopsy?"

"I was only involved in his care for a short time, so I don't know all the details of his case."

"Did you know he was cremated by mistake after his death?"

"Not until recently; his wife met with me several days ago and told me about that. I was pretty surprised."

"And you didn't know anything about it until she told you?"

"That's right."

"What do you know about a company by the name of AmericaHealth?"

"It's a health insurance company that does business in Nashville. They've asked me to serve on their utilization review committee, which I've done for the past couple of years."

"Mr. Kennedy's health insurance was through AmericaHealth."

"They're a good company. I assume they paid all his bills."

"Is there anything else about the AmericaHealth company you'd like to share with me?"

"What is it you want to know?"

"You work for them, don't you?"

"As I mentioned, I manage one of their committees for them."

By this time, Wes's patience grows thin, and he raises his voice as he pulls out several photographs from a manila envelope and drops them on top of the table in front of Edward.

"Look at this picture of you and Dr. Alan Richards at Belle Meade Country Club a couple of nights ago…And here's a shot of you entering the AmericaHealth Corporation this afternoon. We've been watching you…Now, do you want to tell me anything else?"

Under the pressure, Edward stays remarkably calm.

"Alan and I are old friends. We were having a drink together after a long day, and I already told you that I run the utilization committee for AmericaHealth and have to go down there every once in a while. What else do you want?"

Uncertain that he's making headway, Wes tries a different tack.

"Did you know that Alan Richards performed Mr. Kennedy's autopsy?"

"I wasn't aware of that, but what difference could that possibly make?"

From the same folder containing the photographs, Wes reaches for Alan Richards's autopsy report on Butch Kennedy, along with Dr. Chang's analysis just beneath it. He gives Edward just enough time to read both reports.

"It looks like Dr. Richards was trying to cover something up, doesn't it?"

Laying the typewritten pages on the table, Edward, with a slight flushing of his face, looks Wes Straight in the eyes.

"Not having done the autopsy myself, I'm not sure I'm qualified to answer that question."

"Are there any other comments you'd like to make about Mr. Kennedy's case?"

"I'm afraid not, Director Shiels."

Wes then waves one hand toward the two-way mirror glass that makes up one wall of the room. The door then opens, and Martin Trimble enters with a small stack of papers. Somewhat irritated, Wes pushes the documents in Edward's direction, which are copies of bank depository receipts, showing monthly payments to Edward's account from a bank in Fort Lauderdale.

"What do you think of these, Dr. Westmoreland? Do you know anything yet?"

The papers seem to get Edward's attention, but after he looks them over, he refuses to comment on them. Looking over at Martin, Wes interrupts the silence.

"Dr. Westmoreland we've got enough information to arrest you for taking bribes from the AmericaHealth Corporation."

"If that's a formal charge, I will need to call my attorney."

To everyone's surprise, Wes places a phone in Edward's lap.

"Go ahead, make your call, but let me tell you where we stand. We've got a former patient of yours that was cremated to cover up what looks like a manslaughter. We've got a young doctor by the name of Brad Pierson who started looking into the case, and he almost got himself murdered. Not only that, I've got your buddy Dr. Richards in the room next door, and I'm willing to help out whichever one of you comes forward first."

That last sentence makes an obvious impact on Edward, causing him to snap his eyes in Wes's direction. All the while, Wes continues his overt coercion.

"Dr. Westmoreland, I could be quite generous if you'll answer my questions. I can't tie you directly to Butch Kennedy's death, so I'd be willing to throw out the manslaughter charge against you. If you weren't involved in Brad Pierson's attempted murder and didn't have direct knowledge about it, then I can probably keep you from doing any prison time. But I'll need a full confession from you, and you'll have to give up your license to practice medicine."

With his eyes closed, his head down, and his hand still on the phone, Edward's internal struggle is readily apparent. After a lapse of silence, he lifts his head and opens his eyes. At first, the words come slowly and haltingly, and then, with a burst of emotion, the rest flows freely. By the end, perspiration has soaked the front of his shirt.

"About five years ago … I made some stupid investments, and…all of a sudden, I was bankrupt. Somehow, Robert Altman knew about it. He came and offered a deal. He told me that he was under a lot pressure to keep costs down… He told me that he wanted me to do fewer cases."

Wes interrupts briefly. "What do you mean do fewer cases?"

"He offered me cash to turn away a few cases each month."

"What kind of cases?"

"Bypasses mostly."

"You mean heart bypass surgery?"

"Yes, I was to be paid $20,000 for each case I turned down."

"But how does that help the insurance company to pay you that kind of money?"

"Bypass surgery costs a lot. With surgery, plus several weeks in the intensive care unit, and then the rehab required afterward, it costs about $130,000 a case… If I turned them down, they'd get angioplasty or atherectomy and possible stent placement, which costs more like $35,000, and the patient goes home the next day."

Wes is unable to control his shock.

"Holy Moses."

Then, with a remorseful look, Edward looks Wes directly in the eyes.

"After six months, it was more than I could handle. I couldn't sleep. The nightmares started getting to me. I wanted to get out so bad…but Altman, Altman wouldn't let me. He said there was no turning back. I kept on because I was told my family might be harmed if I didn't… Mr. Kennedy was one of those cases. When he died, it nearly tore me apart… The day Brad Pierson came to my office and started asking me questions about his case, I nearly turned myself in. You've got to believe me—I had no idea someone would try to hurt Brad! I would have given my own life first, as miserable as it is."

Now sobbing, Edward buries his face into the sleeve of his shirt, while his shoulders sway up and down. In an act of humanity, Wes allows Edward to collect himself before asking anything else. Nearly ten minutes lapse before Wes begins again.

"Edward, the one thing I need to know is, why was Mr. Kennedy's heart substituted following the autopsy?"

Rubbing his eyes, Edward clears his throat and tries to speak.

"I told Butch Kennedy he wasn't a candidate for bypass surgery because his heart was severely dilated... That was completely untrue; his heart was fine. But when the family requested the postmortem exam, Alan Richards changed Brad's report to make it seem like Mr. Kennedy's heart was severely dilated. The pathology slides had to be substituted to make things look consistent in case there was ever a question."

"Then Dr. Richards is deeply involved also?"

"I'm afraid so."

The intensity in Wes's voice grows as the interrogation goes on.

"How did Altman pay you?"

"Once a month, I got a payment in the form of a wire transfer directly to my account. I don't know where it came from, but I heard Robert comment one time about some offshore accounts. That's all I know."

"What do you know about the lieutenant governor's role in all this?"

"Altman kept that from me; I wasn't even aware he was involved."

Tired, Wes stops there for now. He asks that Edward be moved to a private holding area and that no one else interview him. After Edward leaves, Wes places his hand on Michael Harris's shoulder and asks where Brad Pierson is.

"He's in your office, Wes; he's been there for almost half an hour."

After he thanks Michael Harris, he stretches his arms and rubs his tired eyes and looks for a cup of coffee before going back to his office. The day has been a hard one and, right now, the only thing he really wants is a long nap.

Chapter 27

Finally alone after a terrifically grueling day, Wes Shiels enjoys just standing still in the middle of the kitchen at FBI headquarters, sipping his coffee. With no one there to disturb him, he finds pleasure in his solitude. Unfortunately, his relaxation is short-lived, because all too soon, his mind turns to many pressing matters that need to be discussed with Brad Pierson. His recently completed interview with Edward Westmoreland has left him with many new questions. Crumpling his paper coffee cup and tossing it into the wastebasket, he walks in the direction of his office. Fully expecting to find Brad there when he arrives, he poses his first question while still in the hallway outside his door.

"Hey, Brad, listen. I just had a thought. What do you think about—"

As he rounds the corner, he is a bit surprised to discover that, in addition to Brad, Sandy Starke is seated beside his desk, prompting a remark.

"Well, Dr. Starke, you seem to be a regular around here. If you keep this up, I'm going to have to put you on the payroll."

Laughing, Sandy slaps Brad on the back. "See, I told you they couldn't get along without me."

Obviously in some sort of hurry, Wes then instructs the two young physicians to follow him. It is now approximately 10:00 p.m. On their way to the conference room, Wes explains that a major planning session is about to get under way. George Adams, Martin Trimble, and eleven field agents are waiting for them when they arrive. Wes immediately takes his place at the head of the table, while Brad and Sandy sit down toward the back of the room. The current status of the operation is then gone over, and Wes briefs his men on the latest updates. Then, he reviews their future direction.

Thirty minutes into the meeting, Wes finds himself completely dissatisfied with the plan they've come up with for making a critical assault on Robert Altman and the AmericaHealth Corporation. He solicits suggestions. A long debate ensues, with some heated disagreement among the men. Nothing proposed so far seems plausible. Wes begins to get discouraged. Then, from the back of the room, Sandy Starke pipes in, which instantly halts all conversation. Initially, several agents protest Sandy's presence at the meeting, but many of his ideas appear to be quite good, prompting an evaluation of their merit. Wes, following his usual format, uses a black marker to begin mapping out on the whiteboard the proposed sequence of events for a final sting operation. Another discussion ensues.

After it is generally agreed upon that the plan is feasible, Wes sends everyone home for the evening. At precisely seven o'clock the following morning, the meeting reconvenes, and Wes gives specific assignments to each person. George Adams volunteers to take on the critical role. Five cars, each with two men, will be necessary to carry this operation off. Additionally, officers from the Nashville Police Department are requested to provide backup. A period of two hours is required to get everything in order. Once that time elapses, Wes, Brad, Sandy, and Martin Trimble take their positions in the central operations room as things get under way.

On Wes's command, George Adams, dressed in a gray pinstripe suit, walks through the main entrance of the AmericaHealth building on the first-floor level. After inquiring at the receptionist's desk as to the location of customer service, he strolls leisurely across the lobby in his freshly polished black wingtips. With no line to stand in when George reaches customer service, he is immediately assisted by a courteous college-aged man who is seated across the room.

"I can help you over here, sir."

At the prompt, George walks over to the man's tiny desk and sits down. Not having worn a suit or tie in over ten years, George tugs at the uncomfortable collar, which is buttoned snugly. As soon as he is settled, the young man speaks up. "What can I do for you today, sir?"

"I seem to be having a problem with my insurance."

Reaching into his inside jacket pocket, George pulls out a stack of folded-up papers with a rubber band wrapped around them, and from his wallet he retrieves his insurance identification card. Glancing quickly at the papers, which are billing statements from several physicians' offices and a local hospital, the young man expresses confidence that he should be able to rectify things quickly. While reading George's assumed name off the front of the insurance card, he looks up at him.

"Let's see, Mr. Lundquist. What seems to be the problem?"

Pretending to be irritated, George points his finger at the papers. "You see these bills? Your company hasn't paid them, and they sent 'em directly to me. A couple of 'em are overdue. … That's why I pay for health insurance, isn't it?"

"Certainly, Mr. Lundquist. This shouldn't take long to sort out. Please bear with me."

After spending a little more time looking over the bills, the young man turns to his desktop computer and enters George's Social Security number off the card to verify proof of insurance. Punching key after key, he sighs loudly when he cannot seem to gain access to George's account. Little does he realize that Sandy's idea was to take information from one of the falsified accounts and print up official-looking documents with that information for George to take with him into AmericaHealth. These accounts are hidden deep within the computer system to avoid casual access, so the young man has a great deal of difficulty finding any kind of information.

Fifteen minutes pass. The customer service representative, whose face by now is quite red, excuses himself. Frustrated, he goes in search of a supervisor to help him. On another computer, not even his supervisor is able to gain access to this particular account. Eventually, one of the senior management officers has to be called in to assist. Because of her higher degree of computer security clearance, this woman, after much effort, is finally able to get into the file containing many of the fake accounts. A few minutes later, she locates George's insurance information. While all this is going on, George keeps up the pressure by intermittently asking questions such as, "Does anybody in this company know what they're doing?" and "How come it takes three of you to figure out something this simple?"

Unaware any of this is going on, Robert Altman, in his penthouse suite, receives a phone call from his personal attorney, Joseph Stanmeyer.

"Robert, this is Joe Stanmeyer. ... I just received a strange phone call from one of Buddy Carter's attorneys. He says that Buddy has been arrested by the FBI and wanted me to get word to you. ... I have no idea what this is all about. Do you?"

Barely breathing, Robert feigns ignorance. "I'm not certain either, Joe. It's unclear to me why Buddy Carter would call me when he's in that kind of trouble. We're just casual friends. ... I guess we probably ought to get together with Buddy's attorney later today to see exactly what's on his mind."

"Okay, I'll set it up and buzz you back."

"Thanks, Joe. Oh, and Joe, it would seem prudent not to mention this to anyone else right now."

"Whatever you say, Dr. Altman."

As soon as the phone conversation is over, Robert nervously swivels around in his chair and investigates a series of files on his desktop computer. Desperately searching each screen, he eventually pauses when he finds what he's after. Then, he opens his top desk drawer, pulls out a flash drive and connects it to the computer. After multiple files have been copied, he pops out the flash drive and stores it in his briefcase. He then destroys the information on the computer. Next, he searches other programs. As he reaches for a second flash drive the phone rings. While continuing to work, he pushes the speakerphone button.

"Dr. Altman?"

"Yes, Ms. Jamison."

"Mr. Sanders is on the line. He says he has an urgent question to ask you."

The irritation in Robert's voice at being disturbed is quite apparent. "All right, go ahead. Put the call through.

"Hello, Brian? What's so pressing that you needed to interrupt me? I'm in the middle of something very important."

"Sorry, Dr. Altman, but I've come across a problem I've never encountered before, and I'm not sure how to handle it."

"What is it?"

"Well, I've got a client of ours by the name of Charles Lundquist who is sitting in customer service right now. He's having a lot of difficulty with his health insurance coverage, and I can't seem to figure out why the computer won't let me get into his account."

"You mean you called the CEO to ask me something *stupid like that?*"

"I know it sounds ridiculous, but the computer tells me that this is something called a 'secured account,' and it lists you as the reference."

Unable to believe what he has just heard, Robert drops the phone and again turns to his computer. Escaping from the file he was just in, he enters a series of passcodes that gain him access to the falsified accounts that he had personally established. With eyes glued to the screen and fingers ready to type, he picks up the phone again and frantically asks Brian Sanders a series of questions.

"What's the guy's name again?"

"Charles Lundquist."

"Date of birth?"

"April 25, 1956."

Forty-five seconds later, he locates the file on Charles Lundquist. After Dr. Altman verifies the correct Social Security number, he stares long and hard at the computer screen. Without feeling the need to question his own memory as to his certainty that this represents one of the money-laundering accounts, he stalls Brian Sanders. The communication from his attorney, and now this incident, has convinced him that something is terribly wrong.

"Brian, can I call you right back? I think I've got the problem almost figured out."

"Sure, Dr. Altman. I'll be sitting right here in my office waiting for your return call."

Surprisingly calm, Robert makes a snap decision on exactly how to handle the situation. He summons his secretary by phone.

"Victoria, could you have the limo brought around to the front for me? I've got an emergency meeting I've got to make. And could you get a hold of Jack Carmichael for me? I'll also be needing the corporate jet right away."

While Robert finishes downloading and then erasing incriminating computer data, he rifles through his desk and filing cabinets. Computer disks and papers are haphazardly strewn across his desk as he ransacks his entire office. Then, walking across the room, he nearly rips a European tapestry off the wall in his haste to get at the wall safe located behind it. He then throws stacks of documents and large sums of bound U.S. currency into his overflowing briefcase. By this time, Victoria Jamison is on the intercom.

"Dr. Altman, I've got Jack Carmichael on the line."

From across the room, Robert shouts, "Tell him I'll be right with him."

Stuffing his briefcase under one arm, Robert runs back to his desk and hastily picks up the phone.

"Jack, this is Robert. A high-priority meeting has just been called in Dallas by the president of the company. I've got to get there right away. Can you get the jet fueled up and ready to go in twenty minutes?"

"Yes, sir, we'll have everything waiting for you."

Robert turns around and immediately calls his secretary again. "I've had a change in plans, Victoria. Could you please ask the limo to come up to the executive parking lot on the fourth floor instead of waiting for me out in front?"

Somewhat surprised by her boss's odd request, Ms. Jamison does as ordered. Meanwhile, through telescopic lenses and other surveillance equipment, the FBI is monitoring every one of Robert Altman's moves. From his last conversation that was intercepted through their phone tap, Wes has already dispatched the Nashville Police to the airport to stop Robert's jet. At the scene, the stretch black Lincoln Town Car is observed as it leaves the front of the AmericaHealth building and enters the parking garage. Robert himself is seen getting on his private elevator. Three cars, situated in close proximity to the building, are in position to follow Robert's limousine when it leaves.

Frequent voice communication is made with Wes Shiels. Through video cameras on-site outside AmericaHealth's corporate headquarters, Wes watches the Lincoln Town Car exit the building several minutes later. Excitedly, he yells, "Okay, get on him!" and all three cars drop into place. Wes then sends a dozen agents with search and arrest warrants into the AmericaHealth building. Meanwhile, with three FBI vehicles trailing, Robert's limousine speeds in the direction of Nashville International Airport.

Feeling good about how the entire operation has progressed so far, Wes loudly congratulates his people for having done a fine job. A moment later, while intensive information gathering is under way and everyone is temporarily distracted, something crucial goes unnoticed. From the side exit ramp of the AmericaHealth building, Robert Altman's black Porsche 911 emerges and quietly drives off. Two blocks away, Robert feels it is safe for him to pick up speed. The high-pitched, turbo-charged engine nearly screams as the car flies down First Avenue North on its way to the interstate highway system. Long before the police ever reach the Nashville airport, Robert has made contact with Jack Carmichael on his cellular phone.

"Jack, this is Robert again. I'm afraid there's been a change in plans; you need to meet me at the Murfreesboro Airport in ten minutes."

There is a pause on the other end before Robert hears Jack's response.

"I'm sorry, Dr. Altman, I'm a little confused; you know I don't have routine clearance to land there."

"Well, I'm on Interstate 40 right now and there's just been a horrible accident. I'll be hours getting to you, so I'm turning around right now and heading toward Murfreesboro. I've got to make this meeting!"

The reluctance in Jack's voice is quite apparent. "All right. I'll call the tower to notify them of the change."

"Don't bother, I've already done it. Now hurry along."

"Yes, sir."

At over 120 miles per hour, Robert weaves wildly in and out of moderately congested traffic on Interstate 24. Remarkably, he arrives at the Murfreesboro Municipal's airstrip just as Jack Carmichael touches down. Once the jet has taxied to a stop, Robert drives alongside it and jumps out of his car, barely taking time to shut the car door. With several long strides he is beside the silver-bodied jet. As soon as Jack lowers the steps, Robert is aboard. Somewhat confused by Robert's erratic behavior, Jack feels compelled to ask a question.

"What kind of meeting are you going to that's got you this wound up, Dr. Altman? And what about the limousine that usually brings you?"

"Don't worry about it, Jack. Just get us up in the air."

Less than two minutes lapse before the jet is off the ground. Shortly thereafter, it approaches cruising altitude. Jack prepares to set his compass for a south-by-southwest course when Robert, from the passenger compartment, gives him another set of instructions.

"Change of plans, Jack; I've just received word that the meeting has been switched to Grand Cayman."

Fully exasperated by the unusual series of requests, Jack raises a protest. "We can't do that. I've filed a flight plan for Dallas. I could lose my license."

"It's either Grand Cayman or you're out of a job. Now hurry up and make a decision."

Disgruntled, Jack has no choice but to turn the plane in a southeasterly direction. Robert Altman's erratic commands and unusually aggressive demeanor have him a bit shaken. Uncertain what to make of all this, he contemplates how to handle the situation once they arrive in the Cayman Islands. For now, he pushes aside his anxieties and forces himself to concentrate so as to avoid making any navigational errors during the flight.

Nearly two-and-a-half hours later, Jack Carmichael brings the dual-turbine Beechcraft jet in for a near perfect landing at the Owens-Roberts Airport on the western edge of Grand Cayman Island. In times past, Jack enjoyed the trip to these islands, often surveying the ocean for wildlife on the way in, but today, the events surrounding the trip preclude any sort of enjoyment. With contact having been made from the air, the corporate limousine and its driver await Robert's arrival. Rude to his pilot as he steps from the plane, Robert instructs Jack to be refueled and ready to go again in one hour.

In his office at the Bank of the Caymans, Arthur Smithfield is surprised by Robert's unexpected phone call from the limousine. During their conversation, he reaches for a fountain pen to take note of everything Robert is requesting. The extensive list will be quite a challenge to fill, but he assures Robert it will be accomplished, hopefully by the time he arrives.

Still in quite a state of agitation, Robert Altman is not nearly himself when he walks in the main entrance of the bank. Usually quite friendly with many of the bank's employees he has gotten to know over the years, today he is abrupt and even fails to notice that many of them have spoken to him. Knowing the way all too well, he makes a straight path to Arthur Smithfield's office. There, he forces himself to stay composed in front of his old friend and business associate. Robert's drawn and somewhat unkempt appearance—no jacket and loose tie—gets Arthur's attention.

"Arthur, I'm sorry I couldn't call ahead this time. My trip, well, it was … a bit unexpected."

Gentlemanly as always, Arthur bows his head. "Most certainly, Dr. Altman. I completely understand. Here are the documents you've requested. ... May I escort you to the safety deposit boxes?"

"Sure, Arthur. Thanks."

Usually walking beside his associate as they travel through the bank, this time Robert leads the way, barely seeming to notice that Arthur is behind him. After the armed security guard slides open the large door constructed of shining steel bars, Robert and Arthur step into the moderately confined vault containing the safety deposit boxes. Closing and locking the door behind them, the guard turns his back to ensure privacy. As has been customary, Arthur inserts his key first and then leaves the room. Robert then produces a second key and guides it into the slot beside Arthur's key. The door is then swung open, and Robert pulls out the heavy metal box and lays it on the familiar marble-topped table located in the center of the room.

Hurriedly, he flings the lid back and stuffs the contents of the box—multiple ledgers, paper documents, and large sums of domestic and foreign currency—into an oversized aluminum briefcase. While doing so, his mind is engulfed in other thoughts.

How in the world am I going to get Anne out of Nashville? What is she going to think? Oh my God, what if they've arrested her?

Very abruptly, Robert yells at the guard to summon Arthur as he finishes. Robert does not allow Arthur the chance to retrieve his key but tosses it at him as he runs out of the room, saying only that he's in a big rush to get to his waiting jet. Back in the limousine, Robert berates his driver for traveling too slow and orders him to "step on it." From the car phone, he raises his pilot.

"Hello, Jack? Are you set to go? I'm on my way, so get the engines running and be ready for takeoff as soon as I get there!"

Then, knowing that it will take at least ten minutes to reach the air-strip, Robert raises an international operator to connect him to his home in Nashville. After four incredibly long rings, his wife answers. Robert sounds almost frantic to her.

"Anne, where have you been? What took you so long to answer the phone?"

At first, apprehension is evident in Anne Altman's voice, followed by obvious relief upon hearing from her husband.

"Robert, where are you? I've been looking for you for hours. On the news, there was a story about a police takeover of your company. I couldn't find you. I've been so worried."

"*What?* A takeover of our company by the police? What in the world is going on? ... Unfortunately, I'm down on Grand Cayman right now; an emergency meeting was called this morning, and I didn't have time to call you before I left. I'll get on the phone in a minute and see what's going on in Nashville. ... I've also just been informed of a major business problem that's developed in Australia. I'm being sent there to deal with it. I'll be leaving here shortly, and I'll get word to you when I arrive."

Still emotional, Anne interrupts her husband. "*Australia?* Why didn't the company tell you anything sooner? This seems awfully sudden for such a long trip. How can they expect that of you?"

Calmly, Robert fabricates an explanation. "There's apparently been a substantial breakdown in negotiations on several contracts, and they want me down there to intervene. I wasn't told about any of this until I arrived on Grand Cayman. ... But listen, Anne, I'm going to be down there a week or so. Why don't you come down? We'll have a fabulous time."

"Do you mean it?"

"Sure, I do. ... Go on out to the airport right now. I'll have a first-class ticket waiting for you on American Airlines to Sydney. But hurry. According to my computer, the flight leaves in about ninety minutes."

No longer upset, Anne bubbles over with excitement. "Oh, Robert, that sounds wonderful; I'll see you tonight hopefully. I love you."

"Love you, too, Anne. Gotta go."

"Okay, sweetheart."

Robert puts down the phone just as the chauffeur reaches the airport on Grand Cayman Island. Up ahead, the corporate jet, with turbines running at low speed, is in sight. Before the car has come to a complete stop, Robert pushes open his door. Climbing out, he runs to the plane with his aluminum briefcase in one hand. Sprinting up the steps, Robert pulls the cabin door tight behind him and turns the large knob to seal the airlock. Instead of going to the spacious passenger compartment, he walks instead to the cockpit and takes a seat beside Jack Carmichael. Speaking quickly and nervously, he gives him specific orders.

"Okay Jack, get this thing in the air."

"You haven't told me where we're going yet; how do you expect me to take off?"

"Just get us out of here, Jack."

"I can't do anything until I file a flight plan with the tower, Dr. Altman. You know that."

"This is the last time I'm going to tell you: *get this thing off the ground!*"

"Yes, sir."

As Jack quickly taxis the plane into position and prepares for takeoff, the airport tower makes communication over the radio.

"Beechcraft 791, you are not cleared for takeoff. Repeat, you are not cleared for takeoff, Beechcraft 791. Over."

Robert grabs Jack's wrist as he reaches for the switch to activate radio communication.

"Don't even think about it."

While the jet is out on one of the main runways gaining speed, the tower continues to yell out its warnings: "Beechcraft 791, do not take off! Return to the terminal immediately. You are in violation. Stop at once!"

Now halfway down the runway and traveling at seventy miles an hour, the plane has almost reached enough speed to become airborne. At that moment, Robert notices two black Cadillac sedans accelerating past them on either side. From over the radio, a different man's voice, yelling commands, can now be heard.

"This is the FBI, Dr. Altman. Stop the plane. There's no way you can escape. Stop the plane now!"

Showing no sign of relenting, Robert presses a pistol into Jack's ribs. The jet continues to accelerate. Not far up ahead, Robert can see the ocean coming into view, signaling the end of the runway. By now, their speed has surpassed that of the two FBI vehicles. Robert breathes a sigh of relief. Just as he thinks he's escaped, from behind a small building off to the right of the runway he sees a large fire truck with its emergency lights on backing onto the tarmac in front of the Beechcraft. He realizes that, in less than two seconds, they'll crash directly into it. Instinctively, Jack pulls back the steering controls and manages to get the jet off the ground. It barely clears the truck by angling sideways, and the sharp ascent causes the right wing-mounted engine to stall. Only forty feet off the ground, the plane bounces around and begins losing altitude. Robert panics and yells out as he looks below, knowing they're about to crash. Twenty yards beyond the end of the runway, the jet spirals down, landing nose first into the shallow saltwater. The final thing Robert remembers, as his face hits the dashboard, is Jack screaming out in pain. Simultaneously, in Nashville, communication is made to Wes Shiels about the situation.

"Altman's jet just crashed into the ocean. Status of occupants unknown."

Luckily for Jack and Robert, the plane floats for a few minutes before sinking. A rescue team makes it to the scene quickly. Both men are still alive when they're pulled from the cockpit. Unconscious, they are rushed by ambulance to Royal Saint George's Hospital, only minutes from the airport. By the time Jack reaches the emergency room, he is awake. His workup reveals only several fractures of his right arm, which will require surgery. More seriously injured, however, Robert is in a deep coma following head trauma and is taken immediately to the operating room to stop internal bleeding and to reinflate his right lung, which was punctured by multiple broken ribs. During his workup, he is also discovered to have severe damage to several spinal bones in the neck, which will need to be addressed once he is more stable.

Four hours are required to adequately take care of Robert's chest wounds, and then the U.S.-trained cardiothoracic surgeon who operated on Robert discusses the case with the local police and FBI officials.

"He sustained severe trauma to the cervical spine and needs immediate surgical stabilization. Unfortunately, we don't have a neurosurgeon down here capable of performing the procedure. I'm afraid we're going to need some help."

After a brief conference, the FBI decides they're willing to fly in a neurosurgeon from the United States, the closest available physician being in Miami. In the meantime, Robert is given high doses of steroids to keep his neck swelling down, and he is placed in a spine stabilization device. Being a humane person, Wes Shiels allows Anne Altman to travel to Grand Cayman to stay at her husband's side. Not wishing to upset her under the circumstances, he withholds some of the information regarding Robert's suspected criminal activity.

Shortly after Robert Altman's crash, Wes receives an update from one of his field agents on Dr. Alan Richards.

"Wes, this is Ted McKenzie. We were able to track Richards to the Nashville airport, but instead of getting on a plane, he rented a car in the name of Gustaf Schmidt. From there, he drove to the Atlanta airport and boarded a flight yesterday afternoon for London. ... We found his rental car still sitting in short-term parking at the Atlanta airport—it's clean. No trace of him after arriving in London last night."

"Where are you now?"

"Still in the Atlanta airport."

Accompanying Ted McKenzie is a new recruit to the FBI, agent John Childers. Even thouh he has been on the job for less than six months, he has already accumulated an impressive work record.

Wes then barks out another order.

"I want you and Childers to get on the next flight to London. I'll call the British Secret Intelligence Service in the meantime and have them meet you at Heathrow Airport. You can pick up some extra clothes when you arrive."

"Okay, Wes. We'll get moving right away."

Back in Wes's office, Brad and Sandy are quite distraught when they hear of Alan's escape.

Chapter 28

Two days after his first surgery, Robert Altman returns to the operating room at Royal Saint George's Hospital on Grand Cayman Island. His neurosurgeon, Dr. Mitchell Armstrong, arrived from Miami yesterday and has kept close watch over Robert during the preceding twenty-four hours. Still comatose and on the ventilator, Robert was transported to the operative suite forty-five minutes ago. His wife, Anne, traveled with him nearly all the way. When it came time to release his hand, she sobbed pitifully, wrenching the hearts of everyone nearby.

Now, in the surgical waiting area, she sits tensely perched on her chair, holding out for any word on her husband's condition. The hours drag on, only piquing her emotions. Any time a nurse enters the room to pass along information to any of the families, she stands, hoping it is her turn. Disappointed many times, she is nearly beside herself when, finally, Dr. Armstrong appears in person. As the sentence, "He made it through surgery okay and is on his way to recovery" strikes her ears, her rubbery legs threaten to buckle beneath her. It takes her several seconds to comprehend what was said. Sighing loudly, she asks when she may see Robert.

During the surgery, the experienced Dr. Armstrong went about repairing the two fractured vertebral bodies in Robert's neck and then, using artificial discs, replaced the discs between the bones, which had completely collapsed in the traumatic plane crash. Titanium rods were necessary to stabilize the spinal bones of the neck, and afterward Robert was fitted with a rigid supportive device, termed a halo. The apparatus consists of several long stainless steel rods that run from the shoulders to the head. At the head, they are connected to a metal ring that not only encircles the skull but is also bolted into it at four separate points, thereby preventing any movement of the neck. All told, Robert will have to wear this device for at least three months.

When Anne Altman is finally allowed to see her husband with the large metal halo in place and two large tubes exiting either side of his chest, she nearly faints. Still unconscious and on a respirator, Robert's face and neck are heavily bruised and severely swollen. He is barely recognizable even to his wife. After giving her a few minutes alone with her husband, Dr. Armstrong comes in and advises Anne Altman that there is a slight possibility that Robert may not survive the extensive injuries he's sustained. He also mentions that if Robert's condition does stabilize, he would like to move him by jet to Miami, where his progress can be monitored more closely. The news only brings more tears from Anne. Mitchell Armstrong, an empathetic individual, does his best to comfort her.

Clutching Robert's hand for the next five days while he lies unresponsive, Anne Altman refuses to leave him. She spends nights in a reclining chair in the corner of his room. Although sleeping intermittently, she maintains a constant vigil for her husband's condition. By the end of the sixth postoperative day, Robert finally begins to show improvement, so Dr. Armstrong authorizes the transfer to the University of Miami Medical Center. Both he and Anne make the voyage across the Gulf of Mexico with Robert in the air ambulance.

Long before Robert ever regains consciousness, the grand jury investigation of the AmericaHealth conspiracy proceeds forward on schedule. With more than ample evidence to make multiple indictments, a trial date is set and the jury pool is summoned. To no one's surprise, the highly ethical Sidney Isaacson is appointed to preside over both the investigation and the subsequent trial, resulting in constant communication between him and FBI Director Wesley Shiels.

On a cool and dreary late October day in Nashville, the criminal trial begins its proceedings. Against a gray and heavily cloud-laden sky are the unmistakable profiles of hardwood trees, the nearly barren limbs of which cling on to the few remaining leaves. On the ground, a light breeze tosses about some of the discarded red-and-orange foliage that has yet to lose its brilliant autumn color.

The day is one that Brad Pierson has long dreaded. As he stands in the tiny bathroom of the FBI safe house in Bellevue, he ponders the events of the last several months while paying little attention to the long necktie that lays draped around his collar. With each episode that he will be forced to relive at the trial, he's well aware of the personal pain he'll suffer.

Staring blankly into the mirror, Brad is somehow unaware of his own reflection. Deeply lost in thought, he jumps when he feels someone touch him from behind. In the mirror, he sees his father's solemn but reassuring face, and suddenly he finds the warm hand on his shoulder quite comforting. A moment later, his mother arrives. Sensing her son's apprehension, she instinctively reaches to help him with his tie. Not long afterward, Wesley Shiels, from the hallway outside the bathroom, announces, "It's time."

The home where the Piersons are being sequestered is a small, one-story ranch-style house that maintains a solitary perch on a densely wooded hilltop in the southern Nashville suburb of Bellevue. Parked in front is a navy Ford Crown Victoria with heavily tinted windows. Flanking the car on either end are several black-and-white police cars, waiting to escort the Ford Crown Victoria to its ultimate destination. Cutting a swath through early morning traffic, the Pierson family arrives uneventfully in front of the federal courthouse building at Legislative Plaza in downtown Nashville.

With police officers and FBI agents on hand to push back the camera crews and anxious onlookers, Brad and his family run up the long rows of marble steps and reach the entrance of the federal courthouse building without incident. Inside the courtroom itself, with its eighty-foot vaulted ceilings, polished marble columns, and gilt-edged intricate woodwork, Brad, David, and Jean Pierson are swiftly escorted to the front row of the first-floor seating area. Glancing back before sitting down, Brad sees the huge doors swing shut behind them. Posted at every exit and vantage point are heavily armed police officers. It is not until all security checks are completed that Wes says anything. Then, and only then, he imparts a brief comment to the Piersons.

"Once we've got you and all the other key witnesses settled, we'll let everyone else into the building."

As soon as the entire courtroom, including the balcony, is filled to capacity, the rear doors are sealed shut and locked tight. At Wes's signal, the prosecutors and defense attorneys are then allowed in. The twelve jurors arrive next, and afterward the bailiff instructs everyone to rise. The distinguished Sidney Isaacson then emerges from his chambers and takes his position at the tall judge's platform that looms high over the courtroom, giving its occupant an intimidating stance. After Judge Isaacson gives a detailed announcement of the proceedings, he carefully instructs the jury and then nods at the lead prosecutor.

"Mr. Caldwell, you may now make your opening statement."

The trim, moderately-tall Harris Caldwell gets up quickly from the prosecutor's table. He succinctly overviews the AmericaHealth conspiracy, in which Robert Altman, as chief executive officer of the company, is accused of masterminding a complex influence-peddling, bribery, and money-laundering scheme, along with attempted murder, while attempting to advance his agenda.

"This conspiracy had far-reaching arms, ladies and gentlemen of the jury. It involved well-respected physicians, members of the Nashville police force, known criminals, *and even the lieutenant governor himself!* Dr. Altman utilized all of these individuals to propel his company forward, mindful only of the personal fortunes he would reap, never once giving thought to the innocent people who never got the health care he promised them!"

As Harris Caldwell paces back and forth a respectful distance from the jury box, Brad notes his choppy short strides and his brief but not overly dramatic arm motions. His words are purposely chosen and precisely enunciated, and his tone is an impassioned plea. In his early sixties, he has jet black hair showing only gray at the temples. His brown eyes contain a driven intensity. Well-dressed, he wears a conservatively tailored, dark double-breasted suit with expensive, matching, kiltie tassel loafers.

It was certainly no accident that Harris Caldwell was chosen for this high-profile case. After graduating Yale Law School at the age of twenty-two, he returned to his home state of Michigan, where he successfully indicted members of the Teamsters Union for racketeering. Less than five years later, his string of successes led the judicial branch of the federal government to offer him a position overseeing many of their most challenging cases. Spearheading a probe into drug smuggling out of Central and South America in the 1980s, he was chosen to act as lead counsel for the Manuel Noriega trial. In the early

1990s, he was involved in the investigation and subsequent prosecution of multiple United States congressmen and senators involved in bribery schemes associated with the savings-and-loan crisis.

Once Harris Caldwell has finished his carefully crafted introduction, Sidney Isaacson directs his attention to the defense table, where the sizable team of attorneys are closely huddled together. After a short lapse, one of the male attorneys gets to his feet and announces that he will serve as lead counsel.

As the Atlanta-born Reginald James Carruthers begins his eloquent rebuttal of each point Harris Caldwell just espoused, the differences in the two lawyers become readily apparent. Compared to his more youthful counterpart, the mildly overweight R. J. Carruthers appears to be in his late seventies. His almost completely gray hair is worn a bit longer, and his eyes are partially obscured by horn-rimmed, tortoiseshell eyeglasses. Less formally dressed, he wears a tweed jacket, brown wool vest, and slacks, and he carries an antique gold pocket watch, which he looks at often. Laid-back in his approach, he slowly strides up to the jury box and lays one arm on the railing, speaking to each of the jurors as if they were old acquaintances in his drawn-out Georgia accent.

Despite his seemingly relaxed approach, R. J. Carruthers is a formidable opponent. For nearly two decades, he successfully prevented several Southern states from litigating against the tobacco industry while allowing the companies to continue aggressive national advertising campaigns. The current trial is not the first occasion he has had to do battle with the federal government. Ten years ago, he represented several military defense contractors who had been accused of bilking billions of dollars out of the Pentagon. In addition to getting many of the fines substantially curtailed, he managed to keep many of the companies from going bankrupt altogether.

When summarizing his version of the events surrounding Robert Altman's criminal behavior in his opening remarks, R. J. Carruthers cites a lack of written documents that prove his client's guilt. He also argues that without Dr. Alan Richards's direct testimony Robert cannot be connected to Butch Kennedy's death. Robert Altman has proven to be a master of manipulating those around him; he didn't leave a paper trail connecting the bribes to Edward Westmoreland back to him. Hence, it is Edward's word against Robert's in the courtroom, and the evidence against Edward is damning. It is painfully obvious to Brad that when R. J. Carruthers completes his introductory remarks, the jurors have been partially swayed by his convincing version of the events. At that moment, Brad's attention is distracted by Wes Shiels, who receives an urgent faxed update on Alan Richards's location from one of his men stationed overseas. Apparently, after arriving in London nearly two months ago, Dr. Richards managed to find passage on a small fishing boat across the English Channel. Two days later, he was spotted in Brussels. There, a man fitting his description appeared at one of the more eminent Belgian banks and retrieved 10 million dollars that had been wired from the Bank of the Caymans prior to the time the FBI had frozen the accounts. From there, he rented a car and drove to Paris, where he boarded a flight to Athens. Despite an intensive search, no other clues as to his location have surfaced since then.

Angry about the escape, Wes crumples the printed document and throws it to the floor while the first witness is being called to the stand. In a highly emotional testimony, Elinor Kennedy describes the events surrounding her husband's death. This is obviously difficult for her, and she breaks down often, despite Harris Caldwell's delicate approach. Wisely, at this juncture, R. J. Carruthers declines to cross-examine her, fearing the reaction of the jury. Afterward, Dr. James Sterling, the emergency room physician who assisted in Butch's care on his two admissions to the Deaconess Hospital, is called to testify. Dr. Leonard Peters, Butch's cardiologist, is summoned next. He mentions the echocardiogram that Edward Westmoreland performed, demonstrating that Butch had a severely dilated heart, which excluded him from bypass surgery. When Dr. Peters speculates that the report of the study may have been falsified by Dr. Westmoreland, R. J. Carruthers swiftly halts his testimony.

"Dr. Peters, did you see the echocardiogram yourself?"

"No, but—"

"You mean to tell me that a physician with a reputation as fine as yours didn't even bother to look at the echocardiogram before deciding the best course of treatment for your patient?"

"I don't think you quite understand how things work in medicine. We depend on the specialists we consult to guide us through decisions such as this one—"

Before Dr. Peters is allowed to finish answering, R. J. Carruthers inserts another question. "So you can't say for certain that Mr. Kennedy *didn't* have a badly dilated heart."

"There is a lot of evidence—"

"Answer the question—yes or no."

"No, I can't."

"Thank you, Dr. Peters."

The quick-witted Harris Caldwell moves quickly from his seat and breezes by R. J. Carruthers on the way to the witness stand. He confidently addresses the cardiologist while glancing at the jury. "Dr. Peters, did Mr. Kennedy have anything on his clinical evaluation to suggest a dilated heart?"

The gray-haired cardiologist appears relieved to be given an opportunity to further discuss his thoughts. "No. The usual signs of swelling of the extremities and fluid in the lungs were absent, which made me somewhat skeptical of the validity of Dr. Westmoreland's report."

Looking directly into Dr. Peters's eyes, Harris Caldwell makes a pointed inquiry: "Had you ever had occasion to question any of Dr. Westmoreland's evaluations before?"

"There had been a patient or two before Mr. Kennedy—"

Nearly yelling, R. J. Carruthers interrupts the witness, saying, "Objection, Your Honor! What is the relevance to this case?"

Sidney Isaacson then addresses the prosecuting attorney. "I'm sorry, Mr. Caldwell, but Mr. Carruthers has a valid point. I'll have to sustain his objection."

Resting his eyes on the jurors as he returns to his seat, Harris Caldwell, aware that he's cast suspicion in their minds, smugly says, "That's all, Dr. Peters. Thank you."

At 3:00 p.m. on the first day of testimony, Judge Isaacson decides to halt the trial and announces that the court will reconvene at nine o'clock the following morning.

On the second day of the proceedings, things move swiftly. Brad's heart races when he hears his name being called by the bailiff. Before Brad gets up, David Pierson places one arm around his son, giving him a reassuring squeeze on the shoulder.

"Don't worry, Brad. You've already proven that you're tougher than they are."

As he walks the seemingly endless distance from the first row seating area to the witness stand, Brad feels a bit shaky. Glancing up at Sidney Isaacson, he notes a look of almost fatherly protection in his shining hazel-colored eyes. While getting situated, Brad gazes briefly at the jurors and notes that each face is turned in his direction. One of the women, sensing his uncertainty, smiles at him, and somehow he finds her kindness comforting. Then, he mounts the courage to view the remainder of the people in the courtroom. Several attending physicians and professors from Vanderbilt are instantly recognizable, as are many of his former classmates from medical school. When his glance sweeps across the ground floor, he pauses momentarily on Julie, who gives him a loving, supportive look. Beside her, her mother, Anna, appears quite worried. Sandy Starke merely raises his fist and opens his mouth wide to form the sentence "Go get 'em!"

Harris Caldwell approaches him first. He relates in great detail the complex string of events, beginning with Butch Kennedy's autopsy. The audience rumbles frequently with emotion, especially when Brad describes his encounter with the police at Centennial Park. R. J. Carruthers slyly attempts to shake his testimony, but Brad confidently stands his ground, dismissing each of the attorney's verbal assaults.

Exhausted after his testimony, Brad asks Wesley Shiels's permission to leave the courtroom early. Not long afterward, he and his parents are traveling south to their secure home in Bellevue. Brad misses the only remaining witness of that day, the forensic pathologist from FBI headquarters in Washington, DC, Dr. Nelson Chang.

On an overhead projection screen at the front of the courtroom, the pathology slides from Butch Kennedy's autopsy are shown while Dr. Chang undertakes a thorough discussion of the findings. Afterward, the irrefutable DNA analysis is shown, demonstrating that Butch's heart had, indeed, been switched. Unable to discredit the well-documented evidence, R. J. Carruthers attempts to cast doubt on the presentation by pointing out that Brad Pierson is "a mere physician-in-training and may have accidentally switched the heart slides himself at the time of the autopsy due to his lack of experience." Those statements bring a resounding objection from Harris Caldwell.

"Your Honor, defense counsel is trying to testify. There is nothing in Dr. Pierson's spotless record to indicate that an incident such as this has ever occurred."

Nodding his head, Sidney Isaacson sustains the objection. "Mr. Carruthers, you know the rules. Please limit yourself to asking questions, *not* answering them as well. ... Members of the jury, please ignore Mr. Carruthers's last statement."

Once R. J. Carruthers has completed his extensive cross-examination of Dr. Chang, the second day of the trial concludes.

Having slept only a few hours the night before his testimony, Brad excuses himself shortly after dinner and leaves his parents and his FBI bodyguards to crawl into bed. Several hours later, while in a deep slumber, he dreams that someone is shaking him. He fights, still exhausted, to suppress the dream in an effort to remain asleep. Unfortunately, the shaking persists, and he fully awakens when he hears someone yell, "Brad, come on, get up! We've got to go!"

Startled, he quickly sits up and is surprised to see Wes Shiels standing over him, accompanied by two other FBI agents. Assisting Brad out of bed, Wes Shiels explains, "For the last hour, we've maintained constant surveillance on two unknown vehicles watching the house. We've got to move you and your parents right now."

Utilizing police escort, the Ford Crown Victoria, with its bulletproof body panels, glass, and tires, blasts through traffic at over ninety miles an hour to the downtown FBI headquarters. Makeshift sleeping quarters are arranged for Brad and his family until a new location can be decided upon for the near future. Not surprisingly, returning to sleep is difficult for Brad. Several times that night he is awakened by nightmares, his heart pounding and his clothing drenched in sweat. Meanwhile, back in Bellevue, Wes's men surround the two cars and apprehend their occupants at gunpoint. While in custody at FBI headquarters, Brad identifies one of the men as having been at his apartment the night it was robbed and recognizes another as the driver of the Cadillac that had pursued him.

The following morning, Brad and his family are nearly late for the trial because of their scramble to get ready in the unfamiliar surroundings. They barely reach their seats before the first witness of the day, the blond police sergeant Bill O'Neill, takes the stand. After verifying Brad's account of what occurred that night at Centennial Park, he goes on to describe how Captain Lefevre handed him a photograph and a falsified arrest record for Brad that implicated him in the liquor store shooting. At that point R. J. Carruthers begins his cross-examination.

"Sergeant O'Neill, do you still have the photograph of Dr. Pierson or the supposed record?"

"No, sir. Captain Lefevre kept it."

"So, you actually don't have proof of what you're telling us."

"I was there, and I know what happened. That's my proof."

"I'm afraid that wasn't the question. Do you have physical evidence of any kind?"

"No, sir."

"Then it's your word against Captain Lefevre's."

"No, sir, it's—"

"Thank you. That's all, Sergeant."

Before leaving the witness stand, Bill O'Neill is questioned by Harris Caldwell.

"Sergeant O'Neill, do you see the person in the photograph that Captain Lefevre showed you in the courtroom today?"

Bill O'Neill points to Brad Pierson without hesitation. Harris Caldwell continues and asks Brad to stand up for the jurors to see.

"Have you ever seen Dr. Pierson before, Sergeant O' Neill?"

Bill O'Neill then turns his head side to side and says; "Never."

Harris Caldwell then locks gazes with many of the jurors when he says; "Thank you Sergeant, O'Neill."

Having inflicted a damaging blow to the defense, the lead prosecutor then summons Harry Lefevre from the defense table. The charges lodged against him are read aloud. Practically sneering while being questioned by Harris Caldwell, Harry Lefevre denies all wrongdoing and fabricates a series of elaborate tales to legitimize his activities. In response to the question about why AmericaHealth had paid him such large sums of money, he explains that Robert Altman had contracted with him to set up extensive security systems around the country for many of the company's offices. When asked about Bill O'Neill, he theorizes that the sergeant nearly shot the wrong man following the liquor store robbery and has implicated him to place the blame onto someone else.

Aware of Captain Lefevre's maneuver, Harris Caldwell then asks that prosecution item D be brought forward. After a brief inspection, he instructs the bailiff to play the compact disc over the courtroom's speaker system. The first voice is that of a gruff man with a strong Southern accent.

"Is this Bill O'Neill?"

"Yes sir, it is. Who's calling?"

"I've been told to give you a message. If you go and testify at the trial, someone's gonna put the hurt on you and your family. You wouldn't want somethin' to happen to that sweet little girl o' yours, would ya?"

"*Who is this?*"

At that point, the caller hangs up. Harris Caldwell again directs his attention to Harry Lefevre.

"Capital Lefevre, if your supposition that Sergeant O'Neill is lying is correct, then why would anyone bother to threaten him?"

With an ingratiating look, Harry looks directly at the jury while responding. "Since that's not my voice on what you just played, your guess is as good as mine. Perhaps the fellow knew Bill O'Neill was going to lie and wanted to keep him quiet."

Frustrated, Harris Caldwell thrusts his jaw forward. "And what if Mr. O'Neill is telling the truth and you sent one of your thugs after him?"

The last comment brings R. J. Carruthers up out of his chair. "Objection, Your Honor!"

With minor irritation in his voice, Sidney Isaacson addresses the objection. "Sustained. Mr. Caldwell, you know better than to delve into innuendo."

"Yes, Your Honor. Question withdrawn."

Despite a more than adequate defense, the extent of Harry Lefevre's criminal activity is clearly demonstrated. In a series of private bank accounts on both Hilton Head and Grand Cayman Island, huge sums of money were discovered that were traceable directly back to the AmericaHealth Corporation. R. J. Carruthers is able to forcefully establish that the bribes came from AmericaHealth, but a direct link to Robert Altman was nonexistent. Presumably representing payoffs for illegal services rendered, the multi-hundred thousand dollar accounts were well beyond Harry's explanation, which was that the money had come from setting up security systems for AmericaHealth. Both legitimate police officers and hired criminals had been utilized to carry out Harry's illegal activities, and there was no doubt that he was directly responsible for Brad's attempted murder. In addition to helping Robert Altman set up his money-laundering operation, Harry was directly linked to the intimidation of physicians and patients who filed complaints against AmericaHealth.

After a two-hour recess for lunch, the trial reconvenes, and shortly thereafter, there is a furor at the rear of the courtroom. After Wes and his men expel a large number of excited camera crews and spectators, the reason for the commotion becomes obvious. Emerging from the crowd with his large legal staff and FBI bodyguards, the lieutenant governor Buddy Carter takes a seat at the defense table in anticipation of his testimony. His much publicized misconduct has the entire city of Nashville abuzz. Sidney Isaacson has a difficult time maintaining order in the courtroom.

From the substantial evidence unearthed by the FBI, the role that Mr. Carter played in the conspiracy becomes well elucidated. With illegal funds from Robert Altman's money-laundering operation, the lieutenant governor was offered a series of substantial bribes to shift the state workers' insurance coverage to AmericaHealth by informing Robert Altman of all other bids that had been received. Once the company had landed the contract, Buddy Carter then used his political influence to push through a 15-percent increase in the number of dollars spent on health-care premiums for the state workforce, thereby directly benefiting the company. Additionally, he was instrumental in restricting competition for the state insurance contract by helping to enact specific legislation that prevented several companies from doing business in the state of Tennessee. Finally, through political wrangling, he managed to influence the passage of certain laws that severely curtailed lawsuits against health insurance companies.

Toward the end of his examination, Harris Caldwell approaches the judge's bench and requests that prosecution item P be brought forward for examination. Several minutes lapse. The bailiff returns in a frantic state, stating that many crucial pieces of evidence that had been stored in the courtroom safe are missing. Aware that this item represents a taped conversation between Buddy Carter and Harry Lefevre concerning how to handle Brad Pierson's homicide, Wes Shiels quickly places a call to the downtown FBI headquarters, where a copy of the tape has been stored in the crime lab.

After a brief pause on the other end of the line, a worried-sounding assistant bureau chief, Martin Trimble, comes to the phone. "Wes, we've got a problem! That tape, plus several other things stored in the same locker, have disappeared. The log shows that they were accounted for last night at ten o'clock on our last check."

Slamming the phone down, Wes yells, "*Damn!*" Looking up at the witness stand, he is further angered when he discerns a thinly veiled smile on the lips of the plump-faced lieutenant governor.

Aware of how crucial this information is to the case, Harris Caldwell attempts to have the transcripts of the tape introduced as evidence, but because the original recording is missing, R. J. Carruthers triumphantly blocks Caldwell's motion. This new development has introduced an element of unrest into the courtroom. Amid the bickering between the legal staffs of both the prosecution and the defense, Sidney Isaacson elects to halt the trial for the day.

The following morning, day five of the proceedings, the third defendant, Willie Buck, is called to the stand. Tall, with long, greasy dark hair and a pronounced beard shadow, Willie Buck's attire of jacket and tie does little to cover his roughened appearance. As Willie begins his testimony, Brad glances over at his deeply recessed eyes and heavily wrinkled face and becomes unnerved, remembering time this man stalked him and nearly took his life. His voice harkens back to that awful night at Opryland Amusement Park when Brad was hiding under that bridge and heard Willie Buck standing directly over him.

Under Harris Caldwell's carefully directed interrogation, Willie Buck openly confesses that he attempted to take Brad's life under the direct orders of Harry Lefevre. Buddy Carter's façade of innocence is shattered as Willie Buck implicates him as having had full knowledge of both the plot to assassinate

Brad Pierson and Robert Altman's money-laundering operation. He admits to having received specific instructions from Harry Lefevre to carry out beatings, threats, and harassment against a variety of physicians and patients who registered complaints with the state insurance commissioner against AmericaHealth. He identified Robert Altman as the central figure of the entire complex conspiracy.

After Willie Buck is released from further questioning by Harris Caldwell, R. J. Carruthers expresses his desire to cross-examine. Several seconds lapse while he confers with his team of attorneys. Then, in contrast to his usual easygoing pace, Carruthers forcefully strides forward from the defense table, perching himself in close proximity to the witness.

"Mr. Buck, that's quite a story you told us. You didn't, by any chance, happen to make a deal with the FBI to avoid prosecution, did you?"

Before answering, Willie Buck stares at Wes Shiels, who nods his head. "Yes, sir, I did."

"And exactly what was in that deal?"

Harris Caldwell yells out, "Objection!"

R. J. Carruthers's response is instantaneous. "This goes to credibility of the witness, Your Honor."

Sidney Isaacson glances down while momentarily contemplating his answer. "All right, Mr. Carruthers, I'll allow it, but please be discreet in your line of questioning."

"Mr. Buck, please answer the question."

"Mr. Shiels, he tol' me—"

"Are you speaking of *FBI Director Wesley Shiels?*"

"Yes, sir, that's him. He said that if'n I came forward wid the truth, he'd git my sentence pushed way down."

Turning away from the witness, R. J. Carruthers walks to the defense table, picks up a single typewritten page, and hands it to Sidney Isaacson.

"Your Honor, I wish to submit defense item T."

Once Carruthers places the document before him, Sidney Isaacson slides on his gold-rimmed reading glasses. After he has satisfactorily completed his review, he summons Harris Caldwell. After giving Caldwell several minutes to digest the contents of the page, he asks the prosecuting attorney if he has any objection. With no reservation expressed, the exhibit is returned to R. J. Carruthers, who hands it to each of the jurors in turn. Meanwhile, he peppers Willie Buck with a string of inquiries.

"Do you know what this is, Mr. Buck? It's your criminal record. ... It seems you've had a busy life. Assault and battery, armed robbery, and carrying a concealed weapon. That's quite a series of arrests, Mr. Buck. Have anything to say?"

The witness declines to comment, choosing instead to cast his glance at the floor in front of him. R. J. Carruthers then sweeps back along the jury box and again plants himself in front of Willie Buck.

"Why should the jury believe anything you say, Mr. Buck? You're a thief, and it's just as likely you're a liar. ... You'd do anything to save your own skin, *anything to keep you from going back to prison, wouldn't you, Mr. Buck?*"

Confident that he's destroyed this witness's credibility, R. J. Carruthers turns around and walks with self-assurance back toward his seat. Surprised to hear a response, he listens carefully while barely breaking stride.

"You oughta believe what I said 'cause it's the truth, that's why. And don't you never call me a liar again, or you'll live to regret the day you was born!"

The chilling threat halts R. J. Carruthers in his tracks and brings a swift reprisal from Sidney Isaacson.

"Mr. Buck! There will be no such conduct in this courtroom! Bailiff, return Mr. Buck to the federal jail while I debate contempt of court. Remove him from my sight this instant!"

A two-hour recess for lunch is then announced, at which point Wes Shiels receives a status report on Robert Altman's condition from one of his men in Miami.

"He left the intensive care unit this morning? ... When do you think he will be strong enough to make a statement? ... Two days? Great! Let's ship him up here by private jet tomorrow. I'll get everything ready and have a bed waiting for him at Vanderbilt Hospital."

Fortunately, that afternoon, the testimony is much more routine with no major controversies arising. Several patients who had been insured with, and an assortment of doctors who had been contracted by, AmericaHealth come forward to describe some of the atrocities they've sustained at the hands of

Robert Altman and his coconspirators. Among the list of grievances is denial of appropriate health care, lack of approval for specific critical tests, and suppression of complaints.

In keeping with FBI procedures, at the end of each day the sequestered witnesses are escorted from the courtroom last with heavy police protection. Near the end of the line this evening, Brad is not far behind Edward Westmoreland and his wife, Patricia. He notes the anguished look on the surgeon's face, likely in anticipation of his testimony, which is to begin in the morning. Nearly on schedule this evening, there is only a short wait at the front doors of the federal courthouse building while the news media and bystanders are cleared away.

Once a path down the front steps has been established, Wes nods his head, and Elinor Kennedy and Sergeant Bill O'Neill depart first and make it successfully to a large, black Chevrolet Suburban without undue fracas. The Westmorelands are given the signal to go next, and Brad and his parents are instructed to follow close behind. While hurrying down the several tiers of wide marble steps, Brad is forced to dodge screaming reporters, who thrust microphones into his face while trying to get within arm's length to get their questions heard.

Up ahead, there's welcome relief, with the open doors to the large vehicle only twenty feet ahead. Then, suddenly and inexplicably, Brad sees Edward stumble and fall ahead of him. Lurching forward, he bends down to help him up. As he reaches one hand under Edward's chest to help lift him off the pavement, his concentration is instantly snapped by the sound of shattering glass. Looking over, he sees the windshield of the car next to him explode. Chaos then erupts all around him. While Brad struggles to determine exactly what's happening, the crowd begins screaming and disperses haphazardly in all directions, nearly knocking him down. At that instant, Brad's hand on Edward's chest suddenly feels wet. When he withdraws his hand, *it's covered in blood!* Horrified, he projects his bloody arm straight up in the air, and he cries aloud while still bent over Edward. As if everything were in slow motion, several FBI agents nearby him reach for their weapons and begin firing at the rooftop across the street. Instinctively, just before one of the assailant's bullets is heard ricocheting off the sidewalk nearby, Brad throws his arms out wide and lunges back to knock both of his parents safely to the ground. Overhead, the loud choppy sounds of a helicopter's blades can be heard as the police attempt to take aim at the sniper. From behind, Brad feels someone push him forward. He hears Wes Shiels yell, "Get in the car!" Just ahead, two FBI agents scoop Edward off the pavement and lay him on the backseat of the Surburban. Brad, his parents, and Wes Shiels are only a fraction of a second behind. The vehicle accelerates at lightning speed toward the closest trauma center, Vanderbilt Hospital.

At the emergency room entrance, two surgeons run to the vehicle and begin working on Edward while he's still in the vehicle. Moments later, he's hoisted onto a gurney and then rushed into emergency surgery. After making several communications with his men at the courthouse, Wes posts several policemen outside Edward's operating room to stand watch, and then, with the Pierson family alongside him, he returns to Legislative Plaza. On their arrival, Brad notices a huge commotion still going on. Teams of SWAT police, dressed in black uniforms, comb every square inch of the area with trained German shepherds, while multiple frightened pedestrians remain huddled behind parked cars. Wes instructs the driver to take the Piersons around to the back side of the federal courthouse building, where they enter via a secure doorway. Once they're safely inside, he returns to the command center out front.

One hour later, after the area has been completely secured, the shell-shocked news media slowly emerge from their hiding places and begin to poke around. Wes Shiels is informed that the gunman made a clean escape on a racing motorcycle, speeding away from the scene on sidewalks to evade capture by the police and FBI sedans. The only thing left behind is his high-powered rifle and silencer. Under the circumstances, Wes elects to move Brad and his parents to FBI headquarters for safekeeping. Brad becomes nauseated as he sees them drive off and pass the large pool of Edward's darkened blood still on the sidewalk in front of the courthouse. Safely tucked away in the backseat of the heavily armored vehicle, Brad begins to ponder whether it was he or Edward who was the intended victim. While the Piersons are en route, Wes takes a separate vehicle to Vanderbilt Hospital to check on Edward Westmoreland's progress.

Later that same evening, Edward emerges from surgery and is immediately taken to the surgical intensive care unit. The single bullet that struck his chest perforated a lung and caused a fair amount of muscle damage, but fortunately it managed to miss his heart and all major blood vessels. The team of surgeons who operated on him note that although he is very weak, they predict a full recovery. Given the circumstances, Judge Isaacson has elected to postpone the trial until Edward's status becomes more clearly defined.

Five days later, the proceedings resume. Edward, by audio-and-video linkup, gives his testimony from his hospital bed at Vanderbilt Hospital. Frequent pauses are necessary on account of his pain. At one point, Edward becomes exhausted enough that he requires a one-hour recess. Beginning with his near bankruptcy, he explains the enticing offer made to him by Robert Altman, who somehow knew about his financial situation. For every bypass surgery that he turned down, he received $20,000 wired to his Fort Lauderdale bank account. He then explains the chain of events in Butch Kennedy's case in a stepwise fashion with his frank confession that Butch was denied the necessary bypass surgery that would likely have saved his life. He next makes note of Brad Pierson's astute observations of the inconsistencies in the autopsy report and how unsettled everyone became over his discovery. Loudly and emotionally, he reiterates the fact that he was unaware that anyone would attempt to harm Brad.

Although obviously remorseful about his actions, Edward receives little sympathy from those in the courtroom. Hissing and grumbling comes from the large collection of doctors and patients present. Sidney Isaacson slams his wooden gavel repeatedly in an attempt to maintain order. During Edward's entire testimony, Elinor Kennedy cries silently on her son's shoulder, while many of Edward's colleagues leave the courtroom out of anger and disgust.

After the lapse of another day, Robert Altman is finally strong enough to make his debut in the courtroom. Arriving in a wheelchair with the monstrous metal halo affixed to his head and running to his shoulders, he evokes quite a strong emotional response from the jury. Due to a minor legal technicality, R. J. Carruthers managed to suppress many of the documents that had been recovered from Robert Altman's home and office. Because of that, many of Robert's arguments seem to have an impact on the jury. The money-laundering operation is explained away by portraying himself as the witless victim of a complex scheme orchestrated by Harry Lefevre that secretly involved his company.

When asked about Edward Westmoreland, he theorizes that Edward must have been part of Harry Lefevre's conspiracy and that Edward implicated him only to shift blame away from himself in order to make a deal with the FBI.

With regard to his supposed tie to the lieutenant governor, Robert quite confidently explains that the state insurance contracts were granted to his company because of the superior product he offered. He mentioned that Buddy Carter was well aware of that. He fails to speculate on the legislation that Mr. Carter had enacted to help protect his company.

When Brad Pierson's name is raised, Robert expresses horror over "what that young man must have suffered" and then says, "What a hero he is." In response to the question raised over the 5.7 billion dollars commission he would have received had the deal to sell the AmericaHealth Corporation gone through, Robert makes the observation that, in many companies, the chief executive officer is richly rewarded for running a successful corporation. He then offers a list of specific examples as evidence of that.

Finally, toward the end of his extensive examination of Robert Altman, R. J. Carruthers points to Robert's halo and wheelchair and asks how he sustained such extensive injuries.

"After I had finished wrapping up some business down on Grand Cayman Island, I was in the corporate jet preparing to fly home to Nashville. When my pilot attempted to take off, the FBI drove a fire truck in front of the plane, causing us to crash. I'm lucky I wasn't killed."

At that moment, Robert casts a pitiful glance at the jury, again in an attempt to influence their opinion. Several of the courtroom observers gasp in disbelief at Robert's comment, believing him to be the victim of the FBI. However, many of the jurors recognize Robert's ploy and are not as easily influenced. They have listened carefully throughout the proceedings and have noted the mountain of circumstantial evidence compiled against him by multiple witnesses. Despite Robert's best attempt to cover it, they have also astutely perceived his arrogance and insincerity.

Eventually, the trial approaches its conclusion. It is elected to try the still-unaccounted-for Dr. Alan Richards in absentia. It had been nearly a week since Wes Shiels had last received an update on his whereabouts. Apparently, several days after arriving in Athens, Greece, Alan Richards boarded a small private cargo plane bound for Argentina. Despite the fact that a small team of FBI operatives have been dispatched to South America, there has been little information uncovered as to Dr. Richards's location to date.

With substantial evidence to support his contentions, Harris Caldwell declares that Alan Richards was a critical figure in the complex AmericaHealth conspiracy. He clearly defines his relationship with Robert Altman and says that he assisted in many facets of the operation. It becomes obvious that he had made the substitution of Butch Kennedy's heart following the autopsy to cover Edward Westmoreland's tracks. In addition, multiple other patients' autopsies had been altered to disguise the inappropriate denial of health care, as in Butch Kennedy's case, or to conceal the mistakes of some of the poorly trained physicians whom Robert Altman had contracted with to save his corporation money.

Dr. Richards was also found guilty of switching other pathological material. Certain patients diagnosed with cancer had their written reports altered. Alan Richards then communicated with Robert Altman to give him an opportunity to cancel those patients' insurance coverage before their true diagnosis came to light and expensive medical treatments were begun.

Among the lengthy list of Alan Richards's victims, Tracy Kilpatrick's name surfaced. When she had utilized nearly $200,000 in health-care expenses, Robert Altman seized the opportunity to cut his losses when Dr. Greer innocently performed a biopsy on her cervix. Alan Richards was ordered to ascribe a false diagnosis of cancer to her case and cover himself by switching both the biopsy and hysterectomy slides. With no uterus, Tracy could no longer undergo the expensive in vitro fertilization attempts that AmericaHealth had agreed to cover in their inclusive contract.

The most damning evidence against Alan Richards was discovered in a safety deposit box located in a Memphis bank that had been rented by someone who used an assumed name on the lease. Contained within the large stack of paper documents recovered were the specific details of how Brad Pierson's body was to have been disposed of had Harry Lefevre's men managed to get their hands on him. As county coroner, Alan Richards planned to label Brad as a homeless person when he was brought into the morgue and have his body buried in a remote location deep within the Smoky Mountains.

After the courtroom proceedings convene, and while the jury begins its lengthy deliberation about the evidence, a formal ceremony is scheduled to reinstate Brad into the pathology residency program at Vanderbilt Hospital. Because of the remarkable circumstances, the event is held at the prestigious Faculty Club on the undergraduate campus, and it is well attended. In addition to the president of the university and the dean of the medical school being present, multiple attending physicians, Wesley Shiels, George Adams, and even Jimmy Hill attend. With Julie, Sandy Starke, Joanie, and his entire family circled around him, Brad receives his reappointment graciously from his chairman, Robert Collins, who acts like a proud father during much of the ceremony. At one point, Brad finds himself getting choked up over Dr. Collins's emotional speech, and toward the end, he is overwhelmed when his chairman deems it necessary to openly apologize to him.

Unable to control himself, Sandy Starke can't resist the opportunity to upstage Brad in the middle of the event. With a big smile for the news media who are present, Sandy formally accepts Dr. Collins's invitation to join the Vanderbilt faculty at the completion of his residency training. Well aware that Brad had the same option but instead chose a year of intensive study in the area of hematopathology, Sandy derives great joy in announcing that he'll be "Brad's boss for a year." Irritated by Sandy's inappropriate actions, Brad whispers something in Jimmy Hill's ear while his friend is in the midst of his attention-getting speech. Caught completely off guard, Sandy is speechless when he feels himself being lifted off the small stage and gently dropped to the ground behind a large crowd of guests. Getting to his feet, he is surprised to see Brad standing over him with an annoyed look on his face.

"You sure deserved that one, Dr. Starke. *You're not my boss yet!*"

That evening, Anna Christensen hosts a dinner party for Brad and his family at her home in Franklin. Ecstatic, Julie finally has the opportunity to meet Brad's sister, Kristin, who arrived from Vermont two days ago, and his brother, Matt, who flew in from Seattle last evening. The reunion is a happy one for Brad. In between reading some of Kristin's latest magazine articles, he reminisces fondly with Matt. Brad's siblings pay particular attention to Julie and flatter her by mentioning that Brad has spoken of her constantly during their phone conversations.

Many of Brad's closest friends have been invited to the party. Sandy and Joanie manage to stay most of the evening. To Brad's delight, Jimmy and Grace Hill are also present, as is George Adams, whom Brad saw quite frequently during the trial. Right after dinner, Brad, with one arm around his mother and the other around Anna Christiansen, thanks everyone for their help during the ordeal that he underwent, especially noting the critical roles played by George Adams, Jimmy Hill, and Sandy Starke. The family's time together is good not only for Brad but also his parents, who until now haven't had all three children together for quite some time.

After assisting Anna with the cleanup, Brad returns with his family to their hotel. Back at the Vanderbilt Plaza, David and Jean Pierson turn in early, but Brad, Matt, and Kristin chat until well after midnight. Over the next several days, with Julie at his side, Brad cherishes the time with his family. Much of his pent-up stress that had built over the past several months finally begins to recede, and he once again begins to sleep through the night without being frequently awakened by nightmares.

The day that Brad had fretfully anticipated, the day that Matt and Kristin needed to return to their respective jobs, finally arrives. At the airport, there is an emotional parting. Brad's sorrow is only made worse two days later when his parents leave for Cooperstown. At each instance, Brad is left with a deep sense of feeling lost and an emotion he had never previously experienced, a fear of being left alone, an insecurity. Spending his evenings and weekends with Julie help somewhat, but his major distraction doesn't occur until the following week when he returns to work.

Brad's focus on his own situation is further lessened by another event several weeks later, Sandy and Joanie's wedding. Not surprisingly, Brad was chosen to be the best man, and Julie was chosen as a bridesmaid. Given that the ceremony was to be held at the West End United Methodist Church, no one other than Drew Henry have would sufficed to perform the ceremony. Thrilled over their daughter's marriage, Joanie's parents held the extravagant reception on one of the large riverboats that courses up and down the Cumberland River, the *General Jackson*. By all measures a success, the celebration was well attended. The bride and groom couldn't have appeared any happier.

The following morning, when Sandy and Joanie leave for their honeymoon in the Bahamas, Brad again experiences a feeling of desolation. On the drive back from taking the couple to the airport, he recognizes that the recent events have shaken him quite substantially, and it's only at moments like these that he's fully cognizant of this fact. Sensing his anxiety without commenting on it, Julie remains closely attentive to Brad. She also frequently encourages him to stay in close contact with his family.

It is not until one month after the trial has convened that the jury completes its deliberation, at which point a sentencing hearing is scheduled. With Julie beside him and Wes Shiels and George Adams nearby, Brad patiently watches as each of the jurors enters the courtroom and takes a seat in the long wooden jurors' box. After the foreman of the jury hands the written verdicts to Judge Isaacson, he reviews the sentences and then reads them aloud.

Pursuant to the deal made with the FBI, Willie Buck is to serve eight years in a minimum-security prison, with occasional time off on weekends. Harry Lefevre was found guilty of attempted homicide, money laundering, and accepting bribes as a public official, and of multiple counts of accomplice to assault and battery. His sentence is much more substantial, fifteen years in a state penitentiary without the possibility of parole. Buddy Carter had charges similar to Harry Lefevre's lodged against him, with the exception of political corruption and misuse of a public office to influence legislation. Because of his prominent position, his attorneys have somehow managed to get a preliminary sentence of only five years in a minimum-security prison, but they have already filed an appeal, which may possibly keep the lieutenant governor from serving any time at all.

So compelling was the incriminating evidence against Dr. Alan Richards that little effort was required by the jury to assign his guilt. In addition to having his medical license revoked for multiple counts of intentional malpractice, he was convicted of being an accomplice in the attempted homicide of Brad Pierson. His other crimes included coconspirator in the money-laundering operation, flight of a federal magistrate, and accomplice to Butch Kennedy's manslaughter. The jurors found great personal satisfaction in assigning him a sentence of thirty years to life in prison.

The most difficult task that the jury faced, and what made their deliberation so lengthy, was deciding Robert Altman's fate. It was reasonably clear that he had been the central figure in the conspiracy, but because of the evidence that R. J. Carruthers had gotten suppressed, how much he knew about the attempt on Brad Pierson's life was uncertain. Hence, he was sentenced for only those charges that had been demonstrated beyond a reasonable measure of doubt, namely, conspiracy to commit fraud, money laundering, and the denial of appropriate medical care to hundreds of patients, resulting in the loss of life, pain and suffering, and personal injury. Because many of the charges against him could not be proven, his sentence was much less severe than Dr. Alan Richards'; ten years in prison without the possibility of parole.

During the trial, Robert's wife, Anne, sat directly behind him in a show of support. Her initial reaction to the charges against Robert was frank disbelief. Then, as more testimony was given and the evidence continued to pile up, her heart was broken, bringing on a constant stream of tears.

When Robert's sentence was read aloud, she cried out and ran out of the courtroom with all eyes on her.

Robert Altman's reaction to the sentence was substantially different than his wife's. During his multiyear tenure as CEO of AmericaHealth, he had suppressed his own conscience, knowing that many of the things he did were immoral and illegal. His desire to succeed pushed aside his own conflicted feelings of betrayal to the patients AmericaHealth insured. In the end, he accepted his sentence as just punishment. Prior to the judge's determination of his fate, the judge asked him if he wished to address the court. In a shocking display of emotion, he cried silently while openly expressing his remorse.

Because of the severity and the sheer numbers of atrocities committed, the AmericaHealth Corporation was ordered to pay hundreds of millions of dollars in compensatory damages to the families of patients who were harmed by Robert Altman's actions.

Finally, because of the deal made with the FBI, Edward Westmoreland was never sentenced by the jury. He surrendered his medical license voluntarily and will never serve any prison time, but the personal torment of knowing what he has done will most assuredly haunt him for the remainder of his life.

Several days after the sentencing hearing, Brad and Julie begin packing for a long-anticipated vacation together. Brad had initially requested one week off from work, but Dr. Collins insisted on allowing him two weeks, aware of how badly he needed the time away. Early one Saturday morning before sunrise, the couple leaves Nashville, traveling south in the direction of the Florida panhandle. Eight hours later, Brad's Ford Taurus arrives in the main square at Seaside, where he acquires the keys to their two-bedroom bungalow directly on the beach.

The November weather in Seaside proves to be surprisingly accommodating. Despite cool mornings in the fifties, the afternoons are quite warm, with the thermostat reaching well into the midseventies. The extended break is rejuvenating for the couple. After an early morning run along the beach, Brad often takes Julie for a bike ride or a tour of the colorful, tin-roofed Victorian homes that have made Seaside so famous. Between long walks on the white sand beaches protected by tall dunes, the couple spends many an afternoon nestled up with a book under one of the architecturally unique beach gazebos, with the light ocean breeze streaming across their unclothed arms and legs.

The slow pace of the time away is not only pleasant but also of dire necessity for Brad. Often, after waking in the morning, he lies quietly and listens to the gentle pounding of the surf. In that never-ceasing sound, there is a quiet peace, a comfort.

When it eventually becomes time to pack up and return home, Brad finds himself beset with melancholy. Reaching for Julie's hand, he desperately desires one final afternoon stroll along the ocean, where the crashing waves and the lofting pelicans might once again soothe his soul.

After they've returned to their beach cottage, Brad quietly goes to one of the bedrooms to begin loading his suitcases. Staying behind in the kitchen, Julie organizes many of their belongings while preparing a light dinner. By this time, dusk has arrived. With only a few lights on, the interior of their rented home is dimly lit. When Brad reaches into the closet to retrieve the last of his clothing, he hears Julie call out to him.

"Brad, please come in here right now."

Startled by the apprehensive tone in Julie's voice, Brad immediately drops what he is doing and hurries to see what's wrong. As he enters the kitchen, he sees Julie standing rigidly still, staring intently into a completely dark living room. It is not until Brad is several feet away from Julie that he notices what has captured her attention. At that very instant, his heart nearly ceases beating. In the shadows, with only his haggard face visible in the faint light, is Dr. Alan Richards! In his right hand is a blue steel revolver pointed directly at Julie.

As Brad attempts to move closer to Julie, Alan Richards cautions him: "Stay right where you are, Brad."

Uncertain what to do next, Brad blurts out a question, trying to make sense of the situation: "Alan, what are you doing here? What do you want from us?"

Angrily yelling at him, Alan Richards turns his head in Brad's direction. "Do you have any idea what you've done to me? People are stalking me day and night! I can't go anywhere near my house. I'll never see my wife again. … You've ruined my life!"

Brad then sees Alan Richards raise his arm holding the gun, which is still pointed in Julie's direction. Instinctively, he leaps to throw his body between Julie and the path of the bullet. Just before knocking Julie to the floor, he hears an explosive roar as the .38-caliber weapon goes off. Unclear if either he or Julie has been shot, he pushes her to safety behind the couch. After quickly ascertaining that she's unharmed, he tries to identify Alan Richards's location. Reaching for a brass standing lamp to defend himself with, he cautiously sticks his head out from behind the sofa. When he sees Alan Richards lying facedown on the floor ten feet away, he's uncertain exactly what's happened. Then, from one corner of the room, he hears a familiar voice: "It's okay, Brad. We've got things under control."

From across the living room, Brad then sees FBI Director Wesley Shiels emerge from the shadows with a handgun trained on the now bleeding Alan Richards. To address Brad's as yet unspoken question, Wes Shields says, "That was my gun that went off. But don't worry, I only shot him in the shoulder. He'll be all right."

Over the next several hours, Wes Shiels explains to Brad and Julie that he had been concerned about their safety and, because of that, had decided to order several of his men to protect them while on their vacation in Seaside. When Alan Richards had been spotted several days ago in Miami, Wes felt it necessary to make a personal appearance to monitor the situation. Apparently,

Dr. Richards had managed to dodge the FBI's surveillance up until the moment he entered Brad and Julie's beach cottage, and at that point, Wes and his men moved in.

It is not until well after 3:00 a.m. that the commotion dies down and the FBI and the local police complete their investigation. Unable to sleep after their trauma, Brad and Julie decide to throw on a couple of loose sweatshirts and watch the sunrise. When the first rays of early morning sunlight arrive on the horizon, Brad looks into Julie's eyes, which appear nearly aquamarine in the faint light. After he kisses her softly, he casts his gaze down and softly says, "Thank you." To Julie's questioned look, he explains, "For loving me when I needed it most." While holding Julie in his arms, he gently brushes the hair away from her face and continues in a quiet voice. "You know, Julie, I'm not sure I could ever imagine my life without you anymore." In unspoken confirmation of her own feelings, Julie squeezes Brad tight and rests her head against his chest.

CPSIA information can be obtained
at www.ICGtesting.com
Printed in the USA
FSHW011417140320
67985FS

9 781732 611801